TIDES
of
WAR

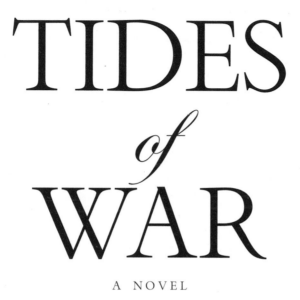

TIDES
of
WAR

A NOVEL

STELLA TILLYARD

A FRANCES COADY BOOK
HENRY HOLT AND COMPANY
NEW YORK

HENRY HOLT AND COMPANY, LLC

PUBLISHERS SINCE 1866

175 FIFTH AVENUE

NEW YORK, NEW YORK 10010

WWW.HENRYHOLT.COM

ORIGINALLY PUBLISHED IN THE U.K. IN 2011 BY CHATTO & WINDUS,

A DIVISION OF THE RANDOM HOUSE BOOK GROUP LIMITED.

LIBRARY OF CONGRESS CATALOGING-IN-PUBLICATION DATA

TILLYARD, S. K.

TIDES OF WAR : A NOVEL / STELLA TILLYARD.—1ST U.S. ED.

P. CM.

"A FRANCES COADY BOOK."

ISBN 978-0-8050-9457-2

1. PENINSULAR WAR, 1807–1814—FICTION.   2. LONDON (ENGLAND)—

HISTORY—19TH CENTURY—FICTION.   3. SPAIN—HISTORY—NAPOLEONIC

CONQUEST, 1808–1813—FICTION.   I. TITLE.

PR6120.I47T53 2011

823'.92—DC23   2011025731

ISBN 978-0-8050-9457-2

HENRY HOLT BOOKS ARE AVAILABLE FOR SPECIAL PROMOTIONS AND PREMIUMS.

FOR DETAILS CONTACT: DIRECTOR, SPECIAL MARKETS.

FIRST U.S. EDITION 2011

DESIGNED BY MERYL SUSSMAN LEVAVI

MAP COPYRIGHT © 2011 BY SANDRA OAKINS.

PRINTED IN THE UNITED STATES OF AMERICA

1 3 5 7 9 10 8 6 4 2

SALLY LAIRD, 1956–2010,

FRIEND AND STORYTELLER

Contents

PART ONE 1

1. Suffolk, London and Spain
FEBRUARY 1812 3

2. Elvas, Portugal, Badajoz, Spain and London
MARCH–APRIL 1812 34

3. London and Badajoz
6 APRIL 1812 62

4. Elvas, Portugal and London
APRIL 1812 84

PART TWO 107

5. Madrid and London
AUGUST 1812 109

6. London and Seville, Spain
SEPTEMBER–OCTOBER 1812 132

7. London and Seville
AUTUMN AND WINTER 1812–13 161

8. London and Freneda, Portugal
WINTER AND SPRING 1812–13   197

9. London and Spain
SPRING AND SUMMER 1813   222

10. London and Norwich
SUMMER AND AUTUMN 1813   248

PART THREE   277
———

11. London and Suffolk
SUMMER AND AUTUMN 1814   279

12. Suffolk and London
AUTUMN 1814–SUMMER 1815   317

Dramatis Personae   347

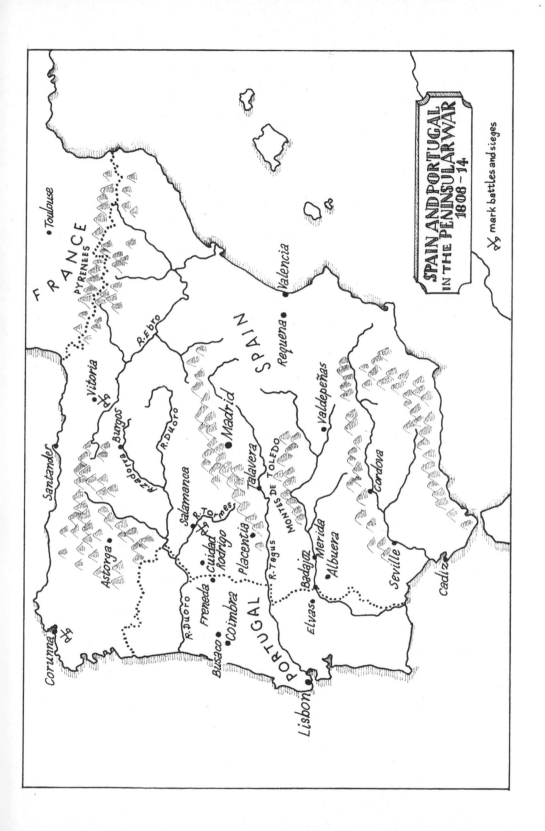

SPAIN AND PORTUGAL
IN THE PENINSULAR WAR
1808 – 14

⚔ mark battles and sieges

FRANCE

Toulouse

PYRENEES

Santander

Vitoria ⚔

Burgos

R. Ebro

R. Duero

R. Adaja

SPAIN

Valencia

Requena

Valdepeñas

Madrid

Astorga

Salamanca

R. Tormes

Cuidad
Rodrigo

Talavera

MONTES DE TOLEDO

Placentia

R. Tagus

Cordova

Corunna ⚔

R. Duero

Freneda

Busaco

Coimbra

PORTUGAL

Badajoz

Merida

Albuera

Elvas

Seville

Cadiz

Lisbon ⚔

PART ONE

1

Suffolk, London and Spain

FEBRUARY 1812

'Now, what am I looking for?'

Harriet scanned the stoppered phials on the shelves, putting a finger to the label of each one. Some of the bottles were dusty, some had marks of recent use. In her father's day the laboratory never had this abandoned look. Sir William Guest's large cabinet stood by the door, its drawers open. Delicate instruments, magnets, loose nails and coils of wire lay jumbled inside. Larger pieces of apparatus and machines were grouped without order against the end wall.

In the middle of the room, its chimney built out through the ceiling, the iron stove sat on a square of delft tiles. As a girl Harriet used to rub the soot off the warm tiles while they waited for an experiment to take, and absorb herself in the story each might tell, a labourer in a heavy smock, a milkmaid with her pail, the blue bridge where they met over a white canal. Black grains of soot coated the tiles now, and a displaced group of bottles with round shoulders and cork stoppers stood on the workbench nearby. In one a lump of yellow phosphorus, Harriet's favourite, lay in water. Ease it out into the air and it would burst into flame.

'Nothing is where it should be.'

Harriet wiped her dirty hands on her apron and pushed a lock of hair under the scarf tied round her head. Her hair refused to stay put; her forehead was covered in an arc of dust where she swept it away. She quickened her search, darted along the shelves and read each label.

'Oh, woe is me, t'have seen what I have seen, see what I see.' She put her hands up to her face.

'*Hamlet*, Act 3, Scene 1,' she said under her breath, and turned to the door. No, there was nobody there; she was alone.

'Ah here, here.'

She took a slender bottle, rubbed it off on her apron and read her father's hand. 'Nitrous acid. Strong.' Further along she found the sulphuric acid.

'I can be quick; besides, it is done in a moment.'

It only took a second to unhook a cup from the underside of the nearest shelf with one hand, and with the other pull open a drawer and rummage for the old silver spoon.

'The last thing: oil of turpentine.'

She found the bottle, tipped a spoonful of the thickened turpentine into the shallow cup and set it down on the hearth by the stove. A stick and string she needed next, and to be careful when she mixed the acids. The world receded.

Harriet loved this experiment for its simplicity and noise, the leap of fire and the sudden creation of a new compound in the flames. Her father told her that he often performed it for her mother, to lift her from melancholy. But that was before Harriet was born.

She remembered her father, his white hair disordered, a hessian apron round his waist and his shirt open at the neck. No matter that they were alone together and at home, Sir William always wore his clothes as if someone might arrive at any moment. How many afternoons they sat in there, with the laboratory full of silence from the park and a gentle hiss from the stove. As darkness gathered, the panel of mica windows on the front of the stove glowed redder. Harriet could see herself, too, hair tied back, her own apron a copy of his. She sat thin and taut on a high stool, proud to hold the scissors to cut litmus paper, or lift a delicate retort over a flame.

''Tis time I should inform thee further,' Sir William would say, and wait for Harriet to add: '*Tempest*, Act 1, Scene 2.'

Each time they began a new experiment, her father consulted his Accum or his Parkes, the pages of the books discoloured with drops of the liquids they made and mixed. He read out what they needed to find, and Harriet ran along the shelves, levered down bottles and phials with two hands or crossed to the cabinet to pull string and nails, a ruler or a measuring spoon from the drawers. With her breath held in, careful not to drop anything, she placed each tool or ingredient on the workbench to make the orderly row as her father had showed her. The longer the line grew the happier she felt. When an experiment was done, they put the bottles back and walked hand in hand to the drawing room and tea. Harriet could still hear her father's voice, with its note of apology, and, in her own chatter, the burden of dissolving it.

Now, she laid a glass phial at the end of a wooden stick and tied them together with several turns of good hemp string. Then she poured in a few inches of sulphuric acid and added in the clear nitrous acid. Her task now was to pour the mixture into the cup of turpentine. She leaned over the hearth, concentrated. When the acid hit the warm turpentine the sudden combustion might throw the liquid fire straight up. Again she heard her father's voice.

'Stand aside, Harry. Watch for the moment when the new compound releases the heat. Are you ready?'

'Ready.'

'*Midsummer Night's Dream*, Act 3, Scene 1,' he said, and they laughed together, her father with a sideways glance at the hearth, while she flung her hands onto her knees and leaned forward to catch his eye.

She began to turn the stick in her hand, filled with the calm that the laboratory brought her. She had come in to allay her fears and walk along the shelves. It was an afterthought, or an involuntary movement, that had led from that to Parkes's manual and its well-used section of practical proofs.

'Harriet!'

The door swung open. Harriet stood by the hearth, the long wooden rod in her hands, about to pour.

'James!'

She turned towards him, her eyes on his face, and forgot everything. The acids fell onto the hearth, some into the cup, some onto the tiles. In the sudden explosion of flame drops of turpentine jumped up and caught fire. Tongues of flame fell onto the tiles and the floor and burned there, blue and noisy.

'There, no harm done,' Harriet said, and pushed her hair out of her face. Now, here was James, in a new white cambric shirt and pressed dress trousers, his hair wet.

'What are you doing?'

'I thought I might come in for a few minutes.' She looked up at her husband, a look of self-containment on her face, a kind of retreat.

'Have you forgotten that we begin in less than an hour?'

Harriet ran towards him.

'Oh, darling James, no. That is why I came.'

James took a step back and put his hands out towards her. Harriet glanced at her dusty apron and the acid burn on her gown. She ran to look in the mirror, a mottled glass oval that she and her father had silvered years ago. It was pitted black where the silvering had been too thin and reminded Harriet that when their experiments had gone wrong, as they often did, she would hug her father tightly to make up for something more than an incorrect mix of chemicals and compounds.

In the eaten silver surface Harriet saw that streaks of dust and soot ran down her cheeks. Fire singed the hem of her old day dress.

'I can get it all off. My gown is brushed and ready.'

James smiled suddenly. A note of warmth was added to his measured, even voice, so that it dropped down a tone to become soft and humorous.

'Dear girl; dearest Harry. You are absurd. We leave for the Peninsula tomorrow. Major Yallop is already here; Dorothy Yallop and David McBride, too. I had thought to take them over to the hotel in half an hour. What is to be done with you?'

Harriet looked at James, at the breadth of his shoulders and the strong push of his calves against the backs of his trousers. Desire flashed up her body like the twist of a fish underwater.

'I shall wash and be down directly.'

'Nonsense, Harry.'

Tears stood in Harriet's eyes.

'Do not say so, James. I have been dressing myself for years. I do not take the hours that other women do.'

James Raven's features shifted, as if it was the first time he had caught the beauty and oddity of Harriet's features.

'I tell you what. I'll go back up and ask Mrs Yallop if she will help you to dress. I shall not say anything to the others. I think that will be best.'

Harriet ran down the corridor that connected the laboratory to the main house. She pulled her scarf off as she went and dashed a sooty hand across her eyes. James watched her heavy hair fall down her back. It would be a considerable labour to brush, pull up, tie back and set with ropes of pearls. Harriet would be late, even in Dorothy's hands. How was it, he asked himself again, that his fellow officers, and even the men, used to a punctual life of rules and self-reliance, made such an exception for her, shrugged their shoulders and smiled?

WHY SHOULD HE ASK? He was one of them himself. From the first time he saw her, outlined against the light from the long windows in her father's drawing room, her narrow face turned to the park outside, he knew he would have to campaign for her attention. There was something about her then, and still now, that was irretrievable. It was nothing she kept apart or hid; but rather as if, long ago, something had dropped deep into her and left no trace, no ripples on the surface, but stayed there, tantalising and out of reach. In all her high spirits, her enthusiasm, and her affection, she was beyond him, a step ahead, or just round the corner.

He had joined the army four years before with the usual portmanteau of dreams: to distinguish himself, serve his king and win promotion. Napoleon had marched across Spain in 1807, invaded Portugal and then turned his attention to his Spanish ally. The British army, under Sir Arthur Wellesley, helped the Portuguese see off the French, but Wellesley was then recalled and Napoleon picked off the Spanish armies one by one. By the end of 1808, when James embarked for Spain, Napoleon had forced the Spanish king to abdicate in favour of his son, confined them both in France and installed his brother Joseph Bonaparte in Madrid instead.

James had landed in Santander as autumn turned to winter, and joined the rest of the 9th Foot with Sir John Moore's small army outside Salamanca. General Moore had been left to command the rump of the British army in the Peninsula and James arrived at the moment when Moore, without reinforcements, could no longer contain Marshal Soult's well-fed French force. He ordered his army to retreat to Astorga and then make for the coast and the British fleet.

Soult's army had pursued Moore's ragged troops all across the top of Spain. In the snow-covered mountains of Galicia the French picked off dozens of British stragglers as a tawny lion pulls down gazelles from the edge of a moving herd. Cold and bad lungs did for hundreds of others. Men lay down on the iced verges and waited to die or to be taken prisoner. The retreat lasted three weeks, night merging into bitter day. Only the bones of Moore's small force were left at the end, men who had stripped themselves into marching automatons and hurled their illusions one by one onto thorny gorse at the roadside.

Sometimes a party of them, officers and men who could still bear the sight of one another, laid ambushes for the French vanguard. In the high mountains above Astorga, where their army split in two to make the journey to the coast faster and confuse the enemy, James knew that he, a soldier who had bought his sword in Jermyn Street and his commission for an inflated price, had become a killer. When he faced the Frenchman, looked into his light blue eyes and saw fear slide into them, he saw himself suspended above life like a bird of prey.

Yet he felt nothing; or only a kind of vibration, a thrum of blood such as a hawk might experience as it waited for the moment to lower its head and dive. Then the moment of thrust, intense as an explosion. With that James was certain that he had reached what lay like lava at the bottom of every man; but afterwards, when he sat round the fire back with the division, there was nothing to say about it. The moment had gone from him, its legacy only a mind picked empty the way that carrion strip a carcass to leave a skeleton white against the green.

His senior officer, Major Yallop, had merely nodded at him, and slugged an extra tot of brandy in his tea. The next day the retreat went on. The regiment was sleepless, the men irritable and petty. They jostled for the best bivouacs at night, quarrelled over sticks for fires and twists of tea. With the French at its back the army became a rabble; but James did not dwell on the brutality. All along the way the lightness accompanied him. He forgot about Lady Lavington and the drawing-room life in London he had left when he bought his commission. Like the others who survived the march he learned to ignore the rain that drove at his face as he rode and soaked through the seams of his gabardine. He came to appreciate the dry humour of his men, their fortitude and acceptance, the way they never dwelt on friends who became too sick to go on and fell back towards the baggage train and the advancing French.

They had reached Corunna before the fleet, and the French were upon them by the time the transports got into the harbour. There was only time to put the sick and wounded on board before they had to turn and fight, but James welcomed the battle. Wounded in the shoulder at the end of the day, after their commander Moore was killed, he was mentioned in General Anderson's dispatches and promoted to Captain.

The next day, with Soult's army beaten back and the British saved, James boarded a worn-out ship of the line. He disembarked at Portsmouth to the approbation of a sombre crowd. The newspapers excoriated

Sir John Moore and described his officers as the bravest of men. By the time he reached Suffolk to convalesce he had grown tired of women who touched his bandaged arm, called him a hero and implied that they would be glad to know how such a man conducted himself on softer ground.

When he was introduced to Harriet at dinner in her father's house, she had challenged rather than invited him.

'Captain Raven, you are welcome. But in your regimental jacket? What happened to the notion that "we are but warriors for the working day"?'

At least he had recognised the line: Shakespeare, though he had not admitted it. But he acknowledged the absurdity. In the early years of the war men changed into everyday dress as soon as they disembarked. Today their jackets were everywhere, drops of scarlet all along the streets.

When Lord Nelson was still alive, a sea captain had been the thing. Now that Arthur Wellesley was back as Lord Wellington and Commander-in-Chief in the Peninsula, army officers were the fashion. With his imperious manner and polished boots, the General was a man to rival Bonaparte at last. The shimmer of war accompanied James down the street and into every room. Yet he knew himself to be a killer in a red coat. War was his companion; it lived under his skin. Women sensed its presence; they offered it, as much as him, the softness of their naked bodies. Harriet appeared to ask what else there was.

He had stood back when he first observed her, walked to the supper table and watched as other men tried to catch her attention. To be sure she was Sir William Guest's daughter, and Sir William was a gentleman, despite the reputation for oddity his interest in science had given him, with a long lineage. But it was not Harriet's prospects, merely, that drew admirers. Neither was it Harriet's beauty, for she could never be described as beautiful, or even pretty. She was too thin and quick, her face narrow and long, her hair always on the point of escape. No, it was something else; around her, the men were like anglers who crowded a river bank, cast their lines into the water, came up with nothing, and cast again.

After that day the simple life war offered him was not enough. He came back to Suffolk at every opportunity, and approached Harriet with care. At first, for every step he took towards her she had taken two steps back. He learned what it was to be the pursuer, though it was always she who determined, by a gesture, a laugh, a question, how far he might advance.

James found, in the end, that it was best simply to be discovered at

Beccles Hall in conversation with Harriet's father. Sir William welcomed him into his house, and seemed to help James in his pursuit. When they talked Harriet often came into the library, seated herself at a distance and then joined in. If the talk interested her she would move to a closer chair and then throw herself on the sofa next to James or her father, forgetful of everything else. Then James might ask her to show him something outside; the large lens telescope in the observatory on the lawn, or the experiments Sir William conducted with different soil types and seeds. Over the weeks, when he was with Harriet alone, James began to add into the conversation a compliment on her dress or the grey of her eyes. She never showed she noticed such remarks, and James began to think that she had no grasp of his intentions or the state of enchantment she had thrown upon him. Then one day out in the park she said as if it had just occurred to her.

'The colour of an eye I believe to be like that of our hair, a pigment which fades with the years. Yours, for instance, appear to be of the purest blue, unmixed with any other colour.'

'Indeed.' James let the conversation run. He loved to listen, not just to Harriet's words but to the sound of her voice, which had a depth and certainty unexpected in so slight a form.

'It is difficult for me to be sure, however, since my vantage point is so far beneath you. If you were to lie flat on the lawn and let the sun shine slantwise into them, I might see better if their blue lies on another tint.'

'You tease me, Harry.'

'I wish to conduct an investigation. Lie down.'

James lay down and opened his eyes as much as he could in the evening sun.

'Quite blue; cobalt, or cerulean.'

Harriet leaned over him. She took her bonnet off; her hair fell across his face.

'You make a fool of me, then.'

'Perhaps.'

Harriet came so close that he could no longer see her face; just feel her breath and warmth, and the moment when her lips touched his. He stayed as still as he could bear to be, and then felt with wonder the entry of her tongue into his mouth.

'Is that an investigation also?'

'In a manner of speaking.'

'What manner, Harriet? You must know why I come to your father's house.'

Harriet stood up and threw her bonnet so it skimmed over the grass like a loaded plate. She followed its path as if nothing else interested her.

'In the manner that, if we wish to mix two compounds to create a new one and have never done so before, we begin with a very small quantity by way of a proof.'

'A proof?'

'That we reach the result we had hoped for.'

James jumped up in a bound and looked down at her.

'And did you, Harry?'

'I think so.'

'Then do it again.'

Harriet came closer. To his delight and amazement she began to unbutton his coat. Her body was hot against his. He wanted to reach down, ease her backwards and put his hands tight over her breasts; but he stood motionless, afraid to make any move that might stop her. When his coat was open Harriet ran her hands round his back, and kissed him again, as if she had been kissing him all her life or as if they were lovers already and she knew everything that he did.

Yet even now, more than a year later, and a month after their wedding, he wasn't at all sure he had got her. He was leaving for the Peninsula again, with a secondment to Headquarters, he thought as he walked up the corridor to the library, and Harriet was still at it, that disappearing act of hers.

Once she said to him, 'You do not know me, James. There are things in me that I cannot think about.'

'There are those things in all of us, Harry. Any man who has been in war knows that.'

She had smiled then, and fallen silent. He did not pursue the conversation; from his own case he knew what he said to be true. At other times she was more simply elusive. 'I'll run upstairs for it', she might say of something she had forgotten, and turn away from him. Half an hour later he would find her under the covers with a book, or in the laboratory, as he had today, covered in soot, when their guests were to arrive any moment.

'AH, DOROTHY,' JAMES SAID when he opened the library door, 'Harriet is a little late. She would be so happy if you might help her. Just to clasp her jewels and so on.'

'The poor thing. She is unhappy, no doubt, at your departure and forgot herself.' Mrs Yallop looked delighted. 'I could use an iron myself, and a pier-glass. I have quite a surprise for you all.'

She nodded at her husband. David McBride, the new regimental surgeon, who was seated next to the Major, saw Yallop blush and concentrate his gaze on the tips of his polished boots.

'My pièce de résistance, I think you would call it. In honour of the regiment.'

DOROTHY YALLOP PRESSED HER shawl and set the iron down flat on the hearth. Behind her through the window the River Waveney spilled out into the meadows and caught the last of the light from the bleached winter sky. A rising breeze moved through the naked willow branches; snow was on the way from the west. In the darkness the current of war came upriver on the evening tide, pushed unnoticed into every rivulet and stream, and seeped into the frosted ground.

'Now, how are you placed, my dear?'

Mrs Yallop considered the young woman in front of her who jumped from foot to foot in the cold while she washed herself. Harriet Raven was eager for life. She might feel the parting acutely but would not suffer for long, would learn how to put the pain at a distance. Mrs Yallop had heard that Sir William had brought his daughter up alone, that Lady Guest had disappeared, had been odd, too, in her way; but many officers' wives had endured childhoods of hardship. It was good drill for the job, the Major always said, and after twenty-five years of service, there was not much that George could not tell you about life in the army.

'Look at me, Mrs Yallop. I ran into the laboratory to forget what was happening, and made everything worse.'

'Nonsense, there is plenty of time. We will have you right in a moment. I have dressed more quickly and in many a worse place I can tell you. Try a frigate in the harbour at Messina, or a bordello in Lisbon.'

Half an hour later Harriet was ready. Her mother's diamonds, set in gold, hung around her neck. Mrs Yallop had brushed her hair and tied it with a loop of pearls, and Harriet stood, quite composed, in her blue gown.

'And now for my masterpiece.'

Mrs Yallop unwound a small, carefully wrapped bundle that she laid like an offering in Harriet's lap.

'What is it? A new creation, I hope.'

'A novelty, certainly. I made it myself. Here is Britannia, our badge; to this side of her, "9th Foot", and there, to the other, "East Norfolk".'

A fat Britannia, embroidered in white and blue, sat with her left hand at rest on a shield. In her right hand she held a sturdy stick stripped from a living tree and sewn onto the backing cloth. Tawny feathers encircled her like the laurels of a victor. Were they pheasant, Harriet wondered, or something more domestic?

'And what do we do with it?'

'Do not tease me, young lady. It will sit beautifully.'

Mrs Yallop lifted her handiwork to her head and tied it with a bow behind. Wiry tufts of hair lay flattened on her forehead.

'I consider it to have an eastern effect that recalls the Major's service overseas.'

'Oh, it is marvellous. You have quite restored my good humour.'

'My dear.' Mrs Yallop tested her headdress for security. 'You take this all too seriously. Tomorrow they leave; I have known an overseas campaign to last a year or two. The Major admires Napoleon and does not believe he will surrender the Peninsula lightly.'

'I know you are right; but I find it hard to be light-hearted. It is shocking to say, and do forgive me, but if my father had not died I should have been married much longer and this parting might be easier.'

'No, my dear. You may be wife, mother, daughter or sister; the misery is the same. Who knows, we may never see them again. It does not do at all to dwell upon it. After the first time, you learn to endure with good humour.'

But Harriet was sure that Dorothy had no idea of her feeling for James. In the nights after her father's death and the postponement of their wedding, the thought of James took her breath away even when grief gripped her; one animal passion vied with another and life got the better of annihilation. Though they had finally married last month those few weeks were scarcely time to learn to live together. Now James could only say he would come back to her, and she could only say she would wait.

Then she was afraid. Suppose, as the months went by, James faded? Suppose he became a kind of ghost, a shadow so indistinct that another man might interpose himself in the space between them? Worse, she might wish one to.

'Mrs Yallop, I will try to endure. But what if I forget him?'

'And fall in love with another man?'

'Not in love; but one might become lonely.'

A keen look crossed Mrs Yallop's face.

'It is easily dealt with. Do not pretend it does not happen. I have experienced it myself, although one must never speak of it; a blow that comes down just like that. You must hold your nerve. Do nothing and it will go away. In a few months you will be as you were before, and the better for it, I assure you. There is nothing to worry about if you love your husband as I see you do.'

Harriet heard a knock at the door. Here he was, then, come to take her downstairs and to the hotel in the square, where the officers of the 9th had assembled in farewell. A vibrant picture of James, tall, fair and muscular, came complete into her mind, like a gloved and golden Florentine on a white horse. She turned to greet him. It was not James who stood there, but Dr McBride, ponderous and solid as a seal, with his hands behind his back and his topcoat made lopsided by a book in one pocket.

'Oh, Dr McBride.'

David McBride watched Harriet's eyes darken and narrow in disappointment. He stood in the doorway a moment and examined her the way he hoped a physician might study a patient. He looked at her mouth, thin and red, the lips slightly parted; her eyes, grey, or perhaps greyish blue; her slight form; her bosom, surprisingly full, its curves just visible above the lace of her gown. He coughed, and Harriet looked at him as if trying to get him into focus. But this examination, for such a thing he permitted himself, did not describe her. No medical man could find it satisfactory, he thought. For a start it stopped somewhere above the waist, and he felt it inappropriate, even for a man of science, to drop his eyes further. But, more than that, the words in his head pinned things down, made a report in fixed ink and lines, and the fact was Harriet Raven was a person of movement, of an upward tilt of the chin, and sudden deep laughter. Not one of her features was of the best. Her mouth for instance—he gazed at it without emotion—was too wide to be pretty; it curled up at the ends in a way that defied nature.

Dr McBride sighed heavily and shifted his shoulders inside his ugly topcoat. Harriet looked at him with amusement; the best way to approach James's friend was to joke with him.

'"Now sits the wind fair?", Dr McBride?'

'A westerly, I believe. It should run us down the Channel and into the Bay of Biscay in no time.' He coughed again, 'Henry V, Act 2—'

Harriet laughed, and David added to his description of her features the fact that when she did so two creases framed her mouth in the way that commas surround speech. How did she guess he liked to be teased?

'You know the source of my nonsense. How is that?'

'I attended the medical school at Edinburgh. In Scotland, and away from home, winter stretches out. I lodged with my grandfather and read a good deal at night.' He looked at his shoes and then back up at her. 'You never know when you might need words to put life at a bearable distance.'

'You do not need a book now, Dr McBride. Mrs Yallop here counsels us to be cheerful. We shall simply dance and say farewell.'

David held out his arm. Harriet slipped her hand through it.

'Lead on,' she said, and smiled at him as if he was not there.

DOROTHY YALLOP ADVANCED INTO the ballroom of the Grand Hotel in Bungay with a buoyant shake of her head.

'The waltz! Gentlemen, I ask you to put away your swords and dance.'

'But first, a toast.' Edward Tillett, a grain merchant with a fortune from supply to the navy, lifted his glass.

'The King!' Tillett took a forward step and paused theatrically, to acknowledge the King's madness, and his audience's understanding of it.

'King George; and the Regent.'

'The memory of Sir John Moore, and Corunna,' Major Yallop added.

'And to the 9th Regiment that buried him,' another officer shouted.

The group of officers around the supper table broke up. Obediently the men unbuckled their swords and laid them in a pile by the fireplace. Orders from Mrs Yallop were tantamount to orders from the Major. Wives and daughters of local merchants came forward to take their hands.

Mrs Yallop's headdress shook with her efforts to organise the dancers. 'Ladies, listen now.'

The waltz was recently introduced from the Continent, whirled from Vienna with the officers of the Allied armies. Familiar only with the twos and fours of marching tunes, the band struggled with the lilts of triple time.

'So, ladies, place your left hand on his arm, just below the shoulder. Now gentlemen, put your right hand flat on her back, and no whacking. She is not a pony.'

She considered the dancers. A few of the men inched their hands round their partners for a squeeze; most stood stiff, as if they waited for an order to advance.

'Now; the other hands come together and out. Stand close together! This is the waltz! Elbows up and out, ladies. Lightly, that's it. Now lead with the left, gentlemen. Imagine you tread round the edge of an ammunition box. Forward, along, back. Lightly now; anticipate the second step. There, you have it, ah ha!'

Mrs Yallop laughed in delight. Her high voice always carried the possibility of pleasure. Britannia nodded on her head.

'Now, off we go.'

One or two couples hurried on to the open floor, afraid they would forget the sequence. Others hesitated and banged into one another, toe to toe. But with the help of the melody, a kind of order soon prevailed. Like novice skaters who clung to one another on the ice, the dancers began to turn, and the defiant gaiety of the music caught them up.

Harriet pulled James towards her till she could feel his jacket buttons through the thin silk of her gown. They launched themselves into the waltz, and circled on its rhythm. She came close, then bent away, and, when she came back, flowed along with him for a moment. Round the room they went, sky-blue and scarlet, past the supper table where Dr McBride stood alone, past the long windows curtained in dusty red brocade and into the open space in the middle. James held his upright poise, light on his feet. He threw off his stiffness beat by beat in the turns and in the music.

'Harriet, you will not forget to call on Lady Wellington when you go up to town?' he said as they turned at the far end of the room.

'James, do not let us talk of it now. It is our last evening.'

'Indulge me, dearest. And do dance with the Major; you will put him in good humour.'

Before Harriet could protest, James steered her to Major Yallop's side, squeezed Harriet's hand and left her.

Major Yallop saw Harriet glance back at her husband.

'Just one turn, eh, to please him?'

'I see I must make the best of it.'

'Well now, you will have him back soon enough. Shall we show them how it is done?'

Harriet put her hand out to the Major. George Yallop was a wiry man, forty-five or so, she thought. She could sense him vigorous and light on his feet when he grasped her hand. His chin, when he drew her close, brushed across her hair. Harriet felt his grip tighten and a new alertness run through him. As she leant back into the turn his body pressed against hers, below her waist, below his belt.

David McBride stood with James by the supper table, his glass loose in his hand. His eyes followed Harriet round the room.

'Your wife is a very fine dancer.'

'Yes. She knows how to lean away; to make it look as if she is yielding, when in fact she makes one follow her.'

David touched the reassuring square of the book in his pocket. Beside James he felt his outline to be indefinite.

'You speak as if she was a strategist.'

'Perhaps she is; but it may be simply that the elegance that others have to learn comes to her by nature. With Harriet one never really knows.'

'To leave now is very difficult.'

'To be sure, we are only just married; but it catches one up, the anticipation to get out and try oneself against the worst. Do you not feel it yourself?'

David coughed. A soldier was trained to kill. His trade could only be the opposite.

'I will come up to death in a different way, if that is what you mean. I go for myself, for advancement in my profession. A surgeoncy is as good a way forward in my line as a captaincy in yours.'

An eager look crossed his face.

'Many of the medical men in Edinburgh learned their trade in the army. They put it this way; a battle will test your skill in twenty-four hours more than a whole year's work in London.'

'And no one will remark your mistakes.'

'You are too harsh on us, James. No surgeons are more skilled than those in the army; but we must experiment also, take risks that may save lives. There is so much to learn, and the future pulls me on.'

David lowered his voice. He turned away from the dance floor, where Harriet still circled with the Major.

'I walked through the churchyard on the way here, and you know what I found?'

'The dead, I should think. Men beyond the surgeon's art.'

'Four small graves, besides; from the inscriptions I believe them all the children of your servant.'

'Thomas Orde?'

'Yes, one after another, year upon year.'

Thomas Orde was a worsted weaver, a proud man put out of work by the collapse of trade between Britain and the Continent. He went with James as his servant to save money for his family.

'Listen, David, that is something Thomas does not speak of, so I beg you do not mention it. After his first son, Nelson, each was stillborn. Nelson is five now. Thomas feels it like a curse and fears they may never have another.'

'It is a phenomenon I wish to investigate. With progress we may understand it.'

'A battlefield is not the site for such investigations, David. Few children, I believe, are born there.'

'No, you mistake me; it is their deaths that interest me; how death may be prevented. In Spain I may learn.'

'Ah yes.' To David's surprise James sighed. 'Your job is to pluck up wounded, patch them up and send them out to face death all over again.'

James straightened up and saw the Major steer Harriet towards them. George Yallop glided like a water-boatman across the floor, composed and not even out of breath. Dorothy Yallop walked up, and pushed the lapsed Britannia up her forehead. The Major lifted his hand from Harriet's back, and bowed.

'Mrs Raven, it has been a pleasure. I shall see you again when I return. Take good care of yourself.'

'I shall have plenty of time to practise my waltz, Major. You will find me an expert when you get back.'

The Yallops made their way to the door, one neat and immaculate in outline, the other disordered and unkempt. George Yallop breathed in a gulp of night air.

'That girl will cause trouble, if I am not mistaken.'

'Nonsense, George. She is charming, that is all.'

'Well, my dear, I leave that kind of thing to you who has much more discernment than I, but there is something in her dancing I cannot quite place.'

'It is simply that the world knows her story; her mother's nervous disposition, and her flight, if flight it was: that she never returned, at any rate. That hangs about Harriet, I think, makes people talk.'

George Yallop squared his shoulders, tightened his arm round his wife and kissed her powdered cheek.

'As long as it does not affect Captain Raven it is not for me to enquire, eh Dorothy? Let us forget it; we have our own business to attend to.'

'TIME TO BE OFF,' James said. He walked to pick out his sword from the careful stack at the other end of the room.

'Good night, Dr McBride.' Harriet did not look up at David. 'I had better find my cloak. I may see you in the morning, perhaps.'

Dr McBride looked at her again as he had done upstairs, with concentration, as if he were considering certain worrying symptoms.

'There is nothing wrong with me, you know.'

'Indeed not. It must be with me. So, good evening, Mrs Raven, and farewell.'

McBride put his empty glass on the table and walked out of the room before Harriet could reply.

OUTSIDE THE HOTEL IN the market place, soldiers sheltered from the snow under the shallow dome of the Butter Cross and lined up along the cowslip-yellow walls of the hotel.

'Eve-nun, Cap-un Raven,' they shouted. Their voices rose with the first syllable of James's name in the East Anglian way.

''Night, men.'

Hunger drove these men to sign up. They did not fight for their king; Suffolk meres and Norfolk broads had never bred a love of crowns. But they were sturdy; in their speech James heard the slow, water-circled self-sufficiency of East Anglia, the dogged stubbornness that, for a few moments, filled him with pride to be one of them.

Down a narrow street off the market place stood the remains of Bungay castle, that had once sat sentinel above the valley. The castle commanded wide views all around, snug on its mound in the narrow neck of the oxbow bend of the river. Now all that remained was the lumpy curvature of the curtain wall and the towers of the gatehouse. Where the castle keep had once risen, clusters of sheep stood amongst the ruins like ancient boulders, luminous in the darkness. Sleety snow soaked into their long fissured coats and water dripped from their narrow bowed heads. War had reached this far before; but now it seemed impossible that any invader would ever threaten this green world. Yet what did they fight for if not to stop Bonaparte declaring that this, too, was a part of his empire?

Harriet jumped out of the open carriage door onto the hard-standing in front of the house and ran in. She held up her long skirts with one hand. James followed; he took the shallow steps in twos and arrived in the hall in time to see Harriet turn into the bedroom at the top of the stairs.

Perhaps he looked at it the wrong way round. The war was not to stop Napoleon invading Britain or turning all of Europe blue in the image of France. No: to the victor would go not just safety but the spoils, the whole world, or all the world where war had reached; the serrated coasts of South America, the pointed Capes in India and Africa, islands in the China seas; the Union flag would rise over them all.

When James reached the bedroom he found Harriet seated at her small table. She fiddled with the clasp of an earring, one hand buried in her straight brown hair. Light from the candles danced over her mother's necklace. James came up behind her and slid one hand underneath the gathered top of her gown and over her breast.

James kept his hand there, and Harriet tipped her head back to gaze up at him. His body, pressed to the chair-back, was already taut.

'You will have to help me.'

'Help you?'

'Get me out of this.'

'Mrs Raven, I shall be delighted.'

The gown slid to the floor with a sigh. Harriet lifted her arms and James bunched the shift with care. He held it out of the way of the points of the necklace and lifted it over Harriet's head. He had seen her naked, how many—thirty times, now, but each time his own body registered a shock. This evening he looked at her with especial care and a kind of detachment. His eyes travelled down her narrow body past her breasts, the slight indent of her waist, and came to rest on the sharp curve of her hip bone. How had he never noticed the way it sat under her skin, and gathered a shadow in its lee like a tarn on a mountainside? He must touch it, kiss it, remember.

In the dark river valley a dog barked and settled. James watched with impatience as Harriet walked to the bed. He had learned from Lady Lavington how to wait, to extend the moment before he pulled her to him.

Usually he could bear it; he could kiss slowly, stretch the time until it nearly broke. But tonight he was different. He felt close to panic; he wanted to dive into her, grab the thing he always sought, and carry it to the surface the way a pearl-fisher brings his prize from the depths of the sea.

~

LOOSE FLAKES OF SNOW floated down into New Court and melted on the flags. They fell like cotton fragments, frayed at the edges. Nathan Rothschild watched them twist out of the sky and remembered winters in Frankfurt. That was real snow: solid flakes, that sat one on top of another till the steep roofs of the Judengasse were dressed in white. The next day he and his brothers would wake, two in a bed, and run to the gable windows to see the street sparkle in the sun. Just west of the Judengasse the River Main froze thick and glittered. Oh, they were skating days, if there wasn't shul; snowball and stamping days with the little ones wrapped up tight and good strong boots on.

Long ago, when he must have been a man of seventeen, with years of Hebrew behind him and a stool in the office already, he had come to the door to see Jakob hard at work piling snowballs in a perfect pyramid like the cannon balls they saw in the Prince's arsenal beyond the zig-zag of the city walls. Lottie with him, under orders; Jakob with a serious look on his face. *'Zehr kalt, zehr kalt,'* Jakob said when he saw his brother, and held up two red hands, palms out. The rascal could not have been more than three years old and he complained already, even at play.

Well, he had been nowhere to rival it since. Frankfurt winters were real winters, blue-skied, with air crisp as starched Virginia cotton. In Manchester, from October to March, the air was soft and wet, like soap, and the sky so dark he had to take samples right into the street to see their quality. Nathan shook his head. In Manchester the winter seeped down into you and never drained away, and summer was unworthy of the name.

But then, he admitted it: cottons had never held his attention. Patterns in calico had none of the beauty of a bank draft, however much you bought, unbundled, retied, and sold on. Clients complained; Harman— old Jacob, who bowed low to him these days—wrote to his father about arrears on his account. Letters from Mayer Amschel Rothschild arrived in England, heavy with his disappointment and admonition.

Nathan had lasted five years in Manchester; long enough to bring a goodish fortune south to London, parlay it into his Hannah's hand in marriage, set up at 12 Great St Helen's, move to better quarters in New Court right in the centre of the City, and so begin. Set up home, some would have said.

Nathan went out of his office and opened the door of his house. New Court was narrow and high. The houses looked close at one another across it. He had chosen New Court not just because it was a few steps from the Exchange, but for its familiarity. In the Judengasse, until the French burned down half the street, scores of families lived crushed together, a thousand souls at least, in a hundred houses set right on the pavements with tiny courts behind where children played and washing hung in sagging lines. Even after the French came, his people were slow to move. He liked life like that, the press of humanity, sounds of children, packages delivered, the street cleaner and lamplighter close enough to see the quality of their britches, a ring of metal on the flagstones.

But home? How people liked to talk of it. English or foreign, it made no difference. You could hear them on the Exchange, solid men from Holland or Riga or the East; watch them turn misty-eyed and vague and begin to picture it; the light off a canal, the dome of the Hagia Sophia, the fall of a particular brook or slant of an apple tree. Nathan shrugged and walked back into his office. He looked with indifference at the blue flames of Newcastle coal in his hearth. Meadows, bricks, country turns of phrase, even the snows of Frankfurt: why put faith in them? For a man of ambition, home was a portable commodity. Keep it in your head, carry it with you, and you can never lose it.

To be sure, he said to himself, one can deposit a little of it here and there; but never the balance. A piece of home now stood above him, in the three upper storeys of the red-brick house, with his dear Hannah, the children, the solid bedroom furniture, and curtains of best damask that he had off Rathbone wholesale at ten shillings the yard before he left Manchester. Pieces about and beneath him, too: his own office on the ground floor, clerks in the back and the reassuring presence of the kitchen below. Underneath me the cooks are at work, he thought, and slid out his watch; and where would we be without the solid comfort of food? You could keep the books in credit—though a clever man always had more money out than in—but he had made a rule in New Court always to run a surplus in foodstuffs. A dinner that ended with empty plates was no dinner at all.

Nathan pulled his small brass bell from under a pile of papers and rang it briskly.

'Moses.'

His clerk Moses Solomon came in through the doors that divided back and front on the ground floor.

'Lady Wellington's accounts, and call down for the coffee to be prepared.'

Moses nodded once and left. Nathan's brother Calmann in Amsterdam had recommended Moses as a man with a neat economy of word and gesture. He had come off the packet already sharp, and now he was done with deference, Nathan noticed with satisfaction. Outside synagogue, where a bow joined one man to another, he himself disdained to bob about. The English rated politeness far too highly; any man could bend and produce a smile.

This afternoon, Nathan expected Lady Wellington. He kept a number of private clients, taken on, why not, with an eye to the future. A junior minister with a promising career, an heiress who had just married well, a merchant with a good balance already at Coutts. Investments, really. He could meet such people once a month, deal in stocks and consols for them in a small way; wait.

BY THE BANK OF England, Kitty Wellington pushed down the window of her cab and listened to stockjobbers swap prices, heads together at the railings: the manly hum of the City at work. Men were everywhere; bankers with top hats; delivery boys who held trays from the chop-houses high above the crowd; printers and newsmen; Frenchmen in exile, Russians in furs, street sweepers in ragged soldiers' topcoats, and mud-larks with pennies up from the river. The colours men wore gave the City of London its palette. Engrossing black, chestnut, creamy buff, the egret-white of cravats and shirts; solid tones, unfickle and restrained, but lit with a flash of buckle and watch chain and the sheen of expensive velvet.

Off St Swithin's Lane, the cab wheels rang on cobbles. The sounds of the city withdrew as they came to a stop in New Court. By no. 2, a groom held a pony fresh from the stable, saddled and ready to leave. Its black hide absorbed the fallen snow. Warm soupy steam drifted from its nostrils.

Kitty climbed the four shallow steps and pulled the bell.

'Mr Rothschild expects you, my Lady,' the footman said, and held out his hand for her cloak.

At the same moment Nathan Rothschild came out into the hall and ushered her inside with an arm that shadowed her shoulders. He slapped his feet heavily on the boards and turned them outwards with each step. 'Come into the shop. It is my honour to see you, and on this good day, also.'

The room was small and panelled to the ceiling. Stacks of paper stood all over the floor like the shaken remains of an ancient empire. Letters and scribbled notes covered the desk, and across them lay a leather dispatch bag, its underside dark and greased with pony sweat. On the back of the chair hung Nathan's fine cotton cravat, pressed and unworn.

Nathan handed Kitty into her chair and eased back onto his calves. His stomach pressed through his waistcoat like a hard-boiled egg. Nathan Rothschild, Kitty thought, was a man born to be fat; largeness became him. The buttons on his silk breeches were undone at the knees as if his legs demanded more room.

'Never mind the disorder. You see how it is; and my brothers deride me for it, though except Jakob they have never yet been here.'

Nathan laughed sharply and banged on the connecting door. His high collar scraped against his jowls. Moses Solomon brought a volume of papers and a maid came in with a silver tray of coffee and small almond biscuits.

Kitty looked forward to her appointments with Mr Rothschild, and sat down with anticipation, as if they were to play a hand at cards. There was something complete about Mr Rothschild's attention that sharpened and calmed her mind and answered to a need. Looking back at the day, she was more glad than usual that she was here in the city surrounded by men and figures.

'SHOW HER IN,' SHE had said to the butler.

'Mrs Fitzwilliam, Piccadilly', the card announced in ornate letters. When Kitty ran her finger across it she found that the indentation was shallow. Up the marble stairs, a minute later, the tread was a soft scrape, slow and hardly audible. Her caller wore court slippers, to show she came in a coach.

'Lady Wellington.'

Kitty's visitor stretched out a hand covered in lace to the fingertips. Kitty did not get up.

'Yes, he told me I should find you cool. You hold yourself back, he said.'

'Of whom do I have the pleasure?'

'I am Mrs Fitzwilliam.'

'I do not believe we are acquainted.'

'Oh, but I feel I do know you; I feel that we know each other.'

'Indeed.'

'Arthur talked of you. I am just back from Spain; an officer's wife.'

Mrs Fitzwilliam glanced at Kitty again, and swayed a little.

'I have known Arthur for three years.'

'Please sit down, Mrs Fitzwilliam. You appear to be unwell.'

Mrs Fitzwilliam sat down promptly on the divan. Beneath her bosom two pink ribbons lay crossed and knotted over her gown in the latest style.

'I knew him since before he went to Portugal; but lately in camp.'

Mrs Fitzwilliam gestured out to Harley Street, as if the leafless trees bent to listen to her.

'Times are hard, my husband on half-pay. The plate is gone already.'

'And so, Mrs Fitzwilliam?'

'And so, your Ladyship, I have been forced to contemplate the sale of my memoirs. Loving Arthur as I did, I kept a diary of his visits. No detail will prove too small for the press.'

Mrs Fitzwilliam pulled a calf-bound book from her pocket.

'Lady Wellington, I am a woman, too; a woman first, I should say. I see how these revelations will hurt you.'

Kitty was silent. On the mantelpiece a clock ticked; a gift from the city of Lisbon to her husband last year.

'I am prepared, of course, to delay publication. It is quite a simple matter, as I am sure you know. The sum would not be large; we could settle on a hundred guineas.'

Mrs Fitzwilliam sighed. She appeared to be surprised at the modesty of her own demand.

'You are not the first, Mrs Fitzwilliam, who has come to me. Some have suggested publication; others have Arthur's letters.'

'Indeed; but, Lady Wellington, Arthur cared for me in a particular way.'

'You may print what you like. I do not read the papers.'

'But your reputation, Lady Wellington, and your children. What of them?'

'I will look after my reputation, Mrs Fitzwilliam. Yours is your own affair. Please go now.'

Mrs Fitzwilliam rose and took a step towards Kitty.

'You leave me no choice, Lady Wellington. I assure you, you will regret what you have said to me today.'

Kitty finally stood up and faced her visitor. Besides Mrs Fitzwilliam's rounded form she felt angular and slight though she could look her straight in the eye.

'You see me as your enemy,' she said. 'But I have long since given up thinking of you, or others like you, as mine. I think you may find in the end that we are on the same side.'

'I will never be on the same side as you, Lady Wellington.'

Mrs Fitzwilliam raised her voice.

'It is not just my memoirs. I have something of his, a precious gift.'

He has given her a ring, Kitty thought, some sort of signet ring which has his crest on it or a seal that all the world knows to be his.

'Goodbye, Mrs Fitzwilliam. I do not think we need meet again.'

Money, money was what she needed, Kitty thought as her carriage turned into New Court. Not the small amount Mrs Fitzwilliam requested, but much more. Enough to give her independence; enough for a life.

NATHAN ROTHSCHILD SAT DOWN, poured coffee, threw several spoonfuls of sugar into his cup, and stirred it with an almond biscuit. The top of his bald head gleamed.

'So, let us begin, dear Lady Wellington. I have been buying three per cent consols on your account, as you requested. But there are better things you may do.'

'Yes,' Kitty said.

'You will never make a fortune with a few thousands laid out in that way. That is why I gave up the textile trade. All is far too slow.'

Nathan thrust a hand into the pocket of his velvet breeches and leant back in his chair. His voice was more modulated than his heavy looks suggested.

'I did not come to London to dabble on the 'Change and hang a few pictures on my walls. Here we trade in something else, much bigger. Risk.'

'Risk?'

'And news, of course. We deal in risk coupled with news, or, let me put it another way, risk tempered by news. To make a good guess, yes? To guess when to move, when to go in, you must know the strength of your forces and those of your rivals. That Lord Wellington can understand.'

He pulled forward a sheet of paper, covered with notes in angular black letters.

'From my brother Jakob in Paris, just arrived with our courier.'

'Good news?' Kitty asked.

The familiar shiver ran across her skin. Any news from abroad might be about Arthur or her brother Ned Pakenham, golden-haired and eager to please. Ned wished too much to prove that his promotion owed nothing to family ties; it made him reckless.

Nathan handed her the paper. Beyond the date of four days ago, Kitty could make nothing out. The hurried cursive was not a Latin hand.

'What is this script, Mr Rothschild?'

'Jeudendeutsch. German with Hebrew letters and a few private words thrown in; very safe from curious eyes.'

He laughed again, a harsh note in his light voice, and threw the letter back onto the heap on the desk.

'We write well, neither of us. Jakob howls down my German, dear lady, and my English is hardly better; but this is good news. My brother tells me the Assembly in Prussia has voted to allow the Emperor across that territory. You understand his meaning?'

'No.'

'The result will be the Emperor marching east to discomfort our Russian friends.'

'Yes?'

'So another game begins. It will be a good one, and long, I think. Would you care to join me in it, Lady Wellington?'

'You must explain it first.'

'Well then: Russia and France will be at war. We must sell Russian bonds now and buy them back later, and at a discount.' Nathan leaned towards her. 'Do you understand me?'

'Not well enough.'

'What I am saying, dear lady, is that we have the information first. The stocks are bound to fall when the news gets out, so we sell now. We place a bet, as it were, on the panic on the Exchange to buy in again.'

'And take the profit?'

'No, no, of course not. We lay out the profit on something else. Bullion, for instance; our Russian friends will be needing of that. Or we might lend it, at greater risk, to the Spanish king in exile.'

'That sounds most adventurous.'

'A bet, merely, on the King's return to Madrid.'

After a pause Mr Rothschild said, 'There is another way, which asks a cooler head.'

'And what is that?'

'We do not, exactly, sell stock, say; but we promise to do so, at a fixed price.'

'Yes?'

'But in this moment we know that the stock will fall, and fall before our buyer must pay for it. So we wait a day or two.'

'What good does that do us if we have already agreed to sell?'

'Lady Wellington, you must pay good attention. We do not own the stock when we agree to sell it and so we must buy it, and then sell it. Our buyer has already made a bargain with us, which he must keep, and he may do very well by his purchase in the end. But we are not interested in the end, but in how we make a profit with speed. When we come to buy we pay less than we will sell for and before any money has been exchanged, we have already a good profit, to which we will add a small commission for the purchase in the first place.'

Nathan drew an arabesque in the air the way a painter makes a stroke on his canvas.

'The fact is this. Because we know the stock must fall, we make our money in that moment; and a lovely moment it is. One such has come today.'

'With your courier?'

'Exactly, dear lady. You are a fine pupil. Now here is still the more beautiful part. Sometimes our information informs merely. Sometimes it has a magic of its own.'

'What do you mean?'

'I mean that a word from New Court can have a shrinking effect upon a stock; or, indeed, it may have the contrary.'

'Forgive me, Mr Rothschild, but that has a whiff of sulphur about it.'

'Yes, yes. It is how we can create the world anew. That is the business I am in; none of the old stuff. But the devil is not always on our side. Rothschilds is not always correct. A clever man is merely correct more often than his rivals.'

Nathan Rothschild considered Kitty. He preferred to help those who helped him, and Lady Wellington did not fuss. She interested him; besides, she had something he wanted.

'What do you say? Should I lay out your thousands in these ways? The risk is with you.'

'Perhaps I should take time to consider the proposition.'

'My dear Lady Wellington, if we are to begin, then we must begin today.'

He threw out a hand towards the dispatch bag on his desk.

'My courier arrived earlier this morning. We should have had the carrier pigeons also, though they struggle against this wind.' He nodded towards the window. 'But tomorrow, or the day following, Barings will have the news, Harman, too; Herr Schroder: yes, even Heinrich, my German friend.' He laughed scornfully. 'They will all sell also. So we must do it today.'

Kitty felt the air thin and her heart sound loud. What risk had women been bred to take? Only the risk of marriage and then the gamble of childbirth when nature rolled the dice. Women of her sort, married women of quality, were never thought to invest, though she was not quite alone. Lady Blessington held money in mining stocks, and had tried to interest her, over tea, in the virtues of Peruvian ores. Lady Lavington had a taste for speculation as well as young men and had hinted that one paid easily for the other. By law no married women could do it; they came to the City with secret accounts or with the connivance of husbands busy with other matters. The money she was giving to Nathan now, bits and pieces of savings, could not be called hers. Arthur granted it her to make the scales a little more even. She had her scraps of cash, he his other amusements.

Kitty looked up at Mr Rothschild. He drew in his solid bottom lip and looked at her steadily. Used to deference or pity in men's eyes, Kitty was surprised to see eagerness in his manner. He was not, perhaps, even thinking about her at all.

'Yes,' she said. 'Yes, then, I will put my thousands in your hands.'

'Good.'

'With a definite end in view the risk seems small,' Kitty added, as if she needed to explain herself.

'An end?' Nathan was suddenly intent.

'Do you not have an end also?'

'My dear lady, this great game is itself the end. But there are certain things; perhaps I shall tell you one future day. As for you; do you play the game for your children?'

'No, not for them.'

'Boys, are they not?'

'Arthur and Charles, yes; they are five and four years old. Then my sister-in-law's child Gerald has lately come to me, and my husband's god-son Arthur Freese has been with me for five years. They are all my sons. But I invest for myself.'

'I am pleased. Let us begin then.'

'You have my confidence,' Kitty said.

Nathan took her hand between his hands and patted it briskly as a boy might pat a sandcastle to keep it standing when the tide came in.

'Not a word to anyone.'

At the door he stopped, and said, as if it were an afterthought, 'You are acquainted with Mr Charles Herries?'

'You mean Mr Herries at Great George Street? Only in a formal way. He has only lately taken up his appointment, I believe.'

Mr Rothschild came a step closer. A childish shriek followed a thump on the boards on the floor above.

'My Charlotte, my Lotte.'

Nathan smiled with delight. Then with surprising swiftness he leaned forward and began to whisper in Kitty's ear, his gutturals dry as autumn leaves. Under the light of the open doorway Kitty caught a kingfisher flash in his brown eyes.

'You will do that for me, Lady Wellington?'

'Mr Rothschild, I am delighted to be able to return a favour.'

Snow fell against a black sky on the way home. In Cavendish Square, before the coachmen turned into Harley Street, she watched her neighbour Sir William Beechey struggle head down through the cold flakes.

Alone in her parlour, Kitty took a card from her writing desk and wrote a few lines. On the cover sheet she added the recipient and address: Mr Charles Herries, commissary-in-chief, the Commissary Office, Great George Street. Then she rang for the footman, and went upstairs to change for dinner.

～

ARTHUR WELLESLEY, LORD WELLINGTON, commander-in-chief of the British army in the Peninsula, had received two letters that morning that whipped up the choppy surface of his temper. Now he rode through the hills above Ciudad Rodrigo and not even the sight of the recently captured fortress down below him could smooth it down. Rigid and imposing, with the town clasped within the embrace of its walls, Ciudad Rodrigo commanded the northern routes from Portugal into Spain; taking it was useless without the complement of its southern neighbour, Badajoz; and Badajoz had resisted the British army twice already. A victory like that of Ciudad Rodrigo only led to the possibility of another defeat. He had little to show for nearly three years in charge of the British army. Most of the time his army had been holed up in Portugal. Now that he had begun to advance, he must go on. He needed, by the summer, to seal off Portugal from invasion and push the French out of central Spain. Then he might advance on Madrid, where Joseph Bonaparte sat in the Royal Palace with works of art about him; a bumbling incompetent promoted by a younger brother blinded by the ties of kinship. That, Wellington thought with a glance to his left, was a mistake with which he could never be reproached.

Ned Pakenham, by the Commander's side, felt his ill humour like a magnetic field. It repelled approaching objects. General Pakenham kept a discreet distance between his horse and Arthur's; they might be brothers-in-law, but their relation made no difference to the cutting remarks Lord Wellington lobbed his way if he attempted to speak too soon.

Pakenham rode bare-headed; the heat of his hatband made his head ache; once out of sight of headquarters he liked to tuck his hat under a saddle flap. A stray crumb from his hasty lunch stuck to his upper lip. Lord Wellington glanced at his brother-in-law with dismay. He disdained to eat when there was work to be done, and contented himself with a boiled egg from his pocket. Worse than that, the glint of silver in Ned's fair curls reminded him of Kitty and her brown hair turned to grey, and then of the letter she had sent; a ramble about household arrangements and investments. Investments! Women presumed to know too much and then talked too much about it. What did he care what Kitty did with her pin money or the savings on the housekeeping she mentioned, when he struggled to find the cash to feed his army? Forty thousand men, doctors and unctuous chaplains, women who attached themselves to the baggage train despite his best efforts, horses and mules, servants, hundreds of cattle for slaughter: all to be fed, every man and beast turned towards him, mouths agape.

It would be better not to hear from Kitty at all. Or, to put it another way, when he did receive letters, he was glad of the profession he had chosen, grateful for war. Here in the Peninsula he could at least forget the mistake of his marriage and soothe himself with the women who came for him after a victory. Who knew what Ned imagined: his officers and staff knew better than to refer to Kitty in his presence.

Then, Kitty was almost forty, and that was another reason not to think of her. It showed him up to be near forty-three. Lord Wellington disliked the thought of his own age; it stood as a kind of defeat. He demanded a bachelor feel to headquarters, insisted on the timbre of youth. His officers, unlike his wife, were always eager to comply; boys as young as twenty aped his manner and copied his dress.

Now, this morning, there had been a second letter that annoyed him even more than Kitty's, a request from a gentleman volunteer to be placed 'where danger and valour most demanded it', or something of the sort. What nonsense these perfumed creatures wrote. This one, the Honourable Robert Heaton, was fresh out from Piccadilly it looked like, with servants, horses, the latest kit and no doubt a volume of Walter Scott in his valise. Or Moore's *Irish Melodies*, a book that he, as an Irishman who knew that wet green wasteland, had special cause to dislike. 'Go where glory waits thee'; that was its first line, its absurd sentiment. They plagued his life, these volunteers. Heaton's letter mentioned 'previous postings in the service of the crown'. The man had most likely been a member of the militia and done a turn round his park on a Sunday afternoon.

Lord Wellington tapped his horse into greater speed.

'I shall march south on Badajoz and establish headquarters at Elvas without delay, Ned, take advantage of the victory here.'

He said nothing about whether he would be taking him south or leaving him with the garrison at Ciudad Rodrigo, Edward Pakenham thought with alarm, and he knew better than to ask. General orders would go out soon and his would be included. Ned had never felt at ease with his brother-in-law. He often found himself addressing him in the formal way, when, out of earshot of other officers, 'Arthur' should have been acceptable.

'Yes, sir. I hear Elvas is a filthy town.'

'Filthy and fortified, Ned. This time I intend to take Badajoz by April and push on across the country.'

Wellington paused. Ned needed something to do. It was irksome to have him so loyally in attendance; besides, he reeked of Ireland and the wastes of County Meath.

'Oh, and Ned; I have a request here from another foolhardy volunteer. Can you place him somewhere where the officers are not at full strength; the 44th or the 9th, say; any regiment off to Elvas soon?'

'Yes, my Lord. I will send out a note to the regimental colonels.'

Edward Pakenham rode back to the battered fortress in silence. The sun fell down the valley behind him, dusty red in the smoke from thousands of camp fires. He felt the General's impatience like a grey shadow. Sometimes he regretted the moment he had handed his sister to Sir Arthur Wellesley in Dublin six years ago, standing in for his father Lord Longford under the ribbons and bows of the stuccoed ceiling. Looking back, he had been apprehensive even then for the happiness Kitty promised herself after the years of Arthur's absence and in the joy of his return.

2

Elvas, Portugal, Badajoz, Spain and London

MARCH–APRIL 1812

As he came down from the border town of Elvas, David McBride looked across a wide, desolate plain. In the sky, eagles skimmed the currents on wings that rippled like cut paper. Far below, three hours' ride away, the grey walls of the fortress of Badajoz stood out in the low spring sun, walled into the side of the city above the meandering Guadiana River. Behind Badajoz a ridge of hills pushed into the Spanish interior and on the horizon a white band of light parted land and sky. To the south, the upland fell away towards Seville and the sea, guarded by a single outcrop.

Beside David, correct and immaculate on a grey pony, rode the Hon. Robert Heaton, the volunteer, new out to Spain, who glanced round like a man at the theatre, about to take a seat. Dressed in pressed grey trousers with his thick wavy hair new-cut and brushed over his forehead, Heaton's air suggested that he expected a fine performance. He appeared to be a man of the world. Eagerness and languor balanced in him to leave no hint of his intentions. Why was he here? Heaton sat to attention as they came closer to the great ridge.

'Albuera, is it not?' Heaton swept an arm southwards. A small dog trotted by his stirrup. The hill of Albuera lay like a beached sea creature, its blue rump lit by the rising light.

David nodded. How peaceful Albuera looked, slumped and benign. Yet it was a graveyard. The dead lay thick on its sides. A year ago five thousand men had died there in Lord Wellington's previous attempt to capture Badajoz.

Heaton looked down on the tiny figures far along the road ahead.

Round the city the zig-zags of entrenchments and enfilades looked like gashes cut into the ochre earth with a giant butter knife. A hum reached them through the still air, the sounds of men as they washed, chopped, dug, shouted, grumbled and sang. Silent in the middle, the city of Badajoz awaited her attacker. Heaton stopped a minute to admire the view.

'Marvellous; quite a panorama.When do you expect the storming?'

'Mr Heaton, as the 9th's regimental surgeon, I am stationed in the rear, as you know. At present I wait and treat the sick as they come in. I shall direct you to Colonel Paston and the 44th, and you may offer your services to him. When the assault is ordered, I shall doubtless be called down, but who knows when the General will judge that the time is right.'

'Quite so. The General; I look forward to a meeting with him.'

David's interest was caught by Heaton's tone. The man's voice had a keenness to it, an edge like steel that was a contrast to the way he held the reins and sat so easily.

'You think, Mr Heaton, that it is the commander who makes the difference between victory and defeat, or something else?'

'You ask me what makes a great general, doctor? I have given the question some thought. A certain detachment, do you think, to make a man able to throw his troops at bayonets and cannon?'

David looked along the clogged road in front of them, the carts and drivers, bullocks and boys, fading into the distance where thousands of men had begun the siege. Could a commander, Lord Wellington or anyone else, really shape all their movements? He shifted his bulk in the saddle, conscious that beside Mr Heaton he cut a poor figure. Perhaps everyone, he and Mr Heaton too, were merely a part of a greater world, where beasts hunted one another without any notion that they obeyed nature's laws? Right now, in the undergrowth beside them, creatures killed one another. Was man so different?

'Do you not wonder, Mr Heaton, how all the species in nature display the same activities? Swallows move back and forth across the world as man has done from time immemorial; the hawk swoops down on a weaker prey.'

He gestured towards the town below.

'I am not apt to think much about nature, I must confess.' Heaton looked bored. 'Much of it seems an unfortunate mistake. All in all, one is much safer in St James's. I cannot abide it for long out of town, Newmarket and the hunt excepted. The races, though; now there one certainly can see the likeness between man and beast.'

'I am inclined from my studies to think the affinity closer than we believe.'

'How so, sir?'

'When I was a student at Edinburgh, a Mr Leacock from Barbados described to me his experiments in the transfusion of blood. When he put the blood of a cat into a dog, the dog died.'

'Ah, now that is cruel.' Heaton was suddenly more interested. 'I keep a few hounds myself, as well as Racket here, of course.'

Heaton's dog, a chestnut spaniel with a mongrel touch, pushed his ears forward at the mention of his name.

'Yet when he took the blood of a slave, and transfused it into a dog, the dog survived. So, too, when the transfusions were given from slave to slave; some died, others lived.'

'What do you suggest, Dr McBride? Sounds a damn waste of good men and dogs to me.'

'The men were ill, I should add. Or so Leacock assured me.'

'And the dogs? Perfectly well, I dare say. What a wretch your Leacock was; but then one can expect nothing better from the son of a plantation owner. I know the type.'

Heaton appeared to be languid, distracted even, but David noticed that his eyes were alert and focused on him. Why would he disguise his interest? Perhaps he was not quite the man he offered to the world.

'What Mr Leacock's experiment suggests to me is that if the blood of dogs and humans is so close in composition, perhaps man and the animal kingdom are too.'

'Are you telling me this Leacock had to torment his poor hounds to show that men and dogs have an affinity? Good lord, sir! Had he not read his Homer or looked in the eyes of a creature like Racket here?'

In response to Heaton's voice, Racket's feathered tail began to swish back and forth.

'Look at the sympathy there.'

David felt the thread of the conversation run away from him.

'I do not refer to the organs of feeling, that is to say the nerves, but the blood.'

'I do understand, and I hope we may be friends. But, Dr McBride, I shall not be able to answer for my conduct if I find you torment a poor animal. The local people are bad enough, as it is. The horses, too, are dreadfully neglected.'

'No,' David said, 'I shall have no leisure for experiments while the siege continues.'

He paused and tapped his pocket. A picture of Harriet Raven came to him, the look of amusement on her face he had seen in Suffolk the night before they left and the sound of her deep laugh. He remembered that she, like him, was captivated by experiment. David sat up on his horse and coughed as he might in answer to a summons.

'Do you leave anyone behind, Mr Heaton?'

Heaton looked along the road ahead as if the answer to David's question might lie there.

'No, I cannot say I do, though here and there one misses a person, of course.'

Heaton's speech tailed away. The two men rode on in silence until they came onto the wide shallow valley of the Guadiana River, and joined a slow convoy across one of the new pontoon bridges. Mr Heaton dismounted and led his pony across with girlish tenderness, a silk handkerchief tied round her eyes, as if she was a child afraid of heights.

'Athena is her name, Dr McBride. She is a dear thing, but skittish over water.'

Once on the south side of the river, they rode round the battlements of Badajoz at a safe distance. All the way round the French had deepened the ditches in front of the walls and thrown up escarpments beyond them. The walls were high and white, the joins between the great blocks of stone deepened into dark crevasses in which valerian and vetches had taken hold. The great fortress itself was Moorish, David realised, built to keep the Christians at bay and the blood of one species of humanity from mingling with another.

After an hour they came into the army encampment. Right to the horizon, groups of men bivouacked under old cork oaks or sheltered from the wind and rain in makeshift huts with roofs of leaves and branches. Up a sandy bank, they ran straight into Major Yallop. The Major sat on a camp stool in the open flaps of his tent. He leaned forward and looked out over the camp of the 9th Foot, while his Portuguese servant watched a camp kettle on the fire. When he saw David, Yallop waved his hand in welcome.

'Dr McBride, punctual to the minute. Come over for tea.'

'Major Yallop of the 9th,' David said to Heaton as they picked their way through groups of soldiers to reach the Major's tent. 'He has been with the regiment since before Flanders in '94 and loves it as his family. Yallop will know where the 44th is in all of this.'

Everything about the Major's encampment spoke of custom, readiness and order. Inside the tent David could see the Major's boots upended on sticks to keep the damp from their linings, a cot with a thin mattress neatly rolled on top of it, and two woollen blankets folded in squares. To one side of the cot stood a large wooden chest covered with papers and an inkstand, to the other a portmanteau on a wooden stool with a seat of hessian webbing. From hooks in the end pole hung the Major's sword in its sheath, a retractable spyglass in a leather case and a square shaving mirror with bevelled edges. Carefully laid on a wooden rack were a mahogany pistol case, a hand hammer and bags of nails, and a hatchet with a handle shiny from use.

David came up to the Major.

'Major, this is Mr Robert Heaton. I have ridden with him down from Elvas and believe you might be able to help him.'

David heard Heaton whistle lightly over his shoulder.

'That is quite a blade you have there, Major. French by the look of it.'

'Ah, yes.' The Major grew suddenly alert. 'It came my way at Busaco the year before last, and waits to be put to good use.'

'Quite so. I am waiting for the opportunity myself.' Heaton pulled out his own sword and laid it across the Major's knees.

'From Reddell's in Jermyn Street.' Heaton's tone was casual. 'I am sure you know that establishment.'

Major Yallop turned Heaton's sword over in his hands and looked with attention at the minutely braided silver wire that bound the grip. Then he handed it back and picked up one of the cups of tea from the flat patch of ground beside his stool.

'And what can I do for you?'

Heaton bowed.

'I am a volunteer on the look-out for Colonel Paston and the 44th where I have been placed. I intend to offer the Colonel my services in the assault. But do tell me what is going on here.' Heaton gestured towards a small group of men who sat on a pile of chopped wood and smoked together in silence. 'It scarcely seems like war.'

Major Yallop considered the men. Their scarlet jackets had faded to a rusty brown, their beards were thick with dirt. He pointed to the walls of Badajoz beyond the camp.

'General Philippon, who commands the garrison in there, has fortified the town to perfection, I must give him that. He is confident we shall not get in, and has every reason to be so. Lord Wellington has tried twice before and failed. Besides, General Soult brings his army closer every day. In another month Lord Wellington will be menaced from the south and east and may be forced to withdraw again into Portugal; yet without Badajoz we cannot take Madrid or begin an offensive campaign, the kind, Mr Heaton, that we all wish to take part in.'

'Indeed, sir. Now what do you do here?'

Heaton gave Major Yallop a keen look and David saw the Major return it. Heaton did not behave as a novice might; he appeared, indeed, to test the Major, and George Yallop to relish the challenge Heaton threw down.

'Take a seat and a cup of tea, both of you.'

The Major's servant brought camp stools for them, and then cups of tea. Yallop went on.

'Day by day we push the trenches forward in parallels, as you will have seen on the way down,' he said. 'There are eight hundred men there, besides the covering force. They work six hours at a time, more sometimes at night, then come back to dry out. It is hard work, the everyday labour of a long campaign.'

Major Yallop looked up and listened to a sudden explosion of sound above the crack of muskets. Then he jumped up from his stool, ducked into his tent and came back with his spyglass. With a flick of the wrist he pushed it out to its full length and handed it to Heaton, who stood up and trained it towards the town as if it were an opera glass.

'Find the church tower, there, square above the battlements.'

'Ah, yes, I have it, and four or five fellows hung in the crows' nest round it, dangling their legs like misses on a swing.'

'Lookouts. They spot movement, or a changeover in the trenches, and signal to the batteries to fire in that way. We pick them off, if we are accurate and lucky, with a twenty-four-pounder.'

'Ah. Can we do that now?'

'I am still without my guns, Mr Heaton, as you can see.' Major Yallop sat down and picked up his tin cup again. David saw that the conversation was at an end.

'The 44th and Colonel Paston; you should find them in the advance headquarters, across the Talavera road. You think you will take to fighting, do you?'

Heaton smiled and made a brief bow to the Major.

'I bid you good day, Major, and hope to have the pleasure of your company again. You have a fine set-up here.' He nodded to David, gathered up his pony's reins and swung himself into the saddle in one supple movement.

Major Yallop watched Heaton pick his way between the soldiers. The few dozen men Major Yallop had brought out with him were camped around him in orderly groups, but the Major missed the rest of the regiment.

'Well, Dr McBride, what do you think? I cannot abide those fellows—but you never know. An extra sword-arm might be useful, eh? I'd take him myself if I knew when the rest of the 5th Division will arrive. I have been here since last week without a sniff of Leith or my men. I am like a mother hen separated from her chicks without them, I can tell you.'

The Major swilled down the last of his tea, then stared at the leaves in the bottom of the cup. After a couple of minutes he looked up as if he had forgotten that David was still there.

'Well, good evening, Doctor. You will be looking for a site for yourself, I dare say?'

'I am setting up behind the lines, yes, but we will use billets or a church as a hospital if we get in.'

'We will get in, Dr McBride. This time we will have them.'

George Yallop smiled and waved David goodbye. Something about Heaton had caught his attention, David saw. Heaton's image, his well-groomed persistence, stuck to him too, and accompanied him as he rode towards the high aqueduct at Elvas that evening. Up the ramparts and through the massive gatehouse with the violet horizon behind him, he turned in at the door of the monastery where the hospital was established. Under the eaves black swifts squeaked in their foul-smelling nests. Inside another smell, the sweet odour of sickness and putrefaction, closed in on him. Heaton drifted out of his thoughts.

Before his eyes adjusted to the gloom, David heard his name called.

'Ah, McBride.'

The soft Highland voice belonged to James McGrigor, head of the medical service.

'Still waiting for the rest of the Division, I see from my returns.'

McGrigor tapped a roll of papers across his barrel chest, and David fell in beside him as he walked along the whitewashed corridor.

'Your sick are all neatly tucked in here.'

'Ague cases, mostly. It is a damned difficult thing to treat despite the bark, carries off some men, leaves others without a trace.'

'Yes, quite so.' McGrigor nodded. 'You are an Edinburgh man, I think? You bought a surgeoncy, as I did?'

'I returned to Edinburgh for my education, sir, but my father has the asylum at Bushey. You may know it. There are still a few soldiers there from the wars in America, men who returned disordered in the head and have never recovered.'

David remembered the atmosphere at Bushey when he was a child and accompanied his father on his rounds, one hand tight in his mother's, the other in a pocket, safe from exposure. He saw himself, a plump, solemn boy, dressed in camel britches and a white smock. His father walked the corridors with a firm step, dark and slender, alert for commotion from the wards. Patients were brought in by relatives, or committed themselves in desperation to the asylum's care. When they died, often at their own hands, new ones came to take their place. Some patients, women especially, sat mute for years, or lay curled on narrow beds. Their fellow inmates would walk past them without a look, as if they had already ceased to occupy any space in the world. Such sights haunted David, but it was the sounds of his childhood that returned most often, the wind in the great trees in the grounds, the unhappy cries that gathered, broke, and withdrew, only to begin again.

The old soldiers lived apart from other patients. For thirty years, since he had been wounded in the bitter skirmish at Eutaw Springs, one gunner insisted that blood seeped from him. Another man, who never spoke, was disturbed by constant explosions that made him jump in fear. A third rolled strips of linen into tight curls for bandages; at the end of each day the servants smoothed the strips out again for the next day's work. The old soldier never complained, never noticed perhaps. The work soothed him and stopped the shaking in his hands. The asylum, paid for by pious and fashionable men of rank, was a barracks, they declared, and their fellow patients soldiers of inferior rank. David sighed; war had made those men lunatics and the whole world their battlefield.

The asylum smelled always of carbolic soap and vinegar. From underneath oozed the same sweet smell of decay that assailed him every time he came into the hospital here at Elvas. In the asylum it was the odour of deliquescence, and old age. One or two patients, fearful of nakedness, refused to remove their clothes. They raged and spat at the men who came to wash them, and lodged apart in their own miasma of cloying humanity. Here, the same sweet smell was the token of sickness and infection. David knew it would be much worse after the assault, when he cared for the wounded.

'Ah, indeed,' McGrigor went on, 'your father is a fine man. I wonder you did not choose to follow him.'

'My father is indefatigable, sir, and has the comfort of religion, though few of his patients recover. I found it a melancholy world, thought the mind incurable, and fixed my energies on the body. I am much interested in disorders of the blood.'

'You will see plenty of that in the next few days, sir, and the best of luck with it.' McGrigor took David's hand and squeezed it. 'Good evening, Doctor.'

David watched McGrigor walk away, the roll of documents, crumpled now, still in his hand.

~

BY THE DOOR OF Durrant's Inn behind Manchester Square, Charles Herries hesitated. Light from the hotel windows fell across the pavement in square gold bars. The afternoon had drained out to the west and ahead of him on the horizon the cut of the new canal at Paddington reflected the last meagre slice of light in the sky. A murmur of voices invited him into the saloon down the hall. This evening, after a day of rumours of war from America and the usual press of demands from Spain, he was on the prowl for sweetness. Something to take his mind off his work, he thought; a glass of Madeira, or a Spanish sherry to go down his throat like nectar.

In the saloon, with a glass in his hand, Herries acknowledged with a shake of his sandy head that what he really wanted was a woman. Dreams—no, they were visions!—of women plagued him, even in his office. Beautiful female forms, some sculpted and angular, others round as fruit, had taken up camp in his mind, and ambushed him when he least expected it. He might scan down a column of figures with a stubby forefinger, and then hear a light voice, or see the firm swell of a hip. Then his brown eyes would soften. Everything could be forgotten in a woman, in the joy of possession and escape, especially when he regretted ever rejoicing in his position as commissary-in-chief to the army, a salary of nearly three thousand a year, in his office in Great George Street or the deference of his staff.

Even today, when news came from the Peninsula that Lord Wellington had Badajoz surrounded, Herries's cares did not take leave. The army in Spain marched on a hundred thousand pounds a month, never less. Lord Wellington's men were fed with food bought with bills drawn on the Treasury. The British army ate the purest sterling, every penny of which he had to supply. In dreams, Herries saw himself stand by a muscular and taut commander-in-chief and offer Lord Wellington his bags of coins, like a pilgrim at a shrine. As he held the heavy bags the General grew taller. No matter how high he stretched, Herries could not reach him.

Herries swallowed the last of his sherry and frowned.

'I am thirty-four, and I think like an old man,' he said to himself. He crept about London bowed by responsibilities; the lightness of youth had deserted him long ago. The bills of exchange he sent south were never enough and bought less and less. Someone, Harman, or Latouche in Paris, was making a pretty sum on them, too; buying bills at a discount in Spain, which kept the price low, and cashing them in at a higher rate in London. Latouche had the contacts, the clients who might act as agents. Harman, too. But it was a big operation, one that required a cooler head than he thought either had.

Robert Kennedy, commissary general in the Peninsula, a man about his own age, treated him with disdain. Did Herries not know, Kennedy wrote, that a full oxen cart fed five hundred men a day? The army was a hundred carts short and needed money to buy them. Tons of food lay in the magazines for lack of transport and complaints rained down on him. What was Herries doing about it?

I am in the saloon of an inn, Herries said to himself, soothed by candlelight, women, drink and the chance to forget. But he did not forget, he remembered. Paris, and Lucia Carioli, every detail; the swell of her belly, how he traced up from it the pattern of her ribs, and up again to her smooth brown nipples, how she threw back her head and laughed. We delighted in each other, he thought, and clung to the memory as if it were real flesh.

Paris, six years ago; he should not have been there at all. He had risked everything to go, just from curiosity. For years Paris was forbidden, and any visitor risked the attention of Pitt's secret police. There was the brief peace a decade ago, but then war came again and obscured the city the way a storm swirls in and blots out the horizon. Few men of his age had ventured there, breathed the rich atmosphere of Napoleon's swagger and glory. He had been on the way back from Leipzig, full of the banking business, and calculated, in his headstrong way, that a detour would never be noticed. A visitor from Hesse, he called himself, a German speaker and an ally of France. Lodi, Marengo, Ulm, Austerlitz—the names of French victories were on every tongue. Napoleon had assembled an empire in the space of a few years. No one in a city awash with men from conquered territories asked about his name or nationality; or so he had thought. Then came Lucia and love.

Ever since, he had sought her in others; he took rooms with any willing women who had Lucia's soft olive skin, asked girls with dark hair to dance and flattered them with attentions; once he even followed a woman for half a day because she swung her hips in Lucia's way. The thought of that now made him hollow. The saloon of Durrant's, no more than a parlour of one of the four houses thrown together helter-skelter to make the inn, was as good a place as any to drink away his past and the anxiety of his present. Marylebone was gimcrack and new, built with the profits of war; a place where courtesans took rooms above colonels and both might be gone tomorrow.

'Are you looking for something, sir?'

Now a woman stood in front of him, small and plump, with a pink ribbon crossed beneath her bosom. A splendid bosom, Herries could see. A man might slide a finger tight into the deep valley between its breasts and hold it there in the warmth. He might at the same time press his other hand on the small of her back to draw her to him, with a certainty of pleasure.

Herries ran his hands down the sides of his trousers.

'No, indeed not, thank you. I am here for a sherry, merely.'

'Someone, then?'

Herries looked round the room. In one corner, glasses to hand, a group of young men played cards. At small tables women waited, creatures of silk and lace, with pretty feet and smooth hands. Blood rose up into his cheeks. She had guessed; he had the incomplete look of a man in need. Yet it was a simple transaction, with no need to add shame to the figures. The greatest pleasure in the world? A couple of guineas. A whole night of carelessness? A few more. Who would not pay for that?

He was unable to raise his eyes.

'You have a room?'

'Upstairs.'

'Your name, madam?'

'Madame Duplace.'

He nodded. It was no such thing, of course, but no matter. The tingling sense he had had all day left him. He knew the form of such encounters. She would go upstairs and wait. He would follow after a few minutes. When he came into the room he would find her there, still clothed, with an open bottle of wine. They would drink, as if the transaction was more sociable than mercenary. She, whose name he would never know, might drink; he would think of what was to happen, and wait. When the wine was low, he might advance, push up her gown and feel the warmth of her come from under the cool layers of silk.

SOME TIME LATER DORA Clark stopped outside the door. When Mrs Fitzwilliam—Eliza she called her now—took the room a few weeks before, Dora had agreed, for a small consideration, to tap softly on the hour as she passed. If Eliza coughed in return then she might knock more loudly and announce a delivery. She must remember to say, 'Madame Duplace, a packet.' It was her habit then to wait until the gentleman came out and ask, politely of course, for a small sum. A tip for not seeing. Sometimes she got it, sometimes not.

This one, she could tell, wasn't finished yet. There was no point in her knock or the wait. She heard him, even through the closed door, grunt like an animal that burrowed and scrabbled; as if he knew Mrs Fitzwilliam, as if he thought he loved her. Then, when he had finished there would be the pleasantries, Eliza said, and men would try to stretch them out. They thought it was only polite to turn human, to get back into their skins, and be seemly once the cloud of lust had lifted.

NAKED ON THE BED, Herries looked down at the rise of his stomach, dusted with pale hair, soft as a jelly. I cannot get away from myself, he thought. I look like a young porker that noses in the undergrowth, pink-skinned and on the hunt for truffles. I push for what I want, and men respect me for it, this quality that I have of blind determination, snout

out in the darkness. It will take me far, this greed, this ambition to be recognised. I am called a man of ability.

But the price weighed heavy. Even now, with the warmth of a woman to calm him, and quiet with her scent on his hands, Herries sensed his duties come back. They lined up as he lay there, like marble children on a tomb. He felt for Madame Duplace beside him and ran his hand up her thigh. Oh that he might do that each day. He might pay for another hour and more oblivion, but his thoughts turned away. The room began to seem overheated. Herries sat up and reached for his shirt and cravat. Across the room he saw his shoes, one turned over in his haste, and his trousers inside out.

Herries sat up. He started to sweat.

'How much can I give you?'

The woman looked at him, eyes blue-blank under the disorder of her curling hair.

'What do you require as payment, madam?'

'Payment? Oh, no, sir, I would not ask for money. A gift merely, let us call it. I leave the amount to your discretion.'

Charles Herries took several coins from his pocketbook and placed them on the consul table by the bed. He could not, as a gentleman, be less than generous, he reflected, as he pulled the door shut behind him and hastily tipped a maid who stood by the door with a pitcher in her hand and an expectant look in her eye; but the sum he left was far higher than anything the woman could have demanded. Never mind. He paid for peacefulness.

Outside it was dark; the air moist and heavy with rain on the way. In an effort to conserve his cheerfulness, Herries hailed a hansom and sat quiet all the way down to the Oxford Road, along Park Lane and on to Cadogan Place. His house was on the left-hand side, new and raw; modest for a man of his means. He had paid sixteen hundred pounds for it, he remembered as he turned his key in the lock. What had he been thinking then; that he might fill its five storeys with the laughter and bustle of a family? When he stood in the quiet hallway and opened his letters he was his daily self again. Worse, there was something to make his hands shake. A note: short, handwritten on thick card with a gold border and bevelled edges: 'Lady Wellington sends her compliments to Mr Herries, and would like to inform him again that Mr Rothschild, of New Court, has news of his family.'

In the gloom, Herries folded the card over, as if to conceal its words. He walked upstairs to the small drawing room, pushed the paper under the coals and watched until it was burned to dust. His throat was tight. He acknowledged no family except his mother here in Cadogan Place. Lady Wellington had sent a note to his office some weeks ago. He had ignored it, dismissed it somehow as nonsense. Now here was another.

Nathan Rothschild, a banker in the City. Of course he had heard of him by way of business. Talk swirled about Rothschild; he had made a fortune with notable speed. Herries knew from his Leipzig days the cleverness of the family. Amschel Rothschild, in the '90s, was credited with rescuing the fortune of the Prince of Hesse when Napoleon overran the kingdom; something to do with letters of credit, buried treasure, smuggled bullion. Amschel's son was reckoned brilliant, and decisive too.

Herries stood back from the fire, fell into an armchair and pulled off his cravat. Smuggled bullion. Nathan Rothschild, it was whispered, had experience in that line and it had lately come to his attention that large quantities of silver bullion and coin were disappearing from the country. But no one, Herries knew, should credit rumours about money. They were almost always exaggerated. He was letting worries about his work cloud his understanding.

What then might Mr Rothschild want? There was something persistent about a second letter. It suggested that Mr Rothschild had something up his sleeve. He would do well to guard against any revelations. Under the cloak of office business he would set a watch on New Court; return Rothschild's interest in kind. He would do it first thing tomorrow. Still, he thought as he tapped on the door of his mother's parlour, he did not like the feel of it.

'AH, PARIS. HOW I wish my dear, that you could see it.'

'Mrs Lefevre, you have not seen it for twenty years; who knows what it is like now?'

Harriet turned on the block in the dressmaker's bright workroom. Late winter sun flowed into the room. Outside, on Dean Street, the pavements glistened with the moisture of overnight rain. London sparkled with the hope of advancing spring.

After James left for Spain, Harriet had stayed on in Suffolk through the thin watery days of March; but the house oppressed her, and the bed, when she flung out an arm at night, felt empty. Even the laboratory, where she had sat out the listless afternoons, could not help her. Suffolk was full of ghosts, or, worse, the anticipation of future days alone.

At the end of March Harriet shut up the house and took the post-chaise to London and her Aunt Cobbold's old house in Hatton Garden. Mrs Cobbold had always made her welcome as a child, and had taken her arrival now with her usual good humour. Both Anne Cobbold's sons were abroad in India and she endured their absence with an acceptance of its benefits and a hope that they would one day return. To Harriet's relief she asked few questions. It was natural, she implied, that Harriet should come to London; she herself had left Suffolk thirty years ago. The country, and life there, had weighed on her spirits. Mrs Cobbold took the view that as soon as a person arrived in town, then life, with all its glorious possibility, could truly begin. Where else could a woman be released from the burdens of house and family and chart her own way in life? And then, in the payment of a few guineas, the whole world might be summoned to one's kitchen or parlour. Silks from India, given an extra sheen by her sons' presence there; coffee from the Americas, soft leather and dates from the Barbary coast, novels, newly translated from the French. She herself had married out of Society, but for Harriet, who arrived with an introduction to Lady Wellington, the doors of London's drawing rooms stood open.

'You need new gowns right away, my dear. The Season will be over if you do not take advantage of it. Do go to old Mrs Lefevre. She dressed all of us in the old days and knows the habits of our family.'

'Did she dress you, Aunt?'

'All of us.' Mrs Cobbold hesitated, then hurried on. 'She learned her craft in Paris years ago, and the skill has never left her.'

Mrs Lefevre was round and small, corseted in a manner quite out of keeping with the times. A hairband, in the style of the '80s, kept her long dyed hair away from her eyes. After thirty years of business she had developed a manner that was at once solicitous yet discreet, though a throaty timbre still sounded in her speech and her sentences lifted at the end in the French way.

'Stand quiet, my dear. Do not jump about so. How can I do my job? Of course Paris became a fearful place, but they say the Emperor has brought back its style. You must think of the golden stone of the palaces, the blue of uniforms, the swirl of the tricolore.'

'I have something made of tricolore ribbon in my drawer. A tiny fan of silk fixed with a button. I believe it belonged to my mother. Did you make that?'

Mrs Lefevre looked vague.

'Ah, a cockade; perhaps I did make it. I sewed one for a hat I remember. A pretty, small top hat with ribbons to tie under the chin. We have lost so much in the years of war. Patterns and bows, patches and powder, lace ruffles, turned heels and shoe buckles—all gone.'

'How did my mother look then?'

'*Charmante*, yes, with your air of hurry too; the same quick movements.'

'Mrs Lefevre, tell me something of her. Do you know where she went? Now that my father is dead, I feel that I might find out.'

Mrs Lefevre considered Harriet on the wooden block in front of her, and sighed. A guarded look came down over her face. She lifted up the skirt of Harriet's gown and let it fall.

'At least the skirt is a little wider than a couple of years ago; but I have so little to work on. We have to show quality in other ways, in the cut of the gown, the lightness of the silk.'

'And my mother?'

'My dear, I do believe it might be best to forget it. You are a married woman now, with a husband to love and wait for. Why turn back to the past?'

'I know you are right; and I do forget her, at least so it seems to me, and then another day I put out my hand and find no one.'

Harriet jumped off the block and walked to the windows. She could not tell Mrs Lefevre anything of the rage that gripped her at those times, the sense of helplessness and danger, and then her own shame when she came back to herself. Beneath her on the pavement two officers walked side by side deep in conversation. Behind them the chop-house boy ran from step to step to collect tins for the night's dinner. Sometimes she thought that her mother was part of all that movement still, that one day she might simply come face to face with her, as she had heard of a man who walked by his long-lost brother on the street. Then surely she would know her: they would know each other.

Mrs Lefevre turned her attention back to Harriet's gown.

'I believe I shall set off this yellow with three or four rows of pearls, on a ribbon under the bosom. You have chosen a fine colour. In candlelight, a blue, such as the gown you came in, can lose its hues and appear reddish. But this yellow, with its carmine undertone, will glow a deep gold.'

Harriet turned round, walked back to the block and stepped up. She pushed her hair back over her forehead and considered her gown. It fell in folds, with straight sleeves and a scooped neckline. Tiny seed pearls, sewn across the bosom in diamond checks, gave the gown a note of subtle luxury in keeping with the times, as if nature had lent to art its irregular beauty. With a bolero or a spencer to guard against the evening air, it would closely match the new designs of Monsieur Leroy that were everywhere this season.

Harriet had never thought for more than a few minutes about anything that she wore, or even looked closely at a pattern or fabric. But the gown suited her. It did not clamour expense or formality, and formality, Harriet knew, was always her undoing because, with her, nothing ever stayed uncreased for more than an hour.

'Yes,' said Mrs Lefevre, considering Harriet, 'you will do very well, my dear, though why we follow Paris and my countrymen like Leroy, especially after so many years of war, is a mystery. I shall send the gown and slippers to Hatton Garden directly. The petticoat and the day gowns will take another week.'

As Harriet tied her cloak and settled it on her shoulders, she leaned over and kissed Mrs Lefevre on the cheek. In that moment, for Mrs Lefevre, Harriet might have been her mother. She had the same talent for the sudden and unexpected, carried delight with her, and bounded away with a dancer's grace.

Diana Guest had taken so well to the new styles. Mrs Lefevre remembered how, in her new simple gowns, white and gathered under the bosom in the Hellenic fashion, Lady Guest, just arrived in London and despite everything, had breathed the spirit of the days before war was declared and there still seemed hope for some in the revolution. Her simplicity charmed the drawing rooms. When she planted a posy of country flowers in her hair, other women hurried to follow her lead. In the short time before everything soured, Diana had what fashionable London wanted: youth, naturalness and grace. Later, her impulsiveness had turned into something else, though it did no one any good to dwell upon that.

WHEN SHE STEPPED OUT of Mrs Lefevre's red-brick house into Dean Street, Harriet felt herself taken up by the swirl of London, where it was easy to forget the poor harvests that weighed on the people of Suffolk. London merchants made money when prices rose, spent it without a care, and went to church on Sundays. Like the spring air, London was redolent with possibility.

Her father used to say that in the coldest days of winter new life already stirred. Roots pushed out between grains of soil while the world above lay immobile. Winter was not an endurance but a preparation for better times. Sap rose up the tree trunks and along the branches, and now April had come, the leaves waited for the signal to unfurl.

Ribbons of talk from a group of clerks outside a chop-house followed Harriet up the street.

'Turn around, pretty thing.'

'Look this way!'

'You all alone?'

Harriet looked at the ground to hide her smile, delighted suddenly with the coming spring and the city itself, where as a married woman she could walk alone. London this morning was to her a huge living experiment in which different elements combined and split minute by minute, where novelty and decay could be found side by side. Back alleys and courts sheltered fanatics and visionaries; in their small rooms a man, or a woman even, might change the world quite unregarded. On the city's pavements a rich man had to look a poor man in the face and know them to be alike. Something was sure to happen soon, the sort of thing only the city could throw up.

If one of those clerks would dance with me now, waltz down this street in broad daylight, I would say yes from joy, she thought.

In Soho Square she waited by one of the big bollards for a drover to pass with his cluster of sheep. The flock swayed from side to side, bustled along by two black collies. Through the gaps between woolly legs, Harriet noticed a man who sat against the railings that bounded the garden in the middle of the square. When the street was clear he raised his stick to her, and she crossed to him, impelled by his greeting and her own high spirits. Why not talk to a man who, like her husband, served his country?

'You are a soldier.'

'Bates of the 52nd, Miss. Back from the war for ever.'

He waved his stick at the ground, and Harriet saw it was carved into a cup-shape at the end.

'The leg's gone from the knee. Last year's gift from Boney.'

Bates grasped a railing and pulled himself upright. He slipped the wooden leg under the stump and strapped it tightly round his knee.

'There you are, Miss; still standing.'

'My husband is in Spain now, with the 9th Regiment. The *Morning Chronicle* reports today that Lord Wellington has the fortress of Badajoz surrounded.'

'The 9th?' Bates raised a hand to his forehead in an elegant salute, and leaned towards Harriet. He brought the war to London; she could smell it on his breath.

'The 9th buried General Moore. They were brave men, the last to leave Corunna. Honour to him.'

'And to you, sir.'

Harriet was lost for words. She pulled her velveteen purse from inside her cloak.

'Mr Bates, take this in memory of Sir John Moore; not as charity, but in payment from your country.'

Bates saluted again.

'My thanks to you. You will see me if you pass this way again. I am always here.'

The yellow jasmine that flowered along the railings in the square now looked sere and pallid. Harriet decided not to walk; she would only think of James and wonder where he was and how many would die when Badajoz was stormed. She stopped a hansom.

'To Hatton Garden,' she said, and pulled up the blinds to shut out the sun.

~

5TH APRIL 1812. BADAJOZ, SPAIN

LORD WELLINGTON STOOD BEHIND a trestle table, arms extended and palms flat to the wood. As the General leant forward, James Raven could see his bare scalp and the light gleaming on the prominent curve of his nose.

'Thank you, McGrigor.' Wellington looked up and nodded at his Surgeon General. The group of young men ranged against the brown canvas of the marquee stood a little taller. There was no formality, yet the General had gathered to himself the attentiveness of each person there, from the servants in the shadows to the golden-haired secretary, who sat quiet and ready to take dictation. At the sound of the General's voice the sentry who stood beyond the open tent door stiffened against the pale morning sky.

The General, James could see, did not measure up as a tall or a handsome man. Had they stood shoulder to shoulder, James would have bulked wider and higher. But Wellington made up for his slightness with a muscular perfection that was a reproach and a challenge to the younger men. Everything about him was taut, from his squared shoulders to his elegant calves. His face was tight and alert and his prominent nose pushed him forward, propelled him into the future in reproach to more languid subordinates. Even the thin, negligent, upper lip, which sat back from its fuller bottom, gave his long face a look of reserved calculation suitable for a man who risked the lives of thousands.

James glanced at the General's blue coat. It was cut above the knee, higher than usual, flapped not pleated at the back. Slim and short, it had the effect of making Lord Wellington's legs seem longer and the whole man taller. Then his boots: in the shade cast by the buff canvas of the tent walls they gleamed like newly fallen chestnuts. James glanced round and saw that a couple of Lord Wellington's aides-de-camp had already cut their coats to match the General's. Despite his new trousers and a fresh cravat, he felt his own dress was slovenly and loose in this company, and knew that he was meant to.

Dr McGrigor stepped back and Wellington's gaze shifted to the dark figure of the Adjutant General who walked forward towards the table.

'General Stewart, who do you have?'

'Captain Raven, sir, 9th Foot. I have attached him to the 5th Division. He has excellent French and will interrogate the officers taken.'

Stewart gestured beyond the canvas walls; in the silence the distant thud of the guns came into the room.

James bowed and stepped forward. Wellington nodded and then stood upright.

'You have a report, I believe?'

'Yes, my Lord.'

At this moment a young officer ducked through the tent door, looked round and handed a note to one of the aides-de-camp.

'Fitzroy?'

A softness came into Wellington's voice. Fitzroy Somerset inclined his head in the relaxed manner of the favourite.

'My Lord: a message from General Leith. The infantry are arrived beyond the bridge and the scaling ladders, too.'

'Good enough.'

Wellington turned back to James.

'You have a report on prisoner numbers. Continue.'

James reached down and pulled his notes out of his pocket. At the same moment he saw disdain and boredom cross the General's face. Wellington brushed the sleeve of his blue coat as if it had caught a mote of dust.

'General Stewart.' Wellington turned to the Adjutant General. 'You know I cannot abide notes. There is no time for them. Have I not made that plain?'

Stewart's dark face turned grey. 'I had intended to leave this with you.'

'No. You know my wishes. Get it by heart, Captain Raven, and then return. Now, Colonel De Lancey, your brief.'

James walked out into the morning. He imagined the eyes of the aides-de-camp on him and pushed his shoulders back. General Stewart, ducking through the doorway, emerged beside him.

'Do not take it too much to heart, Captain,' he said. James thought he could catch in Stewart's voice a trace of his home in the north of Ireland.

'The Beau is short-tempered,' Stewart went on. 'You know his reputation. Sit out here now, and learn it off. Then we will go back in.'

'Now, sir?' James felt like a boy sent out of the schoolroom.

'Indeed,' Stewart said more sharply, 'and remember, our brief is merely to inform. Never try to advise the General. God forbid that one should forget oneself so far as to attempt that.'

For a moment, James thought he saw a flash of bitterness cross the Adjutant General's handsome face. But it was followed by a stern blandness that emptied out his last words of any meaning.

James looked round to see his pony lift her hooves off the ground and turn her head in the direction of Badajoz. Even at this distance the bombardment travelled to her through the earth. Then he sat down beside her on the grass, pulled his papers out of his pocket and began to memorise the figures he had written there.

Inside the tent, the commanders of each division gathered round the small table. General Stewart placed himself to one side as they received their written orders, neat sheets of paper written in columns by the General himself and copied by Fitzroy Somerset and the other aides-de-camp. In the silence that fell Stewart looked across at Lord Wellington. His grey-blue eyes were steady, and passed from one to another of his generals in turn until he caught Stewart's look. Then impatience flashed through them, as if he refused a connection Stewart tried to make, denied any fellow feeling.

It came to Stewart then that in Wellington's repudiation was an acknowledgement of the tie they shared, the history one might call it. Ireland bound them together. The Beau was especially scathing about Ireland and professed to have cast it off. Stewart remembered the General's childhood home, Dangan Castle. Lord Mornington had built his boys a fort in the lake there, as if they might be besieged at any time. Arthur and his brothers practised for hours; two boys to attack, two to defend, with rowing boats, ladders and old fowling pieces without shot. And then there was Trim Castle, built by the Normans, barely an hour's ride away. The General's first school, Stewart knew, looked right at it, across the motte to the castle keep. If Dangan Lake did not turn him into a soldier, Trim Castle would have challenged him to it. Between the school and the castle flowed the peat-black Boyne. From the bridge across you could watch it run down to Drogheda and the sea.

So today the General knew a thing or two about fortresses, and how the river was the key, often, to a successful assault. Ireland had given him the knowledge. England took it, and put it to work, as she took so many of their countrymen who offered to serve. Stewart thought of his own half-brother Castlereagh, taught with intrigue, and then the General's elder brother, Lord Wellesley, hard-shelled and cold. Both of them worn out in Westminster. Yes, we Irish and Scots, how we jostle to fill the seats round the cabinet table or sweat in Calcutta and the Cape. Why? So England will accept us? We wanted to leave our own country, perhaps that is it, more simply; Lord Wellington the fields of Meath flat under their blanket of grey, and I the rock and bluster of County Down.

As James rode back to the camp on the other side of the city he counted off the curved bastions in the walls to settle his spirits. Santa Maria, San Roque, San Juan, each named for a saint, with narrow battlements finished in canine points. With the darkness silence fell all round him. The light shone on the back-buttons of his coat, on his polished boots and on his sword as if his flesh had fallen away and left a skeleton. He imagined that even at this distance the French sharpshooters on the battlements might pick him out. In a whisper he urged his pony on and clasped the handle of his sword to smother its clinking.

His mood had been subdued since he arrived in Spain. The three years he had spent in England on the staff dropped away; he felt himself to be again the man who had walked through snow-covered hills and killed without feeling. Harriet and his happiness had floated off to leave him annealed. Now, tomorrow, the assault would come. Officers on the staff had no need to throw themselves into the fight; but Lord Wellington had called for volunteers to follow up the advance parties, and James had put himself forward to serve with his own regiment.

At Elvas the staff officers were billeted in town. James had commandeered a truckle bed in a grocer's house, while his servant Thomas Orde slept snug amongst sacks of rice in the shop. Now Thomas was back with his tent and the 9th. James found him in the muddle, quiet by a fire. Two mules and his goat stood close by in the dark, huddled like gossips under a cork oak.

'Thomas, there you are. All ready?'

'The Major says it will be tomorrow.' Thomas's hands, callused from the shuttle, grasped a tin mug. 'I have volunteered, sir; and will go with you.'

'There is no need, Thomas. You do your duty here already. Think of Mary.'

'Mary?'

'Did you not come out because of scarcity at home? If you die tomorrow, she will be left quite destitute.'

'But, Captain Raven, there is a chance of riches. The town is ripe for taking, they say, and I may come by more there than in a year of service. Mary will understand that balance; she is a sensible woman.'

Thomas did not say what the men also whispered; that the enemy had teased and tormented them. Two years running they had been denied what they wanted; and again this time the French picked them off in their hundreds, with cannon and musket, with mines and shot. Sometimes the men talked about the French as if they knew them. Thomas had heard stories of men who swapped tobacco and other bits and pieces with enemy soldiers when the armies were encamped close to one another last winter. But now a dull hatred had set in, made worse by the rain and the days under bombardment. Badajoz was at their mercy, heavy with riches and with women. The British were already enraged and triumphant, carried beyond the thought of risk or death. Anticipation ran through them like brandy.

James could feel it too, the nearness of conquest, especially after the attack had been postponed this morning.

'Very well,' he said to Thomas after a pause, 'the Major will issue you with arms.'

'Yes, sir.'

'Mind you stay near to me in the assault.'

'I shall follow you in.'

James stood up and walked over to where the Major, too, sat over his fire. By his side was a well-built man with fashionably combed dark hair. The flames illuminated his grey trousers and a red jacket with no regimental buttons, that appeared not to have seen a day's wear. George Yallop greeted James with a raised hand.

'Captain Raven. Draw up a seat. This is Mr Heaton, a volunteer. He wanted to go to Colonel Paston, but I thought he might lend a hand here, so I called him back. He's like a beagle before the off, I can tell you.'

'The Major tells me he expects orders for an escalade.'

Heaton jumped up, glanced at his hand as if it might be too grubby to offer to an officer, and held it out. He might have been about to set off for his club.

James sensed Major Yallop and Robert Heaton, the one so careful and reserved, the other apparently effusive and transparent, were two of a kind. They had found one another as it was possible to do in an army, where behind the rules and rigidities, at the moment of battle, a man's essence could reveal itself. There were some men who looked forward to fighting the way the Major did a dance, or Heaton, perhaps, a day at the turf. Before a skirmish the Major had a completeness that James remembered only too well.

He said goodnight and walked back to the pearly gloom of his tent, attentive and content. As soon as he embarked for Spain, James had rediscovered the taste for war. From the moment of the first skirmish on the march down from Ciudad Rodrigo the fixity and elevation he knew that opiates brought came back. He felt a kind of joy then, as a man does who is drawn back to his mistress after a period of pretending to himself that he no longer wants her.

Perhaps, James thought, as he took off his sword and boots, he should write to Harriet. He remembered Harriet as he had last seen her, naked and at home. She wore her catlike, faraway look, the sheets pulled up to her throat against the cold, her hair a tangle. Why did she seem to disappear in that way just when he needed her most; why was there no seabed within her, no plateau on which he could rest, only endless and cloudy depths? Anger filled him suddenly; he preferred simplicity, in the end. There was time enough for a letter after the assault.

AT DINNER THAT NIGHT, Lord Wellington sat by General Rowland Hill and watched him eat. General Hill pegged down a roasted guinea fowl with a fork and pushed his knife between breast and thigh, easing his way in as the flesh parted; then he pulled the leg away and carved through the joining skin. Hill was a meticulous man, fussy with detail, Wellington knew. He cut the bird expertly, like a butcher; but he chewed with lascivious abandon, head down to his food. Wellington ate little himself and only kept a good table out of form. Sometimes he wished he might do without food altogether, without its sticky vulgarity and the way grown men clustered round tables with such childish eagerness. The whole business of dining, the exclamations over the aroma of meat, the raising of glasses and swill of wine, the talk about dishes; it all took up so much time.

General Hill's dinners were better than his own and Lowry Cole's better still. Wellington glanced at them; neither man would really manage command. Cole had no capacity for detail. Hill was the opposite: a fusser. Daddy Hill, they called him; or the Soldiers' Friend. He was gentle in reprimand, thoughtful about the welfare of his men. Kindliness never won a war.

Did either man think, as he swallowed, of tomorrow's assault; or did relish see off fear? Wellington knew that Hill would already have memorised his orders, as if they were any more than the most rudimentary of timetables, plans he had drawn up to make sure that for the first hour at least there was no confusion amongst the officers and men. In his experience there came a point in every battle and assault, every skirmish even, when an experienced commander had to throw away his plans, when he found the enemy thicker in one place than he expected, or the munitions ran out too soon to cover an advance. That was when a general showed his quality; that moment of decision when a man could, at a single stroke, turn history to a new channel. Bonaparte had that ability, and he had it too; uncanny, men called it, as if it was a mystery, rather than the result of careful labour.

Tonight, though, he would not show any intemperance. Better to keep himself even-tempered, with his inner thoughts gathered towards the next day.

'Well, Hill; how long do you estimate we have, once we have dispatched this business, before Soult is on us?'

General Hill was stationed at Merida several hours away, to guard Lord Wellington's right flank. No one was more aware than he of Marshal Soult's advance from the south. Hill glanced at his commander. The Beau was all affability and charm, Hill thought. What did he really want to know? Nothing about Soult to be sure; Soult was already at Llerena and could be on them any day. Wellington would not have ordered the storming had he any more time. Hill considered his dismembered bird. Slivers of damp meat still lay on the carcass; he longed to seize the bones and suck the flesh from them until they were as smooth as ivory.

'You know the intelligence, sir. At the least, Soult expects the fortress to hold out.'

'We shall see, Hill. Have you finished picking at that bird? Yes?'

Hill pushed his plate away and threw his napkin down on it. The carcass of his chicken was shrouded in white, his gluttony smothered. He coughed. The General's mood had switched to irritation.

'Might I suggest a tune, my Lord, after the toasts?'

'Music? Dancing?' Disgust now filled Wellington's light voice. Fiddling was as bad as food on such an evening.

'Go on into the parlour after the toasts. I will join you.'

When all the officers had left, Lord Wellington sat on. He stared down the length of the table, his eyes hooded and unseeing. Music. He could never tell them how he loved it. He could never explain how he felt at peace in the lift of a melody or the great mansion of sound that his father had built with his friends when every year on the King's Birthday they performed the *Messiah* in Dublin Castle.

Lord Mornington was dead by the time Arthur was twelve. The Professor of Music at Trinity College. Yes, and a spoiled boy who brought them his glees and sonatas with an air of pampered apology, as if they made up for the family's poverty, the moves from one house to another, the drawing-room doors only halfway open. Lord Mornington, father of six and proprietor of Dangan Castle, had dribbled away his life in tunes. He had left nothing but a querulous widow and a tribe of half-starved children with no clothes on their backs.

So Arthur had refused the hand that music offered, taken up soldiering instead. At twenty-two, when war claimed him, he had burned his own fiddle, snapped its slender brown neck and thrown it on the fire.

Now he allowed himself no leisure or pastime, only the company of women, though he knew how to be affable and take his time over dinner.

At the thought of women the memory of Amelia Freese came to him from India rich with heat and dust-choked air. Oh, my Amelia, he whispered almost aloud. He had loved her, every inch of her; her narrow ankles and sinuous feet, her wide brown eyes with enquiring brows, even the way she teased him. She calmed his impatience, or thought it of no importance.

But it was more than that. When the two of them were alone Amelia was his commander, and he her subaltern. Arthur saw himself in the heavy heat of an Indian afternoon with the warm mahogany floorboards under his knees, and Amelia on the bed above, naked and exposed to him. How she teased him then, goaded him, with a scarlet officer's jacket round her shoulders and nothing else but his belt around her waist. In those moments his vehemence softened and he revelled in his abasement. He knew Amelia for two years, and in his memory, hope and laughter filled them.

Wellington's head dropped for a second, and his arched nose lit up in the candlelight. Then he pulled himself up. She had failed him, like so many others. Why had he thought she might be equal to his need? No, she had died on him, pale and unsmiling at the end, and he had embarked for London rich and heavy with grief. Kitty Pakenham, his incubus and obligation, waited for him. Lowry Cole, who never here made any mention of his past, had proposed for Kitty in his absence. She had refused Cole and made Arthur ever more bound by his promise to return. Besides, it had not mattered; he was sure he would never love again. To let Kitty know his mind he had put Amelia's picture up, over the desk in his study. She mocked him, after dinner, dead, with her smile and curls.

So of course he agreed to take Arthur Freese when he was orphaned and alone. Orphaned? Well, so they said, and he did nothing to dispel the notion, though any fool knows, he thought, that no one takes in a child from outside his own family. Arthur was still a boy; time would tell if his young face would thin to resemble his own, his nose grow more aquiline and his mind more acute. Wellington remembered the night he brought the boy home. It was dark as the Styx, and the deer in the Phoenix Park stood blinded and transfixed by the lights of his carriage as it swayed up to the doors of the Secretary's Lodge. He had lifted Arthur out, wrapped him tight in his arms and felt a heart beat loud against his own.

Kitty had taken Arthur and made him hers. He should have known; none of the boys seemed truly his, not his sons Arthur and Charles, not Arthur Freese and not Gerald, the mewling bundle Kitty had rescued from the wreckage of his brother's marriage. Arthur, Amelia's son, was afraid of him. The boy cowered when he came into the drawing room, and held out his schoolbooks with a hand that trembled. For his diffidence Kitty loved him all the more.

Wellington stood up and threw aside his napkin. It was time for bed, not tunes or memories. He would lie awake and ready until the morning.

3

London and Badajoz

6 APRIL 1812

Anne Cobbold turned the handle on her niece's door almost before Harriet could answer her knock. Harriet sat at the writing desk and gazed out at the morning sun. Apple trees stood in the spring grass, survivors of the garden's country days. Now cobbles and flags covered old paths and hedges; clockmakers and jewellers worked where the well and the vegetable patch had once been. Across the slope at the bottom of the hill and past the open space that lay beyond it, Harriet could see the start of the Great North Road, where it rose through fields to the village of Islington. This morning Harriet woke to the sound of cattle. Herds came down the hill to Smithfield and gathered by the market. They were auctioned at dawn and slaughtered by noon. On market days the Fleet turned blood-red and the ferrous smell of slaughter hung for hours in the air.

'I intend to visit Lady Wellington this morning, am in a hurry to get ready, and still dreaming.' Harriet laughed and turned to her aunt. Together, arm in arm, they walked down the wide oak stairs and into the small parlour that opened off the hall. A new front had been put on her house some years ago but the square rooms inside took its age back more than a hundred years. Instead of the curled bas-relief of today's ceilings, Mrs Cobbold's house had smooth plaster overhead and her parlour was panelled right up to the cornice. The fireplace was wide and open, with a basket grate. Even on a warm spring morning, a fire burned there and drew the ear to its soft inspiration.

Tenderness filled Harriet at her aunt's touch. Mrs Cobbold was her father's sister, a small compact woman with a brisk tone in her voice, who made up for the discomfort of modern fashions with an avalanche of bows and ribbons down her front. For thirty years her husband had sold grain to the great brewers by the mills on the Fleet River that ran its last yards to the River Thames at the boundary to their orchard and garden. Fields had stretched away to the north when they first arrived, but now the city leapt over Hatton Garden. The great rubbish tip at Mount Pleasant had given way to the new penitentiary. The spas built over springs that bubbled up on the clay strata along the Fleet River had sold out to bricks and progress. But the Cobbolds stayed on in their old-fashioned house, and now, as a widow, Mrs Cobbold declared that she had been through too much there ever to leave.

'Before I go out, Aunt, might I ask you a question?'

'Of course, my dear, you must place all your trust in me.' Mrs Cobbold settled herself by the fire.

'It concerns my mother.' Harriet stopped and brushed her hair from her forehead. 'I always felt when I was with my father that he expected her to return, or that he felt in some way that he was the cause of her flight.'

Mrs Cobbold frowned. There was no profit, she had always found, in dwelling on difficulties in life that could not resolve themselves well or had no solution.

'You must understand, my dear, that I was not in Suffolk at the time. The subject was painful to your father, and all I can say is that we must presume that she is no longer in the land of the living.'

Harriet dropped her head onto her aunt's shoulder. The tears came up in an instant, unasked for. She bit her lip.

'So much of life is simple endurance, Harriet. Mystery is everywhere, and I have always felt it is better to accept what we cannot know.'

'I do not wish to accept; I cannot.' Harriet sat back on the sofa. 'A man of science does not accept mysteries, Aunt. He looks for an explanation that he discovers through patient examination of the natural world before him. In the same way I am determined to discover what happened.' She did not say what was in her heart, a feeling that when she reached out her hands she encountered only empty darkness. Mrs Cobbold might not understand.

'There is nothing to discover, my dear.' Mrs Cobbold sounded weary. 'Your father has spoken to you of your mother's disposition.'

Mrs Cobbold had always felt uncertain before Diana Guest. She liked a woman to be definite, liked to see a firm outline and know that was where a person stopped. Beyond her enthusiasm, her sister-in-law had been vague. One could not imagine her seated before the household accounts or taking an interest in spring-cleaning. William had indulged her; it was no wonder she remained so difficult to approach. But then, Mrs Cobbold reflected, she had always preferred a salted to a delicate flavour; a woman like dear Dorothy Yallop, who would arrive any day for a visit. Dorothy was somewhat beneath her own rank in society, to be sure; but a major's wife was perfectly acceptable, and Mrs Cobbold worried less about social proprieties than her own pleasure, especially now she was a widow and had no wish to cut a figure in Society. Dorothy looked straight at the world and did not flinch; Mrs Cobbold liked to do the same.

Harriet, she thought, had not been tested by the waiting that makes up a woman's life, the dragging days before childbirth that carried the fear of catastrophe; the horror when it came; the never-ending hours while, as a mother, she would barter with death for sick children's lives in whispers. Her niece would have to learn how women tied themselves up tight, carried themselves about like that, bound with restraint. There were worse things in this world than losing a mother when you were too young to remember.

Harriet stood up.

'I must go, Aunt. I have sent a note to Lady Wellington and should arrive before noon.'

'An excellent idea.' Mrs Cobbold patted her niece's hand. 'I will call for the carriage.'

THE DRAWING ROOM AT Harley Street was a necessity that Kitty had learned to bear. Here she was, alone by the fireplace, in grey moiré silk slippers at the end of a long morning of visits. She stood to greet a delegation from the City and to accept, on Arthur's behalf, a silver model of the fortress of Ciudad Rodrigo presented by the Worshipful Company of Goldsmiths. At the base ran a rippling inscription: The Hon. Arthur Wellesley, Lord Wellington, Earl of Douro, Duc de Fuentes de Onoro; then the battles won: Porto, Busaco, Fuentes de Onoro, Ciudad Rodrigo.

Future victories, like that they expected at Badajoz, the Aldermen pointed out, might be added where the silversmith had left a blank in confident anticipation. Kitty thanked them and swept clean a space on the mantelpiece next to her Lisbon clock. A troop of the boys' blue-and-white French soldiers, fallen in the last fireplace cataclysm, toppled into a posse of scarlet dragoons and clattered down onto the hearth. Behind her, the City merchants shuffled and coughed. They did not know whether they should laugh at the sight of leaden redcoats thus swept away. Kitty needed two hands to hold the model safely. With the fallen soldiers clustered round it, Ciudad Rodrigo now had heaps of dead about its walls.

'I shall write to Lord Wellington directly and inform him of your most generous gift,' Kitty said, 'and I shall send notes to all the papers, to thank you on his behalf.'

The Aldermen bowed.

'I bid you good morning, gentlemen.' Kitty inclined her head to show that their interview was over.

The butler was at the door again as soon as the Aldermen left.

'A Mrs Raven asks to see you, my Lady.'

Kitty sighed.

'Her business?'

'I do not know, my Lady. She says she is here with an introduction from Lord Wellington.'

'Then show her in; but this is the last. Are there others?'

'The hall is quite full, and more wait on the street.'

'Dismiss them with my thanks. Lady Wellington can receive no more callers this morning.'

'Mr Rothschild's runner is among them, madam.'

'Ah, I shall write a note to say that Mr Rothschild is welcome at any time.'

Harriet waited in the hall. She pulled her gloves at the fingertips and then pushed her fingers back in. Brass banisters marched up the marble stairs. This house is new and cold, she thought, with none of the wooden warmth that Mrs Cobbold draws around her. Her heart jumped with her up to the first floor.

Inside the drawing room, Harriet stumbled on the carpet.

'Lady Wellington. I have a letter of introduction from your husband. I hope it is proper for me to bring it myself.'

Lady Wellington stood by the pianoforte. One hand rested on the slatted diagonals of the music-holder. Her gown had the silver sheen of the sea on a sunlit evening. Lady Wellington, Harriet thought, did not invite or repel. There was nothing out of place about her, nothing fly-away. She simply stood, as Harriet longed to stand, or, more precisely, as she wanted to be.

Kitty held out her hand for the letter. Harriet regretted her lace gloves and magenta gown. They demanded notice, as if she were skittish and uncertain.

Arthur's note had nothing to sting in it. It was short and to the point:

'Dear Kitty, James Raven, Captain in the 9th, posted to my staff, has asked for an introduction on behalf of his wife. They are apparently recently married and she has only a small acquaintance in London. Any kindness you can do her would therefore be appreciated—Wellington.'

'What can I do for you, Mrs Raven?'

'I really cannot say.' Harriet pulled off her gloves and stuffed her purse full with them. She forced the button over the bulge.

'Then why are you here?'

Harriet knew the blood ran into her cheeks and made ragged patches. A lock of hair fell onto her neck in disarray.

'Captain Raven, my husband, wished me to deliver the General's note. But I see already that I am improperly dressed for a morning visit.'

To Harriet's surprise Kitty laughed.

'Ah, but fashions while away the hours for women of quality who are allowed so little else to divert them. Do you not agree, Mrs Raven? We have undress for lounging at home, then a gown for morning visits. Change after midday to a walking outfit, or a riding habit, with boots not slippers. Two hours fly away there at the least.'

'Then we change again for dinner, whether we dine at home or out.'

'And again for an assembly or a ball.'

Harriet began to feel at ease.

'But the theatre demands something between; neither a ballgown, nor a supper dress. We have not even spoken of jewels, or coiffure, Lady Wellington.'

'Or gloves.'

'Or stockings, or slippers and shoes, reticules and bonnets, purses and parasols.'

'So, Mrs Raven, we are given fashions to consume half the hours of the day.'

Harriet stopped. 'But I am never bored,' she said and came to a halt.

'Then tell me, Mrs Raven, what it is that you wish to accomplish in London?'

'Oh, I shall attend the Royal Institution, go to Herr Mozart's opera at the theatre. Perhaps I might even meet Lord Byron himself. I am sure to find something.'

'That depends, I believe, on what one looks for.'

Kitty paused and considered her visitor. Mrs Raven was a girl, more than a woman, who held herself ready for flight. Her hair had escaped already. There was something charming about her, Kitty saw, compelling even. She wished immediately to know her better, to draw out her wonder and curiosity, see them unfurl and expand.

'I find it is advisable to make my own life. We cannot simply wait for our husbands to return. Should you wish to meet Lord Byron, I have an open invitation to Holland House, where he is often to be found. You might accompany me tomorrow evening.'

'Tomorrow evening?' Harriet laughed. 'When I have scarcely made your acquaintance?'

'And why not? Two women together need not stand on ceremony. Besides, we can get to know one another on the drive.'

'I should like that of all things.' Harriet paused. 'This was a merry message.'

'What did you say?'

'It is my habit to remember phrases from Shakespeare; something my father taught me. I do it without thought. Forgive me, Lady Wellington.'

'There is nothing to forgive. My habit is to see in too many things an opportunity for my stocks. Might I call you Harriet? You must call me Kitty; I never use Catherine.'

As Kitty spoke the drawing room was flung open; first Arthur then Charles ran in, followed by Arthur Freese, who walked behind them with the gravity of a ten-year-old who wanted to distinguish himself from the children around him. Last came three-year-old Gerald, who dangled a cup in his hand and dripped milk across the carpet. Charles ran to his mother.

'Arthur stole my pen!'

'I did not. It is mine; you took it from me.'

Charles pulled at Kitty's gown.

'He did.'

Kitty took her son's hand.

'We will find new pens, one for each of you. Now, please say good morning to Mrs Raven, who has come to pay a visit.'

The boys looked solemnly at Harriet. Arthur Freese blushed and bowed.

'We're pleased to meet you.'

Harriet smiled and returned the greeting.

'She's not the pink lady.' Gerald tugged on Kitty's free hand.

'The pink lady?'

Arthur Freese spoke up.

'He means the lady who came before; who promised to return.' Colour swept into his face and covered his freckles right up to his brown curls. 'She said she had something for us. I never believed so, but the others did.'

Gerald's mouth wobbled.

'She will come back.'

'Come now.' Kitty began to usher the children towards the door. 'Let us say goodbye to Mrs Raven and then find new pens.'

WHEN HARRIET HAD LEFT and the children returned to the schoolroom and the nursery, Kitty let the sound of the street drift through the open windows and settle round her thoughts. Mrs Fitzwilliam. Kitty had forgotten Mrs Fitzwilliam, though the children remembered. Perhaps she had found a man who could give her more money than she might ever make from her memoirs or whatever else it was that she threatened Kitty with.

The children's mention of Mrs Fitzwilliam brought Arthur back too. He strode purposefully into Kitty's mind, but it was his voice that sounded loudest. Arthur's voice mixed beauty and menace. She had loved it more than anything else about him. To listen to Arthur when they first met, and again when he claimed her after his years in India, had been like listening to honey run through glass. She heard him say now that Holland House was a disgrace. The Irish met there, talked their brogue and boasted of dissent. Lady Holland had ordered a bust of Napoleon from Canova and planned to display it openly. Her limping husband acquiesced in everything with a soft smile. Naturally, Arthur forbade Holland House.

Kitty smiled. Distance and liberty loosed the chains of Arthur's displeasure. He was gone, and she found, when she thought of it, that she was happy. She might order her carriage to take her to the ponds by the village of Highgate, and watch larking children stir up mud. She could stroll into a hellfire sermon or dance with a widower until dawn. Mr

Rothschild had lent her determination and the war gave her lightness. She wanted it to last for ever.

～

THOMAS ORDE GRASPED EACH rung of the ladder, rough underneath his palms. He followed close behind Captain Raven as they pushed upwards into the darkness. He felt nothing, as if fear and their earlier merriment had floated away and left him weightless, and rose up the wall without any effort. Yet he could hear his own heart beating, and see, when he looked up as he moved his feet, that the battlement was thick with the enemy. Either side of him, close enough to touch, men pressed onto the ladders. Some grunted to themselves; others shouted out. Thomas could see their mouths opening in the flashes of silver that split open the darkness.

They must have been twenty feet in the air and nearly to the top, when the ground beneath them exploded. The earth rose up towards them. Thomas half-turned on the ladder and looked down.

'Keep going, man,' someone shouted. 'Get up, get up. You will kill us all!'

'Why has it become so difficult to breathe?' Thomas asked himself. He could hear his heart beating right up in his throat. A picture of Mary got into the way of his vision, at home, with Nelson pale and thin beside her. He forced his hand onto the next rung of the ladder. He could hear the shrieks of wounded men piled on top of one another at the bottom of the wall.

When Thomas stretched up again, he felt nothing but the pitted rock of the wall. The ladder was not tall enough to reach the top. Just as he was about to sway round again, he felt a hand touch his own. He grasped it and swung himself through the pointed teeth of the battlements. In the darkness he landed on the stone floor of the rampart amongst a tangle of limbs. Captain Raven was up and gone already.

'Go forward,' an officer shouted.

Off away to the right, where the main assault party was gathered, the sky had joined in the battle. A whole firmament of bright moons and exploding planets threw itself on the attackers. The town shook in great convulsions of force. Half blinded by tears, Thomas stood up and ran along the narrow bastion after the man in front. All he could see was the red of a jacket, hazy in the acrid smoke. He felt light-headed again, afraid he might fall, and forced his attention not on the fortifications that fell away to his right, but on the dark bowl of the town inside the inner walls.

Musket balls flew past him, humming like bees. Heavier shot whistled in the still air, or whined and twisted through the distance. In the smoke and noise he could see none of the enemy. He heard a man scream and bellow like a heifer. It was some time before he realised that it was himself, though he was untouched and unwounded. He hurled himself forward along the rampart. A group of enemy artillerymen stood just up ahead of him.

'Are they running away or about to fire?' he asked himself. Was the whining shot from English muskets or from the enemy's? Thomas crouched and then ran forward. His musket with its bayonet blade weighed nothing. In the flashes that lit the darkness he jabbed and poked. Had he struck anything? Were they even close to the enemy? He stopped, and doubled himself up, unable to move. Next to him he saw a man he knew.

''Ham, Abraham.' He whispered, as if even his breath might be heard by the enemy. Abraham turned round, a powerful man dressed in grimy overalls.

'Can you not talk, bor? See we are up. That counter-attack there; General Walker has beaten them off easy.'

Thomas was brought round by Abraham Greene's strong Norfolk voice. When he stood back up, he could see the enemy pour down from the next bastion into the darkened alleys of the town. Exultation and relief ran through him.

Over the noise of the bugles and the shot, Thomas heard the Major. 'Form up,' Major Yallop shouted.

'We have taken the bastion,' one of the officers cried. His words echoed round the walls.

'By God, it will all soon be ours.'

'Form up!' Major Yallop's voice was hard.

The men formed into a narrow column, two by two. When Thomas came to a stop he realised that the smoky air was empty. All the noise, the shrieks and the whiplike cracks, the explosions of light and the shocks under his feet, were coming from the direction of the main assault.

'Now we clear the town. Turn to the right.' The Major was brisk. 'Follow General Walker's men in front.'

'To the breaches.' The order passed round as the column marched towards the battle. At his left hand, downhill towards the river, Thomas could see groups of Frenchmen running to the safety of the bridge. Every few yards a ripple of light slipped out from under a door or through a barred shutter. They looked like streams of honey that waited to be tasted. All around him the men had fallen silent, taut as lions on a night hunt. Above the breaches, flashes and meteor showers of shot and light slackened and passed over.

Squashed together, scarcely able to raise their arms, the column marched up the narrow alley. Above the shouting and the screams Thomas heard a distant bugle answer the call of Leith's column just up ahead. Through the darkness the waves of sound echoed and joined one another. The man next to Thomas turned to him. A leer spread across his face.

'Picton's bugle. They are up onto the castle ramparts. We have them now.'

The defenders heard the bugles too, lifted their heads to them as hunted beasts do when they hear the snapping of the hounds. Worse than bullets, the shrill cries told them they were surrounded and helpless. As Thomas came into an open space he saw the inner ramparts of the fortress up ahead alive with men from the 3rd Division waiting to pour through the narrow gate. In the space between them dozens of the enemy threw their muskets on the ground. Some lay down and begged to be taken prisoner.

'How long have we been at them?' Thomas asked a soldier standing nearby.

'Must be three or four hours since the order came to attack.'

Another man nudged Thomas with an elbow. 'Over there. Officers and their wives. They have come out to surrender.'

Two or three families walked from the open door of a house. In the square, children, wives and officers in blue jackets mixed together. One baby was sound asleep in the racket, leaning with his face squashed against his mother's breast. A little boy in a long cloak howled with fear. Thomas leaned forward; the fabric was a worsted twill. A well-made piece, something he might have woven himself in better days.

One of the women held out her jewel case and tried to speak. Did she say her prayers? It made no difference. One redcoat grabbed the jewel case, another the woman. Then the screaming started. Soldiers rushed forward and pulled the women and a couple of girls away out of the square, followed by others who pawed and scrabbled at the women. The men retreated, but the fellow feeling that took them up the ladders and through the firestorm was frayed and thin. Thomas felt a surge of joy that he was alive, that he had survived. No one had seen that he was afraid.

A charge of energy ran through him, and when he saw a French soldier run down another steep jagged alley, Thomas ran after him into the darkness. Elation made him fly. Down a hill he ran, across an open square and into a dark labyrinth of streets, where the Frenchman suddenly turned to face him. Thomas nearly ran into him, carried forward by the incline and his own charge.

'Surrender!' Thomas heard himself shout. 'Put down your arms.'

The Frenchman was silent. Did he not understand? Thomas levelled the musket the Major had given him. He could not remember now how to fire it. He ran down on the Frenchman. All he could hear was the roar in his head, then a grunt and a rasping sigh. The Frenchman slid to the ground. Thomas saw with surprise that his bayonet was in the soldier's body right up to the end of the gun barrel. They were alone and almost joined together. He let the musket go and stood back.

'He was the enemy.'

Thomas spoke aloud, as if he had a witness. From one pocket in the man's blue breeches he pulled a small silver flask; from the strap over his shoulder he cut a plump leather water bottle, still full.

'Where are the rest of the men? I have lost the Major and Captain Raven.'

All around he heard crashes and shrieks, new thuds, the crack of muskets fired into the air. Back up towards the square he could see smoke and flames. The town was opened up and defenceless. Through a lighted window he watched two English soldiers drag a table across a room to blockade the door of a house. Peering in past the broken shutters he noticed rows of bottles, a heap of plates and glasses, hams and loaves of bread, fat blue plums in jars; a hoarded feast from the larder. In the next house two young officers drank plundered wine by the fire and counted Spanish dollars onto a small table. They fed the fire with smashed floorboards and chairs, nonchalant and at home.

Thomas turned away and ran downhill through a long open square. Fires hissed under the doorways of the houses and into the darker area of the town by the river. The streets were wider here and soldiers roamed in bands, swords out. Thomas heard the cry of a woman and, as he passed by a lighted window, the lust of her attacker, a curdled drunken cry of possession and rage. His own lust rose and he knew he would kill for it.

He ran through the doorway and saw a girl on the floor, half dressed, her face blackened. Her arms were held to the ground by two men, one on each side. Thomas recognised one, a Captain Townley of the 95th.

Another man was on the girl, a ragged scarecrow grey with powder and dirt. As soon as he cried out, Townley pushed him off. The third jeered and grabbed at the front of his trousers. Tears trickled from the girl's eyes. Her mouth opened with a rattle; no sound came out.

The second soldier forced the girl's legs up off the floor, pushed them wider apart and threw himself in. He grunted louder and louder, head back. Thomas watched. Rage and desire coursed through his body until it acted on its own. He tore the second soldier off the girl and hurled him against the wall, where he slumped down with a single groan.

Thomas turned to the girl. She tried to twist away, but he held her. Blood seeped out between her legs. Her sudden moan of pain brought him to such a pitch that he scarcely had time to grab her hair, steady himself and push into her before he was overcome himself.

He could not leave; the rage came through him again in waves, part of him and outside him too. On and on he pushed. He felt the girl tear. She cried and screamed till he saw himself screaming too, in excitement and cruelty and joy.

WHEN THOMAS CAME TO, the house was empty. It must have been long past noon; the sun burned above him in a sky that swam in a sickening blur. Soldiers blocked the alley outside the house, fast asleep. Some clutched bottles, others were drenched in wine. As the world turned dizzily again, Thomas forced himself to concentrate on one man, a private from the 3rd who had come up through the breaches most likely. Sunbeams glanced off the buttons on his singed scarlet jacket; blood and red wine pooled together at his side. Had he died drunk, or was he sleeping off the effect of the wine and his wound together? In the distance, Thomas could hear shouting, musket fire and screams; more than once, soldiers appeared at the top of the alley, then turned back. When he looked up again he saw an early lizard, with its tapering tail in grey-green winter colours. It paused in the sunshine on the wall, and swayed from side to side. A hooded green eye, close to his head, flicked to catch movement. Could it smell blood or did its eyes see merely a fine spring morning?

The alley was blocked with debris and drunken men. Captain Townley sat amongst them as if he was at a picnic, except that his leg was bandaged.

Thomas half raised his hand to him; he had seen him somewhere before, he was sure. Captain Townley seemed to have survived the assault and been wounded in the town.

Chunks of masonry from the houses and shot from the bombardment littered the flagstones. Houses gaped wide, their contents strewn on top of broken shutters and smashed doors: women's clothes, ripped up and trampled, chair-legs, glass tumblers in splintered heaps, smashed plates. Thomas ran a hand through the grit and stones on the ground beside him, and felt the warm mound of a water bottle. The rough leather, like lichen to the touch, was familiar. He had taken the bottle off a dead Frenchman yesterday, or earlier today—he could not remember. Relieved to find it was half full, Thomas tipped up the bottle and let a trickle of water sluice across his face.

Hazy fragments of the night passed across his memory as if he watched scenes in a lantern theatre. From a distance, from far away, he saw maddened men fire their muskets into the air, their skin blackened and singed by exploding powder. Bullets whistled and snapped off the house fronts. A group of enemy prisoners cowered, their hands up on their bare heads. Screaming British soldiers fell amongst them. Others smashed through the windows of the houses, hurled shattered masonry at the brown shutters and then clambered into the dim interiors. Thomas saw himself follow. But he could remember nothing.

Coming round again, Thomas saw that his left hand, loose against the stones, was closed tightly around something. He opened it out finger by finger. Flat on his palm lay a twist of black hair; more than a twist, a whole handful of hair, pliable and young. Silk-soft. He had pulled it from her scalp, and blood and flesh clung to it.

He forced himself to look again. How long the strands were, each delicately curled and sprung. He wanted to touch the hair with his lips, gently. He could put it back, reassure her, stroke her. He felt the desire rise in him again, and closed his hand.

All about soldiers lay dead to the world. The man whose ankles he had rested on still snored victorious sleep. Thomas laid the hank of hair on the doorstep behind him. It captured the sun and gleamed like tar. He stared at it. In the light of day it became horrible. Why was hair saved as a reminder of the dead, put in lockets, twisted into rings? She was not dead. The blood on the hair where it had parted from the scalp was fresh and bright.

Thomas forced back the nausea that jumped up from his stomach. He glanced round. No one watched him. He pulled up the corner of a smashed paving stone and scraped out a narrow hole in the compacted earth beneath. When it was a few inches deep, he pressed the hair down into it as far as his fingers would stretch, covered it with earth and banged down the flag again. Then he stood up and walked away, down through the town to the river.

'It is gone,' he said to himself. 'No one will ever know; I will never know.'

HE DRANK THE LAST of the water and threw the bottle aside as he marched out of Badajoz, across the old bridge and round towards the new pontoon and the baggage train of the 5th Division. He marched like a soldier, and passed two men who sweated under a rolled silk carpet that sat on their shoulders. Their legs had tangled with a flock of geese tied neck to neck and driven by a gunner from the Engineers. They swore and cursed. Six men from the 38th carried a model of the Madonna, her hand raised in blessing. A halo of golden stars garlanded her head. The men walked three each side of her, swayed with her weight, and laughed as if she were alive. What would she give them: forgiveness or a blessing? Would they pray to her that night?

Thomas trudged on. He kept his eyes on the stony road and ignored the shouting and jostling crowds and the wagons loaded with sheep and sacks of flour. He had lost his musket somewhere, the one the Major had issued him. Now he was not carrying a thing, not even a memory. The Madonna would see to that; he would see to it too. He felt light as a feather that drifted down to earth. Nothing had happened, just the storming. It had lasted only a few hours.

He saw his own Mary, like a picture, the gathers of her gown tight under her bosom, her bonnet in her hand. She might have been framed in gold. Nelson stood beside her. The grey-green willows by the river wove shadows into the background. Nelson's yellow hair shone bright and he planted his sturdy feet safe on the ground.

'I have taken part in a glorious victory,' Thomas told them. He saw his words travel across the high plain, down to Lisbon and out to sea, like the ribbons that came from saints' mouths on the wall of Bungay church. 'We have stormed the fortress in a great assault. I played my part.'

In the muddle of camp he made for the bivouacs of the 9th.

'Ar yer awright, then?' He spoke to the first East Norfolk man he saw.

'Awright, an' you?' The soldier shrugged. He sat by a mound of what appeared to be women's clothing, lace and bolts of cloth.

'I'm awright.'

'Brought nothing back?'

'Just myself, and I reckon that is enough.'

'Soon as Bob comes back an' relieves me, I'm gorn for a swim in the shallows. Bugger's running a shop up there, seems like. Like to wash off the dirt, then?'

'Yes.' Why not, Thomas thought. One thing was as good as another.

'Yes, I'll do that.'

~

NATHAN ROTHSCHILD STOOD BACK on his heels and let his stomach sit out over fresh air. It was some years since he had seen his feet when he stood up, he reflected; but he had no time for elegance. The prevailing habit of combing the hair forwards round the face was absurd; he allowed his side tufts to grow outwards to the horizontal. He glanced about the great drawing room at Holland House. Awkwardness was useful for evenings such as this. Like guttural English and directness, it threw men off their guard and allowed him to see them as they were. He could see such anxiety in the manner of George Fawley, a young man in the Treasury.

'This business of armies, Mr Fawley; what a costly way to defeat Napoleon. Manufacturing will have the same effect in time.'

'It is an affair of national honour, sir,' Fawley said, 'and not England's alone, but that of Spain and all our allies.'

Fawley had not come to Holland House to banter with German bankers like this one, but hoped for cards and to get an early look at the Duchess of Bedford's daughter, not yet out, and reckoned a beauty. He needed a wife now that he had a government post, and the matter of the Duke's disagreeable politics might be lost in a sizeable dowry. Disappointment clouded his evening; the Bedfords had not come, and the Hollands had set no card tables.

'I am talking of a new kind of power, more powerful than any yet invented. It is one that your government might have need of.'

'What might that be?' Fawley looked incredulous. 'Our government is sovereign, I believe.'

'I call it the power of credit, sir.'

'You are perhaps using a figure of speech, Mr Rothschild. There is no credit greater than that of the government itself. The funds back our war against tyranny, and have the trust of all who invest in them.'

'But are the funds sufficient, or even fit instruments for all the needs of a government? There might come a moment, forgive me, when a nation finds itself no more powerful, no more capable in the field even, than the services and credit it can call upon from its banks.' Mr Rothschild bent over and looked with interest at the pattern in the carpet.

'You are asserting that private individuals, men from the 'Change such as yourself, might hold the fate of the nation in their hands?'

'Not this nation alone, Mr Fawley.' Rothschild paused. 'Any nation; or many.'

Fawley remembered that Mr Rothschild's father was credited with rescuing the fortunes of the Prince of Hesse. They had come out of it handsomely, too.

'Princes, nations, even individuals,' Rothschild went on, 'might come to the end of their credit and become debtors to the banks.'

Fawley began to feel uncomfortable. He only kept up the conversation from politeness.

Mr Rothschild glanced across at him.

'I mention the matter as an example merely, but should you also have a certain urgency for credit, so to say, or find your personal drafts trading at something of a discount, Rothschilds might help.'

The devil they might, thought Fawley, whose credit at Coutts was nearly out. He stared at Nathan. What was it he wanted? An introduction to the Prime Minister, a couple of other doors opened?

'The thing works the same way with nations,' Rothschild said. 'I am at New Court, Bishopsgate, most afternoons, as you might know. Or your man can find me on the 'Change in the mornings.'

Nathan bowed to Fawley just as Lady Holland came up, followed by a tall young man in a dark green coat and a fashionable wide cravat. Fawley nodded in return, and took advantage of Lady Holland's arrival to walk away. Mr Rothschild, he thought, wore evening dress damnably and carried his belly like a butcher.

Lady Holland grasped Nathan Rothschild by the elbow.

'Now here is a young man, a compatriot of yours, too, Mr Rothschild. He is on the look-out for credit.'

Nathan Rothschild nodded and considered the young man in front of him.

'Herr?'

'Friedrich Winzer.' The young man dropped into German. 'I have judged it best to call myself Frederick Winsor now that I live in London.'

'Why so? Are you not proud to be German?'

'It is not the best moment to be a foreigner. I do not wish to be taken for a spy in Bonaparte's pay.'

'I cannot think that likely; but tell me, Herr Winzer, what you propose by way of business.' Attention tightened across Nathan's face.

Lady Holland left them together and walked away to check on her evening. One after another she looked into her grand state rooms. Ah, there was Mr Blanco White (she preferred to call him Giuseppe y Blanco as she had in Seville) leaning close over Mr Allen, her librarian. Here was the Austrian Ambassador, marooned in London since his court went into exile, talking to bald old Lord Moira about the chances of a French victory in Silesia.

By the supper table under the three great mirrors in the drawing room, Lady Wellington, who never came, talked about Ireland with a cousin of Lord Holland's, back from the Peninsula with an arm off at the shoulder. How she loved these conversations; they gave a distinction to her assemblies and set her apart from those who refused to receive her.

Lord Holland limped up. His face wore its characteristic cover of benevolent distraction. His wife squeezed his hand.

'It is going as well as possible, my dear Henry.'

'Good, good.' He patted her arm and raised thick eyebrows in acknowledgement of her success. Most evenings he would have preferred a few hours in his study, where his history of Spanish literature waited, stuck at Cervantes.

I HAVE GOT MYSELF separated somehow from Lady Wellington, Harriet whispered to herself. I must appear as if I know how to conduct myself in such a house, though it is surely evident to everyone that I have dressed quite wrong again.

She glanced down at the straight folds of her new golden ballgown. She was got up for dancing and saw there would be none. Apart from a couple of officers in the jackets of the Light Brigade, there were few young people here. This great house, with its French furniture and resident thinkers, was a relic from another age, an age when men really thought that knowledge and reason might persuade the world to perfection.

Now we know that we cannot trust what we see or think we understand until we have tested it. Observation and experiment: that is what I must remember, and remember here too. *Macbeth*, Act 1, Scene 7: "Screw your courage to the sticking place."

She shook her head and walked over to a tall young man in a green coat who stood by a fat man in black.

The older man dropped into English and nodded at Harriet's approach. 'A pretty scheme, but too fidgety for me. I like to do a deal here and now, as the English say it. A man brings me a bill of exchange. I offer him a price. He can take it or leave it and there is the end. I am known for my quickness of decision. But go on with it. Work is the thing after all.' He patted the young man's arm and walked away.

Harriet found she was standing not in front of, but next to, the younger man. He was much taller than she was and looked straight down at her, into her eyes. His own were mint-green, flecked with gold. They sifted the colours of the spectrum and now caught the yellow candlelight. He looked more like a magician than a man of any church.

'What is your work, sir?' Harriet could find no other way to begin.

'It is not work, but a calling, if I say it right.'

'Are you a priest?'

'A priest! No, I am a man of science, merely, an explorer of the natural world.'

He smiled, and Harriet saw his long brows rise upward. A wide streak of white wound through his dark hair up and away from his forehead.

'I must introduce myself. I am Frederick Winsor.' His bow was shallow, as if he scorned the politeness. 'Lady . . . ?'

'I am Harriet Raven. My husband Captain Raven is serving with the 9th Regiment in Spain.'

'And you?'

'I have come here tonight with Lady Wellington, but have somehow parted from her.'

'Captain Raven? Lady Wellington? You are here in your own capacity, Mrs Raven.'

'Sir, you must know that the law of this country does not permit a married woman any such thing. Perhaps in your country it is different.'

'Where is it you imagine, Mrs Raven, that I have come from?'

'I cannot say.'

'Good, that is very good. I like the mystery. You flatter my English and the way I speak it. I come from Brunswick, and lately Paris.'

'You are a German, then. And your discovery?'

'I propose to light London using inflammable air.'

'Inflammable air?'

Winsor looked away from her. His voice was almost a whisper, his accent just touched with traces of French and German. Harriet had to come close to hear what he said.

'It is simple, Mrs Raven. We heat coal and collect the gas that emanates from it. It gives off a strong light. That much has been done already. You have perhaps heard of the installation of gas in manufactories in the Midlands. They are pretty things; but none does more than light a single building and benefits the manufacturers only.'

'I have read of them in the *Monthly Magazine*; and also of the lighting of the Regent's House in Pall Mall for the King's Birthday, I believe.'

'That was my work; and what made it different, Mrs Raven?'

'Tell me.'

Winsor stood back. The cut of his coat and the strict fall of his white trousers were impeccably up to date, Harriet thought; but he was out of place, mysterious in this setting of paintings and ormolu.

'What I have made is a means to transport power from place to place, so that it may light our streets and houses, and boil our water too.'

'Do we not have oil lamps, tallow and coal for all of that?'

Frederick Winsor put his hand on her arm. His skin was dark, almost golden. Insistence came through his quiet voice.

'Look about you, Mrs Raven. At how much would you estimate the evening's light?'

Harriet said nothing. It was a folly to calculate the cost of candles for such an assembly, or to imply that Lady Holland might make such a calculation. Besides, she had no idea.

'For less than half the cost of wax,' Winsor said, 'my National Light and Heat Company will, in future times, illuminate all these rooms, and light up driveways and walks.' His hand stayed on her arm.

'See that poor fellow there?' Winsor nodded his head at the footman, who, every two hours, snuffed out and replaced the burned-down stumps of beeswax candles.

'I will do away with him, and all his labour and dirt. My coal gas is, besides, quite without soot. It is not mere industry, Mrs Raven. It will be art. One that will show women to their best advantage.'

'My father was a lover of natural science and much taken with an account of Lord Cochrane's lighting his hall with an urn that burned coal vapour. He made something like it in his laboratory when I was young.' She remembered her father's attempt at a pottery vessel. They had laughed at it together, she with an eye on his apologetic air. 'He wanted a delicate two-spouted vessel such as you see on Greek vases, but we never achieved the effect he desired. You yourself have experiments on hand?'

'Experiments?' Winsor looked disdainful. 'No, no, I am far beyond the point of experiment. You may not know that I have been in your country some time. Five years ago I lit Carlton House and Pall Mall by gas. Now I propose to my investors something quite different: to light the whole city. My company is already granted a parliamentary charter.'

Winsor's eyes had a tigerish look. Their golden flecks glinted in the candlelight. He is beautiful, Harriet thought. She felt something quicken inside her.

'You will allow me to demonstrate it to you.'

'I should like that, Mr Winsor.'

Harriet pushed about in her purse for her calling card. She was aware of Winsor's attention and for a moment she thought he might kiss her hand; but he slipped the card into the pocket of his coat without a word.

'Mrs Raven.'

Harriet looked up. What was he like? Mercury, from which was made vermilion, cinnabar, Chinese red; that on a touch broke into a myriad iridescent spheres, shining globules of liquid, or liquid solid. Quicksilver: yes, that would be a good element for Mr Winsor.

'Please, call me Frederick.'

'Yes, thank you.'

'Mrs Raven, I think we understand one another. Can I think that we will?'

Then he was gone.

CHARLES HERRIES STOOD IN a stone window embrasure and looked out at the American pines in the park, black as widows against the night sky. The trees reminded him disagreeably that the United States threatened war. It was a wretched attempt to make off with Canada while Britain was busy elsewhere.

'Mr Herries,' Kitty said.

'Lady Wellington, good evening.'

'You received my notes.'

Herries bowed.

'Indeed.'

'I sent two, I believe.'

'Quite so.'

Herries felt Kitty's steady gaze on him. He looked at the floor.

'Most kind, Lady Wellington, but there must be some mistake. Mr Rothschild can have nothing to tell me of my own mother—my family—that I do not have myself. Our life is quietness itself, I assure you.'

'Mr Rothschild is here, Mr Herries. You might like to speak to him.'

I have no choice, Herries thought to himself. He bowed to Kitty and let himself be guided into the drawing room. At least his chestnut-brown evening suit was correct for the occasion. There was Mr Rothschild, corpulent, unmistakable.

'Lady Wellington, who do you have here for me?'

'Mr Charles Herries, Nathan.'

Nathan Rothschild lost his languid air. He leant forward on the soles of his feet and put down his glass on the top of a Louis XV writing desk. Lady Wellington moved away.

'A good evening, Mr Herries, is it not?'

Mr Rothschild, Herries thought, did not sound merely genial.

'I have some news about your family which I believe you may value.' Nathan paused.

'I have a young girl, you see, my little Charlotte. She is quite the charmer.' He smiled, his eyes empty; then appeared to start and recollect himself.

'But now is not the moment to talk of it, sir. Not here. Why not pay me a visit at New Court?'

Herries knew that he would have to go. If Mr Rothschild knew something, oh then, he wanted to know it too. He felt the blood rush to his face.

'I shall be pleased to wait on you tomorrow, sir.'

'Good, good.'

Nathan put out his hand. The face of his signet ring, half-buried in soft flesh, was blank. Herries offered his own hand, and Mr Rothschild enclosed it, top and bottom, for a moment before Herries walked away with so much confusion that he banged the door frame as he passed through.

For a man in charge of supplying the army with all the money necessary to continue the war, Nathan thought, Mr Herries appeared a little highly strung. His palm felt unpleasantly moist. Nonetheless, his history was pleasing. Herries, he found, had studied at Dresden and risen by his own talents. He liked that. When a man has got on by himself he can be trusted to help others get on also. It pays to study each man with care. An unlucky man, now, that is a man he would never act with. If a man cannot do good for himself, he will never be any good to others.

Nathan nodded at the company and walked out into the hall.

'My carriage,' he said to the butler. He fidgeted by the great open door. Lady Holland insisted that her footmen dress in the buff and blue of the American rebels of thirty years ago. Her enthusiasm for the past and for Napoleon was absurd. Never mind; Nathan smiled to himself. The encounter with Herries had put him in a good humour. He disliked such gatherings, usually, but this had been a pleasant evening: profitable, even for a man who shunned poets and pictures. His coach drew up and Nathan hopped in with a lightness and grace quite at odds with his size.

4

Elvas, Portugal and London

APRIL 1812

'Wipe down the table and bring the next man.'

As his assistants worked, David arranged the instruments of the craft in familiar order. First, on the left, the saw and knife; then the metacarpal saw, two scalpels and a screw tourniquet: with them he could cut a leg off in minutes. Next, a pair of forceps and a couple of curved needles already threaded; the first to extract bullets, the other to sew up flesh wounds. He touched each one, and ran his hands over them as his grandfather, in the drawing room in Edinburgh, extended his fingertips over the keys of the pianoforte before he started to play. For two days after the assault he had cut and stitched, lost and saved. Hundreds of men passed beneath his fingers; he no longer saw them as anything more than bundles of nerves, blood and bone. Exhaustion pulled at him, closed his eyes to the sight of men about to die.

'Dr McBride, not the best of circumstances.'

The familiar voice made David concentrate. He looked down at the man on the operating table.

'Ball in the ribs, is my guess.'

Robert Heaton lay there. Froth sat on his lips, red and bubbled. He breathed quickly and coughed blood. David took Heaton's hand. It was white and icy.

'Examination!' David nearly shouted at his assistant. He was shocked to see Heaton so pale.

'Pulse feeble, tendency to syncope, extremities very cold.'

Heaton tried to speak, and David bent close to hear.

'I got into the town but missed everything thereafter. Just as well; it was quite a scene, the Major tells me.'

Heaton's grey trousers were torn and charred, his hair half burned off. One bright blue eye stared out of his swollen face; the other was closed completely. David stood back.

'I have to get this ball out, Mr Heaton. It may move around, and it looks from the wound to have entered between the fourth and fifth ribs. It is too near the heart to leave.'

'I should not want to lose my heart, Doctor. It would be the first time.'

Heaton lay back and closed his good eye. His skin was sheened with sweat, quite cold. He spoke in a gurgle.

'To work, then, Dr McBride.'

'Will you take a draught of brandy?'

'No, later, I think.'

'It is customary, also, to bind the patient's eyes.'

David picked up the muslin sheet from the table. It was grimy now, but still serviceable.

'Ah, yes.' Heaton tried to push his hand into his trouser pocket. 'I cannot seem to do it. Could you lend a hand, Doctor?'

David slid his hand into Heaton's pocket and drew out a silk handkerchief. It was like fine wine to the touch in this rough place, and came with the smell of hay and perfume.

'That's it. I use it to blinker Athena at bridges and fords, you remember. Just lay it across my eyes, will you, though I have half a mind to keep them open. Or the good one, at any rate.'

'It will be best not to, Mr Heaton. I will endeavour to find and extract the ball right away.'

One of his assistants grasped Heaton's legs at the ankles. Heaton flinched and sighed. He was losing quantities of blood. David needed to work fast. He counted off the ribs one by one, and through them felt the weak beat of Heaton's heart. He put his finger into the wound and pushed it as gently as he could up to its whole length. Nothing.

'I shall have to go in with the forceps.'

David wiped Heaton's chest again. The rag left a rich red smear over the ribs. Still the blood flowed. Heaton said nothing, but lifted up one hand, and sighed again. Blood from the wound dripped off the table and pooled on the floor. Heaton was weak, and probably light-headed from the loss of blood. He would not last long. David pressed down with one finger either side of the wound to hold it open, then felt for his forceps, pushed them in and, with a sudden leap of his own heart, felt metal touch metal. He grasped the ball in the spoonlike forceps and pulled back. The bone gave and the ball came away with a viscous suck.

David dropped the bloodied forceps and the loose ball into a small bowl on the table. If he lived, Heaton might want it to keep with him. With his right hand he felt along the row of instruments until he came to a needle.

'This one is going, Doctor.' His assistant whispered in his ear.

David stitched quickly with the curved needle, as dextrous as any seamstress. He tried to ignore the haematic smell of the room. If gangrene set in, the sweet smell of blood took on a foetid edge. David was afraid that he might catch it now. He gestured to his assistant to remove the handkerchief from Heaton's eyes. The whole face, once so handsome and alert, was now slack and drained, the cheeks sunken and grey. Behind the grey was a yellow tinge. David was alarmed; he could see through the skin, beyond the empty and collapsing veins to the fat layer beneath. Colour and blood had drained from his patient.

Heaton opened an eye and closed it again. It was an involuntary gesture, surely. Or might it have been a wink?

'You are losing blood, Mr Heaton.'

Heaton was obviously beyond speech. His wink was given to David to interpret. Very well; he would see it as an agreement, a sign that trust had passed between them.

'I intend to give you a transfusion. You will remember we talked of my interest in the blood.'

There was no time to explain. Heaton had sunk beyond hearing. Later, when he reflected, David knew that he had at that moment forgotten the man under the skin. Desire took hold of him. If he saved a life there would be no murmur against such an experiment. Heaton would certainly die if he did nothing.

'I will take it from myself.' He picked up the catheter he had ordered for the purpose, a narrow silver tube with open points at either end. 'Find the tourniquets.'

When the assistant had tied his left arm tight above the elbow, David did the same to Heaton's right, then sat down behind his shoulder on the camp stool. He picked up the catheter with his right hand then plunged one end into his own vein and the other into the prominent vein in the soft blue swelling in Heaton's inner elbow. David waited until he could see the vein swell with new blood, and then loosened both tourniquets.

How much blood did Heaton need? What would be its effect, he wondered. Leacock in Edinburgh had boasted of reviving slaves with blood from others; but is the make-up of an African the same as that of an Englishman? Was Heaton even an Englishman, he wondered. Well, it was too late to ask him; his hunch must be put to the test.

'Enough,' he said, after a few minutes, 'bandage the arm and bring two cups of tea with brandy.'

The assistant tied the tourniquets and walked off. Heaton was motionless, his eyes both closed. In all probability he was already dead.

'Move this patient to the cells and bring me the next. Give Mr Heaton the tea if he comes round.'

David stood back for a minute to clear his head. He turned to see the Chief Inspector, Dr McGrigor, by the table, dapper and clean. 'What is going on here?'

McGrigor stared at David's catheter.

'This is no time, Dr McBride, to be using untried methods on your patients.'

'Dr McGrigor, it is an honour to receive you.'

'What do you mean an honour? I am in charge here, and do my duty much as you do. Now tell me what you are up to.'

'Sir, the man was dying. He is an amateur, a gentleman volunteer. It is a different case, I hope you will agree, from the use of such a method on a line officer.'

'Or any man enlisted in the service of his country.' McGrigor was no lover of pretension.

'Quite so, sir; and Mr Heaton gave me his consent.'

'Ridiculous, Dr McBride. Do not try to fool me. Blood loss would have robbed him of judgement long ago. That is, if the pain had not already.'

'I needed to do something, sir. I learned much of the procedure from Mr Leacock in Edinburgh.'

'Never heard of him.'

McGrigor glanced up with a look of interest. He tapped his fingers on a bloodstained book that lay on the chair by the table.

'Ranby on gunshot wounds. Good. A very sound text. I am glad to see it is still useful after all these years.'

'Dr McGrigor, you have read of Richard Lower's experiments at the Royal Society?'

'Indeed. But that was a century ago, Dr McBride, and poppycock. This idea of transfusion; upon what theory do you base your belief in it?'

'I do not have a theory, sir. Rather I am doing as we doctors have done for so long; observe, test and conclude. The blood of our species is still a mystery.'

In his eagerness David took McGrigor by the shoulder.

'Dr McGrigor, that is why we are here, is it not? We do our duty, to be sure; but I long to find new cures.'

He gestured round the room and at the soldiers who lay thick on the floor.

'If we believe in progress, surely all this must belong to the age of barbarism.'

'It is war, Dr McBride, the exercise of power by one nation upon another. Not our business to question or disdain. We merely make good the consequences if we can.'

David nodded.

'And then we send them back to fight again if we succeed. But the imperatives of war are not my province of thought. It is my hope that our work might not only impress our names upon the public, but be of benefit to mankind besides. I should like to make a mark in the world.'

McGrigor looked round the crowded room. The patients seemed too far gone in weakness and pain to overhear the doctors who muttered in the corner. Still, he lowered his voice further.

'I wish you well, sir, but ask that you remain discreet. The army does indeed encourage such experiments, though you will make more enemies than friends if others know what you do.'

'I believe Mr Heaton will live.'

'Should he do so we will never know if it is owing to a robust constitution or to this transfusion.'

'Perhaps both, sir.'

McGrigor seemed to cheer up. He slapped the cover of Ranby.

'Ranby now. They are fifty years old, these operations, and we still learn from them. He finished up as Surgeon General to the King, I believe.'

In the gloom of the monastery, David thought he saw McGrigor smile.

'Well, good day, Dr McBride.' McGrigor turned to go. 'And the best of luck to you.'

~

AT TEN O'CLOCK, UNDER a weak sun, Charles Herries walked with purpose round the corner into New Court and checked the doors for no. 2. Five storeys, he thought: but a modest old house for a man with such a fortune.

When the door opened, the manservant took his hat and cane and laid them on a chair.

'Mr Rothschild asks you up, sir. Please follow me.'

Heavy brocade curtains looped across the windows on the first floor. Despite the hour, the drawing room seemed to be in darkness. Herries stumbled forward and made out not just Mr Rothschild but a woman too.

'Good day, Mr Herries. How pleased I am to welcome you and with me Hannah, my wife.'

Herries bowed as Hannah Rothschild came forward. She took his hand and looked into his face. Her eyes, Herries saw, were deep blue, clear and steady.

'Good morning, Mr Herries. You and my husband have much to discuss, so I shall leave you.'

Herries noticed that Hannah was full-bosomed and -hipped. I cannot help myself, he thought, even here, with my life in the balance, I am at it.

When Hannah had left, Nathan Rothschild indicated a chair for Herries.

'Paris,' he said in a soft voice, when Herries had sat down. 'Paris and Napoleon. I suppose you do not know, Mr Herries, that I myself have been under French rule? Yes, we all became citizens in a manner of speaking when Hesse fell.' He paused. 'You yourself have visited Paris more recently, I believe.'

He knows everything, Herries thought. The man is preternatural.

'I was a younger man when I went to Paris, sir. I now pay heavily for my folly.'

'To smuggle yourself into the enemy capital at a time of war, you mean, I dare say.'

'All that I did there.'

'A man makes such decisions in an instant. There is nothing to regret,

I fancy. Sometimes one loses on the transaction, sometimes there is a profit. And in your case, Mr Herries, how could one compute it as anything but the latter?'

Herries did not answer; the room swayed before him. He felt held to account, although he had attempted to do his duty. He had written to Lucia, sent money, asked for news. Nothing had come back but years of emptiness and so he had stopped. Perhaps Lucia had changed her lodgings. More likely, he had thought, she had a new lover and wished for nothing more to do with him, even by letter.

Nathan Rothschild's gaze held him immobile. He waited.

'A family, however we find it, is a blessing. My brother Jakob writes me word from Paris that your Louisa begins to write and read.'

'My Louisa?'

'Your Louisa, Mr Herries.'

A stillness came over Herries as if a tempest had swept through a forest and left nothing behind.

I am going to faint away, Herries thought, and clung to the arms of his chair, I shall fall onto Mr Rothschild's knees, and then his fine India carpet, and make a fool of myself.

Herries swayed a little. A child. He had a child. He was a father, father to a daughter. Louisa; a beautiful name. Then another shock: Lucia. He and Lucia had a daughter. Father, daughter, mother: familiar, ordinary words. He had used them a thousand times for others. Now they hung, yoked together in Mr Rothschild's drawing room, aglow with joy and fear.

Herries summoned the control he used to master the figures that were set before him every day. Mr Rothschild did not deceive him, he was quite certain. He began to calculate. Six months in Paris he had stayed. So Louisa must be five by now—four at the very least. He glanced at Nathan again. The man was motionless and in complete command of himself. The thought came to Herries that they must be about the same age. How then had he let Mr Rothschild have the advantage of him?

'My Louisa. Yes. She is five years old—five, or is it four—and a lively girl. It is some time indeed since I have had news of her.'

'I can assure you of her good health.'

'Might I ask how you are aware of that, sir?'

'We have made enquiries. They live, it is true, in modest circumstances in the rue de Grenelles. Two rooms, front and back, no more.'

'And Lucia?' Herries forgot his reserve.

'Continues to work at the Opéra, but has engaged a governess. Your Louisa speaks the purest French, Mr Herries. She will be a credit to you.'

'Oh that I might see her.'

Herries swallowed, brushed his hand across his face, and wiped it behind his back on the tails of his jacket.

'Impossible, my dear sir. You will be aware of all the reasons.'

There it was then. He would not last a week in the Commissary Office if word went round that he had been lying in the arms of a singer at the Opéra, Lucia Carioli, on the very day the Grande Armée entered Berlin six years ago. It was not the nature of the indiscretion, of course, but where it took place, and when. Who had been in Paris six years ago but spies and traitors? He stood to lose everything when he had nothing to fall back on, and a mother to support besides. A man of no family, even a man of ability, was easy to dismiss and slow to be forgiven. Every such man had enemies, gentlemen who resented those whose salaries were earned with work rather than bestowed by rank.

Nathan leaned towards Herries. His voice was light.

'But now that she learns her letters, Louisa might send a note to her Papa. Couriers arrive frequently from Paris to New Court, two a week at the least. I have other means, too, if you wished to send her something by return. For more substantial items, that is to say, I have a packet standing by at Folkestone. The Cullen family there are in my employ.'

So that was how the Rothschilds conveyed their bullion to the Continent, Herries thought, and this is how he ensures that I will tell no one that I know. He felt tired, worn out by the effort of probity.

'To hear about Lucia has lifted one of the stones that weighs me down. I cannot thank you enough.'

'Do not thank me, Mr Herries. I intend nothing by the information other than a favour to you. I shall get word to you at Great George Street when something arrives.'

Nathan Rothschild stood up.

'I wish you a good morning, Mr Herries.'

Herries bowed and withdrew. Outside the sun still shone. He trotted up to Threadneedle Street and hailed a hansom beside the Bank.

'Great George Street, the Commissary Office.'

As soon as the cab bounced off he changed his mind. The old desire for a woman came down and imprisoned him. He leaned back against the horsehair seat and determined on self-control; but in an instant his resolution flagged. Why should he keep himself tightly shut up? What did it matter? Joy and fear mingled in him. For a minute joy might be uppermost, winged with the thought of Lucia and Louisa. The world appeared crystalline, perfect, in tune with the morning. Then fear pushed forward and he felt hunted and alone. He might lose his position; Mr Rothschild might compromise him at any moment. He had henceforth to learn to live with both; there could be no resolution, at least while the war lasted. He needed Rothschild. Yet he could not hate him; still less despise him. Herries was sure that Nathan would never reveal what he knew. His genius was to probe a man, find his weakness and work it. He had done him a favour, as he said, in the continental way. He would expect something in return—a contact, a word on his behalf—that was all.

Herries shrugged and tapped on the glass.

'Durrant's Inn.'

The day for himself, and for a woman, then. There was no news from Spain. The War Office could wait until tomorrow. Crossing Cavendish Square he saw the neat small figure of Lady Wellington alone. That woman led a wretched life by all accounts, forced not just to attend interminable drawing rooms in the General's place but to ignore the chatter that came out from behind the ladies' fans. Still, was he any different? When he leaned back against the cushions, images and thoughts of Lucia came to him, mingled now with the anticipation of Madame Duplace. What was that woman's real name, he wondered idly, lulled with anticipation and relief. That was another thing he must find out. The knowledge might come in useful. But not today; today was for joy, and oblivion.

～

AT NOON, THE DAY after Badajoz was stormed, Lord Wellington called the Adjutant General.

'You have the returns, Stewart?'

'As well as the regimental colonels could give them, my Lord. The situation is still confused.'

Stewart gestured towards the devastated fortress. Haze hung over Badajoz and from the city flames and black smoke rose into the morning air. It was a fine spring day, bright after the rain.

'Officers killed?'

'Dozens, my Lord, so they say.'

'Lesser ranks and privates?'

'Thousands, sir; four or five thousand at first count.'

Stewart noticed the General start. Wellington's head shot up; under his three-cornered hat, light caught the arch of his nose and his broad forehead.

'What did I tell you, Stewart, after Ciudad Rodrigo? Spare the garrison, as I did there, and the enemy will take advantage of clemency again. My men pay the price.'

'General Philippon surrendered to Fitzroy Somerset, sir, offered him his sword at seven this morning. My congratulations. The victory and the town are yours. Somerset brought Philippon out of San Cristóbal under escort, bareheaded with his two daughters.'

'Have them taken to Elvas and given suitable quarters.'

Stewart coughed.

'It was an affecting scene, my Lord. Men—our men—tried to pull the girls away, rip them from their father's hands.'

Wellington was silent. Fitzroy had acted well.

'We had best view the damage. General Picton, I commend your gallant action. Your assault at the castle carried the day. I trust your wound to be slight enough to allow you to accompany me to the breaches.'

General Picton limped up. Shot in the foot, he had spent much of the night laid up and doubted he had the strength to walk far.

'Sir, I beg leave to retire.' Picton's voice, hoarse from an old gunshot wound in the throat incurred in a duel years before, was weak.

'Very well, sir. Ned?'

General Pakenham stepped forward. His jacket, Wellington noticed, was torn and blackened. He would excuse his brother-in-law: he had been courageous last night, taken charge of the 3rd with credit when Picton could not continue. Still, he needed, in the next few months, to rid himself of Ned somehow.

'My Lord?'

'Oh come now, Ned; we can for once forget ceremony. You will ride with us?'

'It will be an honour, sir.'

At the main breach Charles Stewart thought he might faint away. Blood had collected in the inclines, brown and muddied. Heaps of debris blocked the approaches to the walls of the fortress. At intervals among the rows of criss-crossed bayonet blades planted by the French at the bottom of the walls hung dead men with open eyes, impaled like sides of meat ready for the spit. The living and the dead tangled together under fallen scaling ladders and rubble. Men still alive cried and moaned. Up above, the shattered walls gaped; a great glacier of wood and masonry flowed down the breach. Blackened limbs of soldiers caught in the collapse stuck out at intervals up the slope. Here and there blue smoke rose into the sky and shafts of sunlight fell through it as if the heavens wished to illuminate the horrors that man had made. Over everything the stench of seared flesh, charred wood and gunpowder settled like a pall.

'Good God,' General Pakenham exclaimed despite himself, 'it looks like the day of judgement.'

The three men dismounted and walked towards the edge of the debris. They passed doctors and their assistants, working to pull men from the masonry and encircling sabres. Silence fell as Lord Wellington walked among the heaps of bodies; soldiers doffed their hats. Stewart, who struggled to control himself, felt rather than saw Wellington bow his head. He turned to see that the General had halted, hands over his face.

'My Lord?'

There was no reply. Stewart saw the General dip slightly at both knees; in the silence he heard him groan and moved to take him by the arm.

'Sir, do not despair. It was a great victory and the men brave beyond words.'

'And the cost, Stewart. Look at the cost.'

Wellington took his hands from his face and glared at Stewart. His face was wet with tears.

'I tell you, Stewart, I shall never again allow myself to pay for victory in this way. Did I not inform Lord Liverpool of our shortages? How am I expected to carry on with an army that walks on the soles of its feet, without boots, and without ammunition? My masters in Spring Gardens, men who have never seen a battle, never smelled death the day after? I should bring them here to see what they have done.'

'Indeed, my Lord.'

'Well, what are you standing there for like a stuffed doll, Stewart, like a marionette who cannot move?'

Stewart judged it best to stay silent.

'You have no answer? Come then; let us go. I have letters to write.'

Not a man moved. Wellington turned away from the carnage and walked briskly to his horse. His eyes, Stewart saw, were now dry.

'DAVID, I MUST LEAVE you to get on.'

James Raven stood with David McBride at the door of the monastery in Elvas that served as the main hospital. Two French officers, captured during the assault, lay in a cell set aside for them. They had nothing of importance to tell James; he was content for them to be taken down to Lisbon and swapped, in due course, for English or Portuguese prisoners.

David grasped James's hand.

'You yourself are unscathed, it appears.'

'Not a scratch on me. I live a charmed life, David. Fighting suits me.'

'So I observe. You appear invigorated.'

'You are right; but it is not just invigorated. Life here is more concentrated. It suits me.'

'Though you must feel the absence of Harriet; the loss of companionship and home.'

James considered the idea, then looked closely at David as if he had just noticed his presence.

'No. I tell you in confidence as my friend. Harriet is dear, but far away. When I look back at Suffolk now, it appears dull and insignificant.' He shrugged. 'Perhaps it is merely that I am busy here, and my service to the army valued. Do you not find something similar?'

'Indeed. Every day I learn something that may be of use.'

'David; I really must go now. I bid you good day.'

David McBride watched James stride away down the dirty street and round the corner into the main town square, his red jacket bright against the dirty white walls. Even among the press of officers here, he stood out. James carried himself well, held his fine frame upright, shoulders back. The sun, up above the houses now, picked out the golden glints in his hair. Yet something was unsettled in him, David could see. The ease that James had had in Suffolk was gone.

AFTER BADAJOZ WAS TAKEN, wounded soldiers with a good chance of recovery were removed on bumping carts over the hills to the River Tagus, where they would be transported to the hospitals in Lisbon, or shipped home. By the fourth day after the assault the hospital at Elvas was left with the worst cases: the dying and the feverish. David made his way round the crowded cells. Where one monk had prayed, now men lay on pallets laid side by side, four men to a cell, crammed so closely toe to head that David had to squeeze between them, retching in the foetid air. In one narrow cell lay an officer with severe dehydration. David watched as the man's servant dropped water through his swollen lips. He had fed a fallen fledgling in Bushey once that way and remembered how the creature widened its beak at the approach of the smallest spoon he could find. Drip by drip he had restored the bird to life while its mother called from the trees close by, and then lifted it into the thicket and walked away. For years he wondered if it had lived, or if his tenderness had been in vain.

With the wounded divided between Elvas and Badajoz, regimental surgeons swapped patients. Down in Badajoz, Dr Bennett, the surgeon of the 95th, took on two officers from the 9th and here he was now, David thought, with two in return, young Lieutenant Grant and Captain Townley, a man who took everything with a lightness David envied. Heavily bandaged across one eye, Grant lay flat on a camp bed brought across from his billet. His arms supported his head. Captain Townley sat up with a pipe, which he waved over a bandaged leg.

'I find that smoke keeps off the flies,' he said when David came up to him.

'It cannot do any harm.'

'I say, Doctor, have you looked up there?' Townley took the pipe out of his mouth and waved it at a crucifixion scene that was painted on the wall of the cell. 'We have had enough of it, I can tell you, what with the wretched chaplain who creeps round just when we are ready to scream with the dullness of it all. Prisoners to his enthusiasm we were this morning, though God knows, we made it clear enough we had no time for redemption unless it comes in a female form.'

Drops of blood hung in the air below Christ's feet. Behind the cross olives grew beyond the wall in neat lines. Few soldiers worshipped or prayed. Most ignored the comfort belief might bring. Death was commonplace, devoid of the sublime. David looked at the fresco or rather the blood in it. He looked at it as a doctor might, but then blood ran through his mind at night; not the unreal pipette drops from Christ's wounds, but full pails, thrown over his dreams. In the last few days his eyes closed to it even in the daytime.

'Let us forget all that nonsense, Doctor.' Grant stared at the ceiling. 'We are compiling a list of beautiful women in each country we have passed through. Townley here says none compares with Camille Florens at Lisbon. Have you encountered her, Doctor?'

'No, indeed. Unlike Dr Bennett I arrived only a few weeks ago.'

Grant lifted his bandaged head. 'Señora Florens is a firm ally of Great Britain, the Captain says, and more enchanting than you can imagine.'

Townley waved his pipe again.

'I have seen nothing like her, and I have been at Paris, Dresden, Naples, Vienna, Rome. Dublin, too. She came to Lisbon to pass on information, so they said. At any rate she is in Seville now, beyond the reach of your paws, Grant.'

'Then, if you have such experience, you can tell me how she is different?'

'A man can see a hundred beautiful women, Grant, but then you see one who invites you to admire her, who has none of this chaste hanging-back that women pretend to these days.'

'You are telling me this Donna Florens takes lovers like Lady Oxford?'

'Not at all. That's the devil of it. She appears quite demure, but she tempts one to hope.'

On the far side of the open space where he had operated, David saw Robert Heaton, who half-raised a hand in greeting. Heaton was propped up in bed, a crisp white tablecloth over his knees and Major Yallop by his side. On the floor beside the bed stood a bottle and two fine cut-crystal glasses. Racket lay on the rough blanket, his nose on Heaton's leg. At David's approach the dog opened his eyes and raised his nose.

Major Yallop looked sheepish; the splendour, he implied, was none of his doing.

'I brought up something for Mr Heaton to eat. Believe it or not, his servant had glasses packed away somewhere.'

David ignored the wine, which might do the patient some good.

'What is this dog doing here, Mr Heaton?'

Heaton stroked Racket's silky head.

'What a question. Racket here does me more good than anything, though wine is also a fine restorative. Perhaps you could squeeze that glass into my hand, Doctor. I confess I feel a little light-headed.'

He leant back, and then made an effort to go on.

'The Major tells me that the whole encampment is now a fairground.'

Yallop snorted. 'A pantomime I should call it. Lord Wellington handed the men the town, and the debauch went on until this morning. I saw

Captain Raven's servant asleep in an alley. I tell you, Mr Heaton, it was shameful to see my men dressed like whores, wrapped in silks. I would have marched them to the breaches if I could, to dig out the wounded from the dead.'

The Major paused and looked at the floor.

'I am happy that Mrs Yallop is not here. The dear soul would hate to witness such things.'

'But the men were maddened, Major, I felt it myself, it takes hold of one.'

Heaton nodded at David.

'There, Doctor; there is your connection to the beasts. We have to be schooled not to run amok. Even dear Racket would start after a hare and tear it to pieces if I did not speak to him about it.'

'How are you feeling, Mr Heaton?' David sat down on the end of the bed. 'I need to take a look at your wound.'

'Yes, do, do. I am faint still, though confident the wound is clean.'

'Lean forward.'

David unwound the gauze from Heaton's chest. An opaque wet film spread across the opening of Heaton's wound, and glistened in the sunlight. David looked at it in silence for a few moments.

'It looks raw but has already begun to close.'

Heaton squinted down with his open eye.

'Dr McBride, I thank you,' he said. 'You have done me a great service.'

'I believe it was the transfusion.' David lowered his voice.

'Ah, yes, that is most interesting. We are in a manner of speaking now mingled together; that is to say your blood is mixed with mine. What might that make us?'

'I have an idea that living organisms within the blood can flourish in many of us; yet some patients die within minutes of a transfusion, as if they have been poisoned.'

'I was fortunate, therefore. We must have some chemical affinity, or an elective affinity as Goethe calls it.'

'I do not in this case use chemical experiment. I base my observations on the humours. That notion is long discredited, but perhaps unwisely so. Scotchmen you see are melancholic. We are full of black bile, fond of sadness and drink. East Anglians, on the other hand, are phlegmatic, slow to anger.'

George Yallop started.

'Indeed I am not, sir,' he said. 'Mrs Yallop would say I am heated and choleric. Besides what has that to do with giving Mr Heaton a transfusion?'

'My idea is to match the humours of the giver and the receiver, so I have thought to pair countryman with countryman. In Mr Heaton's case I had to be the giver myself, for lack of anyone else, though I am a Scotsman by birth and he is an Englishman—at least I have presumed so.'

Heaton looked bored.

'Good, good. I should not want the blood of a Spaniard, certainly. Still less that of a dear creature like Racket here, a circumstance I think you mentioned before. It is disagreeable to dwell on it, especially since the whole episode is over.'

With his free hand Heaton tried to reach the flat pocket sewn into the silk lining of his jacket, which lay on the bed beside him. When his hand fell listlessly down Racket jumped up and began to lick it.

'I cannot manage it. Major, can you help? You will find my card case in there.'

Heaton looked fondly at the small ivory case Major Yallop pulled out. It was carved all over into a fantastic oriental landscape with weeping willows and Chinamen underneath them, the bone dug out to make a bas-relief with shadows and depth.

'Neat piece of work, eh? I had it off a trinket merchant in Paris a dozen years ago. Ah, there now. Doctor, take my card. One never knows what might happen in a war and I should like you to have it.'

David took the card. A feminine copperplate flowed across it, so fine that it was hard to read. 'Hon. Robert Heaton, Arlington Street.' Nothing else.

Off Piccadilly, David thought. London, as it might be that April morning, rolled out before him. The eastern sun that shone straight down the Strand and swung round to pick up the silver river light; the rumble and clatter of morning; mercuries out on the street, redoubtable women with slabs of folio sheets over their arms, who shouted the news and sold it to passers-by; milk- and fruit-sellers, beggars and old soldiers, the slap of metalled boots on the flags, the screech and creak of laden carts and lighter carriages. Children everywhere in the side streets, organised into companies that raced round corners, hung off the ladder rests on lamp-posts, sang and skipped; some barefoot, others scarcely clad.

In Portugal white walls cracked and peeled in the bright sun, mud-splashed at the hem. Cornfield-yellow cornices ran round the doors and windows. Elvas crammed its grid into the great star-shape of its high bastion walls, a town built for war and guard duty. Inside the bastion of São José, a new cemetery was dug. Dead officers' bodies settled fresh into the stony ground there. Beyond the walls, plum trees flowered at the edges of olive groves and new emerald grass was long in the ditches.

From afar, the air itself shimmered. In another month the deep heat, day- and night-long, would spread over the country. Summer heat entered the body like liquid, indifferent to the waste of hours. It warmed flesh into languor, merged the blue sky into the white horizon, turned curiosity into desire, resolution into torpor. Put a Riga merchant in Portugal, David thought, and would the heat, after a year or two, melt his sharpness?

'Mr Heaton will be back with us soon,' George Yallop said with decision. 'After all there is a good bit of fighting to come.' He grinned with pleasure, as if he chewed on a fine cut of beef. 'We no longer have our backs to the sea; we can turn north and harry the enemy, begin to push him out. The General will want to tackle Marmont now, cut him off and take Madrid. Besides, Boney has withdrawn fifteen thousand troops for his Russian adventure, I hear, and that leaves him light here. We will sweep them away, Doctor, I am sure of it.'

～

AT THE END OF April Kitty drew up by the high columned front of the Royal Institution in Albemarle Street. On the pavement outside stood two lamplighters, each with a pair of scissors tucked into his belt. One carried a ladder and a lighted taper, the other a can of oil. Up on the ladder propped against the crossbar, the lighter lifted off the lamp cover and lit the oil-soaked wick. Sometimes he trimmed a blackened wick with his scissors or handed down an empty cylinder to be swapped for one new-filled. The glutinous odour of whale oil lingered in the street, and reminded Kitty of assemblies and dancing. It was just the hour to attend a lecture.

Kitty noticed Harriet in a velvet cloak on the other side of the street. Harriet stood alone looking at the last of the day's light fall through the trees of the garden opposite the grand new building. The green pockets of London were filling with bricks and noise; the memory of the farmers who once worked these orchards would soon be covered over in lime-stone and tar. Future generations would struggle to think that salad grew in the back yards, and plums and apples once lay on Mayfair streets.

'Harriet, I am here. Not too late, I hope.'

'No, I have the tickets. There is quite a crowd.'

'A visit from William Herschel is a rarity. He scarcely ever ventures away from Slough and this may be the last occasion he is in London.'

'Let us take our seats, then, Kitty. I am impatient to set eyes upon him.'

Fifteen tall Corinthian columns, rising forty feet and painted in the buttermilk-cream that distinguished the newest architecture, measured out the new façade of the Royal Institution. Inside, a double staircase with narrow banisters ran up from the centre of the entrance hall. Members of the Institution and their guests, politicians and peers, serious black-coated men of science, lady authoresses and famous hostesses greeted one another on their way up. Several officers wore the scarlet jackets of full dress uniform. Kitty nodded to acquaintances. From the murmurings about her she knew that many present were not sure who she was, though they noted the respect in the way she was greeted.

The theatre was very small, cut across at the podium end to make a horseshoe, and steeply tiered in dark mahogany. Green velvet covers, stuffed with horsehair and corded in gold, made the wood a little more comfortable. Tucked into their narrow seats, knees to backs for the taller men, the audience waited. When no space remained, an usher closed the doors and then opened them. A sigh, half-expectant, half-bored, ran through the audience; everyone stood.

'His Royal Highness, the Prince Regent.'

All you could say of the Regent, Harriet thought, was that he did not look well for a man of fifty. The Prince's face was mottled and flushed after the walk upstairs. His dress coat was too tight, and the single Garter star that glittered on the convexity of his chest did not lie flat. His feet, cased in white silk pumps topped with silver tassels, looked too delicate and short to support the swell of his thighs and stomach. At any moment, Harriet thought, he might topple over.

The Prince held his hand up in acknowledgement of the standing crowd.

'Charming, charming.' With an audible groan of effort, he lowered himself into the chair set for him by the front row of seats.

'Now, the great explorer of the skies,' the Prince said with a languid flourish of his hand.

The doors opened again and a tall thin man walked with purpose into the lecture theatre. It was impossible not to switch one's gaze onto him, Harriet thought. Herschel concentrated the attention of the audience as one of his own great telescopes concentrated light. Even now, as an old man, his long straight mouth was set with determination. But there was nothing ponderous about him. Herschel stood behind the lecturer's desk and swept his look up and round the theatre with an innocent eagerness. Then he began to speak about the life of the heavens, the great organism of the sky above that, like everything in nature, might bloom in one place and decay in other, and, like the earth itself, was restless and alive, moving and turning in an infinity of time.

In soft waves of accented English Herschel's voice rose and fell. Though he had come to England dozens of years before, German vowels added music and gravity to his speech. New galaxies, just swimming into the very limit of our sight, were constantly being born, he said. Others were dying, or had died long ago. Light, which signals life and germination, might in fact come to us from stars long dead. Nothing was what it seemed at first. Great tracts of the heavens that seemed on cursory examination empty might in fact be full, replete with the ghosts of dead stars. Yet these ghosts seemed now, to him, not to be insubstantial or a mere absence, but to have a strange existence of their own. Night after night he and his sister had observed the sky. There were places up there, stellar graveyards, round which nimbler stars dipped and swerved. Why? Here on the earth's surface we might see such places as mere uninhabited spaces in the great firmament. Young stars knew better. They avoided the dead and dying the more to cling to life.

Herschel paused. So, Harriet thought, planetary corpses haunt the firmament long after their bodies have melted away. Nowhere is there peace, though the heavens seem so quiet at night. Comets and shooting stars, that we think of as celestial prophets, streak through the skies on a mission to scorch their presence in the firmament, hurtle through a darkness that vibrates and shudders, is born, shines and dies. Nothing can be fixed or last for ever. Like the particles that make up solid objects, everything everywhere is in motion. Even time itself might one day decay or come to a stop. Change was man's condition, foretold in celestial convulsions.

Harriet clasped her gloved hands. To hear a man like Herschel, who twenty years ago had seen a new planet and changed the look of the heavens for ever: that was why she had come to London. It was for that she had read Mrs Marcet's *Conversations on Chemistry* in her father's study, even though Mrs Marcet assumed that the girls she wrote for had no mathematical knowledge.

She looked down at the Regent, who sat with his legs splayed and smiled with vacant bonhomie at the benches around him. He affected a gaze of sincere and proprietorial interest. It was, after all the Royal Institution; everything that took place there pertained to him. Then he lifted his slippered foot off the floor and glanced at his ankle with obvious pleasure. A bead of sweat ran down the side of his cheek.

William Herschel dipped his voice to indicate that he was reaching a conclusion. The audience sat up in readiness for the end, and then applauded. Herschel bowed first to the Prince Regent and then to the audience. The Regent stood up stiffly, walked to Herschel and put his arm around him. Herschel seemed to flinch under the Prince's soft bulk. From her seat on the first row, Kitty watched him stand to attention until the Prince released him. The Regent, Kitty thought, does not wear kingship well; he never manages to play the King as he should. He fails to convince even as an understudy, hair combed up and dyed, eyebrows plucked and lips suspiciously red. With his arm on Herschel's shoulder the Regent looked like a Drury Lane actor whose best performance is long behind him.

Arthur, now, knew how to wear the mantle of the General to perfection. Men might ape his carefully tailored clothes, but they saw through them to the muscularity beneath, and deferred to it. Then Arthur's comportment, chin up and eyes hooded, commanded attention. Everyone feared him; she used to herself, and to live in awe of the care he took to remain young. Lately, however, her thoughts had shifted. She sought out rounder men who did not seek to hide a fold about the waist. Why had she come to long for plumpness, to think, even, of laying her head against it? She dismissed the thought; there was no gain from it.

IN THE LOBBY OF the lecture hall, above the heads of the crowd, Harriet saw the dark head of Frederick Winsor. His hair had been tamed, cut in the manner of Lord Byron. Its white streak glinted from underneath.

'Mrs Raven.'

Frederick came towards her in his quiet way and bowed to Kitty.

'Lady Wellington, I am pleased to see you here. Sir William is my compatriot. He honours Germany as well as Great Britain with his discoveries. I hope to do the same. My National Light and Heat Company has new premises and begins the production of gas shortly. I should be flattered to demonstrate the properties of my inflammable air for you both at my house.'

Kitty, Harriet saw, was amused and interested.

'I am at 97 Pall Mall. The tickets are half a crown, but I have here two which you may present at the door.'

Frederick slid a case from his pocket and handed Kitty two small cards. They showed a lamp surrounded by a halo of rays on a dark ground, and underneath it the name of his company.

'I perform the demonstration with my assistant every Monday and Wednesday at 7 p.m.'

'Then I shall come when I have an opportunity, and I hope that Mrs Raven will accompany me.'

Harriet nodded as they said goodbye and made their way out to the stairs and the street.

'This chemical impresario,' Kitty said, 'do you think, Harriet, that he is a visionary or merely a showman?'

'Perhaps he is both. We shall no doubt discover if we go. You remember that I met Mr Winsor at Holland House?'

'He interests me, like so much these days. Let us go and judge this gaslight for ourselves.'

'He is looking for investors, I am quite sure.'

'Very good. I am an investor myself, as you know.'

Harriet said goodbye to Kitty and pulled on her cloak. She would walk back to Hatton Garden. Once down the length of Piccadilly and across the spongy grass of Leicester Fields, she made for the Piazza of Covent Garden through King's Place and the back of the churchyard. Mrs Cobbold would be horrified if she knew she walked down a street so renowned for its bagnios and courtesans of all descriptions. King's Place, at this time in the evening, was quiet and muffled. In one of the parlours she saw a youngish woman, fashionably dressed in a white silk gown. Her red hair was loose round her shoulders, a waterfall of spiralling ringlets. Their eyes met for a minute with only the glass of the window between them; then Harriet walked on.

On the south side of the green field by Lincoln's Inn, a grand new building was rising by an encampment of indigent soldiers. At night, fires burned in the fields, where the men slept in bivouacs as neat as anything they had built on the plains of Estremadura or the volcanic slopes of Sicily. In the daytime, lawyers in tight wigs threw pennies into the soldiers' hands by the railings of New Square.

Harriet walked round the field and up onto the dilapidation of High Holborn. Frederick Winsor came back to her mind. There was something about him that made her hesitate. She had felt unsettled after their talk at Holland House, unable to place him within any catalogue of her acquaintance. His quiet voice was insinuating rather than powerful. He appeared soft and uninterested in what went on around him. Perhaps he believed that quite without exertion he was the most powerful phenomenon in any space. At any rate she had thought it better to forget him. But now Kitty had declared her interest in his business and she was inclined to go along with it. Mr Winsor reminded her of all the hours she had spent in the laboratory and of everything that enchanted her about chemistry, natural science and astronomy: that there was a world to discover. Well, here was her chance to start again.

'Like greyhounds in the slips, straining upon the start.'

She smiled into the darkness, shook her head, and hurried along almost at a run. 'I might find something in an unexpected place,' she told herself, 'a detail of life, a nugget that will gleam in the dark.' Under her breath she added, like a charm, '*Henry the Fifth*, Act 3, Scene 1.'

PART TWO

5

Madrid and London

AUGUST 1812

Francisco Goya did not like horses. Years ago, before King Carlos had stupidly abdicated in favour of his idiot son, Goya had done him a favour, a considerable favour, considering his fixed aversion to equestrian life. He had painted Queen Maria Luisa on horseback, sitting on her favourite, Marcial—a hulking chestnut with shifting yellow eyes—in the vainglorious pose of Caterina la Grande of Russia. Her riding habit he had trimmed with gold. The most delicate of his sable brushes, touched across the rough canvas, pulled the light onto the Queen's collar and cuffs. Oh yes, he was paid to draw attention—and he had, quite literally—to her fine small hands and the plump forearms of which she was so unjustifiably proud. After all, he was not court painter for nothing. He mixed flattery with truth on his palette. That was the way he had seen off King Carlos IV (a kind enough man, and a good shot into the bargain) and Carlos's father, and now his son Fernando, that halfwit fat-thighed dwarf.

For Maria Luisa, who sometimes shared a joke, he waved his magical brush with deference and a swagger. He gave her a standard studio background, it is true: rolling hills, misted mountains, a country palace. But the Queen herself? Oh—she got twinkling golden stirrups, a scarlet cockade and the saucy air of a woman who sucks at the fruit of life. Greed became her better than delicacy.

But Marcial, that brute of a stallion. He, Goya, had no need to give him any special treatment. The horse did not appoint him, ask him to paint his lover or pay him to design tapestries by the yard. So Marcial became a flat cut-out, a paper horse, one front leg raised as a child would do it, back legs blotched into shadow, ears like a kitten's and the round forehead of an ass.

Not everything on four legs lacks charm, Goya thought. Dogs now—ah dogs. Look into a dog's eyes and he looks back. He tries with his eyes, as if he knows he cannot speak, to tell you what he feels. Peer into those brown pools and see how sadness washes through the pupils; notice the jump of fear, and liquid joy when the master returns.

Have a good look at the hound in the portrait of the old king's father he, Goya, had done twenty years ago even before he became official court painter. How tired the dog is, flat out, on the ground, curled up soft like the leather of the king's glove. From sympathy he knows his master is old and ill. He will come into the sickroom, where fear circles like a night-moth, place his damp suede nose on the king's dry hand and lie quiet until death comes. Look too at the floppy-eared retriever in the portrait of Carlos IV himself, how his nose turns up in trust and love. Sadness and hope balance in him; if the king were in danger his dog would try to reach him. No tempest, no flood or fire would stop him; on and on he would swim, uphill and alone, until he found his master.

Pity, then, that humanity so little deserves a dog's devotion. Today any-way, was not a dog's day. Here he was, this morning—an airless August morning, bone dry in the great palace, thirsty for autumn mist—with another horse, and he, Goya, obsequious and truthful as always. He had lived out the years of Carlos and Carlos's father, and now that slimy ass Fernando too. The kings and princes were gone; one dead, the other two over the border into France and the captivity of Bonaparte, a Corsican thief who pretended he did not have an Italian name. But there was still, and always, the horse.

The fact was, the commission of the victorious General and liberator demanded equestrian grandeur and Goya was short of canvas. Then, since he did not like horses, why paint another, why round the flanks and dot with white those dull and stupid eyes, when he already had one finished?

Yes, this mess of a horse that he painted on this morning had already had another rider. To be truthful, two. Goya had started it years ago for Manuel Godoy, when he was chief minister and ruled the country. Godoy was a man with a good eye for a woman and a picture. They called him Prince of the Peace before war swept him away; and he did not murmur, or even laugh, when he, Goya, put a horse's bottom plumb in the middle of a canvas and stuck a fat gold stick straight up between Godoy's thighs. No, he paid up; the King's money it would have been; but why should he, Goya, ask about that, when one gold coin looked and bought the same?

When Joseph Bonaparte got his hands on Madrid he wanted a portrait in his turn. Off came Godoy with a scrape of sand and oil. Up went fat little José, quite the dandy; red ribbons, silver star and black cocked hat. Now here is Lord Wellington, Duke of Ciudad Rodrigo, come into the city quite the hero, and he, Goya, got the summons to paint him of course, never mind that he has given his canvas linen to the army for bandages and dislikes horses.

Vanity makes his sitters blind, Goya knows. This lord for instance—Nosey, the General—whatever name they give him, does not notice that the brute is far too small for him, a merry-go-round pony with a tail like a witch's broom. No matter. The General will look at himself, and be satisfied by the seen-it-all look in his eyes, the extra hair added to his head and a well-fitted jacket.

Goya watches uniformed young men come uncertainly into the room. The Duke's upper lip thins in disdain when they speak. These English know nothing, and will ask nothing, of the other work Goya does at night in his lodgings. The English speak another language and think themselves invisible even to him, the painter. Because he is deaf they think he is blind also.

In his house Goya has left a canvas just finished, to dry in the heat. A lunatic asylum, someone will call it, though it could be this room, or any room, where naked men jostle and fight imaginary monsters in the gloom. There, in the middle of the picture, in sepia and buff, a man who thinks he is a king, a crown on his head, who roars commands to a cellar full of madmen who do not listen. Here is a lunatic bishop, there a nearly naked muscular man who spars with the air, a prizefighter at war with the invisible. A bare-breasted, would-be general has a stick for a sword and three feathers for a tricorne hat. No matter: a cloaked man still kisses his hand. In the shadows one lunatic—or maybe any man—fumbles with another, forces himself upon him with bestial greed.

In the time of war, the world narrows to that darkened cellar. Grown men scrabble in the dirt and strike senselessly at one another. Outside under the open sky, a village looks on as a peasant who had shared a plough with his neighbour now gores him like a matador. The cries of women go unanswered; limbless corpses hang over lakes of blood; nature itself is mutilated and dies.

'I saw it,' Goya said to himself. 'I looked right into the mad black heart of it. Nothing came out.'

With a sable brush he touched light onto the golden belt round the Duke's tight waist.

ASTRIDE A CHAIR IN an equestrian pose, Lord Wellington went through the morning's business. Over the falls of his new white cravat he kept an eye on the painter, who stood half-hidden behind a giant canvas balanced across two easels. A little man, run to fat. He would speak French, perhaps some Italian; but English? Certainly not. They might as well be alone.

'I do not expect much from the exertions of the Spaniards, despite all we have done for them,' he said.

'You mean exertions in a military way, my Lord?'

Fitzroy Somerset smiled discreetly. The General spent his nights with the most beautiful women in Madrid. With the opposite sex, particularly if they were young, Wellington became charming, though these days it took little more than a hand slipped round a waist to conquer. The victor of Salamanca could be a hunchback and never have an empty bed.

Somerset had had his share of women since they had arrived. Desire flooded him at the thought of them; plump married ladies who had let their servants go hungry rather than lose their own roundness; ecstatic half-starved beauties picked up on the hot streets; the modest-looking wife at his billet who without a word offered herself to his golden hair and scarlet uniform. Each of them had lifted her hips to him in passion. The whole city, it seemed, was open for the liberators. The Madrileños were crazed with hunger and wild with relief.

At a ball last week he had tangled his spurs into his partner's gown at the height of the waltz, and fallen over. Two other couples whirled into them. In the heap a woman took his hand and placed it on her breast. Fitzroy remembered it with a gasp, as if he had taken a shot of aqua vitae before breakfast.

'But, sir,' General Stewart was saying, 'should we not take into account the efforts of the guerrillas? By all accounts Chaleco and his band harried Joseph all the way to Valencia.'

'These irregulars can never win a war, cannot form any idea of a real campaign.'

Wellington scowled at Goya. 'They are ignorant of military affairs, even here in their own country.'

'I think you do the partidas an injustice, my Lord.' Stewart was insistent, lulled by the heat and the unfamiliar sensation of sleeping between linen sheets on a feather mattress.

'Do not cross me, Stewart. I am tired enough sitting rigid for this monkey of a painter. The Spaniards are incapable of exertion, quite incapable.' Wellington's voice fell, full of menace.

'Very well, give me your report.'

'On receiving intelligence that Marshal Soult has left Seville with the whole of the French army of the south behind him, I issued orders to any guerrilla bands operating in Andalusia to—'

'You issued orders?'

'I did.'

'You issued orders without consulting me?'

Wellington looked straight at Goya and began to shout.

'You know perfectly well, sir, that this is my army. This is my army and no one, certainly not you, Stewart, gives orders without coming to me first.'

'There was no time.'

'No time! There is always time, you idiot. Why must I be surrounded by fools? You know my wishes. You know that I am answerable for the conduct of the army. Will Parliament strip you of command if we lose the war? It will not! Will a parliamentary commission turn your life-blood into ink for the newspapers? No again! Day by day it is I who will take the blame; but it is you, and fools like you, who will lose me this war. No time! No time, when you stand here in front of me bone idle!'

In the silence that followed, Fitzroy Somerset lost himself in the motes of dust in the sunlight that came through the windows. Goya laid his brush on the easel shelf.

To paint a man's portrait you must push him to let you into his secrets. Some sitters are transparent fools. Others are generous with their weaknesses or vain enough to think them attractive foibles that the world will want to see. This General was difficult. He might show his anger, but he guarded what lay behind it. With him, Goya thought, some diversion was necessary.

Goya threw his arms out wide and stared at Stewart. He turned full face towards him so that he could read his lips, though the man made his words in the loose flat way of the English and was difficult to understand.

'I have done something wrong?'

He spoke in Spanish, and put a horsey whinny into his voice.

'Lord Wellington is displeased with my work?'

He could see the tears in Stewart's eyes. Stewart stepped towards him.

'No, no. Please do not think so. It is I who have displeased him.'

At the thought of it, Stewart was overcome. He covered his face with his hands and sobbed.

Goya watched the General. A look of haughty satisfaction crossed Lord Wellington's face. Then it softened like a clean sky after rain. No one spoke.

'You will dine with me tonight, Stewart?' Wellington said.

Well, then, I, Goya, have seen him. A man cruel enough, in the act of winning—and he must win—to abase another man. Then he will change utterly, as if two wheels must turn in opposite directions to balance a delicate mechanism. This General will never ask forgiveness, but will admit a wrong with a kindness. Drive a man to tears and then ask him to dinner. Surprise him into gratitude. Oh, now there is an exquisite power that not even Godoy in his pomp knew how to use. Womanly almost, the painter thought. And behind that fury, something else, locked for ever.

'Our intelligence continues to be sparse.' Wellington went on in an even voice, as if nothing had happened. 'We need much more of it. Do you have any useful report, Stewart?'

'Ah, yes.' Stewart was steady on his feet again. 'I have word from Seville. Camille Florens. You know she has been a most reliable source for us. She now offers to liaise with her brother, Felipe Odonnell, who has the ear of most of the partidas in the north where the French have the advantage of us.'

'Odonnell, you say? An odd name for Spain.'

'The family is of Irish origin, I believe, my Lord; Odonnell the hispanic version of their name.'

'Good. And Señora Florens, is she in Seville?'

'Indeed. She sat out the French occupation there by posing as a Bonapartist, and now asks that we send down a suitable officer.' He paused. 'That is to say a man with whom she can communicate safely.'

Wellington nodded. Stewart gulped in relief.

'Major Yallop of the 9th—you remember that he was commended after Badajoz—a most worthy officer, has suggested Captain Raven for the mission, sir. Raven has excellent French. He distinguished himself at Badajoz and can, moreover, pass for a French officer should he encounter any of Marshal Soult's forces on the way down.'

'Pack him off without delay, Stewart, and I shall see you at dinner.'

Stewart bowed and left the room. Lord Wellington looked at Goya, who picked up his brush and began to paint. He would not add what he knew to this work; he would not paint it. The General would see it and then, he, Goya, might not get his fee. No, he would put it somewhere else, in time, that mixture of guilt and sentiment, haughty superiority and clever pity. Some other sitter would wear the General's soul.

Just now he had a horse to finish, a canvas horse who would carry no one into battle, absurd enough to mock a general's power. He would make this cut-out brute carry Wellington all right, and what a punishment for the four-legged beast. As for Camille Florens, he knew her too, and could tell these English what he knew; but they would never listen. He, Goya, was just the painter, invisible; and deaf besides.

STEWART HAD NO IDEA how thin it was, his hold on Madrid, Wellington thought as he stepped out into the stone-flagged courtyard of the Palacio Real. The midday sun struck the top of his head. He clenched and unclenched his hands round his cane. He was surrounded by fools. His young men were inattentive, sun-sozzled and soft with passion.

The walls of the Royal Palace, white and smooth, stretched away either side of him. They sucked up the heat and threw it out at him. There was no good reason to be in Madrid in August, indeed, except to show these wretched Spaniards his face, and demonstrate that he could march into their capital at will. That and the pages it would command in the English newspapers. The capture of a capital resounded with achievement; the public was not to know that Madrid was not a fortress; not, even, a crossroads, just a hot and intolerable town in the middle of the country.

Once he had marked his presence here he might have to leave. The battle at Salamanca in July had been a victory, but not as resounding as his dispatches painted it. Although he had driven Joseph Bonaparte out of Madrid as a result, six weeks later forty thousand Frenchmen now marched at him from the south and east, and might close in on the city in a very few days. Worse, his men had not been paid for seven months. The case was a simple one: his quartermaster had no money and the army could not last the winter without it.

A cream-coloured parasol caught his eye: another woman come to offer him flowers and an invitation. She was dressed in emerald muslin and through her skirts the sun picked out the form of her hips and a waist so small his two hands might circle it. In this heat every inch of her would be warm to the touch.

Wellington walked with his brisk step towards his visitor. The look of the woman reminded him of Kitty. He ought to write to her, but the very idea brought his impatience back. Kitty, cool and grey, could not fit into Madrid in summer, where passion rose from every sun-baked surface. In London, he remembered with annoyance, she seemed more at ease than he, straight-backed and still by the pianoforte, or seated at her desk.

Wellington took the flowers offered him, bowed, and strode on. Kitty had no idea of the difficulties he faced. A few months ago she had sent another letter about investments; some nonsense about Russian consols. He had not answered it; he had nothing to say. Kitty could do what she wished. He was distant, indifferent. As long as she kept up the form of their marriage it mattered little how she frittered away her days. Besides, except for mornings like this, when he had been insulted by the follies of his staff and cooped up in front of that bullish little painter, he rarely thought of her.

By the gatehouse in the corner Wellington came to a halt. A line of carts stood by the railings. Soldiers bought milk and bread, pipes and tobacco, brass buttons and tea there. One woman sold almonds by the dozen: sweets for summer, baked hard in sugar tinted with the colours of roses. Fitzroy Somerset, coming out of the great door of the palace, was in time to see the General hand over several small coins to the almond-seller and take a twist of paper in return.

As Wellington walked, waves of heat engulfed him. He wobbled before Somerset's eyes. Once out of the frazzled air, and into the shady lee of the palace, the General turned and looked towards the groups of Madrileños who strolled across the courtyard. By the immense wall the master of sixty thousand men appeared slight, fragile, even. In one hand he held a bunch of carnations, the pink and white splashed over the grey of his trousers. Then, as Somerset watched, the General squared his shoulders, popped a sugared almond into his mouth and came towards him.

'LADY WELLINGTON, YOUR BUSINESS.'

Nathan Rothschild settled against the horsehair back of his chair. Its legs creaked in protest. He was, unaccountably for this late hour in the morning, in undress. A Prussian-blue dressing gown over his shirt and breeches gave him a cannon-ball look, though the fabric, Kitty noticed, was thin, fine silk.

'I have found another thousand, and hope that you can use it well.'

'Would I do anything else? Even if it were not your money, I should treat it with respect. But as it is yours, double respect to it.'

Nathan Rothschild laid Kitty's draft on his desk with care. It looked lost in the drift of papers already. He glanced across at her. Really, Lady Wellington was a fine woman; charming even when you looked at her closely. She had besides the skill of invisibility, self-effacement; might make an excellent agent, or a courier of sensitive communications. Suitably dressed Lady Wellington might slip through Europe unseen, and without a shadow.

Beautiful women demanded you look at them. But women used to doing without that shining mirror were more valuable. Modesty and lack of show had made them self-reliant and watchful. Discretion, that was it; discretion ran through them like their own lifeblood. Umsicht, he might call it; prudence. Lady Wellington had it in good measure. He could have used her, in another life.

'Is that thousand to be followed by another? You are aware, I am sure, that America has declared war, thinks she can make off with Canada while Lord Liverpool turns his face to Spain? There are opportunities for us there.'

The Times newspaper on the desk carried news from the Peninsula. Nathan tapped the front page, where Kitty could see an advertisement from the commissary-in-chief's office. It requested tenders for contracts to supply grey kersey for britches and bread for barracks.

'Mr Charles Herries stays busy.' Nathan followed her glance. 'I have made his acquaintance.' He paused. 'And am quite sure he will prove a man of substance.'

'You have a plan for him?'

'No, no, I extend the hand of friendship merely.'

He had indeed done no more, Nathan reflected. There was nothing he needed from Mr Herries. That is to say, nothing now, or nothing more than the assurance that he would be left alone. Mr Herries might give that by an incline of the head, by his silence even. Silence did not disconcert Nathan. Indeed it could be as valuable as news. He could listen to its meanings while others merely waited; almost all the most important things were hidden or quiet. One needed to pay attention to silence and what was left unsaid. That was where subtlety and discovery lay.

'Now, your own affairs, Lady Wellington.'

'You have a competitor for my funds, Mr Rothschild.'

'A rival?'

'Yes, let us put it that way.'

Nathan hummed and pulled off his cravat. His mornings were rarely so full of pleasure.

'Impossible! No one can give you my terms.'

'How can you be sure?'

'I know every offer of the men who work next to me. I work faster and with better results.'

'This is not about quickness. It is an opportunity to invest in the business of a young man whose acquaintance I made in April.'

'A man younger than me, Lady Wellington? More handsome too? What does he offer?'

'Light. He sells light.'

'Ach, I know him. Herr Winzer.' Nathan drew out the name and rolled a German tongue around it. 'Winsor to you; his plan to illuminate the world.'

'I believe it will succeed. The light from inflammable air is brilliant. I visited Mr Winsor's house and attended a demonstration; I have since then deliberated upon an investment.'

Kitty hesitated. Had she merely been enchanted? Frederick Winsor was more than persuasive; he had been a magician, dressed in blue and nearly invisible against the walls of his basement in Pall Mall. In the darkness he ran about and turned tap after tap so that the gas hissed in the darkness. When he put his taper to them his marvellous creations came to life, given form by dozens of murmuring jets. First a golden palm tree grew against the night-blue of walls and ceiling, then a bowl of flowers bloomed on the table.

'He pointed out that he has advanced considerably on his predecessors Lord Cochrane and Mr Murdoch at the Soho Works.'

'In what way, Lady Wellington?'

'Mr Winsor puts everything underground. The gas runs in tinned iron pipes; thus the light can travel anywhere. Now he proposes to light whole streets in the same way from the manufactory he has been building at Horseferry Road. No man has done that until now.'

'He suggests, moreover, that his gas will heat as well as light the world?'

'He dreams to change the seasons, to replace the weak light of our winter sun with everlasting day and an eternal summer, so that we may grow the fruits of the Mediterranean all the year round in our hothouses.'

Nathan laughed. Kitty saw that he looked more incredulous the more she spoke.

'Well, I have understood it. All of us from Germany are masters of the intangible; money men, poets, astronomers, chemists, the tiresome musicians who come and ask me to commission their tunes; all deal in magic, dear Lady Wellington. We are the alchemists of this new century, who make something from nothing, pure gold from something unremarkable.'

'Information, in your case, Mr Rothschild, if I am not mistaken; and I have learned the lesson you gave me. I have had Mr Winsor bring me his accounts. They are all in order. It is true he needs the addition of another engineer. But the balance of costs is so clear; the installation of gas lighting will save every parish money.'

'Ach, have it your own way. We shall see. I am not a man of the turf, Lady Wellington. I keep my distance from most creatures, two-legged ones especially. They all want something from me. But I would lay a considerable wager against that young man's success.'

Kitty was silent. She did not say that she had no wish to put her faith merely in Mr Winsor himself. It was his idea she liked, the notion of a great lattice-work of pipes that reached out beneath the city like fingers and let invisible light slip underground. If London, why not other cities; why not indeed every town and village? No, she had not tied herself to Mr Winsor; she had bought stock in the National Light and Heat Company. A good portion of it. She could wait; Mr Rothschild's coolness would not deter her.

'Shall we see, Mr Rothschild? Meanwhile you may tease me as much as you like.'

'I should never presume upon our acquaintance in that way.'

'Oh, come, come. We understand one another.'

Since their first meeting, Nathan Rothschild had felt his interest in Lady Wellington grow. She was a woman prepared to launch herself into the current of life; but she planned with the utmost care. His own language (his fourth language, or was it perhaps his first?) of consols and credit, bills of exchange, sterling, louis d'or and gilts, came easily to her. Like a talented musician she understood the form in which she worked. He merely had to teach her its grammar.

He watched Kitty stack and slide her papers into a leather portmanteau. Of course, he had not told her that her account was absurdly small. It was not, for him, business at all; more a means to conjure gratitude. For a woman such as Lady Wellington he might offer one kind of service. For some other person—Mr Herries came into his mind, pink and freckled—the service was more delicate. From neither did he expect an immediate return. Lady Wellington had no idea that his charges were so low as to yield him almost nothing on her business. What did he want? Merely to tip the balance in his favour when the time came, when all the insular pride of the English weighted it the other way. That was sensible business. Nathan looked around his office. What he did was also the operation of natural justice; his right, his duty, even as an outsider, to give merit its due.

With Kitty Wellington, now, there was more. Her mind was congenial. Nathan Rothschild steered her to the door and as she left lifted her hand and brushed his lips across it. A woman in a thousand, he thought, and hitched his blue dressing gown back onto his shoulders.

～

ALTHOUGH IT WAS STILL summer, the nights in Madrid already promised an autumn respite. When the sun went down, magenta through the violet horizon, the city's buildings breathed out the heat of the day. By midsummer's night the city sweated through the hours of darkness. But now on the brink of September the heat curled away and daylight came on the heels of a faint breeze; hot and exhausted by its journey across the shimmering plain round the city, but a breeze all the same. At five in the morning David McBride opened his window, put a candle on the sill and watched until the yellow flame bent inwards on the wind. In the greenish first light he wrote letters by the open shutters.

'Tuesday, 1st September 1812, Madrid. My dear father—though at a

much greater altitude than Bushey or even Edinburgh, this city is remarkable for its unhealthy climate—too hot even now in late summer, too
damp and cold in winter and the spring and autumn so short as to pass by
before the citizens have enjoyed or taken advantage of them. The people
here suffer extremely from pulmonia, as they call it, and other diseases of
the lung, for which I can prescribe nothing but onion soup and brandy.

'The starvation of the citizens is remarkable, though they welcomed
us as liberators, and all this month have been nothing so much as skele-
tons dancing.'

He stopped, hesitant to tell his father of his excitement, how the days
after a battle were worth months of tepid work at home. He must have
carried out two hundred operations after Salamanca, where four hundred were killed and four thousand wounded in a single day; amputations, incisions and extractions, cleaning wounds and binding them.
Once the cutting was finished, he administered such medicine as the
progress of the patient required. The distillation of willow bark, softened
in water, eased the suffering of men with bruises and incisions that
would heal. Belladonna and a mash of poppy seeds helped them through
greater pain and to the moment of death.

David came to life in those emergencies. After Salamanca he had
accompanied many men to that moment. He noticed that sometimes a
dying man was determined to reassure those around him with the touch
of an outstretched hand or with words pulled one by one from pain and
confusion. Then there were those who, out of a sense of duty, perhaps,
asked with their eyes for permission to die. So he learned to hold a soldier the way a mother holds a tired child before sleep, and feel death walk
kindly in. In the midst of such suffering, he was amazed to admit that
sometimes joy coursed through him with a force that he could only liken
to a galvanic shock. It tracked him down in a hot corridor with such
strength that to stay upright he had to press his hands against the wall,
or came over him as he sat in the evening with a notebook before him,
unsuspecting and alone.

Dr McGrigor, when he met him a week after the battle, seemed to
understand his elation.

'You have found purpose, if I may say so, in the flesh, Dr McBride. I
have seen that often in a young man. First the apprehension that comes
with an open body, some determination to find the soul or its site. That is
followed by the certainty that there is nothing else.'

'You mean to say the certainty of no deity, sir?'

McGrigor lowered his voice.

'You have noticed that few old soldiers give much time to prayer?'

'Indeed I have, and conclude, after seeing so many go, that a man's soul, if he has one, dies with his body. But might I tell you something else, Dr McGrigor?'

'Another observation?'

'It may be men of science who will find answers to the mysteries of life.'

'Life's mysteries are a fool's pursuit, David. Alchemists believed they could find the elixir of life in a base metal and some are still looking. A clean incision, neat stitches and a little kindness: that is what we medical men are good for.'

'No, I do not mean that we will come to the end, merely that one answer will lead to another question and that to another. Imagine, sir; all life and the tiniest crevices of the body will become our laboratory.'

'My belief, the belief of a man who has seen too much, is that the mystery will remain.' McGrigor tapped his chest. 'Something, perhaps, to do with the human heart. Find, as La Mettrie did, that the body is just a collection of parts, and that our nerves and feelings are just a series of chemical reactions: still the heart remains. Benevolence and fellow feeling persist. Good day, Dr McBride. Do not forget to write up your experiments. You have a fine career in front of you.'

FOR SEVERAL WEEKS IN Madrid David had lain invisible like an egg in a sac. He felt himself grow in secret, nourished by the heat. Even his own hand, as he dipped his pen again, seemed more vigorous and certain. 'I send you two musket balls saved from my haul at Salamanca. The first I cut from a medical man who got tangled up with his regiment's advance on the battlefield at Salamanca—a melancholy task, my dear father, to operate on a member of one's own profession with scant hope of success. He did not recover from his wound. The misshapen one is removed from a French gunner left for dead and taken up by my assistant. In all probability the ball came back off the gun barrel and entered his shoulder, from where I cut it with no difficulty.'

David heard a decisive tap on the door. James Raven walked in. A pressed white shirt showed beneath the cuffs of his scarlet jacket. Thomas Orde kept his master smart with devotion and darning.

'David. Still in your night gown?'

'To catch a breath of air before the sun comes in and I have to close the shutters.'

David looked his friend over. James had the same hurried look that he had noticed at Badajoz after the assault.

'Sit down here in the window, James, and tell me how you are. I've not seen you since I got into these lodgings.'

'I am well enough.'

'You fought with honour at Salamanca, I have heard.'

James sat up straighter.

'Indeed, but the whole army acquitted itself well. I looked down from the heights as General Pakenham and the Portuguese cavalry charged into General Thomières's infantry. What a sight! Forty thousand men were driven back; two French divisions broken in forty minutes. Yes, I played my part, David, but I should have wished to be with Pakenham then. I have no fear of battle. It is something else that worries me.'

'What is that?'

'How can I explain? It is that I have lost my sense of balance here. I came to Spain sure that I fought to rid Europe of tyranny. Now I find I fight for quite other reasons—ones so ignoble that I hesitate to mention them. Then, I wonder how many others are here from the same motives.'

David closed the shutter, pulled the casement to and slid down its brass catch. 'Forgive me, James. I do not wish to interupt, but in a few minutes it will be hotter outside than in, and I try to preserve the cool. Go on.'

'The General is not here to free Spain from the tyrant as the papers say, but to save our own dear Regent from exile. As for the Spaniards, they are fighting another war, besides being our allies.'

David thought of the group he had seen when they entered Madrid, francescados, they were called, followers of Joseph Bonaparte, set on by their countrymen, pushed into a dark alley and only saved by the arrival of British officers. He had come across several doctors, avowed believers in French progress, who now feared for their lives. Many did not want the Spanish kings to return without reforms. So Spain now fought two wars, one with France, the other with herself.

James stood up.

'No matter; I can continue to serve with honour. Shall we walk a little?'

'A pleasure. Give me a moment to throw on my clothes, and I shall be with you.'

Outside David's lodgings they walked down the wide streets until they reached the Paseo del Prado, which had once been a thoroughfare alive with male voices and the ring of boots on the flagstones. Madrid now, David thought, was a city of women and absence, the absence of all the young men killed by war and disease and of the children they would never have. A superstitious man might see all those souls hanging in the air like dust, a dust that obscured the future and thickened the choking atmosphere that widows and spinsters breathed.

From the Paseo del Prado they turned into the abandoned Botanical Garden. Blue solanum and paper-white oleander flowered still, though nothing grew in the herb beds and the evergreen borders had turned ragged. The gardeners had long gone; war degraded everything. At the far end of the garden, the magnificent greenhouses stood empty and streaked with dirt.

James walked without any care for David's loping, hesitant stride.

'I have some news. I am to leave Madrid shortly. I am appointed to go south to Seville. You know how we are menaced here on all sides and lack information about the movements of the French. I am to meet a woman there, Camille Florens. She works, I am told, on our behalf.'

'Ah yes, I have heard her spoken of. I treated Captain Townley of the 95th after Badajoz; he mentioned her.'

'What did he say?'

'Merely that she visited Lisbon last year. Then, something else that I cannot remember. You may ask Townley himself; he must be somewhere hereabouts.'

'No. I go incognito and do not wish to call attention to my absence. Besides, I know all that is significant about Señora Florens already. I wanted to ask, David, if can I leave Thomas Orde in your care? Badajoz altered him, as an assault might any man, and I hesitate to leave him simply with the regiment. It is not that he is surly, or difficult; quite the reverse. He has turned silent, when he used to be a man who kept up with the times, took an interest in the world. I took him on for his ability, but to help his family also. War had robbed him of the means to feed them and he felt it keenly.'

Like a soldier preparing for battle the next day, David saw, James had ordered his affairs to leave nothing to chance. Was his mission really dangerous or was some other fear in possession of his mind?

'And another thing. Can you assure me you will write to Harriet if I do not get back? I should not like her to receive bad news from any other man.'

David wished he might take James's hand in his own. But something in James's manner forbade him and he walked on by his side.

'You may count on me in every respect. Thomas and I may even be a help to one another. My father used to direct soldiers who were disordered in the head towards practical tasks. I have some animals here in Madrid; Thomas might look after them.'

'Animals?'

'For my experiments.'

ON THE WAY OUT of the garden, David and James ran into Robert Heaton and Major Yallop. The two men were often now to be found together. Racket pushed between the two men like a jealous lover.

'A fine morning to you, gentlemen,' Major Yallop said. 'Captain Heaton here is on the trail of a priest, thought he might track him down behind the bushes. He saw him beat an ass, and set off in pursuit without a word.'

'It is nonsense, Doctor, do not believe a word of it.' Heaton bowed to both men as he spoke. 'Though I must say I have no high estimation of the priests. I have yet to see a thin one. They have hung on to their stomachs while children starved. I am billeted in their wretched monastery and there is not a scarecrow amongst them.'

David held out his hand to each man in turn. Heaton looked well, he noted; better, even, than the Major.

'Major Yallop, good day. I have not seen you since Elvas. Do you like Madrid as much as Captain Heaton seems to do?'

George Yallop shrugged. Cities, except those under siege, did not hold his interest for long. He took no notice of plants like those they walked amongst, unless they could go into the pot. Heaton replied for him.

'The Major hopes to be sent north. He is kicking his heels here. I thought a turn between the flowerbeds might do him good. But it's a sad sight, nothing like our Orto Botanico in Florence. Now that's a treasure for a medical man such as yourself, Doctor, bursting with herbs to cure and salve. They plant balm for the eyes, too; climbing roses, all sorts of treasures.'

'*Your* Orto Botanico?' James asked.

'I was born there. In the city, I mean to say.'

The three other men looked at him in surprise. The Major raised his eyebrows, but none of them said a word.

Except for his blue-grey trousers, Robert Heaton had abandoned the civilian suit he came out in. He was now dressed in what looked to James like a newly tailored scarlet jacket, with the yellow facings of the 44th Foot. Chestnut boots gleamed on his heels and he carried his shako delicately under his arm. As always, Racket was with his master, and Heaton looked round for him from time to time, as a mother does for her child.

Against Major Yallop's orders at Salamanca, Heaton had pursued the stragglers from a French infantry regiment when they retreated into the scrubby forest. He came out half an hour later leading a line of prisoners as silent and docile as orphanage children on a Sunday walk. At the end of the battle he handed them to General Leith without a word. The French Captain never explained how his troops had surrendered.

When the dead were accounted for the day after the battle Heaton was offered the commission of Captain Pitt of the 44th. At the auction of Pitt's possessions Heaton bought every lot. He paid, so the story went, in local currency, tossing 100-real coins and the lighter Napoleons into a heap on the table, which prompted Hugh Kennedy, the commissary general, to throw down his cards and say, 'How the devil did he get all that?'

The next day Heaton rode out of the camp by himself with a mule behind his horse. The animal swayed under the pile of Pitt's trunk, sword, pistols and writing case, topped with a cloak neatly folded in the Spanish manner. Up there in the hills brigands and partidas, one and the same, patrolled the passes. Few ventured out of camp without an escort. But Heaton came back two days later, and told the Major quietly that he had sent Pitt's effects down to Lisbon to be shipped to his widow.

'A couple of children too. They live in Colchester, it seems, from the address on his letter.'

Major Yallop had met Pitt's wife once or twice when he had been down at the headquarters of the 44th on business. She ran a drapery shop and had no need of money.

'She will thank you, no doubt" he said simply.

In the army there was no real grief for the dead beyond a week or two, the Major found; just an accumulating cloud that cast a shade when he sat with nothing to do. He felt displeased with Pitt, more than anything else. Heaton had been a useful, and free, addition to the ranks of the 9th. The Major regretted having to give him up. Further than that he would not go, although he had, since Salamanca, fretted a little when he took his tea alone.

In Madrid Heaton lived in the Convento de la Encarnación and slept, not often alone, the Major guessed, in the great hall of the refectory. He had acquired a carriage which he kept in the stables at the back of the building. Through its windows, soldiers said, they saw drifts of black lace, or a slender hand that had never been the Captain's drawing down the blinds. No one knew how else he spent his time.

Heaton, James thought, is a man without a past; but here in Spain, and in the army, all our pasts drop away from us. Stand in line though we do, the ranks invisibly rearrange themselves so that the ribbons of standing and wealth that tied us together at home fall away. The army makes us ourselves; here is a man who likes to decide and issue orders; here another who will complete the task without complaint. One finds a talent for cooking, another for stories. One was a brute, another learned to reassure his companions that this world was worth the void beyond. But Heaton was still a mystery. Like a water-boatman beetle on a summer pond, the task he set himself appeared to be to skim across the surface with elegance, rarely to alight, and to make light of every circumstance.

Back at his lodgings, David wrote a note to Dr McGrigor.

'I have just encountered Robert Heaton, now a captain. He is the volunteer, sir, you will remember from Badajoz. He is perfectly well. I am collecting a few small creatures to continue work upon, though I have as yet had no opportunity to repeat the experiment of the transfusion of blood at Elvas. Heaton's health will, I hope, persuade you of the value of what I did that day.'

'DO YOU NOT WONDER sometimes, what our menfolk might be up to this very minute?'

Dorothy Yallop sat by the back parlour fire in Hatton Garden that evening, a length of white cloth across her knees. She looked into the fire, as if the flames might have an answer, and wagged her needle at Harriet. Beyond the windows the sky was already drained of light.

'The Major writes that he cannot abide Madrid, my dear. So I wonder how he passes the time.' Mrs Yallop jumped up. Bobbins and thread scattered across the floor. Pieces of finest cotton lawn, cut into pieces to make a shirt for the Major, floated to the ground as if a group of giant moths had come to rest on the carpet. At the window she turned south and put her hand up to a pane.

'To know he is down there, the dear man, and be unable to reach out and touch him.'

Mrs Cobbold, long becalmed on the lee-shore of widowhood, looked up at her friend and was surprised to see the sadness in her bowed head and shoulders.

'Dorothy, he has always come back and he will again. The Major is such a tidy man; how can you think he might leave anything over there, least of all himself?'

'I must believe you are right, Anne.' Mrs Yallop turned round. 'Let us consider where the 9th is now.' She pulled off her bonnet in one vigorous tug and drew from its interior a crumpled paper map of Spain, folded into four. 'I always say, Harriet, my dear, that you cannot lose what you carry with you. Now: Madrid. I feel to love it because George is there, though he calls it wretched hot and dull in his last letter. Captain Raven will be sitting it out too, I dare say.'

Mention of the Major brought back to Harriet the memory of dancing with him, her blue gown, the golden candlelight, rain against the windows, and then the feel of her hand on James's shoulder. Why was it that, unlike Mrs Yallop, she could not feel her husband's proximity? Perhaps it was simply that Mrs Yallop had so much more experience of solitude, had faith that it would end and had learned how to keep the Major in mind. She herself found James an insubstantial presence, at times a ghost too weak to stand beside her at all. She lowered her head; was she shallow, or fickle?

'What is it you read now?'

Mrs Cobbold gestured to the volume on Harriet's lap.

'Another stupid book.' Harriet put it down. '*First Impressions* is its title; and by A Lady, as usual.'

'It does not divert you?'

'Divert me, Aunt! I have no wish to be diverted, though it is witty and charming. This lady authoress believes that girls think only of marriage and a husband.'

'And they do not?'

'I do not. I am quite certain of that.'

'You mean to say, my dear, that you did not, while still unmarried.'

Harriet was silent and Mrs Cobbold stood up to let down the blinds against the dark that gathered outside.

'Do you not acknowledge that the lady knows the ways of the world? Is it not the case that the only way we women have of securing a future is to marry? How else can we get a home and family?'

'What do you intend to say, Aunt; that a husband is merely the means to that end?'

'My dear. I am quite sure your lady authoress does not neglect love. She has to secure the devotion of her readers. No, I mean that any girl of sense will consider her own future along with the brown eyes of her beloved, and the best way to check a man's balance at the bank is often to walk with him through his own grounds.'

'So girls do not look for a companion so much as a heap of bricks and mortar.'

'Consider, my dear, that most girls stand to inherit nothing,' Mrs Cobbold said. 'Is it not quite right and forgivable in them to seek to marry well?'

'And what might marrying well mean, Aunt?'

'Obviously your case is quite different. With your own house and fortune you were free to marry for love. But money, safety, and a degree of happiness go together.'

'So it certainly is not about the husband.'

'The man and the money are joined, my dear. One comes with the other. Who ever heard of a woman making money on her own in any respectable fashion?'

Mrs Cobbold looked around her cosy back parlour. One of the satisfactions of widowhood was that of ownership. A married woman owned nothing, not even her person. But a widow was the equal of any man. Mrs Cobbold thought with fondness of the lengths of red brocade that lay in her chest upstairs and her best china in the kitchen cupboards. Next year she planned to redecorate her two parlours in the latest styles, though she would by no means sacrifice her comfortable old panelling.

Yes, a widow could build her own house and put her money where she wished. She might visit and travel wherever she liked and never had to go through the tedious charade of asking permission of even a devoted husband. She herself would never give up that state, not for the most agreeable man in the world. A discreet friendship, perhaps; that she might countenance, but never anything more. Life, all in all, had dealt her a good hand and she was not inclined, at the fine age of fifty-six, to gamble it away.

'And what of grown women?' Mrs Cobbold heard the irritation in her niece's voice. 'Why do these lady novelists never write their diverting comedies about them? I have never read a book entitled *Second Thoughts*.'

'My dear, do you not ask too much of literature?'

'Is it too much to ask that an author might tell us something of our real life?'

'What can a married woman do that can interest a writer? For there must be a story to tell, and married women, unless, I am afraid, they misbehave, really have very little to add to any story. In old-fashioned story books lovers were quite the thing; but now the temper of the times is certainly against them.'

'Even the officers in these books, Aunt: how absurd they are. How much time they have in barracks or at balls, as if there is no war to be fought, or as if we must be protected from any mention of it. And then she writes that a country surgeon could not be introduced to a lady when I know perfectly well it is possible.'

To her aunt's surprise Harriet brought her hands up to her face and burst into tears.

'Calm yourself, my dear.' Mrs Cobbold leaned forward towards her. At times like this, when Harriet was distracted and upset, Anne Cobbold saw traces of her mother in her. Lady Diana Guest was delicate, too delicate for the world in the end; it would not do for Harriet to take after her in any way. She frowned.

'Your lady authoress no doubt writes of the counties about London. In Suffolk we know the case to be different.'

'And then we sit and wait. What is there about that in this book, about the widows and the poor men we see on the street? Have you not noticed that there are beggars everywhere, soldiers with limbs off, and prices too high for them to afford bread, even?'

'Yes, times are so very hard. All the more reason to pass your time profitably and with pleasure. In difficult moments, my dear, a story book is surely a distraction. Besides, it is to poetry that people look for an account of the times, is it not? Mr Southey, or your Lord Byron.'

'He is not my Lord Byron, Aunt,' Harriet said and smiled for the first time that evening.

6

London and Seville, Spain

SEPTEMBER–OCTOBER 1812

Charles Herries had only pretended, for form's sake, to leave London in the summer. He had nowhere to go. Besides, he told himself, he worked well with only his clerks in the office and enjoyed the vacant city. Children took over the streets of Mayfair and Piccadilly. They larked and played at soldiers on the pavements. One August morning, under the sandstone colonnade in Covent Garden, he stood to watch a sweetmeat-seller drip hot orange barley sugar from a ladle and twist it as it hardened into ropes and bows. Hung on a string above the cart the sweets glistened in the sun. Lazy clouds drifted over the Piazza. The *Morning Chronicle*, folded under Herries's arm, announced that the Grande Armée had crossed the Dneiper River on the way to Moscow.

Several ragged children approached; hungry, no doubt. Herries breathed in their sick sweet smell. None had shoes and their clothes hung stiff with grease. Herries pulled out his handkerchief and put it to his nose; bile rose in his throat. The children crowded round, insistent and determined.

'Give us a penny, sir, for a treat.'

Herries stepped back, felt round in his pocket and pulled out a coin. With a smile that indicated his generosity and its finality he handed one of the boys a penny. The boy looked into Herries's eyes and grinned. His hand remained stretched out. With a sigh Herries found a shilling and added it to the penny. The boy's eyes widened.

'No more, no more. That is enough for you all.'

The boy curled his fingers over the coins and the children turned their attention to the sweetmeat-seller. Those children neither knew nor cared about the progress of war. Herries walked back to Great George Street, and it pleased him to be able to supply them, at least. The thought that there were children who followed life's immemorial patterns of want and satisfaction made him cheerful the whole day.

While ministers and Parliament took the country air, Herries had made himself master of office business. By the end of the summer he was confident that the commissary office was as efficient as any in the country. Now, in the middle of September, as the clerks gathered in the war office and exchanged summer talk like schoolboys returned to class, he watched the first dry leaves outside the windows gust up and spiral down on the wind.

'How light they are,' he thought, 'to float up and sideways like dancers. They lean back against the wind and waltz to earth. Yet each leaf falls in its own, unrepeatable way.'

Earl Bathurst, the new Secretary of State for War, was just back from three months in the West Country. The importance of his appointment gave him a straight back. He disliked his juniors, young men who crawled up the trouser legs of their betters to arrive at this table. He preferred not to think of himself as a man in a crowded office with heaps of papers and files closed with red sealing wax, but as a minister of the crown who served his country. Unfortunately the news from abroad, after a good spring, dispirited him, though he addressed his officials in a tone intended to convey progress.

'Lord Wellington, as you will have read in the newspapers, left Madrid on the first of this month and marched north in order to consolidate his success. He is now encamped at Villa Toro outside the fortress of Burgos and intends to take the castle after a short siege. General Hill remains in Estremadura. It appears that the French intend to consolidate the armies of the south and the centre at Valencia where King Joseph Bonaparte is now encamped. We understand that General Soult has left Seville and moves to join the King. You will all have seen in the newspapers that Bonaparte moves eastwards still. America, too, calls for our attention.'

Intelligence suggested a wholesale Russian withdrawal. Lord Bathurst was surprised to see that Russian bonds remained stubbornly high; on the 'Change they perhaps overestimated the strength of the Tsar's position. Moscow was defenceless, at Bonaparte's mercy. The Tsar was bound to sue for peace.

Each morning, as his valet shaved him, Lord Bathurst reminded himself of the responsibility and dignity of the secretaryship, but by the time he arrived at Spring Gardens he was apt to feel overwhelmed. Lord Wellington's displeasure sat with him at his desk. After the exhilaration of Badajoz and Salamanca, the army's stay in Madrid had served no purpose. The people of Madrid still starved, the British soldiers could only share in heat and scarcity. Now the General's dispatches had taken on their familiar tone of high-minded hectoring. Wellington was disgusted with the sloppiness of his troops, and as dissatisfied as ever at the lack of ready money. His demands for more ordnance sat in a pile on Bathurst's desk. He complained that his own allowance of £10 per diem was insufficient. He doubted that he had the resources to mount any major campaign in the next few months even if he could take Burgos, and managed to imply that any failure in Spain, or, it seemed to Bathurst, any failure at all, was the fault of the Secretary for War.

Bathurst cleared his throat and scanned the circle of men round the table.

'We have, as usual, the problem of specie. Lord Wellington reports, in his latest dispatch, that the return on bills of exchange is intolerably low, and his chest is almost bare of coin. Pay, as you know, is seven months in arrears. We need to investigate new sources of supply, do we not, Mr Herries?'

The Secretary for War leaned back in his chair, stared at Charles Herries across the shining mahogany expanse and felt his mood lighten. Responsibility for the shortage of cash was one thing he need not, and did not intend to, take. The paymaster could shoulder that burden alone.

'Furthermore,' he added, by way of emphasis, 'I have reports that large amounts of sterling coin and bullion are leaving the country, which, as you know, will make collection and shipment to Spain all the more difficult and expensive.'

Herries forced his attention inside. Did Bathurst allude to the Rothschilds' activities already? Herries had put a watch on New Court over the summer, and he now had a better, if incomplete, understanding of what Nathan was up to. Couriers, carrier pigeons and messengers arrived and left New Court many times every day. The Rothschilds dealt in all sorts of goods: indigo and silk, jewels and valuables, cottons and timber, as well as currency; though Herries suspected that bulky goods were traded more as convenient cargoes to accompany coins and gold than as interests in their own right.

The scale of Nathan's ambition and risk impressed Herries. In a very few years he had easily surpassed his closest rivals, the Barings. Harman was a mere coffee-house trader beside him. Hundreds of thousands of guineas, in the last few months alone, had arrived at New Court to be weighed, bagged and smuggled out from Folkestone. Nathan owned or leased at least five boats, ready at any time to cross the Channel, among them the *Hannah*, the *Anthony* and the *Lionel*. But not the *Charlotte*, Herries thought distractedly, not a boat named for his beloved Lotte. Perhaps he had missed it; perhaps there was a whole fleet lurking offshore that his man had not spotted.

Once the consignments arrived on the other side of the Channel, Rothschilds' agents sold them on in France, Holland and Germany. Nathan's four brothers, who criss-crossed Europe in unmarked carriages, took the profits and bought up bills of exchange. Sent back to London, the bills could be redeemed when Nathan judged that circumstances favoured him.

Herries pressed his damp palms together and began to speak.

'In my capacity as paymaster, my Lord, private correspondence sometimes falls into my hands. One family, in particular, seems to have contributed to this shortage of specie and gold.'

Bathurst stared across the table at the commissary general. Mr Herries evidently took him for a fool. Who was Herries, in fact? A man come from nowhere on the strength of a few years in some continental banking house. He might be well versed in double accounting, play a good hand at faro, even, but Bathurst was not so sure he had any real understanding of the tyranny that threatened the country.

'We know a good deal about Mr Rothschild's continental operations, Mr Herries; including the detail that he refers to guineas as "pictures" in letters to his brothers. As if that's not enough, bullion is called "Rabbi Moses" or "the fat man", and London is "Jerusalem". I should have thought that comes near to sacrilege in any faith.'

'Indeed so, my Lord. However, Mr Rothschild's networks are extensive, as you know. Should his Majesty's government need assistance in buying up specie, it seems to me that the Rothschilds might be of use to us.'

'How can you consider him a man suitable for a government to do business with, Mr Herries?'

'I observe merely, sir, that the family have agents in every corner of this country and across Europe. They have boats to transport goods and bankers and merchants to receive and pay for them. They operate with discretion and secrecy.'

Herries shifted in his seat. Despite the coolness of the room his trousers stuck to his flesh. At least Bathurst seemed to have no idea that he himself had had any entanglement with New Court.

A young man who sat further down the table spoke up.

'I must say, my Lord, that I believe Mr Rothschild to be a man of his word.'

'You have had dealings with him yourself, Mr Fawley?'

Fawley coughed.

'A matter of a loan, merely. I found him to be quite a gentleman.'

'A gentleman?'

'The terms were generous, my Lord, and Rothschild has asked for nothing in return.'

Lord Bathurst glanced down the table. War had promoted many men beyond their capacities, and Mr Fawley appeared to be one of them. He shrugged again. These days so few seemed to have any grasp of what was happening in the world, what threats they faced and how to ward them off. In his mind's eye Lord Bathurst saw his great house at Cirencester held safe in the folds of the hills around it. New plate-glass windows caught the afternoon sun at the front and blue light from the lake on the garden side. Years ago he had walked round the water on a winter's day, arm in arm with his betrothed. Wrapped together in the frosty mist, they had talked of their future life, its pleasures and duties. A thousand acres of walled park ringed the garden, and groups of fallow deer, buff against the green, ranged through the meadows and copses. His whole view was so English and pure that he once wept when he rounded the bend and the lake came in sight.

Bathurst turned to Mr Herries again.

'Mr Rothschild is a smuggler.'

'Indeed, my Lord; but we have allowed some outflow of bullion, have we not; connived in it?'

Bathurst was silent. It suited the government to have the profits from smuggling invested in sterling bonds, and allowing the specie to leave the country gave Bonaparte an impression of British wealth to boot.

'Mr Rothschild is also a German, a fact that disqualifies him as some-one the British government might do business with.'

'I beg your pardon, sir.' Fawley spoke up. 'He took particular pains to assure me that he had been naturalised an Englishman several years ago. I think we may rely on his having the interests of our country at heart.'

'As you wish. He is still a smuggler and a Jew, besides a man who I should have thought profanes his own religion. However, we can keep him in mind.'

After a pause Bathurst smiled.

'We might put it another way: any one of those facts might equally encourage him into our arms. Would you not agree, Mr Herries?'

Herries nodded and gathered up his papers. He longed to get out into the air. Across Horse Guards, through the streets beyond the park, he trudged, head down. At Horseferry Road a sweet stench from some infernal works made him reel and reach for his silk handkerchief. In Cadogan Place the house was dark and empty. Even from the hallway Herries heard the light tick of the gilded clock on the drawing-room mantelpiece. His mother was out; half her day was spent a few doors down, gossiping with old Lady Napier. Blind Lady Napier, waited on by her son, boasted of three others in the Peninsula, each, it seemed to Herries, more gallant than the last. Mrs Herries had only himself to offer in return, a single plump government official, trained in the business of banking. She sat and listened.

Herries left the front door open a minute, and leaned back towards the street in an effort to catch a flutter of life; the click of a single pair of heels, the rustle of brocade. There was nothing. Silence enclosed him. He closed the door and dropped his portmanteau to the floor. If his mother lingered, as she often did, dinner would be cold.

Then, on the hall table, a letter; no frank or stamp. 'À Monsieur Herries, 21 Cadogan Place, Londres. Par main.' Herries turned it over.

'The first consignment. In anticipation of more.'

Mr Rothschild had not signed his note. Herries tore off the cover and unfolded the single sheet inside.

'I am past hope', he said to himself.

'35 rue de Grenelles,' Louisa had written in a clear cursive hand, and then: 'Mon cher Papa. Je suis très heureuse de vous écrire une lettre.'

Herries scanned the lines with the practised eye of an office-holder; but the paper shook in his hand.

'This is the first letter I have written. I thank you, and Mama adds her thanks to mine, for the money we have received. I have now a dancing master and I ride out two times every week. I have a new gown with ribbons and practise at the pianoforte every day. We hope, mon cher Papa, that you will visit us when the war is over. Your daughter, Louisa Carioli.'

Herries carried the letter into the library on the first floor, looked round to make sure he was alone, shut the door and kissed the paper. He could not see her; might never set eyes upon her. But might he not, in the letters she had written, trace the lineaments of her features as a blind man beholds by touch the face of his beloved child? There her hand had moved in curves and sweeps, there her eyes, which must be dark as berries like her mother's, had rested.

Absurd sentiments, a wretched mingling of despair and joy. But he knew himself to be transparent and as frail as tissue paper. The Rothschilds had given them money. Should he offer to pay it back, advance more himself? But he did not want to think about money now. He slid into happiness as if it were a bath of milk. 'In anticipation of more': those were Mr Rothschild's words. Louisa would write again. Jakob Rothschild in Paris, younger than his brother, and more slender he was sure, would go to the rue de Grenelles himself one evening, collect her letter, add a cover to it and tuck it in his courier's bag. Might he now write back, and as her father? And what about Lucia? He must ask for news of her also.

Herries sat back and stared through the drawing-room windows. Mist had come up from the river and hung in paper-white sheets outside. He could not deny his love. No, he would write back in a general way, leave his letter unsigned and send it round to New Court. Nathan would understand; he was a man who would never undervalue the joy of a father in his child, the way it stopped life in its tracks, as a great star shooting across the sky stops a traveller by its beauty. Herries knew now that such a love could drive a man to anything.

∾

'I VENTURE TO SAY, my Lord, that despite our failure so far to take Burgos, we hold the best part of the country.'

Fitzroy Somerset looked up at the General from the writing table. The Beau paced about. He had come in from inspection of the guards, still dressed for horseback. Somerset spoke to take an edge off the silence.

'Fitzroy.' Wellington stopped. He stood over the golden curls of his aide-de-camp. 'You mean to humour me; I thank you.'

Why was the Beau so unexpectedly soft, Somerset wondered in alarm. It was obvious that their position was disastrous. Having sent three divisions south to protect Madrid, Lord Wellington had come north with a shrunken army to seize Burgos, and failed. Somerset knew that the enemy had more than a hundred thousand men ringed about them, closer every day. It was almost October. Even if they took the castle, how could they hold it? Retreat, opprobrium from London; those were inevitable. They would have to track back to the Douro and into the safety of Portugal again; and here was the General pliant and charming.

'Do you consider, Fitzroy, that I am your friend?'

Somerset hesitated. It must be some trick, a manoeuvre to trap him. If he agreed, the General might hoot and turn away; he might look down over that curved nose with disdain. But Somerset knew that if he said no he risked real displeasure.

He said nothing.

'No, you cannot.' The General stopped pacing. Fitzroy was surprised to see a look of sadness cross his face.

'You will need something from me; not now, perhaps. Now you are one of my young fellows here, always in good cheer, anxious for my favour.'

'My Lord.'

'Yes, yes, do not interrupt. You have everything you want now. But later, after the war is over, it will be a governorship perhaps, some sinecure at the Cape or in Gibraltar, or a seat in Parliament, the presumption that as you once served me so I must reward you. If I agree, and press your case, you might rise, even in the army, too fast for your experience, or beyond the brink of your talent.'

'I shall never ask for favour, my Lord.'

Lord Wellington snorted. 'Even out here the letters reach me. To subscribe to a charity, a new edition of such and such a book, to accept the dedication of a wretched symphony. They forget I know something about music and will not lend my name to a bagatelle. If I ignore them—ah then the opposition will get wind of it and brand me a man of overweening pride. If I refuse one, I must refuse them all; comply with one, comply with all.'

'If I may say so, sir, that is an accoutrement of your fame that does not touch on the matter of friendship. It is the duty you owe renown.'

'Wrong, Fitzroy.'

Fitzroy pushed back his chair. With the Beau in this mood, the softness gone all of a sudden, one had to sit it out.

'Wrong, Fitzroy. No matter how much sense I have I shall never be able to divide the two; my renown is my skin. I shall never make another friend.' He paused. 'Unless I should fail here.'

'That is unthinkable, my Lord.'

There it was, the General's whooping laugh, more triumph in it than lightness or joy.

'You flatter me already. My case is made. Ah, my golden boy; if not here, where am I to search for sincerity?' He laughed again.

Fitzroy looked down at the pile of papers.

'I have a letter here, my Lord, from Lord Bathurst. He suggests, after consultation with officials, that you consider the idea of recoining Spanish dollars so as to gain an additional eight in the hundred.'

'Preposterous.'

'My Lord?'

'A simple fraud, Somerset. Word would get around and the price will fall even further. Last week he suggested I obtain supplies by requisition. What does he think my men will do?'

'I cannot say, my Lord.'

'I'll tell you then. They will neglect every supply but that in barrels and that they will drink or else destroy all property that falls in their way. I do not have the Emperor's army, Fitzroy. I have the mob; a great fighting force, perhaps, but still, the mob.'

JAMES RAVEN'S ROUTE FROM Madrid to Seville took him over the hills and up to the high windswept plain beyond Valdepeñas. Spanish broom, summer-tired and bent eastwards, gathered dust from the unceasing wind. Vultures followed their progress from the sky. The barren upland, still brown after the dry summer, was almost deserted. Soult had marched his great force through these hills a few weeks before.

Nothing in James's outward appearance identified him as a captain in the British army. He rode head down in the wind, cocooned in a black cloak like his Spanish guide. One saddlebag held a letter of recommendation to Mr Wiseman, a Seville banker, the other a set of Stockdale's Spanish maps, printed in London before the war.

For years the partisans had ruled this empty land, at once Spanish soldiers and lawless bandits. Concealed in stands of cork oak in the valleys, they built camps where they baked bread, cast shot and brought their prisoners. No outsider was welcome there; neither the British nor their Portuguese allies could pass through without fear. Some partisans regarded British soldiers as friends; others, James suspected, fought for themselves and would leave him naked and alone without a second thought.

Once gathered in a band under the command of Juan Palarea, the partisans of the southern uplands now lived in small, scattered encampments, ambushed passers-by, and stripped them of goods, weapons and mules. Now they fell upon the tail of Soult's army, the Spanish families, friends of the French who had fled Seville and Cordova with jewels sewn in their clothes, the women and servants who straggled for miles behind the main force. James and his guide moved warily through the sun-soaked woods, and watched the dappled trees for movement. Once or twice they saw convoys of mules and carts in the grey-green distance wind round the mountain roads that led across the plains to Albacete and the safety of the coast.

At night when the sun went down behind the mountains a glittering ocean of stars rose up to take its place. Sometimes the constellations dissolved before James's tired eyes and all of Spain became a landscape of dreams and imaginings; at others the moon shone and the stars retreated before its mineral light. Then he felt a coldness inside himself, the same fearless equilibrium he had experienced on the retreat to Corunna. At night he revelled in this bone-white self; but in the morning he often had the sense that everything he had learned with Harriet, everything that had made him more complete, had fallen away.

The road from Madrid to Seville ended at the Puerta de Carmona, an ancient gatehouse with Moorish turrets. A few weeks before, the French had dragged their battery from the gateway and wheeled it away. James could see fresh white scars where the axles on the gun-carriages had bitten into the stone blocks. He pulled his horse up and while she drank at the reservoir by the gate he looked up at the walls that belted in the city. Sevilla, Hispalis to the Romans—Ishbiliya the Moors called it—city of sibilants and veils. The dead never left it, they said, but wandered enchanted through its orange groves and gardens in the heavy scented air. Jews and Moors, long gone, could be heard murmuring in the blue shadows. As a boy the Emperor Hadrian, who conquered the world, walked its streets and dreamed of Rome.

Opposite the cathedral, in the shade of Moorish arches, scribes offered their services in Latin or the language of Castille.

'Señor Wiseman?' one said when James asked the way in French. 'He lives on the Calle Genova. Are you an Irishman?'

'A British officer.'

'You are welcome here.' The man pointed the way and watched James lead his horse down the shaded half of the street round the corner and out of sight. The pall of silence that fell over the city in the afternoon heat would soon lift. He would sit here until it was cool enough to sleep. Custom was slow in these days. The French occupation had been bad for business; the British would be no better.

James followed the *escrivano*'s instructions to Patrick Wiseman's house. At intervals water-sellers sat impassively by their bulbous ceramic jars of filtered water. Otherwise the narrow streets were empty. Even the shade seemed to burn the skin, and the whitewashed walls looked hot to the touch. Before sundown, with the mercury up above 100 degrees, the hours crawled, and the flesh with them. The hottest part of the day was an unendurable wait for the darkness, and brought with it a fear that the night would be torrid also. By the time he found the Casa Wiseman, James felt invaded by sunshine.

Ushered into the salon on the first floor of the house, after the footman had taken up his letter, James saw Patrick Wiseman seated at a harpsichord in the centre of the room. Wiseman put down the lid and stood up. He was a squat man with a round chest and the remains of pale hair.

'Captain Raven. Yes, you are welcome.'

Wiseman spoke English with an unmistakeable Irish brogue. His manner was genial.

'I have read the letter you sent up. You will stay with me of course, and draw for any funds you need. I have supplied all the British visitors to Seville, and will respect your privacy, as your letter asks. Now you must bathe and rest. This is no time to be out.'

Wiseman accompanied James to his room, where a flowered carpet covered the pink brick floor.

'The maid will bring you water to wash. Do come out when you are ready.'

'Thank you, sir,' James said and bowed.

Left alone James stripped off his clothes and lay down. Slowly the heat drained out of his body. Outside the shutters he heard scuffles and cheeps. A caged canary, he thought, as he fell sideways into sleep.

~

'MRS HARRIET RAVEN, AT Mrs Cobbold's, Hatton Garden.' The cursive ran right across the cover sheet. Alone in the parlour, Harriet tore the letter open as she stood. 'Dean Street, 18th September, Monday', it began. The hand was neat and elegant, like the even small stitches that made a flat seam. No blots or scratches marked the paper.

'Dear Mrs Raven,' Mrs Lefevre wrote: 'At your last visit, you asked about your mother, Lady Guest. In the weeks that followed I considered what you asked, and my own reply. I write now only to assure you again that in everything Sir William acted for the best. I remain yours, Marianne Lefevre.'

Harriet sat down by the fire and let the letter fall. She stared into the flames; the coals settled and sighed.

'Carbon, with the introduction of oxygen, will produce heat.' Her father's words came back to her and she remembered how he tossed handfuls of common salt onto the fire to turn the flames blue. What was it that he had done for the best, that Mrs Lefevre had heard about or knew about? Her letter answered nothing.

'If there was a rumour; if something happened, then my aunt Cobbold must know of it,' Harriet said to herself. Mrs Cobbold was out, gone to choose wallpapers for her back parlour with Dorothy Yallop. They had fussed over samples after breakfast and then agreed to look at lengths in Trollope's Gallery in West Halkin Street. How wise Dorothy was to while away the time in diversion.

She must do something. She would not find anything in Suffolk, if she went back there. After her father's death James had cleared out the house. They had kept only Sir William's scientific papers and the family silver and portraits. The papers had been turned over time and time again; they contained details of all their old experiments and drafts of the papers her father had sent up to the Royal Society or planned to write. There was nothing in the laboratory, she was sure. No, she must look here. If Sir William had confided in anyone, it would surely have been his sister. He had loved Mrs Cobbold, Harriet knew, felt a closeness to her despite their different stations in life. Mrs Cobbold would surely have kept any correspondence that came from Beccles Hall.

Harriet had plenty of time. West Halkin Street was beyond Piccadilly along the Knightsbridge turnpike, a good half-hour's drive away, and once there, her aunt and Mrs Yallop would be hours in happy indecision.

Between the windows in the front parlour stood Mrs Cobbold's writing desk. It was a sturdy bureau with a row of small cubby-holes inside the lid and three drawers below.

'Oh, I shall do such things,' Harriet said under her breath.

The first drawer was stacked with engagement diaries and books of household accounts, arranged with care year by year. In the second lay piles of schoolbooks with covers of dark blue sugar paper. The bottom drawer, when Harriet eased it open, was crammed with bundles of letters, each tied with red ribbon. Scraps of paper tucked beneath the bows gave the year. Two dozen parcels, she reckoned, one for each year her aunt and uncle were married. The first letters were in the old form before envelopes became common, wrapped in cover sheets and sealed with wax.

She opened the first bundle and then another. But she could find nothing in her father's familiar disorderly italic; each was instead in her uncle Cobbold's neat copperplate. The series ended with his death ten years before. Harriet began quickly to open some of the later bundles. Perhaps in letters of those dates, she might find a clue. Mrs Lefevre had said she had sewn her mother the ribbon cockade in the early years of the revolution in France. She started in the pile for 1789. There was nothing revealed there, or the two following years, and nothing from 1792, the year of her own birth.

Nowhere could Harriet find any reference to her mother or herself, or even her father or Beccles Hall. All the letters, as she scanned them one after another and tossed them onto the floor, were filled with news of the Cobbolds' sons or their business. On every anniversary of their wedding, Harriet noticed, Samuel Cobbold, a man of scant education though great sense, wrote his wife a page of verse in rhymed couplets. To see them so awkward and full of love touched Harriet's heart. She remembered her father say that his parents had discouraged their daughter's marriage to a man so far beneath her. But Sam Cobbold had made his wife happy, told her of his affection; could any woman ask for more?

One of the notes, dated simply 'Sunday morning' and stacked in a pile with letters from 1793, had no cover sheet. It had not been consigned to the post. The hand was small and careful, as if the writer had made a special effort to be understood.

'Dearest Anne,' Harriet read: 'I now must leave to go about my business, and trust you find this when you wake. I can only say that we should have adored our little daughter. She had the face of an angel, and delicate tiny hands. I kissed her pretty fingers one by one, still warm to my touch. From what I could see, her hair was fair like your own. But Mr Adair judged it necessary to sacrifice either mother or child. I will forbear to describe how he saved you, only thank God that you are spared.

'Your loving husband, Samuel.'

Harriet put the letters back and pushed the drawer closed with hands that shook. To lose a child and say nothing; how was that possible? She thought of her aunt tucked tight in her carriage as it jogged down Long Acre and Piccadilly. Mrs Cobbold had always been kind to her, and made it clear that, as she had no daughter of her own, Harriet was especially welcome in her house. She had never hinted at the death of a baby or how she must have suffered. For the doctor had killed the little girl, nameless and breathing, to save her aunt's life; that was obvious. How did a mother live with such knowledge, or how forget? Would the doctor have killed a boy baby, or might he in that case have killed the mother to save the child? Macduff, yes, *Macbeth*, Act 5, Scene 10, Harriet whispered to herself. Macduff 'was from his mother's womb untimely ripped'.

Everything, then, was different for a man. A baby girl could die, but to save a son the mother might be killed. A man might go out into the world to assuage his grief, or like Childe Harold, wander abroad and quell his misery with new wonders. But a woman could only endure. Perhaps her aunt had dissolved her grief inside herself, as sharp crystals dissolve in warm liquid. She would respect Mrs Cobbold's silence; but her own composition was different. In her something submerged threatened, especially now, to push to the surface.

When she peered into the past, Harriet thought she could remember her mother in the laboratory, a third presence, faint and ghostly. How could she test her vision, or her other memory of standing by a great bedpost, just tall enough to look across the silk sea of the coverlet to where her mother lay propped up on her pillows? Perhaps that moment was merely a story that her father had told, or a dream she had shaped into memory.

She knew from the portraits and miniatures at Beccles Hall that her mother had honey-brown hair and blue-grey eyes, but she could never see in them the movement of life. There were no more memories in her head. Her mother had gone and her father never spoke of her. It seemed of the utmost importance that she had something about her mother that she could lean on, but how could she be sure?

The morning wore on; when Mrs Cobbold and Dorothy Yallop came back they found Harriet still immobile on the carpet.

'What have you done, my dear?' Concern and shock filled Anne Cobbold's voice.

'Oh, Aunt, I have been lost in thought.'

'You have pulled the threads out of the carpet.'

Harriet looked down. A pile of golden wool lay next to her hand. Dorothy Yallop, dressed in a violet cloak with a matching bonnet, bustled over and put her hand on Harriet's shoulder.

'Do not fret, my dear. You know what a fine seamstress I am. I can simply follow the pattern and have it mended in no time.'

Harriet leant back against Mrs Yallop's sturdy legs. She wished for a moment she could stay like that, with the warmth of Dorothy's solid body next to her.

'I have been thinking of my mother, Aunt. Do you know what my father did when she went away?'

Mrs Cobbold's voice was firm.

'No, Harriet. Do not let us return to this subject. It does none of us any good. I know only that your mother was ill.'

'Did she die?'

'She left your father's house and never came back.'

'Where did she go?'

'I believe William spoke of a better climate.'

'Did my father send her abroad? Did she die in France or Spain?'

'I cannot say, Harriet. Remember it was a terrible time; sedition everywhere, the start of the war, business disrupted. I know no more than I have told you.'

Mrs Cobbold's face was a plumper version of Sir William's, though she carried herself with an air of determination that her brother had lacked. Now, sadness washed through it, and Harriet felt the past sweep into the room. She saw again the way her father would look up when they were alone together and glance at the door as if he expected someone.

The year 1793, when the war broke out: that was the date of Samuel's letter about their daughter. Harriet pushed her hair back and jumped up.

'Thank you, Aunt. I shall ask no more. I have decided to walk off my bad humour.'

'You will be back for dinner?' Mrs Yallop preferred an early dinner in the style of the last century. Army life had taught her never to neglect victuals.

'Of course, yes.'

Harriet left Mrs Cobbold's house by the garden gate, came onto Holborn, turned west and made for Soho. In Dean Street, she saw Mrs Lefevre through the window. She stood over her table; shining cloth with broad stripes of grey and yellow covered the surface.

Mrs Lefevre straightened up when Harriet came into the room.

'Ah, Mrs Raven. Do look. This is to be a day gown for a young girl.'

'I have come to talk about your letter, Mrs Lefevre.'

'I know, my dear. I can see from your countenance that you wish to talk of it. I wrote because I wished you to be at peace. But I have told you all that I know.'

'You wrote that my father acted for the best. But what did he do? Do tell me, Mrs Lefevre. I am tormented by the idea that my mother might have died not in England but in France or Spain and that my father sent her away.'

Mrs Lefevre stopped. 'I have never heard that Lady Guest was dead. I keep her patterns here still. But I can tell you nothing else.'

'Do you believe her to be alive?'

'My dear, it is not for me to speculate about my clients. I sew for many women, from all walks of society. How would my business fare if I made public every rumour that I hear? In the early days of the Revolution I had royalists and republicans alike as my clients, some sworn enemies. I have not prospered by breaching their confidences.'

Mrs Lefevre lifted the piece of taffeta off the table and shook it out.

'But here, Mrs Lefevre, there is no confidence to breach. My mother and father are both dead.'

'It makes no difference; history does not respect mortality. Consider the possibility that your mother, were she alive, might wish to remain undiscovered.'

'But that is impossible. Surely she would long to know me.'

'We know so little of the human heart.'

'You suggest that she ran away from me and my father?'

'I do not know, Mrs Raven. Please do not let it trouble you any more.'

Mrs Lefevre came round the table and took Harriet's hand. Harriet could look right over her head. Outside the dark obscured the trees. In the houses opposite spots of light stood in the windows.

'Now, tell me what you think of this stripe. It is so charming for a child. I hope that when Captain Raven returns you will have the blessing of a family.'

Harriet found she did not wish to talk of a family. On the contrary the thought jarred her. She gestured towards the window.

'See out there, Mrs Lefevre? The candles and the oil lamps cast the beautiful light of evening.'

'Every dressmaker must work with it in mind.'

'I have seen a new form of light that will change much, though few will notice at the beginning.'

Harriet remembered the demonstration of gaslight at Mr Winsor's house in Pall Mall. The forest of tiny flames left no penumbra as candles did, no wells of light that faded into the darkness. How forgiving oil and candlelight were, and how bright and critical the new world made by gaslight would be. Peccadilloes and eccentricities hitherto lived in shadow would be dragged out from dim corners. Dusty and reticent spaces would be cleaned up and tidied away. Modern life would be without pity for age or blemish. Wrinkles and scars, the waterfalls of old necks and jaws would stand out in undulations and crevasses, as Arabian deserts do when the sun comes up. Even taste would be made to accommodate the new luminous air. The fine damask wallpapers and long silk curtains of the last century, which caught and held candlelight in folds and stitches, would come to seem vulgar and harsh. Bright colours, white carved plaster ceilings that deepened and became beautiful in shadow, golden brocades, glinting buckles and embroidered sprigs of particoloured flowers; all had candlelight to thank for their popularity and feel of luxury. All would be swept away in new colours and designs that gathered light in instead of throwing it out.

What then of her newly painted dining room in Suffolk? Its Pompeian red, made to glow under lamplight, would not survive the scrutiny of gas. In the new white light it will turn brackish and dead, she thought, like blood. The colours of this new world will be dense and pearly, able to give something back to the whiteness or take off its probing edge. Sage and mauve, deep maroon and bottle-green; under the new light they will come into their own.

If gaslights were fed from pipes that coiled through the plaster and snaked round door posts, nowhere in their houses need stay in dusk or mystery. Time itself would change without a candle to burn away during the night hours, and a new sound would attend them down corridors. The whisper of gas would accompany their evenings; music and conversation would be raised to sound above it.

'My dear,' Mrs Lefevre said when Harriet had explained, 'if a young woman such as yourself can feel a nostalgia for what will be lost, how can an old woman of my sort look forward with enthusiasm? No, I shall still use my oil lamps and my candles at night. It is all I know.'

Harriet stood up and tugged on her bonnet.

'Mrs Lefevre, I predict you will be one of the first when the gaslight comes into the street. Think how much better it will illuminate your sewing table. You will be able to work even when the sun sets early.'

The old dressmaker watched her visitor walk up the street and out of sight. Mrs Raven's bonnet hung on its strings halfway down her back. She had not pinned her hair up and her gown was creased. Mrs Lefevre had hoped her letter would stop Mrs Raven's enquiries. Perhaps it was an error to have sent it. She shifted on her feet. Knowledge took the edge off sleep. It was a pity to hide the truth of Lady Guest's disappearance; but Sir William had asked for her silence and left a handsome sum in his will to continue the work after his death. Besides, Mrs Raven could gain nothing by the knowledge except unhappiness and such a beautiful young woman should know nothing to weigh her down. Life would do that job well enough in time.

~

IN THE EARLY DARKNESS Seville began to breathe. In the daytime its narrow streets were torrid canyons but now, when he crossed a wide square as the sun went down, James felt a faint wind stir from the river. Water, sluiced over every step, drew off some of the heat. Over his head palm fronds picked up the breeze and clicked in the gloom.

The Casa Florens stood on Seville's grandest street, a fine stone house with a garden behind. James arrived light-headed and prickling. Inside the double doors a wide courtyard was covered with a great green cloth stretched between the first-floor windows. Underneath it a submarine silence spread through the house. James heard his boots echo off the tiled walls as he took the shallow stone steps up to the first floor. Down a brick-floored corridor the maid knocked at a tall panelled door.

'*Entrez.*'

With the door held open for him, James walked into the darkness. Camille Florens was sitting by an open window that overlooked the courtyard.

'Captain Raven.'

Señora Florens turned and held out her hand. James guessed her to be well past thirty, nearer forty, perhaps, but she was slender and narrow as a girl. A white gown dropped off her shoulders; pearls ran tight round her neck. She did not get up and James bent his head down towards her.

'Señora Florens, I come from General Wellington. I carry no letters for the usual reasons.'

'Bring up a chair and sit with me.'

Señora Florens talked English, in a low voice, and her flattened Spanish consonants added a hiss to her speech. James picked up a chair and walked over to the window. From below mingled sounds came up: running water, pans, the chock of a knife against a board, cutlery, voices, bars of a song, murmurs of a great house on a summer night with doors and windows open.

'Let us begin,' Camille said. 'It will be best to go straight to business. You know that I have helped the British before?'

'Indeed, Señora Florens, I have been told that you travelled with information to Lisbon last year.'

Against the deepening darkness in the window Camille's muslin dress stood out an almost unearthly white. James saw that her skin was pale and shadows gathered round her eyes.

'It is my wish to help the British army. You know, I am sure, that my father was a subject of His Majesty?'

'I am told he was an Irishman.'

Camille smiled and James noticed that her upper lip was very full and pressed back, almost open. It gave her mouth a bruised look.

'Yes and no.' Her English now seemed to have an Irish lilt folded into it. 'Like Lord Wellington himself, my father became a citizen of Great Britain with the Union. He had come from Kildare to the Irish College here. But they closed the College, tossed out the Jesuits, and then he found the priesthood not to his liking and married. I am a Spaniard, but Britain is my second country, dearest to my heart after Spain.'

She gestured to the far wall of the room.

'There is my father. Do you see him?'

Above the fireplace, just visible in the gloom, James could see the portrait of a light-skinned man, painted in a severe classical style. He wore his grey hair cropped and set it off with a deep green cravat. In the curve of the frame at the left ran the words 'Eugene O'Donnell, 1796'. To the right the painter had written his name: Girodet.

'My father was a good man,' Camille said. 'A patriot. It is my earnest desire to rid Spain of the French and to honour his memory.'

'It is for this reason that you help General Wellington?'

'Yes, indeed, and for other reasons, too. I have many friends amongst the British. You know Lord Holland?'

James stiffened. It was well known that Lord Holland admired Napoleon.

'I know him by repute, of course. His house is not one I could frequent, nor could my wife possibly do so. Lady Holland is shunned by society.'

Camille laughed.

'They are my good friends, Captain Raven, and were my neighbours here for many months. Though they may be thought to be dangerous Napoleonists, I know them to be patriots who wish only the good of their own country. For their sake I support the British cause. But let us not dwell on them. I imagine you have come about my brother Felipe, who calls himself Odonnell in the Spanish style. You know he is in the field with Villacampa, the guerrilla leader. They harry the French wherever they find them. Hundreds of enemy soldiers are now required to guard the smallest French convoy.'

General Stewart had warned James to make sure of Señora Florens's intentions. Informers in Seville reported that her salon was the favourite resort of French officers. Men hung about her like wasps at a fruit tree.

'I am told that French officers enjoyed your hospitality during the occupation.'

Camille turned her head to look out of the window.

'My house has the best cellar in Seville,' she said, and smiled again at him. 'Sometimes General Soult himself made use of it, and to be sure I encouraged him. Would you not yourself, Captain Raven, when you might learn something to your advantage?'

'Your husband, Señor Florens. He is also here in Seville?'

'Herr Florens, Captain Raven.'

'Herr Florens is German?'

'A silk merchant. You have seen the mulberry trees all around the city no doubt.'

'I rode through them on the way in.'

'They supply our manufactory. Satins, velvet, silk stockings. My husband makes them all, and sells them on in Hamburg.'

Camille paused. 'Those he gives to me excepted, of course.'

James blushed through the darkness. He felt the heat rise to his cheeks.

'We do indeed wish to establish contact with your brother Felipe, Señora Florens. We know that he has large forces at his command, and it is Lord Wellington's wish to work more closely with the guerrillas.'

'He knows their value, then.'

'Indeed, and that they know the terrain. He wishes to prevent convoys and reinforcements reaching Joseph Bonaparte's army in Valencia. We presume that after the winter the French will march north, and Lord Wellington is anxious to limit the size of their army.' James hesitated. Wellington's views on the Spanish would not help his cause.

'Were your brother to come across any French troops or convoys we might confront them with a force large enough to deal them a blow on the spot rather than pick off small groups.'

'What you are asking,' Camille said, 'is that my brother, or the partisans up towards the border, refrain from attacking the enemy.'

'He will understand that such a strategy will hasten the war to a conclusion and liberate Spain as both you and I wish.'

'To hold off when the opportunity is there to strike seems to me a perhaps unnecessary restraint. You are aware that partisans like my brother have killed far more of the French than any of Lord Wellington's armies?'

James had heard Lord Wellington say with impatience many times that the partisans were a distraction, nothing more. They might disable the French, bleed them of men; but only a pitched battle would get the invaders to abandon Spain. Bonaparte and his generals cared little for the daily loss of soldiers. Hundreds of thousands might die at the hands of the partisans, but a battle was something different. A real battle, fought according to the rules of war, was a duel decided then and there, not a crouched creep forward inch by inch that did nothing for a man's reputation and earned him no plaudits at home. Children, hundreds of years hence, would long to have been at a great battle and felt the booming of the guns. Besides, Bonaparte, no less than Wellington, wanted to join the pantheon. Julius Caesar had fought in such a way, Alexander conquered the world once. So, in this way, would the contest between Britain and France end.

Camille leaned back in her chair. The room was in darkness now; points of light from the candles gathered in the pearls round her neck. She seemed to consider.

'Lord Wellington may not understand that Felipe fights a new kind of war. But no matter. I will send a courier to my brother; I cannot say what he will decide to do. He will send me back word in a week or so. You intend, I hope, to stay in Seville?'

'In accordance with my orders, yes.'

'I shall devise some entertainment for you in the meantime. Something to amuse and instruct.'

'Thank you, Señora Florens.'

Camille stood up, crossed the room and rang a brass bell that sat on the mantelpiece. A maid came in immediately; she must have been sitting outside the door.

'Bring more candles and then fetch my girls.'

'Do meet my daughters before you leave.' Camille turned back to James. 'With my husband in Hamburg they are my only daily companions.'

In a few minutes two girls came in, dressed in white silk like their mother. The elder wore a dark blue velvet ribbon across her chest, the younger a tight sash of scarlet silk, with a bow and long ends behind. James guessed their ages at eight and four.

'This is Laura.' The older girl came forward. 'And here is Corinne.'

'Good evening, sir.' Laura spoke in English and looked steadily at James with her mother's black eyes.

'Are you my mother's friend?' Corinne said. She came up to James and put a plump hand on his thigh.

'I am a British officer,' James said to Corinne in Spanish.

Corinne laughed as if James had told her a joke. Her skin was pale like her mother's, but her hair was thick and brown, cut straight across her forehead.

'She is called Corinne after Madame de Staël's book of that name.'

Corinne stretched two hands up to him.

'I have not read it.'

James bent down and lifted Corinne into his arms. She pushed her hands round his neck and grasped it tightly, then leaned back and smiled at her sister in triumph. James wondered how he could set her down on the floor again.

'It tells the story of an English lord, forced to choose between duty to his betrothed and the charms of a beautiful woman. Do let me send a copy round to Señor Wiseman's.'

'Thank you, Señora Florens. I cannot promise to find the time.'

'Oh but you must.' Camille smiled at him. Her eyes remained still, black as beetles' wings. 'I shall wait to hear your opinion.'

James bowed and took his leave. Outside, the hot night stifled him. In the darkness the face of Eugene O'Donnell floated towards him.

∼

'MR HERRIES.'

Kitty stood in the print room of Mr Hatchard's bookshop on Piccadilly. Hatchard sold books in the panelled room at the front of his shop, and prints and toys at the back. New prints were pinned up on display. One group of visitors stood bunched round a wall of rural scenes tinted with pale colour. Others peered at dozens of black-and-white cartoons. An old man examined the portrait of a well-known courtesan with his eyeglass held close to the paper. One or two people stood back to admire large-scale maps and panoramas assembled from several plates put side by side.

'Are you searching for something in particular?'

Herries seemed startled. He held up a package in his hands as if it contained an explosive charge.

'I have bought one of Osborne's maps.'

'Ah, yes. My boys delight in them; fitting the countries together to make a continent. They are at present at work on the Americas and all those islands of the Caribbean.'

Now Mr Herries looked alarmed. Did he think she referred to recent successes of the American navy?

'Perhaps you have the counties of England instead?'

A hunted look swept across Herries's freckled face.

'I have bought the map of France. I believe it comes in a hundred pieces.'

'How charming. You have children of your own?'

'Indeed, no. I am unmarried, Lady Wellington.'

'A nephew who follows the progress of the war, perhaps?'

'Just so; in Yorkshire.'

'A sister's child?'

Herries nodded. Why have I begun, he asked himself? One falsehood led him to another; he would end with a miasma of lies that lay like smoke between them. Then the truth would come out. He did not wish to deceive Lady Wellington. Indeed, he thought as he screwed up his eyes and looked across at her, she seemed a charming and collected woman. Her hair was streaked with grey and cropped short in the modern manner. It framed her face and drew attention to her still eyes. Perhaps he should confide his secret to her; not Mr Rothschild's part in it, of course, but simply that he had a daughter. The wish to tell someone choked him. She would share his joy, his wonder at Louisa's beauty (with such a mother she must be the most beautiful child in the world). Did she not have two or three boys of her own?

Herries started to speak and then stopped. Now Lady Wellington put her gloved hand on his arm.

'Might I ask, Mr Herries, whether you feel well? Your office carries great responsibility and the work must tax you.'

'Indeed I am quite well, Lady Wellington; just a little wan with care, as the Bard puts it. I have pressing business to attend to.'

'Do not let me detain you.'

Herries bowed his reddish head. He has his reasons for secrecy, and I have mine, Kitty thought, as she watched him walk off. The greater a woman's husband becomes, the more hidden her inner life must be. One had to manage it alone, calm its turbulence and curb its joys. She glanced round to be sure she was not watched. Two well-dressed women leaned over a table on which fashion plates were laid out.

'How *charmante* that fur is. Quite in the Parisian manner.'

'I shall demand one like it for the winter.'

'This lining, now, in saffron. Do you think, Lady Lavington, that such a colour could catch on?'

'Your complexion, my dear Lady Orford, is a little darker, if I may say so, than my own. You will wear it very well, but I am so pale. I shall have to select something a little more forgiving.'

Kitty moved past them. Three weeks ago the Regency that governed Spain had offered Arthur control of the Spanish army to add to his British command. Where previously the Spanish and the British had fought as two separate armies, now there would be only one, with Arthur at its head. So his empire expanded, and with it her own unwanted fame. Men and women stopped her in the street to offer congratulations. Many wished to touch her, as if they could reach through her to her husband, and extract his greatness.

She glanced over the wall of prints, some black-and-white, some coloured in with the familiar watered-down palette of ultramarine, dark green, golden-yellow and pink. There it was: in the foreground a mantilla-clad woman who lay in disordered skirts on a chaise longue. From her mouth came the words, 'Oh, I am taken. I surrender!' Behind her, in unmistakable profile, caught by Mr Rowlandson in a few sinuous lines, stood Arthur, his frock coat washed with dark blue, his boots chestnut-brown. Inside an irregular bubble, his declaration: 'My sword is out; I will ram it home.' On the wall hung a map of the Peninsula; next to it a print of a well-known courtesan.

So there she was, Mrs Fitzwilliam. She had finally turned her experience to the profit she had threatened months ago. Arthur would take no notice of such a thing. He might even buy the print for himself. In London, perhaps only the old King was spared the attention of the cartoonists. Bawdy prints, from the expensive bedroom drawings of Mr Rowlandson to etchings scrawled overnight and turned by the dozen in St Paul's Churchyard, were everywhere. Women of modest demeanour might have drawers full of images in the most questionable taste, and laugh over them with acquaintances. Married men and women practised what the pictures showed them. Underneath the new airs of the capital, concealed in the dark folds of war, scandal flourished like a forest flower.

Kitty looked at the print, and Arthur in it, with equanimity; not indifference, she thought, but as something that no longer had the power to hurt her. She felt that she now faced forwards, and could take tentative steps into the future, as someone does who emerges from the sickroom after a long illness and sees, with gratitude and amazement, the beauty of the world.

AFTER HER VISIT TO Mrs Lefevre, Harriet promised herself that she would try to resist the pull of the past. Sometimes on the way to Kitty's she looked at the women who passed and wondered if one of them might have met her mother. But as autumn wore on she felt her mood lift. She began to correspond with Frederick Winsor about new discoveries in chemistry and visited his manufactory at Horseferry Road. There Winsor had connected cauldrons and cylinders to washers that filtered coal gas through water and removed noxious sulphur from the pipes that would push the gas beneath the city. One day in mid-October he suggested that they meet. He had something he wanted to show her.

At noon on the agreed day, Harriet walked the short distance from Hatton Garden along Holborn to the gate into the court of Gray's Inn. Beyond the court lay the garden, and there, through the black and gold of the great wrought-iron gates, she saw Frederick. He stood against the trunk of a young plane tree, planted by the railings along Theobalds Road. When she reached him, he threw his hands skywards, and bounded into the weak sunshine.

'Harriet, good day. You are wrapped for winter, when we still have warmth in the sun.'

'One can feel the change in the air.'

'Not yet, I hope. I have much to show you, as I promised, and I require a fine day for it.'

'Forgive me, Mr Winsor; you seem quite different; light-hearted, I mean.'

'And why not? I have waited here and watched the lawyers pass in their wigs and gowns. We are to take a walk together. Is that not enough to make me cheerful?'

'Indeed. Of course. But your topcoat!'

Frederick turned back the front of a long maroon coat to show its mustard silk lining. A white cravat in the finest muslin lay loose against his dark skin.

'Do you think it in good taste?'

Frederick did not wait for an answer. He turned and walked through the gate on the north side of the garden and Harriet found herself half-skipping every few steps of her walk to keep up with him. By the time they reached the high wall of the new house of correction at Coldbath Fields and an arched brick bridge that ran over the oily Fleet River beyond, she was almost running. When they scrambled up the steep eastern bank of the Fleet, Frederick stretched out a hand to help her. She took it without a thought.

They seemed to be walking along an invisible edge to the city. To the north, elders and hawthorns crowded along the bank of the river, and the ground rose up in gentle hills, grass-covered, scarred here and there with incongruous building, but recognisably a part of the countryside still. On one side of the river two bottle chimneys of a brick-works stood above a huddle of buildings, on the other a simple picket fence ran up to the garden of a farmhouse reached by a wooden bridge. Sheep grazed the river banks and nibbled at gateposts where grass grew luxuriant in the marshy ground. Southwards the muddle of fields and pleasure houses with wells and spas gave way to the old streets around the Charterhouse and beyond it the great nave and dome of St Paul's Cathedral stood across the horizon with the lesser spires of the city churches in attendance.

All the way Frederick piled up thoughts and questions one after another. Harriet might have thought he did not listen to her answers if she had not felt his eyes rest on her now and then. He picked late daisies, pulled off the petals and threw the yellow centres away. At the bridge he cast a bundle of grass over the low parapet. They stood on the shallow summit and watched the leaves drift away towards the Thames.

A windmill rose in front of them, its wooden arms dilapidated. Behind it stood an irregularly shaped building constructed in the narrow red bricks commonly used two centuries before. They walked round the perimeter of the great pond.

'This water is the same you drink in Hatton Garden and I in Pall Mall. The men who control it own the most profitable company in the whole of Britain.'

From the reservoir, square elm pipes carried water to the city and the distant streets of Piccadilly and Mayfair. A plume of smoke rose from the red-brick building; from inside came the clatter of metal on metal, the sound of a great steam engine at work.

'The engineers who built the pumping house and the great pond came from Holland; Dutchmen understand water. Then, someone has to show the English the way. Clocks and jewels, silks and shoes? Made by the French. Your ceilings and walls? Plastered by Italians. Those grand operas and oratorios? Written by anyone but yourselves. Now it is the turn of us Germans.'

Harriet let the noise engulf her. Perhaps it was true that the peculiar talent of the English was to recognise the industry of others, give it a home and use it for themselves; they had little genius of their own. Even the army, James often said, was the creation of the Irish and the Scots.

'We English are good for a few things; telling stories; making plays.'

'There is very little profit in that, or not enough for me, at any rate.'

They leant over the fence that ran round the pond; downhill to the south the land was streaked with trenches. Workmen had begun to replace the old elm conduits with cast-iron pipes laid underground in the clay. As they stood side by side, Frederick took her hand in his again, laid its back onto his outstretched palm and stroked upturned fingers one by one. Both of them gazed ahead. Then just as suddenly he folded up her hand and dropped it by her side.

'Your profits might be slow to come,' Harriet said aloud. Why did Frederick pick up and then abandon her hand? Was his gesture merely an accompaniment to his speech, in the way a man strokes a cat to smooth his thoughts?

'I do not believe so.'

'You have a great trust in yourself, Frederick.'

'Yes.'

'And what of him, what of that old soldier fishing?' Harriet gestured towards a man who sat by the pond in a patched red jacket. The stump of one leg lay stiff out before him, the other hung down over the bank. He cast his line and pulled it in time after time, placid and imperturbable.

Frederick shrugged. He looked older than Harriet had imagined him, weary.

'What of him? Why should I repine if Napoleon becomes the master of Europe? Does it matter which power wins out, democracy or monarchy?'

'My husband is there, in Spain.'

'And what interest do I have in him?'

He looked at her sharply and tugged on the lapels of his maroon topcoat.

'To concern myself with him would be tedious; vulgar even. Now it is late. I have to go.'

Frederick stood up, buttoned his coat and hooked Harriet's right arm through his left as if it was part of the same movement. They walked down the hill so close together that an observer might have thought them one person, not two.

7

London and Seville

J ames sat in his room at Señor Wiseman's, where palm fronds rustled outside the window. Though it was October and autumn was in the air, the afternoons hung hot and heavy still. Madame de Staël's novel, *Corinne*, lay loose in his hand. Camille Florens had sent the book round the day after their first meeting, with a note attached.

Read this, Captain Raven, and understand me.

When James next saw Camille it was at a soirée, with people crowded round her. She asked him, with a smile, and her head tilted to one side, whether he had received her present, and added, 'There is no word yet from my brother Philipe. It seems, Captain Raven, that you may be here some time.'

'Indeed.'

'It is a delicate matter; we shall have to talk alone. Will you come back tomorrow in the evening?'

Madame de Staël's story did not hold James's interest. Corinne was a beautiful poetess dedicated to Italian liberty, a white-clad statue quite unlike Señora Florens. Thoughts of Camille swarmed across the page and blotted out the type. James let the book slide onto the floor and sank under the surface of the afternoon, grateful for sleep. He had only been in Seville a couple of weeks, but already he was overcome by torpor. Days had been passed in idleness, evenings at houses where he was welcomed, or in talk over wine with his host.

When he woke, some hours later, it was nearly dark and late enough to set off for the Casa Florens. By the fountains water-carriers, the *aguadores*, sat on their empty water casks. Drivers who waited for fares leaned back against their carriages and blew the smoke from their makeshift cigars up into the sky. At the house two lanterns dangled from slung chains by the great doorway, and the courtyard was lit up with octagonal lamps hung from the eaves. In the drawing room Camille Florens sat on the divan, paler than ever, her black eyes impenetrable. James stumbled as he approached. Camille held her hand out to him. It was clothed to the elbow in black lace, her skin visible through the pattern. James leant over to kiss it.

'Captain Raven. How good to see you again. I mean alone.'

'It is indeed a pleasure.'

'And how have you passed the time while we wait?'

'Wait?'

'For my brother's reply. I expect it any day now.'

'Ah, yes.'

James hesitated. He wanted to tell her that at the Casa Wiseman he had sat out the hours in a stupor, that he felt possessed by her. Felipe Odonnell, indeed his whole mission, was already a chimera. Though he knew that he must exert himself to get the information that General Stewart asked for, it now seemed to matter little.

'You have at least found time to read our incomparable Madame de Staël?'

'The first chapters only. Those in which Lord Nevil falls in love with Corinne.' James now wished that he had tried harder. 'In Rome.'

'Ah yes, Corinne. I am like her in so many ways. And you, Captain Raven, have you ever fallen in the way Madame de Staël describes so well, when at the sight of another the world is utterly changed?'

'I am a soldier, Señora Florens. My profession demands a cold heart.'

'But it may not always get it.'

Camille moved along the divan to indicate a space.

'Sit down and tell me about your cold heart, Captain Raven.'

'I come about the mission only.'

'Do you not wish to talk about love?' She bent her head towards him. 'Where would our literature, our art, be without it? Think of Antony without Cleopatra, Orpheus without Eurydice? How would they interest us, those men?'

Did Camille tease him; or worse, mock him? Her face was impenetrable and mysterious, as if she thought of something far away.

'I believe I am here to discuss our cause. It alone concerns me.'

Camille laughed.

'You are right, of course, though you may be less than sincere. Nothing is more important than the future of Spain. But we must fill up the wait somehow. Can you not help me do that too, a little?'

'Since you ask it of me, Señora Florens, it is my duty to try.'

'You must call me Camille. I insist. And your own name?'

'James.'

'Ah, James.' She said it with a perceptible attempt to thicken the first syllable so that it came out soft and flat. 'That is charming. A Stuart name I believe.'

'Stuart?'

'James Edward; you call him the Old Pretender.'

'And you?'

Camille paused.

'Some called him the King.'

'Never my own parents, I do assure you.'

'They had no time for kings?'

'They were loyal subjects, and the Old Pretender was a Catholic. Besides they were unschooled in history.'

'Perhaps they were wise. To remember is to court trouble.'

'Then we must look to the future.'

'Indeed I do.' Camille looked at James. 'And you, what future do you look forward to?'

She teased him, James knew. She tipped up her chin and mocked him. More than that, she invited him to take her in his arms, to crush her, kiss her. Worse, he wished to do so; there was no future beyond that.

'I can see no further than the present, Señora Florens.'

'Let us look forward at least to pleasure.'

'Pleasure?'

'Yes,' she said and leaned forward again. James felt the rough lace of her gloved hand move across his wrist.

～

'I DO ENDEAVOUR, KITTY, to pass the time with profit, but I am so restless. I long for your serenity.'

Kitty Wellington had left Harley Street in the summer for a new house north of Piccadilly, by Hyde Park. Kitty sat in a small armchair, upright and still. Harriet ran her hand up and down a stripe on the damask of the sofa; she paused sometimes to listen and then began again.

'My serenity, as you call it Harriet, may not last.'

'I never found it; not even when James was with me. Now I try to look upon life as something unknown, unexpected. People too; I mean to see whether different people combine well together. My aunt and her friend Mrs Yallop for instance. They are composed quite differently yet they do not grate upon one another. Together they form a new whole. Then there is Mr Winsor.'

'Frederick Winsor?'

Harriet blushed.

'It is quite different from my aunt and Mrs Yallop, of course.'

'Indeed. You are two very different substances, dear Harriet. He is a man, you a woman.'

'Oh it is not like that, Kitty. You misunderstand me. I learn from Mr Winsor, that is all.'

Kitty raised her eyebrows and turned her head to one side the way a robin does to get a better look. She does not believe me, Harriet thought, and with good cause, though what I have said is true enough.

'He took me to the New River Head. He plans for his company to supply light just as if it were water, to every household that wishes it.'

'Ah, yes. The National Light and Heat Company. Many people, I believe, have become interested in it since it came to the market.'

Harriet shifted the conversation to more certain ground.

'Have you bought more shares yourself, Lady Wellington?'

'Indeed no, Harriet; but my holding is already substantial.'

A WEEK AGO, ON the way out of Mr Rothschild's house, Kitty had found herself face to face with a soldier, resplendent in a new scarlet jacket—not an uncommon sight in the City these days, but unusual, she thought, in New Court. Nathan Rothschild, who had gone inside to take a message from a sweating courier, came back a minute after her and called through the open door.

'Moses! Lady Wellington, may I present my brother-in-law, Moses Montefiore.'

The man bowed. He towered over Kitty, magnificent and barrel-chested.

'I am glad to meet you, Mr Montefiore.' She looked at the epaulette on his right shoulder. 'Captain Montefiore.'

Moses Montefiore glanced at his epaulette with delight. He wore his captain's uniform at every opportunity and cleaned his ornamental sword in the parlour at night.

'Of the 3rd Surrey Militia, at your service.'

'Not my service, I venture to say, but my husband's.'

Nathan Rothschild came out onto his steps and looked down at them.

'Moses is now, in every way, a member of the family. He acts as my broker, so should you require any shares it will be he who buys them, though he deals on his own account as well; did before he came here to New Court.'

Moses Montefiore bowed and lifted a hand. He held a bugle that nestled in his huge palm.

'Moses made off with my Hannah's sister Judith, in June. I thought it best not to let the rascal run too far. They have moved into no. 4; and still I can do nothing to stop him taking lessons on that infernal instrument. He torments me with the sound and pretends that it is his duty as a militiaman.'

Nathan smiled a wide genuine smile that showed the gaps between his teeth. Kitty felt immediately at ease.

'And what might you recommend me today, Captain Montefiore, in the way of stocks?'

'I am looking into the National Light and Heat Company. It is now capitalised to a million sterling in eighty thousand shares. The company has a new wharf building at Cannon Row and a plant in Horseferry Road. A gamble, to be sure; but a risk that might be worth your consideration, Lady Wellington.'

Kitty turned round. 'Mr Rothschild!'

'Moses tells me that the shares are already at a premium. As one of Mr Winsor's first investors, you may already have turned a profit, whereas Moses here will have to wait a little longer.'

Nathan Rothschild stood impassive on his step, one hand on the door jamb. His eyes twinkled.

'Moses is a different sort. Plans, companies, dozens of men to worry about, shareholders, directors; all these things interest him. Whereas I, as I said . . .' He shrugged. 'Moses has solidity.'

'And you, Mr Rothschild?'

'Hannah tells me I am a dreamer, that I can forget even to eat in the press of business. Worse, that my mind drifts to business on Shabbos. She is a little mistaken. My best decisions are taken after a good dinner; but I say nothing.'

Nathan took Kitty's hand and kissed it.

'Ah, my best news for last. While you have been looking my brother-in-law up and down, I received a visitor.'

'He ran in.'

'He has good news for us about our Russian bonds. You will remember we added them to your business some months ago.'

'When Bonaparte crossed the Elbe, I believe.'

'Indeed, my good lady. The Emperor has left Moscow. He will crawl back to France.' He waved his hand. 'But the Emperor is not our concern. No, it is Tsar Alexander who interests us. Now he will have his kingdom back, and his stock will rise. But he is a beggar, my dear Lady Wellington. Soon, not now, but before too long, my rivals will realise it. Alexander needs credit. He will have to borrow more. There, I think, is an opportunity. I hope you will join me in that, Lady Wellington.'

'Let us wait and see, Nathan.'

'Moses, do listen when this dear lady speaks.' Nathan threw his head back and laughed. His shoulders shook and then stopped abruptly.

'I shall stop this idle chatter. I bid you good day, Lady Wellington; there is work to be done.' Nathan nodded at his brother-in-law.

'Adieu, Moses, and do not worry about Bonaparte. He is too busy to think of invasion; you can give that damned bugle to one of your charity boys.'

With another wave of the hand Nathan stepped inside no. 2 and closed the door behind him.

MR ROTHSCHILD CERTAINLY HAD the habit of surprise, Kitty reflected as she looked across at Harriet. It was one thing to feign no interest in her investment, but to let her know he had passed the information to his brother-in-law: that was quite another. Perhaps Harriet had that habit too. Certainly there were many things she held back despite her air of openness.

'So, you pass the time with Mr Winsor in debate?'

'We talk. But Kitty, can I tell you, he sometimes takes my hand and puts my arm through his.'

In Harriet's eyes Kitty noticed a look that was hooded and defiant; but at the same time she smiled broadly.

'Perhaps if my mother were alive I might talk it through with her; but then I wonder if such an experiment, for that is how I think of it, should be the subject of discussion.'

'I wonder if anyone can ever advise another on what they should do, Harriet.'

'But why not? I delight in advice.'

'When I was about your age, a little younger even, Arthur proposed for me to my brother Tom, and was refused by him. Perhaps you have heard that story.'

'It has been in all the newspapers.'

'Of course; no matter. While Arthur was away in India I made a new acquaintance, Lowry Cole. He is a general now, but then he was a book-ish colonel, neat and unobtrusive. Who knows whether we might have been suited to one another. He is quiet, as I am, and mindful of others, more than I can claim to be. I encouraged him and we walked out together. He made his interest clear, but when I told my dearest friend, she assured me that Arthur had written to her of his continued sense that he was bound to me. She counselled me to abandon Lowry and wait for Arthur.'

'But did she not think of your happiness?'

'I cannot lay any responsibility upon her; Arthur was a rich man by then, the victor of Assaye. She thought of my standing in the world. We both, perhaps, believed that when Arthur spoke of being bound, he intended affection rather than duty. No matter, Harriet. I was by then a grown woman. My happiness was at my disposal, and I threw it away. I refused Lowry.'

'Oh, Kitty. Do you think of him still?'

'I no longer wonder what might have been. My life has taken a differ-ent turn. I lacked courage, then.'

Kitty paused.

'If I may say so, circumstances are now more advantageous to you.'

'Can you explain?'

'In war old certainties dissolve. There are few to watch you, Harriet. You may have your experiment. Besides, you have done nothing wrong, if wrong there is in it.'

'Oh, nothing.'

Kitty took Harriet's hand.

'Believe me, Harriet. War is a time, perhaps the only time I know of, that women can do what they wish. I do not intend to waste it. Why should you?'

Harriet jumped up and searched round for her gloves, before she remembered that she had left Hatton Garden in a hurry and without them.

'Is that a piece of advice?'

To Harriet's surprise Kitty threw her head back and laughed.

'No, no. Just to listen to your own head and heart.'

'I call that advice. But I will, Kitty, I will.'

The butler came in and handed Kitty a note. Kitty scanned it with a practised eye. 'Mrs Fitzwilliam wishes to inform Lady Wellington that she is a widow. She would further be pleased to show your Ladyship the gift she mentioned when she visited Harley Street.'

'Is Mrs Fitzwilliam still below?'

'No, my Lady; but she asked me to draw your attention to the address she has written on the other side.'

Kitty turned the card over.

'Ah, yes.'

'May I venture to say, Lady Wellington, that she appeared less well dressed than on her last visit.'

On the reverse of the card was written simply: 'Eliza Fitzwilliam, 15 King's Place.'

'Is there anything amiss?' Harriet noticed that for a moment Kitty was discomforted.

'No. Upon reflection I believe I may have been given an opportunity that will serve me well. But it is a private matter.'

When Harriet had gone Kitty opened her writing box and put Mrs Fitzwilliam's note inside. That address was a beacon. For a hundred years King's Place had traded in only one commodity: female flesh. If Mrs Fitzwilliam had set up a bawdy-house she would not be in need of the small sums from the print she had put out a few weeks before. No, this was to tell Kitty something else.

I shall pay Mrs Fitzwilliam a visit, Kitty thought. 'There is more in her note than a simple request for money, and I may benefit from the knowledge of what it is.'

◦

IN THE DAYS THAT followed his last visit to Camille, James's languor turned to a restlessness that drove him outside. In the mornings he threw a few *reales* into his pocket and walked Seville's narrow streets. At midday he moved to the gardens of the great Moorish palace, the Alcázar, where once scholars in long robes had sat in tiled rooms and turned the pages of the Qur'ʾan. Now green oranges ripened in tubs under the windows and officials tried, in a desultory way, to resume city government after the long occupation by the French. In the evenings, when the sun went down behind the hills, he returned to the Casa Wiseman and hoped to find another summons to the Casa Florens.

Each day in October the heat receded a fraction of a degree. Towards the end of the month Stewart wrote that Lord Wellington had abandoned the siege of Burgos. The French armies from the south and east marched towards him and he would be forced to retreat west to the safety of Ciudad Rodrigo and Portugal. He needed information about the south and east urgently, Stewart wrote. Had James any news?

James read the letters and put them aside; they seemed like messages from a distant world. From Camille, however, came only silence. James filled it with desire. Waves of longing rolled through him like Atlantic breakers. He wanted to touch her eyes, her lips, her hair, to pull her towards him until his flesh became hers. He walked towards her with an inevitable step; she drew him on. Today or tomorrow he would go to her; he refused the idea that she might not want him.

One afternoon, as he walked out of the city in the mulberry groves by the great aqueduct it came to James that he had never felt that way about Harriet. He sat down under a tree and pulled from his breast pocket the miniature that he always carried. The girl it showed, impassive under the weight of her drawn-up, honey-coloured hair, looked almost unfamiliar. The light in her grey eyes was docile and sweet, nothing like Harriet's living, lively look. But James could not bring Harriet to mind, or, when he tried, hear her voice.

James decided, when he looked at Harriet's picture, that what was going to happen, what he would do, did not concern her. He need never tell her; should not, indeed. He wanted another woman. That was all, but such desire was foreign to Harriet's nature. She lacked his decisiveness; she would never throw her soul open for all to see as a gambler throws his most prized jewel on the table and stakes it to win everything with his last hand. Though she had courted and teased him once, Harriet was now his wife, and happy to be so.

In the evening, when he got back, he found a note from Camille.

'Come to me on Sunday at three.'

At the Casa Florens that Sunday, James found Camille dressed in a black gown trimmed with scarlet. Laura and Corinne sat either side of her as they had the first time he met them. All three were dressed to go out and the girls held twists of autumn flowers, white and golden and red.

'Mama, we are late already.'

'You will accompany us, Captain Raven?' Camille said.

'Are you going to Mass?'

'Please come,' Laura said and jumped up. 'We are going to the bull-fight.'

James glanced at Camille.

'Do,' she said. 'This is the first fight since the liberation of the city and the Maestranza has selected bulls with a value of ten thousand *reales*.'

'The Maestranza?'

'The noblemen of this city in association. They own the bullring and run the bullfights. You will see that the riding master, when he comes into the ring, asks permission of the Maestranza to begin.'

James thought of Robert Heaton. Did any Spaniard feel as Heaton did towards the animal kingdom, with unashamed sentiment and tenderness?

'You know, Señora Florens, that the very idea of hurting such a noble beast is frowned upon by British officers?'

'The same men who pursue a hapless fox for hours on end and then watch the hounds tear it limb from limb? Come, the girls will begin to fret.'

James followed Camille out into the courtyard at the back of the house and climbed into her open carriage. The two girls faced them. As soon as they left the house the carriage was caught up in a crowd that flowed towards the bullring. The women carried flowers, and wore mantillas against the sun; the men walked bareheaded or in wide brimmed hats. The mood was festive but subdued, as if the crowd had come from the solemnity of Mass into a fine bright day.

Left to himself James might have declined an invitation to the bullfight; but he did not think about the slaughter. His mind jumped over the next hours. Camille sat next to him silent and self-contained. The crowded benches, the hum of talk, the sunshine that fell across the sweep of the ring as they sat down in the Florens family box; everything appeared distant and indistinct. Only Camille stood out. She leant forward on her seat, one shoulder warm against his.

To the sound of trumpets a man in court dress rode into the ring, two footmen before and two behind him. An expectant hush fell over the ring, as the riding master bowed to a gold-framed portrait. James turned to Camille.

'Who is that?'

'He is the riding master of the Maestranza.'

'And why does he bow to the picture?'

'He asks leave to begin the contest. That portrait is our old King, Carlos. You know he is in exile now, Bonaparte's prisoner. Though he has abdicated in favour of his son, the most powerful men in the Maestranza prefer to keep faith with him, and show it thus.'

As the riding master caught the keys from the balcony of the gilded box of the Maestranza, the banderilleros, the picadors and the matador entered the ring to more music. The eyes of the crowd were all on the gate.

Camille leant into James.

'Now the bull will come in. You will see that he is nervous. He has been bred like a racehorse, for his strength and power, and tested in the fields for months. Yet he has never seen a standing man before, only men on horseback, so he cannot know what sort of creature the matador is when they come face to face. That is the contest that we wait for, and the bull is the most important figure in the spectacle. This is his moment, his theatre; man is merely his accompaniment.'

'*Toro!*' Corinne shouted in excitement.

The bull loped into the ring, confused by the brightness. James was surprised how small he was; not like the shambling bulls in Suffolk who stood higher than a man. This animal was compact, the power bred into a great chest and shoulders. A knot of ribbons rippled along his back as he turned this way and that, attracted by the coloured sashes of the picadors on their horses, the flash of their lances and their broad white hats. When the music died away the bull backed his rump against the safety of the wooden barrier that ran round the ring.

When the four horses saw the bull they shifted on their hooves in the sand. Silence spread across the arena. The bull noticed movement and turned to face one of the horses.

'*Toro!*'

The picador challenged the bull with a shout and raised his lance. The animal charged, and found himself turned by the lance, which plunged into his neck up to the crossbar. Across the arena another picador attracted his attention, and he turned and set off in pursuit, with a rivulet of blood down his muscled shoulder. This time he ignored the glint of the lance. Head down, eyes half-shut against the sunlight, he hurled himself at the horse. Tossed up and turned like a sheaf of summer hay, the horse bellowed and fell. A rope of grey intestine fell out of the gash in the horse's stomach and lay in a pile beside it on the tawny sand. Blood gushed down onto it. The crowd jeered; children pointed and laughed as the old nag staggered and fell.

Immediately the six banderilleros, each with a different coloured manteau, ran into the ring. Some ran to the aid of the fallen picador; others distracted the bull.

'*Viva toro, viva toro,*' the crowd chanted.

'*Viva, viva,*' Laura and Corinne shouted too, and jumped up from their seats.

'The bull is applauded when he unseats a rider.' Camille leant towards James. 'We know this bull is brave, that he gores with the right horn, and that he will challenge the matador to the height of his powers.'

James looked at the stricken horse. It had already given up the struggle and waited for death with resignation.

'It looks like a battlefield already.'

Corinne laughed.

'Then, Captain Raven, it is a situation that you understand.'

'Though in this fight there is only one winner.'

'You are quite wrong. The bull may sometimes garner an honour equal or superior to that of the matador.'

'He dies all the same.'

A look of scorn passed over Corinne's face.

'He will not surrender if he is brave, but die with honour. The matador too faces death and looks it in the eye.' She caught James's gaze. 'It is that that makes the matadors so interesting to women.'

'Indeed.'

'We value a soldier from the same motive.'

Harried by the picadors and weakened by the wounds in his neck and shoulders, the bull refused to charge at the horses any more. Instead he stood immobile against the boundary fence, his back legs tense, waiting for an assault or a new target to charge.

'Now is the turn of the banderilleros. They will tire the bull.'

The six banderilleros, dressed in breeches, waistcoats and wide sleeves, arranged themselves at intervals round the ring. They teased and played the bull, goaded him to charge and then, before he could reach them, they leapt over the parapet. More than once the bull ran straight at the wooden fence, smashed a horn through it and turned anew to face a new assailant. When the bull was distracted and tired, the banderilleros darted up to him and planted their gaily coloured sticks into his neck. One after another they tormented him until the bull lowered his head in confusion.

'Now the matador will perform the final act, that we call the act of death.'

Camille turned towards James and smiled. Her voice was remote and impersonal.

'He has to master the bull and prepare him for killing.'

James took the bull's side. The magnificent creature was bred merely to fight and die. What absurdity that he should be accorded honour or respect; words could mean nothing to a corpse, doubly nothing to a dead animal. He wished that the matador who bounded across the sand might suffer as the bull did.

'Sometimes the matador dies himself?'

Camille shook her head. 'Only if he fails in his task, does not break the animal's spirit and confronts him when he is still strong.'

'We will not see that today.'

'I do not believe so, though we have a brave bull. Look how he comes closer and closer to the man. He has learned that the manteau is a trick.'

James watched the animal charge time and again. The matador directed the bull, as a male dancer directs his partner, and forced him to run and turn at the rippling red manteau. Once the two curled horns, dark and polished, grazed the cream silk and silver braid of the matador's jacket. The matador stood still each time the bull passed him, his sword concealed behind his back. Closer and closer they whirled, came together and parted. Pushed on by his weight and speed, the bull strained to stop, turn and run again, maddened by his failure to gore his tormentor. Blood poured from the wounds in his shoulders and flowed in scarlet streams down his flanks.

As the bull went round, the matador shifted his weight from leg to leg and held the scarlet manteau out, now across his body, now to the side of it until the animal tired of the dance and the pursuit. Confused and exhausted, the bull stopped before the matador and confronted him, his great head lifted in enquiry.

Slowly the matador lowered his manteau and slowly the bull's sad eyes followed it, until he stood as docile as a supplicant before an altar. For a moment the matador faced the bull. He forced his mastery upon the animal and upon the spectators. In hushed anticipation people leant forward. Then, with every eye concentrated upon him, the matador struck. He lifted his right arm and jumped high and forward over the bull's neck. In one strong hit he thrust his sword in. The shining blade pierced the blood-mantled hide, and travelled straight into the beating heart.

The bull staggered and then sank. From his heart the lifeblood poured into the great cavity of his chest and down to his lungs. James followed the animal's death breath by breath, transfixed by his struggle. In a few seconds the bull had collapsed, pooled in gore, a mound of lifeless meat. Then the matador moved and bowed to the bull, to his spirit and fight. Next he turned and bowed to the crowd, to the rich in their boxes and the city poor crowded along the wooden seats all around the ring. People crossed themselves at the sight of the lifeless bull. Trumpets sounded and a great sigh floated up, an expulsion of death and inhalation of life.

Next to James, Laura and Corinne stood up and applauded the matador. In company with the women and children they hurled their flowers, singly or in bunches, into the bullring. Some littered the sand; others fell on the carcass itself, and lay bright against the blackened streams of blood that matted the curly hair of the bull's shoulders. The crowd stirred and shook itself. All around them people praised the animal and his adversary.

'The flowers are a tribute to the bravery of the bull,' Camille said.

We too lay flowers by corpses, James thought. We offer the dead that gift of fragile life against the darkness. He was angry at the sacrifice of the bull.

'Why cannot his life be spared?'

'Sometimes you will see it; but the beast would then be wise. He could never fight again. But we prefer the artistry to be complete. We like to finish the drama.'

'And to witness the death.'

'Acknowledge death and revere it; that is our tradition.'

The trumpets sounded and the next bull threw itself into the ring.

James was light-headed. The smell of blood rose from the ring and clung to his nostrils. The brassy, metallic odour brought back memories of all the battles he had fought. Only the wish to appear dignified kept him in his seat.

By the end of the fourth fight Camille's daughters fidgeted.

'Mama, it is time to go home.'

Laura pulled at her mother's gown. Camille stood up and offered her arm to James. Together they walked behind the girls to the carriage. James looked down into Camille's black eyes. They were hooded, almost sleepy. At the Casa Florens the evening air shimmered round the lamps in the peaceful courtyard. Camille called the maid and sent the girls to their nursery.

'Captain Raven and I have business to attend to,' she said.

Corinne stretched up two plump arms and kissed Camille as she leant over. Laura held out her hand to James in imitation of her mother. When the girls had gone Camille led the way up the stairs and into the great room where James had first met her. On the side, laid out with cold food under covers, sat a decanter and two glasses. Corinne poured and handed James a glass of light red wine.

'And now to business,' she said.

'What is our business?'

'Really, Captain Raven, do you not know why you are here this evening?'

'I hope that I do.'

'Good. Then why is it?'

'To serve you.'

'How will you serve me?'

'In any way you wish.' James knew he must now speak out. 'I have longed for you for many weeks.'

'Have you?'

'You know that I have. You must have felt it, heard it in my voice. Everything about you is exquisite, mysterious. I cannot explain it better. Does it need explanation? You see how I am.'

'Captain Raven, I have observed nothing.'

'Oh, do not torment me. You have made me yours.'

'I have done nothing.'

'As you wish. I shall put it another way. I wish to make you mine.'

'Then kiss me.'

He knew it was a command. He drew his finger across Camille's top lip as he had imagined doing so many times. In his eagerness he pulled her to him. Camille drew away.

'No. Come to me slowly.'

James found he had sunk to his knees before her and put his hands round her ankles. He bowed his head and touched her satin gown with his lips. With joy he felt her hand come down on his neck.

'Like this?' he said.

'Like that.'

Camille lifted her hand up. Obediently James rose with it. As he stood, she came towards him. When he put his arms around her, he felt not mastery but surrender.

~

'WELL, DOROTHY, I MUST say I approve of Harriet's high spirits. It is so delightful to see her transformed from the sad creature who arrived back here after the summer. London has that effect I find; it pushes one on. But it is more than that.'

Anne Cobbold and Dorothy Yallop sat at either side of the dining-room table. Squares of silk, each one sewn from two dozen strips, were scattered across the surface. Twists of thread hung out of a sewing box lined in green velvet. Glass-headed pins stuck out from a pincushion embroidered with the words 'Success to Trade, my Boys', one of Mrs Cobbold's earliest attempts at fancy work, and perhaps, she thought now, not in the best possible taste.

They had agreed, when Sir Arthur Wellesley first went out to the Peninsula nearly three years ago, that they would make a quilt together. 'It will be a tribute to our friendship and a pastime for the years of war,' Mrs Cobbold said. 'If Napoleon is defeated fast we will have a child's crib cover on our hands; the longer he holds out the bigger it will be.'

Mrs Cobbold did not admire quilts. They belonged in her mind to the country, to patching and making do, bottles and preserves, blanket chests and oak bedsteads. A quilt was a cloth of memories, or dreams, and Mrs Cobbold had little time for either. Her own town rooms demanded damask on the beds and at the windows; her fabrics looked forward and out, to India and the east. And then, a quilt, like the bits of fancy work that littered her friends' parlours, was diverting to make but less so to display. After years of labour many finished hidden in cupboards. She was relieved that this was to be Dorothy's quilt; they worked on it when she came to town and collected scraps and ideas when they were parted.

In the very centre Mrs Yallop placed a calico handkerchief, thickened with quilting and printed with a portrait of Sir John Moore. In the white sky behind floated the words 'Hero of Corunna'; the battlements of the town and the British fleet could be seen in the distance, stamped in blue.

Mrs Yallop patted Sir John Moore's padded head.

'There now. He looks good in the middle. My notion is to sew two rows of squares round him and then to begin a new section of embroidered scenes, one for each battle. Do you have the prints?'

'Yes, and I found a job lot in St Paul's Churchyard, besides, some new, some a few years old.'

Mrs Cobbold took out a print of Lord Wellington astride a cannon and turned it over. Such a scene was quite inappropriate on a bed cover, she was sure, and Mrs Yallop could scarcely wish to see such a depiction of the commander of the army of Great Britain.

'Here are a couple of Chelsea Pensioners with wooden legs and tankards of small beer. There are several charming naval scenes too: Aboukir Bay, Cape St Vincent, the Nile. How about them, Dorothy?'

'My talent is for the army line; but, the navy, why not? I can try my hand at anything, red or blue.'

Mrs Yallop pulled the prints to her side of the table.

'The death of Nelson. Dear me, all that rigging. Still, a challenge is what we are after, is it not, Anne? Spars and mainstays will keep me on my toes, and the Major will laugh to see them when he returns. But not those wounded men; no, I think we should set them aside.'

'Good, good.' Mrs Cobbold wanted to return to her earlier theme. 'Harriet and Lady Wellington have become fast friends. They spend time in the park with the children. Four boys, she tells me; such a good taste of family life.'

Mrs Yallop was silent. She was content to be childless herself; she and George were sufficient for one another. When women talked about their children, or praised those of acquaintances, she assumed an interested expression and thought about something else. But today Anne's chatter caught her attention. She had never heard Harriet speak about a child or seen her look with longing at the urchins who ran through Hatton Garden and stole Mrs Cobbold's apples in the autumn.

'Are you certain, my dear, that Harriet wishes for a family?'

'Wish it or not, Dorothy, she is likely to get it, and I am delighted that she is acquainting herself with the facts of family life.' Mrs Cobbold pulled several twists of silk thread from her sewing box and arranged them in a pile.

'Then, she has begun to read. You have no idea, Dorothy; books of chemistry such as my brother always had about the house. She has Sir Humphry Davy's *Elements of Chemical Philosophy*, quite new, she says, and Lavoisier's *Treatise*. Odd books too, such as a history of Brunswick.'

'What prompts this study, Anne?'

'She attends the lectures at the Royal Institution, and has a new acquaintance, who directs her reading. My brother would be charmed to see how diligent she is.'

'This acquaintance, who is he?'

'A chemist, I believe.' Mrs Cobbold had never asked Harriet about Mr Winsor though she knew he sent books; beyond his name she knew little about him.

Dorothy Yallop remembered her earliest married days, when George was a lieutenant and posted abroad. She had waved him off from the castle in Norwich and promised never to forget. Neither of them had a way with language. George showed his affection in deeds and in loyalty that was never spoken and as for her, she had never been one to mope about or make up things with words. George had written, of course, notes of military matters and observations of the country about him; but most of his letters were lost and those that did get through did not capture his spirit.

She had learned to wait and keep herself busy. But for every woman like herself there was another who simply disappeared, or turned flighty. Harriet, now, was more in that humour than in the mind to study. She was distracted, hurried, often out of the house.

'Will you lend a hand with these squares, my dear?' Dorothy Yallop asked when Harriet came into the parlour later in the afternoon. 'The bigger strips I am mistress of, but the smallest give my old fingers a deal of trouble.'

'Nonsense, Dorothy.' Harriet laughed. 'You love to affect old age, when I cannot figure you to be more than forty-five.'

'Add two years to that.' Mrs Yallop looked pleased. 'Perhaps you are right; but I should welcome your company.'

Harriet sat down and began to lay strips of silk one round the other to form a spiral square. A mustard stripe next to a pink was ugly. She pulled the strips apart and in a desultory way began again. Sewing, with its thimbles and delicate thread, had none of the satisfactions of chemistry. What could she discover? Nothing but the best way to achieve a tiny regular stitch or copy and quilt a print of the Duke of York on parade with the cavalry. A pastime was just that. Chemistry, or astronomy, changed the world.

Mrs Yallop held her needle up to the light, licked the end of her thread and pushed it through the eye with a steady hand.

'Anne tells me that you have undertaken a course of reading with a friend.'

'Mr Winsor; he shares my interest in experiment, but is a practical man of science. He intends to light London with gas, and will soon open his new works on Horseferry Road.'

Harriet threw down her needle and leaned towards Mrs Yallop.

'It is like nothing you have ever seen before; by the river at the old horse ferry, coal is unloaded onto ponies' backs and at the entrance to the works great tumbrels roll it to the burners. Once inside the works it is as if a hundred laboratories are put together, but in clouds of dust and steam. Mr Winsor is a man of science; he has thought of everything to make his venture a success. You know, Mrs Yallop, that if coal is burned, a noxious smell mingles with the gas produced?'

'I know nothing about gas, my dear, and hope I never have to. I have enough trouble to keep up with developments in artillery and explosives. There my knowledge stops.'

'Never mind; you will enjoy the light it produces soon enough, I am sure.'

Harriet rushed on. She was sure that Mrs Yallop took an interest despite the way she waved her needle in the air.

'The odour is produced by sulphuret of hydrogen. Mr Winsor has now built several great tanks by the furnaces. When the gas passes out of the retorts, it enters these wash tanks and the sulphuret is filtered out. It is a beautiful sight I assure you; great glass storage vessels sit in a line and pipes wind away from the top of them and into the gas pipes. One day even your house in Norwich will be lit by gas.'

'I am not sure Norwich has any need for such monstrous works.' Mrs Yallop did not listen closely to Harriet, but saw her animation, the way she had jumped up from the table and now stood by the fire as if she were held inside against her will.

'This Mr Winsor; who is he?'

'He comes from Brunswick, and has worked besides in Berlin and Paris.'

'Is he a young man then, or a man with a family?'

Was Frederick young? Shadows gathered round his eyes, but his voice, with its modulations like shallow Baltic waves, was ageless and light. Harriet had not considered his age.

'I believe he is here in London alone, Mrs Yallop; but I have given little thought to the matter. He is a man like Prospero with a "magic art". I learn from his knowledge; that is all.'

Was it her place to ask such questions, Mrs Yallop wondered when Harriet had left the room. When the Major had come back from America, the time of her inattention to him dropped away. Love, to her mind, was something like sewing, the work of care and patience. She frowned and gathered up the strips of silk scattered on the floor. Perhaps, when Captain Raven returned, Harriet would find her own way.

Up in her own room Harriet sat by the fire with a new biography of Frederick the Great on her lap. She did not read it. Mrs Yallop's question sat in her mind. She had been less than candid in her reply. Of course she had considered Frederick's age; or rather, not his years, but the way he looked. Twenty-five, thirty, forty, even. It did not matter. He was beautiful. She was drawn to him not simply because of his knowledge. It was his voice, too, and the way he put his hand on her arm to explain something, leaned towards her and opened his eyes a little wider. At those moments she urged him silently to bend to kiss her. She wanted more; the feel of his skin, his hand on the small of her back as he pulled her close in greeting, and though Frederick had given no hint of his intentions she felt sure that his interest in her was not that of a friend.

When Frederick sent books to Hatton Garden, Harriet returned the packages with her card in the loose paper wrapping. Soon she began to write notes on the back. 'I shall be by the north lodge of St James's Park today at two if you wish to walk', or 'I intend tomorrow to drive to Mr Soane's new Picture Gallery now going up at Dulwich, and would welcome a companion.' When they met Frederick kissed her on both cheeks in the continental style. He often linked his left arm through her right as they set off to stroll side by side. Harriet did not tell Dorothy or her aunt about these meetings. Their secrecy was one reason she knew that Frederick was more than a friend.

One December day they walked through the fields above the New Road where Harley Street came to an end until they reached a crowd of Irish navvies, a hundred strong, who laboured to dig the bed of the new canal that would run round the border of the Regent's Park planned by Mr Nash and join the Thames to the navigations already built northwards from Brentford locks. Frederick was elated by the sight.

'If the Prince consents, his new palace to be built here by Mr Nash may be lit by gas from the outset. I can run the pipes from Horseferry Road to Whitehall and the Haymarket, and then up the length of Mr Nash's new thoroughfare to the park gates.'

The National Light and Heat Company was about to open for business. After a tour of the premises, complete with a perfect demonstration of the process of extracting and storing gas, the clerk to the Parish of St Margaret's, Westminster, had signed a contract with the company to begin work. In a few months, Frederick explained, every street in the parish would be lit by gas. Other parishes would want the same. For now the Light and Heat Company must expand in this way, adding irregular segments of the city map to its reach. One day, perhaps, there might be a Board of Light and Heat, just as there was now a Navy Board or a Treasury Board, for was not the creation of power every bit as important to the nation as the rule of the waves and the collection of taxes?

In the week before Christmas, Frederick insisted that Harriet accompany him to Newton's in St Martin's Street.

'It is not one of your London chop-houses or inns, or a coffee house to sit with strangers and discuss the news.'

'And not a hotel, Frederick?'

'Above yes, but below, a pleasure house of food.'

'Named for a natural philosopher.'

Frederick laughed.

'I do not know why it has that name. It is run by an Italian, Pagliano.'

When she peered into the windows of Newton's, Harriet saw a large room, decorated in the light pastels of the end of the last century, and scattered with tables and upholstered chairs. Branching candelabra and pier-glasses with candles in the frames gave the space an intimate look. Pagliano, a fair northern Italian, sat at a desk in the hall, and jumped up when they came in.

'Signor Winsor. A delight.' He bowed at Frederick and then turned to Harriet. 'Madam, you are welcome. I do not believe to have seen you before.'

'No. This is new to me.'

'You will give me your cloak? And then I shall find a table for you.'

Seated in the corner of the room, Frederick shook out the cuffs on his fine wide-sleeved shirt and loosened his cravat. He looked at Harriet through the candlelight.

'Now we surrender ourselves into Pagliano's hands.'

'What will Signor Pagliano do with us?'

'Wait and see.' He paused. 'You look beautiful tonight.'

Harriet was silent. She felt breathless. Frederick took her hand across the table and drew it to his lips.

'So English, and yet there is something else too.'

'Nothing, I assure you. I come from Suffolk. But I do not want to think of that now.'

Frederick leaned forward then, and with a gentleness Harriet had never noticed in him before, tucked a stray strand of hair behind her neck. She felt his hand linger at the nape, and lightly run across her back.

'No, indeed. We have better things to do.'

The silence that fell was interrupted by Signor Pagliano, who came to the table with a waiter behind him. Together they unloaded onto the small table glasses, cutlery, a bottle of wine, a plate of meat, a dish of white beans in oil and napkins as white as snow which they flicked open and handed to Frederick and Harriet with a flourish.

'Now eat.'

After that, all through the veal, as soft as butter, through the vegetables and potatoes baked in cream and with every sip of the light wine, ran that other thing. Harriet let it happen, go along with their conversation, entwine itself around every word and gesture.

'Ice cream.' Signor Pagliano brought the dessert. Frederick scooped a spoonful from the porcelain dish.

'Taste it.' He leaned forward, his eyes on her. 'Cream, flavoured with vanilla, packed into pots and surrounded by ice and salt, so that it freezes itself. Cold as winter.'

The ice cream, granular and honey-coloured, was like nothing Harriet had ever tasted before.

'Delicious.'

Frederick caught her eye, and smiled, a lazy, sensuous, happy smile. He ran the thumb and forefinger of his right hand up and down the narrow stem of his wineglass. Harriet smiled back.

When Signor Pagliano brought Harriet's cloak a few minutes later, his hands stayed on her shoulders for a moment.

'You have enjoyed everything, madam?'

Frederick answered for her.

'It was just what we required.'

Then they were out in St Martin's Street, into the darkness. When he said goodbye to her, Frederick kissed Harriet on one cheek and then the other. His mouth brushed over hers so gently that she thought she might have imagined it, but wished she had not.

IN THE WEEKS THAT followed, London began to change before Harriet's eyes. The streets became grander, more luxuriant and latent with possibility. London burned golden and red. Grey old courts and houses sprang gilded fringes. Beneath the pavements the ground turned into a moving sea, and the ancient city, once so solid, now floated like a flagship on the tide. Worms sifted the friable soil as they bored their underground pathways. Slow and tender, roots pushed through the clay to drink the hidden rivers. Moles made honeycombs and water sluiced through new iron pipes. Soon, when jets were turned on in faraway streets and houses, inflammable air would dart away from the storage jars in Horseferry Road. The whole world tipped and spun. Who could know what anything was any more, when solids turned out to be in constant motion and high above them stars, planets and the infinite skies turned without pause. One thing she was sure of: she was part of this ceaseless movement, caught up in its agitation. Somewhere down over the horizon, so far away that the moon rose in a different part of the sky, James sat out the days of autumn. He was no longer a part of her, but a different being. She had allowed Frederick to come between them. She had wanted him to.

≈

JAMES AND CAMILLE LAY on her bed. Camille twisted James's golden hair in her fingers.

'There is good news from Felipe.'

James only half listened. He had left Madrid almost two months ago; after a couple of encouraging notes, General Stewart at Headquarters must have forgotten him. The war had washed back north and taken most of the army with it. Only General Hill was left south of Madrid, encamped along the north side of the Tagus River. Hill blocked the way to Madrid and from Madrid to the north of the country. King Joseph Bonaparte, the newspapers reported in the third week of October, had left his headquarters in Valencia and marched to join up with General Soult's army as it came up towards the south side of the river. The French planned to force Hill either to fight or retreat to the north or to Portugal. In the marshy lands south of the Tagus and in the Montes de Toledo beyond, the partisans moved about at will and struck at the French wherever they came across them.

'One of his men arrived this morning with a note. Felipe and his men came across a French convoy from the stores at Requena; twenty loaded wagons sent by King Joseph's quartermaster to relieve the scarcity in Soult's army.'

Camille sat up in the half-darkness. She turned to him and ran her hand down his cheek and onto his chest. James stretched out again, his head under the window. In the flicker of the lamplight he saw a vein beat in the soft concavity beside her hip bone. Beyond the open shutters a tangle of stars travelled the sky.

'I am proud of my brother. You know how hungry his fighters are, and winter is almost here. He sent a courier to the British at Fuente Dueñas, as you have asked. The British came out, crossed the Tagus where it is still fordable, took the whole convoy and dozens of prisoners too.'

James felt weary when Camille spoke about the war. The French were weakened more by their own withdrawals of troops to other countries rather than by Lord Wellington's efforts and Spain turned against itself. True enough, the General still held Ciudad Rodrigo and Badajoz, and Madrid, for the moment, was free; but after four years of war, hardened soldiers might have expected more, let alone their paymasters in London. As for himself, there was nothing to be done but his duty as an officer.

'That is welcome news. I shall wait to hear from him and trust that General Cole at Fuente Dueñas will in turn inform General Stewart at Headquarters. But I do not want to think about the war now.'

James stretched a hand to Camille and ran a finger over the sharp angle of her hip to the warmth of the thigh beyond. He put his ear to the milky skin of a wrist; heard the heart beat and blood pulse beneath her skin. He looked at Camille's eyelid and noticed at its edge a shallow wrinkle, a gathering of her flesh that was new to him. The sight made him shift sideways with tenderness. That small tributary depression would deepen and branch as time advanced and the years stamped their mark on her flesh. Why, he thought, do we give the laurels to youth, when age and endurance are so precious?

'You are beautiful, Camille; you are so beautiful.'

Camille smiled and said nothing.

'I ADORE YOU,' JAMES said to himself as he walked home through the narrow streets. He wanted to shout the words, or sing them, so they rang back off the stone walls. Seville shone in the moonlight. Even the beggars, many in ragged remnants of the Spanish army uniform, huddled in doorways and along the great wall of the cathedral, were touched with silvery enchantment. Surely, James thought, there is nowhere on earth so fine as Seville tonight; nowhere, from Rome to the cities of the Orient, so luminous and graceful. At the Casa Wiseman he poured himself a glass of wine and watched the ruby red carry the light down into its depths. For the sake of form rather than taste he dashed a few drops of water into the glass, and lay back on his bed.

As James fell asleep his thoughts travelled over the Peninsula to Harriet. He saw her in Hatton Garden with a muslin nightdress, gathered and frilled at the cuffs, tucked under her legs. A strand of light brown hair lay across her eyes. Her face was serene, unmarked by time or sadness. But the picture did not hold him. At once he allowed another vision to replace it; Camille, with her exquisite smallness, the bottomless black of her eyes, the round curve of her spine in the silk expanse of her back, the sharp ringing laugh that echoed through the room.

As WINTER TOOK HOLD, Felipe Odonnell sent word that Marshal Soult's divisions had crossed the Tagus and attacked the British at the Puente Larga. From the safety of the high ground Felipe watched as General Cole repulsed the French regiments and forced them to fall back. Then, in the night the whole British force began to retreat. By the morning they had gone. Madrid was open to the French, and three days later King Joseph Bonaparte had returned.

General Wellington, it appeared, had withdrawn from the country around Burgos and sent for Hill and Cole to join his army at Salamanca. Harried by the French all the way, the two forces were united on the banks of the River Tormes and prepared to push on towards Ciudad Rodrigo and the safety of Portugal.

'Felipe tells me that his work here is done. All of Spain south of Madrid is free. He intends to move with the war, perhaps, and begin again in the spring. He has not forgotten his agreement, and will work with General Cuesta and others to find the French and hand them over.'

By the beginning of December, with the British army in winter bivouacs, James still waited for orders to leave Seville. The war had left him behind. Did anyone at Headquarters remember where he was? Had the Major, even, put in a demand for his return to the regiment? With the whole of Spain south of Madrid left to itself, did anyone give the mission more than a passing thought? Nothing, now, would happen before the spring. He might stay on in Seville unregarded; indeed he had no choice until he could find out where the 9th was quartered and be sure it was safe to travel alone.

And so he stayed on at the Casa Wiseman. Each day a manservant arrived from the Casa Florens at the same hour. Each day James followed him through the narrow streets that darkened a little every day as the year advanced and winter took hold. He lived for this moment. At the Casa Florens he would fold himself into Camille as if he bandaged them together. Once or twice he waved her servant away and told himself he would not go back; but the longing always overcame him. After a day without her he felt broken and incomplete; an hour after he left her he wanted to return.

～

FROM SEVEN DIALS KITTY walked through the maze of streets and courts that opened into Long Acre, where the atmosphere was coloured by the closeness of Covent Garden. She felt more curiosity than trepidation about her mission. No one recognised her in this teeming place. Straw and vegetable scraps from Covent Garden market lay underfoot. Gentlemen walked with discretion, their hats pulled down, and barrow boys raced one another down the flagged streets now their day's work was done.

King's Place, behind the churchyard, had an air of paint-thick prosperity. The houses were a hundred years old, smaller and squarer than those now favoured by men of property. Their panelled doors, with oblong toplights and fluted wooden surrounds, stood open in invitation. Paint peeled off them in tongues. Behind each door sat a madam, on a chair or at a desk, to welcome custom and keep the girls from escape. Glimpsed through ground-floor windows the parlours gave off the temporary grandeur of ornate divans and ormolu side tables.

Kitty rang the bell of no. 15, pushed back the half-open door and walked in as any man might do. A woman about her own age, dressed in a red gown in the latest style, came out of the back parlour. Her lips were stained with cochineal and the scent of eau de roses followed her in a sweet cloud.

'Good afternoon, madam. I am here for Mrs Fitzwilliam.'

'Mrs Fitzwilliam? Your business, madam?'

'A private matter.'

'Very well; your name, if I am to send for her to come down?'

'I should like to be shown up. You may tell her that I am come from Hamilton Place in response to her note.'

Kitty felt the woman's shrewd gaze pass over her velvet cloak and soft leather shoes.

'Mrs Fitzwilliam is unwell; and behind with the rent. They only stay here on my charity.'

So someone is with her, Kitty thought.

'You do her a service; I understand.'

'First floor, at the front. If you wish to see her you may go up.'

There was no reply when Kitty knocked at the door. She walked into the half-darkness. The remains of daylight, filtered red, seeped through the thin curtains. A bed with tousled covers stood against the back wall. Mrs Fitzwilliam sat in a greasy armchair near the fire. Her pale skin was flushed; two bright spots of fever burned in her cheeks, and her lustrous curls now lay matted against her head. She gazed at her visitor with no recognition.

Kitty knew that look; the heat and the green tinge beneath the eyes. She tried not to draw back. Consumption might pass from person to person in the air. No one knew, but it flourished in tight spaces and the courts and alleys of old cities. There was no cure. Some, with strong lungs and in a dry atmosphere, could expel it. Mrs Fitzwilliam, by the look of her, was past that hope.

Next to the armchair was a battered crib made from dark oak.

'Mrs Fitzwilliam; it is I, Lady Wellington.'

Mrs Fitzwilliam did not acknowledge her greeting.

'You have a child.'

Kitty looked down at the baby, angry and red-faced in the crib. The blankets were dirty, and the child had scabs round his mouth and raw patches of red on the backs of his hands. He gazed at her with empty eyes.

'He must be three months old. It is a boy, is it not, Mrs Fitzwilliam?'

'Ah, yes. Lady Wellington.'

'His name?'

Mrs Fitzwilliam struggled to sit up straight in the chair. Her breath came in long gasps, like the retreat of the sea over pebbles. Kitty found she held her own breath in, and exhaled with her. Perhaps Mrs Fitzwilliam breathed more easily with her sympathy. But when she was composed she turned her flushed face to Kitty.

'Joseph Arthur.'

This time, Kitty heard no calculation in her voice.

'Arthur; for him.'

Shrunk against the back of the chair, absorbed by fever, Mrs Fitzwilliam showed no interest in her child. The sleeve of her gown was covered in blood. She wore no stockings and shoes. Yet, as the widow of an officer, she ought not to be so utterly destitute.

'Do you not draw a pension, Mrs Fitzwilliam? It will not be much, I am sure, but enough to see you through.'

The gurgle that came from the chair might have started as a laugh but became a cough on the first indrawn breath. Mrs Fitzwilliam leaned over and struggled for air. A rope of blood and mucus fell from her open mouth. Kitty picked up the chamber pot that stood on the floor, put it on Mrs Fitzwilliam's lap and stood back.

For several minutes Mrs Fitzwilliam coughed out all the air she had drawn with such difficulty into her lungs. Her face flushed and her thin body bent over in pain. When she became quiet Kitty began again.

'You are the widow of an officer.'

'You mean Captain Fitzwilliam?' There was a rasp of irony in the thin voice. 'Lady Wellington, you know the procedures of the Pensions Board. Every widow must produce a copy of her marriage lines from a parish clerk. You think I have one? I never went near a church with the Captain. I took his name and his money, but I am still Eliza Parker.'

She smiled, a smile half bitter and half childlike. Red spots had returned to her cheeks.

'Besides, it matters little.'

'You will please accept something from me in my private capacity?'

Sunk in her fevered world, Mrs Fitzwilliam seemed not to have heard. Would Mr Rothschild give money to Mrs Fitzwilliam? Kitty wondered in the silence. She was sure he would not. At New Court one afternoon he had said to her, 'I have met many clever men who had no shoes to their feet. I never act with them. If a man cannot get shoes for himself, what use can he be to me?' But then, this was not business. Did she think, then, to give money on her husband's behalf? Arthur did not need, and would not want, her protection. His opinion had always been that a really great man would ride out any insults to his reputation. He would never yield to any threat from a woman, or any entreaty either; but then, he did not think any woman worth his pity. She need not soften on his account. On the child's then, on the off-chance that it was his? There was no means of telling that, and though Mrs Fitzwilliam had tried, with a vestige of her old spirit, to interest her in the child, it was obvious to Kitty that she was beyond caring either for herself or for the little boy. Very well, it mattered not. She would give the money as a kindness from herself and leave it at that.

'Take this, Mrs Fitzwilliam. It is a banker's draft. Do not sell it on the street at a discount; take it to Messrs Coutts in the Strand, or send the woman with it. Make sure she cashes it there for face value and does not pocket more than the rent you owe her. The remainder should see you through the next few months.'

Mrs Fitzwilliam stared at the meagre fire in the grate. She glanced at the bank draft that Kitty placed on the arm of the chair.

'You may take the child. I swear, Lady Wellington, it is his. I was with the Captain when I met him, to be sure; but never after.'

'No, indeed I shall not take him. Your child has need of you, Mrs Fitz-william, and he will be the greatest joy to you when you are better.'

'I shall not get well. Cannot you see that yourself?'

'There are often remarkable cures of those with your condition, Mrs Fitzwilliam. Take your child to the country, where the air is dry. There you may rest and get well.'

'I cough more blood every day and struggle for breath. Besides, what do I have to live for? Mr Fitzwilliam is dead and I am too weak to work.'

'Your son.'

'His son.'

Kitty turned to look at the baby. She could see nothing of Arthur in his small angry face. He opened his eyes. They were still that indeterminate milky colour, somewhere between brown and blue. He is not Arthur's son, she thought suddenly, or it matters little if he is or not. I have allowed my anxiety to get in the way and taken no notice of the most important thing.

This little boy is a scrap I should take care of, and not just as a helpless parcel of humanity. I must look upon him as an investment, and no ordinary investment at that. She smiled to herself. No, I must regard him as a real risk, not as a gift that yields a small steady return, as charity does for the philanthropic. He will do much more for me than that, and at no cost to himself, if he will stay alive.

'I cannot say anything about that. But do not despair, Mrs Fitzwilliam. I will not lose sight of you, or your baby.'

Even in her fever Mrs Fitzwilliam sensed that something between them had changed.

'When you are well, we shall meet again. Remember what I said in Harley Street, Mrs Fitzwilliam. You and I are on the same side.'

Mrs Fitzwilliam had let the banker's draft fall to the floor. Kitty picked it up and put it on the greasy table by the bed.

'Goodbye, Mrs Fitzwilliam. Try to take care of yourself.'

Downstairs, Kitty stopped by the parlour door.

'I wish you good day, madam,' she said into the silence. 'You asked my name. I am Lady Wellington. You may remember one day that I have been here. If Mrs Fitzwilliam's circumstances change I trust that you will send for me. I shall not leave a card. It will be easy enough to find where I live if the need arises. Should you go to such trouble I shall naturally make it worth your while.'

∼

By mid-December in Seville the last of the swallows that gathered in the trees outside the Casa Wiseman had flown south. One day Camille's servant did not come. James waited in the gathering darkness, baffled. At first he consoled himself.

'She has an unexpected visitor and cannot send me word.'

He was unwilling to leave the house in case a message arrived, and paced his room back and forth all afternoon. Once he heard steps in the corridor and snatched open the door. The maid had already passed and turned down the stairs.

'One of the girls is unwell and needs her attention. She herself may be indisposed.'

By evening, as he dressed for dinner, James had begun to doubt his own reassurance. How little he knew of Camille beyond her life at the Casa Florens. He told himself that that did not matter. Women were the spoils of war; his time with Camille meant no more than that. As he slipped on his dress shoes and pulled down his shirt cuffs inside his jacket, he almost believed it.

In the brick-floored dining room the winter carpets had recently gone down. The Wiseman family and their guests talked politics with their fish.

Patrick Wiseman spoke pure Castilian as well as the local dialect, but his pale countenance was unmistakably Irish. He liked to ask questions and answer them himself, with a mournful air.

'Where do we live now, I ask you, dear friends?' He pushed his glass back and forth in front of him. 'Let me tell you. Our country is trampled over by warring powers and carved up by the partisans for their purposes. We are starving and helpless. What a disaster.'

'We have the new Constitution,' said Mr Wetherall, an English leather merchant.

'And what use is that? The Cortes sits in Cadiz, making castles in the air. The wretched Regency is terrified of the Cortes and will refuse to enact any legislation. We are a country with no government.'

'The Constitution offers our country a path to a moderate monarchy,' said Señor Mantero, a visitor from Madrid.

Wiseman sniffed. His face was flushed and his blue eyes darted about.

'Monarchy? Our dear king, our useless Fernando, is Bonaparte's prisoner. Who have we instead? The Regency—or, if you prefer, Joseph Bonaparte, who runs in and out of Madrid like a mouse in a hole, and waits for orders from his brother the Emperor.'

Mr Wetherall leaned forward over the table towards his host.

'Señor Mantero refers perhaps to the liberation of Spain by the British and the establishment of a monarchy along the English lines. Fernando will come back and work with the Cortes to rebuild our country and regain control over the colonies.'

'You place too much faith in your British countrymen,' Patrick Wiseman said.

'You do not trust the British, Señor Wiseman?' Mantero asked.

'No Irishman has ever had cause to do so. The only liberty the British love is their own. They may talk of freeing this country from tyranny, but Spain for them is no more than a battleground. Lord Wellington is an enemy of democracy and will never allow your famous Constitution to stand.'

'You are saying our countrymen fight in vain?' asked Mantero.

'I merely ask what we have achieved after four years of war, and I see nothing.' Wiseman looked round the table. 'Will Spain be different at the end, whenever the end comes? The same wretched country scorched with new hatreds, family against family, father against son. When the war is over, and Bonaparte removed, what will the partisans do then? Join the government, whatever it may be? Some, perhaps. Others will be reluctant to give up their forces or cede back the territory they now control. If they do disarm they will nurse their hatreds. Even when peace comes war will smoulder for generations.' He shook his head. 'Rage in a hot country; it never dies. Very bad for business, too.'

James was silent. The talk washed over him. Where was she? He excused himself and went to his room, to sit out the night in the darkness. His duty and his career as an officer: they seemed as remote and cut off from him as the talk round the table.

The next day, as early as an officer could be seen on the street without exciting comment, he walked to the Casa Florens. The tall narrow windows onto the street were shuttered, the huge gate closed. He pulled on the bell and waited. After a few minutes he heard footsteps and the heavy half-door scraped back. A footman stood behind it.

'Please inform la Señora Florens that Captain Raven is below.'

The footman peered at him from behind the half-open door.

'La Señora Florens ha marchado al campo.'

'She has gone into the country?'

'Se ha ido a su finca.'

'To her country estate?' James had never heard Camille speak of a house in the country. He did not even know she had one.

'Y las señoritas?'

'Toda la familia.' The footman took a step back as if he wished to end the conversation.

'The whole family. When do they return?'

The footman stood impassive. Beyond him the water in the courtyard fountain fell in flounces from one tier to another. The great house was silent, the upper gallery deserted, the far door into the garden closed.

'She will return when she sends word. We never know when that may be. I bid you good day, sir.'

'Wait. A message.'

No. No message. What was there he could say? James thanked the footman and turned away. With his first step he heard the door swing closed on its oiled hinges. Then the great iron bar came down across it.

Once in the street he could not think of walking back to the Casa Wiseman. He took the opposite direction and at the northern gate struck off from the Madrid highway onto a rutted unmade path, one of the *caminos de perdices*, roads for partridges, the Spaniards called them, sandy tracks that wound through the fields and across the hills, familiar to shepherds and their dogs.

With no care for the time, James began to walk through fields of leafless mulberry trees towards the blue line of mountains. Beyond the peaks lay the uplands, Madrid, the road to Christian lands that had escaped centuries ago from the enchantment that gripped Seville; lighter sky and the Biscay coast. Up there were the General, the army, and the tattered remnants of his own career that must be patched and darned for his survival.

Hours later, as the sun went down and took with it the crystalline glimmers from the rock, James sat down on an outcrop by the side of the path. With horror he realised that tears streamed down his face and he could not remember when he had begun to cry. He sat for some minutes, his head in his hands, and let the tears fall; then he pulled out his handkerchief and rubbed his face dry.

A tide of dust rose up his boots. Even to himself he looked dishevelled. But what did it matter. Camille had gone, or found another lover, a Spaniard with a country estate near hers. Somewhere up in the hills, with the fires already lit against the evening chill and flames dancing in shoals across the darkening walls, Camille was with him, her laugh deep in her throat and her white neck tipped back.

The more James dwelt on Camille the more she dissolved into the anger and emptiness in his heart. He felt with certainty that he would never see her again, and never lie next to her. Was she simply a sensualist?

he wondered. Had she built a bulwark against the knowledge of carnage, as many seemed to do here in Spain; passion against blood, love against the losses of war? He could not tell. Perhaps it mattered only that whatever purpose he had served was finished for her.

It was almost dark now, ink-black over to his left. James knew he must reach the outskirts of the city while some light stayed in the western sky. The path seemed to wander and narrow as he walked. Gorse bushes clutched at him and pulled tears in his clothes.

'AH, GOOD EVENING, CAPTAIN Raven.' Out of politeness Señor Wiseman kept his eyes on James's face. 'You have a visitor in your room. Now I must dress for dinner. I shall see you there.'

Camille waited for him. James saw her in his room. She would rise from the bed and come to him, embrace him. Already he could feel the smoothness of her skin as he pulled up her gown, the moment when the barrier of their flesh was melted and they became one creature, whole and light. The last two days would be erased; everything, everything he wanted would be there in that small space. The emptiness in his heart filled in that second with joy and forgetfulness of himself. He turned the door handle. Major Yallop, dressed for dinner, stood by the fire.

'You are surprised to see me, James.'

'George. Major Yallop.'

The Major's familiar scarlet jacket brought the 9th Regiment, and the whole of James's life in the British army, into the room. He forced his mind back to the surface and was surprised to feel nothing but a faint jolt, as if he had been asleep for a second.

'Why are you here?'

'Might I sit down?' Major Yallop took no notice of James's clothes but he sat down with care.

'I volunteered to come with your recall papers. You know the General has lifted the siege at Burgos and taken the whole army over into Portugal. The French dogged us closely on the retreat. It was a miserable march I can tell you. I left the men in Captain Heaton's hands, persuaded him to leave the 44th and come over to me for a few weeks.'

'There will be no more engagements this year, you say?'

'Not until the spring; you know the rhythm of war. I have everything organised and the men fed and exercised. Heaton is a careful man. A brisk ride down here was certainly preferable than to stay and pace about.'

The Major had kept James in a corner of his mind all through the autumn. When a letter came from Dorothy with a mention of Harriet he seized the opportunity to come down and find him. Now he considered him; left on his own, Captain Raven had let his appearance go. He seemed distracted, too, as if he had quite forgotten the war, and that beyond Spain other nations still fought against the encroachments of the French. It was time to take him back to camp.

'I thought I might take in a dance or two while I was about it; but perhaps it might be as well to set off before the worst of the weather sets in. It can be bleak up in the mountains, and I never like to leave my men for too long.'

'Retreat into Portugal is a setback.'

'Indeed; but word is that the General will use the winter to put pressure on London; point out that the government is wasting millions on subsidies to Spain; threaten to stay put until he has the promise of cash. And to prove his resolve he has encouraged diversions; balls, games and hunting. You know the kind of thing. He will make sure reports of our idleness get into all the newspapers.'

Yallop glanced at James's torn trousers and then down at his own immaculate uniform and polished boots.

'And you? What have you been doing? Kicking your heels?'

James gazed over the Major's head and out into the night city. On the far side of the street a man and a servant stood wrapped in dark cloaks. The servant held an oil lamp. The man waited for a woman, perhaps. James wanted to watch until she arrived, until they kissed, stood back and walked away together.

For a little while James was determined to tell Yallop everything. A fellow feeling, gathered from the scene across the street, swept over him and settled on the Major as he sat neat and reserved by the fire. He, too, must carry secrets. Then he remembered Harriet, Mrs Cobbold, Dorothy Yallop. No, he must remain silent at all costs, though his heart was sacked and empty, its chambers open and bare.

'Indeed, I have become a rambler. Today I lost my way.' He gestured out of the window. 'It is, as you say, Major, time to leave.'

'What do you say to tomorrow? There is nothing to keep either of us in this place. One more thing. I took the liberty of bringing your manservant with me.'

'Thomas Orde? Is he here?'

'He has been useful, I must say; a quiet traveller, too. But now we should be gone. I should like to reach the valley of the Tagus before the rains make our passage too difficult.'

'Is Thomas below?'

'I left him at the inn. I thought here you would have men enough to wait on you. What do you say to an early start?'

There was nothing James could think of in objection. His old world seemed to close in on him. He could not escape it.

'You go down, George. I shall wash and change and be with you in a moment.'

'Very well.'

Alone in his room, James sat motionless. To leave the next day; it was impossible without some word from Camille. He needed to confront her—no, to beg her if he had to. But to what purpose? He felt limp and exhausted, hollowed out by longing and loss. Perhaps he and Camille had been engaged in some sort of struggle or contest. Whatever it was had been decided decisively in her favour.

He pulled off his ragged trousers and dirty shirt and washed himself. When he lifted the lid of his trunk he saw the copy of *Corinne* that Camille had sent him three months ago. He had never finished it, or even read much beyond the first few chapters. But it was too late to read it now, and what good would an explanation do, that understanding she had spoken of, but tell him what he already understood, that she no longer wanted him.

A clean shirt and trousers lay ready in his trunk. He pulled them out. To dress for dinner, and the rest of his life. That was as much as he wished to accomplish this evening. If he could act that part for the Major he might, in time, perfect it for himself.

8

London and Freneda, Portugal

WINTER AND SPRING 1812–13

At the beginning of February Harriet walked to visit Frederick at home in Pall Mall. She arrived at the end of a dank afternoon when the grey sky dripped to sooty night and the new triple gaslights glowed in haloes of mist. When the door of no. 97 was opened, she saw that it was just as dim inside.

Frederick sat at a table in his library, dressed in a brown suit. His coat and trousers merged into the gloom.

'You live in the shadows, Fredcrick.'

Frederick said nothing but continued to sit and look at her.

'Or in various depths of shadow, I should say. Why do you not use your own lights in this house? I hear that in a room like this one it would be light enough with gas to read in any part.'

'I should never desire that.'

'But you have said that you wish to eradicate the shadows.'

'In my own house I live as I choose.'

'Indeed I find it admirable that you do so, Frederick.'

'Let us light the lights, then, since you wish it.'

Phosphorus, she thought, suddenly, not mercury, was Frederick's real element. A picture came to her of the phosphorus in the laboratory, the way it lay in its liquid, docile and quiet. Pull it out and, with a rush of air, it burst all at once into flame. The bearer of light, it was called. The devil's own element, her father used to say, though it was not until she studied Latin herself that she understood what he meant.

Frederick stood up with a stiffness to his movements that Harriet had not observed before, took a taper from the table beside him and lit it from the candle flame. Then he walked with decision round the room, turned the handles to the new candelabra one by one, and put the taper to the gas. In a minute the whole space was bright and merciless.

'We must look like ghosts to one another now,' Harriet said.

'That is what you want, is it not, a change of scene?'

'Yes, quite a new life.'

Was that what she wished for? What she wanted, was him.

'You wish to touch me, Harriet.'

Frederick finished his tour of the room and stood by her side. Harriet could not look at him.

'No, indeed, Frederick.'

But she knew that she did, and that ever since their evening at Newton's hotel she had wanted to touch him, to put her hand on his sleeve and feel him turn towards her.

'Harriet, I can feel it.'

'How can you feel it?'

'I am a man of science who observes effects, in the case I speak of an effect upon myself.'

Frederick's voice quietened; its German rhythm became more pronounced.

'I believe you have felt those effects too and therefore we already have the answer.'

Harriet said nothing. Frederick took her face in his hands, bent his own down towards it and kissed her. He drew her towards him with decision. She heard herself gasp and pull back. Frederick laughed.

'I admire you; shall we leave it at that? I shall turn off the lights in this room. There is a fire in the bedchamber; it is warm there. Should you like to go through?'

'Yes.'

'Then wait for me.'

Harriet crossed the hall from the library and went into the room on the other side. She sat down on the very edge of the bed and looked at her own hands. They lay in her lap as if they belonged to someone else. Should she leave? At such a moment a woman, and a married woman, ought to consider, take stock, and act with dignity. She had time to gather up her things and go. A picture of her cloak as it lay over the back of the sofa in the drawing room came to her. If she stood up now, she might pick it up, and go out without a word.

But was it not she who had sent notes to Frederick, she who had arranged their meetings? Had she not longed for this moment without saying it aloud to herself, planned for it step by step? In nature nothing could stop the conjunction of two elements with a chemical affinity once they were placed side by side.

'Do not leave,' Frederick called out from the other room. He anticipated her thoughts.

'No. I am here.'

'And please, do not remove your clothes.'

He came through the doorway into the shadows.

'You know why I say that?'

'No.'

'I wish to have the pleasure myself.'

'COME AND SIT WITH me, my dear,' Mrs Cobbold said after dinner the next day, 'there is a good deal of the evening still to while away.'

'Oh, thank you, Aunt, but I cannot. I have letters to write.'

'Write them in the parlour, Harriet. There is something about you, something feverish that I cannot put my finger on. Are you brooding about the war?'

They walked into the old-fashioned parlour and sat one on each side of the fireplace.

'Now, do tell me what worries you.'

'It is nothing. It is just that everything has turned out quite differently from what I expected. There seems to be so little that I understand.'

'Nonsense, Harriet. You are an accomplished girl.'

Mrs Cobbold flicked specks of dust off the maroon velvet of her gown with a plump, worn hand. She considered her niece by the firelight. Harriet looked a good deal thinner, perhaps. She had been out too much lately, who knew where. I have been remiss, Mrs Cobbold thought, I have allowed myself to forget the delicate health and nervous disposition of her mother. All this talk of science has confused me; I have been thinking of dear William, and not enough of Diana, who was charming, but quite wrong in every way for her William. Bad blood, it is said, runs in families. I must be alert to it.

'You have been tiring yourself, I dare say.'

What could she reply? Harriet asked herself. She could not tell Mrs Cobbold how her amusing, chance acquaintance with Frederick had turned into something else, and she had wanted it to. Even now, this very minute, as Mrs Cobbold sat with that look of benevolent concern on her face, everything that had happened the evening before was with her. She felt taut and alive with excitement. Frederick's voice, light and insistent, sounded in her head and flowed through her body like a liquid. Was it the sensation of her hands on him that she remembered or the feel of his hands on her? Everything had turned inside out; her skin, her body and time itself were peeled away. A feeling of exultation accompanied her home.

Tired? How should she be tired? She remembered that her father had taken her aside after her betrothal. There were certain things she should expect as a married woman, he said, and glanced into her eyes to be sure she understood. A man's infidelity must be looked upon in the same light as drunkenness; nothing more. Whereas a wife who betrayed a husband . . . Sir William had stopped and leaned away from her, as if the horror of such a thing needed no explanation.

But no; delight filled her. She wanted Frederick. Nothing that had happened last night could be submitted to the judgement that her father had hinted at. It was the force of life itself, its great electrical charge. There was no shame in that.

'Harriet, I asked if you are weary?'

'Perhaps so, Aunt; but it is more that I find this life unexpected.'

'It is the wait for news from the Peninsula, I dare say.'

'Yes, indeed.'

When had she last had a letter from Spain? Harriet could not remember; how could it matter, especially today? A picture of James came to her in his captain's uniform, buttoned up, and far away.

'You have surely heard from James since Christmas, though now we talk of it, I can recall no mention of any letter.'

'That is true, Aunt. I have not had a letter for some months.'

'Well, that accounts for your dejection.'

'It does indeed depend on proximity to a port, or a friend at Headquarters who will send a letter with official business. I have heard from Dr McBride, who has made a friend of Dr McGrigor, it seems, and has ready access to the post. He assures me that all is well.'

David McBride wrote with an elegance that must have come from the need to describe his patients' conditions, and in something of the same spirit, Harriet thought. David seemed to know nothing of James's whereabouts, and yet wrote to reassure her. Harriet had not shown Mrs Cobbold his letter. There was something in its tone that made it a private communication despite its formality and reserve. Besides she had soon set it aside. She felt easier when she did not think of her husband, and she had no wish to be reminded of him by Dr McBride.

'Perhaps, my dear, you will come with me to church on Sunday. To take in a sermon does me the world of good and I am sure you will benefit too.'

MRS COBBOLD ENJOYED THE consolations of religion. Sunday service was a fixed point in her week, and although her attention might wander to the housekeeping or her neighbour's gloves the sermon was always a pleasant pause. She did not listen exactly, but she imbibed the spirit of the preacher's message, and sometimes, when she wore her old poke bonnet, she took the chance of a discreet sleep. The chapel of St Etheldreda's in Ely Place just down from her front door was a peaceful place and held reliably to the old ways. Mrs Cobbold liked to vary her Sundays; she went every now and again to hear the fine organ at St Anne and St Agnes in Gresham Street or to gaze at the fine stained glass in the windows of St Andrew's on Holborn. She disapproved of too much enthusiasm and for that reason avoided her nearest chapel in Cross Street where crowds came from the most fashionable parts of town to listen to the Reverend Lucas denounce the evils of luxury. Mrs Cobbold sighed when she thought of it. Sunday was a day of rest, not excitement. Besides, why muddle up God and Mammon? The Good Samaritan could not have done his work without a full purse.

Harriet had often accompanied her aunt to church. She felt safe in the old oak pews at St Etheldreda's. Nothing was demanded of her there; she could be a child again. But since the autumn she had not returned; Sunday worship had ceased to make any demand on her mind.

London, Harriet realised, was awash with sermonisers and parsons. At Spa Fields one Sunday after Christmas she and Frederick had joined the crowds that swarmed about impromptu preachers. One declared the end of the world; another railed against speculators; a third turned on his listeners and denounced the idleness and luxury that imprisoned them in earthly enjoyments. Frederick squeezed Harriet's arm and turned her in the direction of a couple of men in black frock-coats who moved through the crowds.

'They are agents of the government.'

He demanded that they leave.

'How can you be sure?'

'I have seen men like them before; always in pairs, always silent.'

'If they are agents of the government, how does that concern you?'

'There are men who wish me ill.'

'Men who are in the service of the government?'

'Perhaps, I cannot say. Where there is invention and money, there is often also subterfuge. I left Brunswick; I left Paris. I have seen it before.'

Frederick refused to say more. They turned away and began to walk out of the fields towards the curved bridge over the Fleet River and the looming wall of the new penitentiary.

'What of your family, Frederick?' Harriet stopped, surprised by her own question. She had never asked Frederick about his life beyond London.

'What of it?'

'Frederick, do you have a mother living?'

'Why do you ask?'

'Do you write to her?'

'I choose not to think of my mother. Who she is or was is a thing of the past.'

'Is she not then alive?'

'Harriet, why do you ask? It is of no importance.'

Yet suddenly, to Harriet it seemed important that Frederick, at least, should have a mother, should know and love and have lived with her. She ran her hands over her face in distraction.

'But, Frederick, it is. If you have a mother, you must treasure her, write to her. Surely you wish to make sure that you can hold her in your mind, picture her at home and hear her voice.'

Frederick laughed and took her arm. He did not answer her question.

'Do not think you can understand me,' he said later, 'I do not seek to understand myself. Besides, you cannot always get the answer that you wish for.'

Harriet knew it. Sometimes in the laboratory they had set out to follow an experiment, to prove a truth already understood and confirm that nature followed its pattern. Sometimes, however, she and her father agreed to explore. Then, she knew, there could be no confirmation at the end, and what happened was often a surprise.

She looked up at her aunt. Mrs Cobbold's face was understanding, but Harriet could not think of telling her what was in her heart. She remembered lying with Frederick yesterday, her arms around his neck and his skin warm to hers. In the darkness she had felt his voice vibrate through her cheek as it lay on his chest.

'Oh, Aunt,' she said, 'I can't feel much of the consolation of religion in these days. I shall go and read.'

ALL THE WAY UP through Spain to Mérida and on to Badajoz and the border with Portugal, where he and Major Yallop turned north up the Tagus and struck out for Freneda and the British army, James conducted upon his heart what he told himself was a necessary surgical operation, a process of incision and extraction.

'I have to be my own doctor,' he said to himself each day as their horses wound through meadows where the grass now lay windblown against the stony soil. His passion for Camille, the feelings he had, were not those of a serving officer. How beyond control he was, how like a woman, and the worst kind of woman, too; a heroine in a romantic story book.

James watched the man who loved Camille recede as the days passed, and said goodbye to him with relief and the sense of a door shutting. He would never open that door again. Once in a lifetime was enough for any man, or any man of sense. From now on he would maintain a wary distance, lock himself in; he could achieve it, after a week or two without her.

When he talked to Major Yallop, discussed their route or where to break for the night, he congratulated himself that he was still a man of practical intellect. His folly had been his alone, an autumn of foreign madness. No one had witnessed it; no one had heard the words he said to her, or read the foolish poems he had written in his head. Camille alone had seen his fall. How grateful he was for that now. Camille, who had the means to destroy him, could tell no one. No married woman could reveal such things without expulsion from polite society.

She had most likely already burned his letters, made a pyre of his confessions. James remembered with a shock and a tug of sadness that although he had written to Camille every day as he sat in the Casa Wiseman after dinner, he had never had a letter from her. True, she had sent notes with her servant to bring him to her; but he saw now that she had given him nothing that could compromise her. Provided that she said nothing she was safe.

Before he left Seville James threw Camille's notes one by one into the fire. When he stirred the ash with his boot it collapsed into the grate; a veil of dust rose from it and dissipated in the heat. Not a single word could be read there. Now, on this journey, he could digest and expel his shame and passion, and rid himself of them for ever. By the time they arrived at Freneda and he greeted General Stewart he would have become the same officer who had left Headquarters five months before.

As time went on he pushed the images of Camille further into the darkness too. Her picture shrank, as if he saw her in the Panorama in Oxford Street, he on the platform above, she part of the sculpture seated by the painted backdrop far away. He could move round and see her from different places, a waxwork that glowed in the light of the hanging lamps. If he was not so exhausted by the day's ride as to fall asleep immediately, he was sometimes caught unawares by the sound of her voice, by the sense that he might reach into the darkness and feel her warm beside him. Then his body shrank into itself and sleep eluded him.

When he was oppressed James dropped back and rode with Thomas Orde, who sat astride a mule loaded with blankets, a tent, and cooking equipment. Thomas rarely spoke and James was grateful for his silence.

'You and I are remarkably quiet, Thomas,' he remarked one afternoon.

'I have seen things, sir, that cannot be made into words, or at least that a man such as I am cannot speak of.'

'There are things that we, I no less than you, had best leave unsaid. They account, I believe, for the general high spirits of hardened soldiers.'

Thomas paused.

'What do you intend by that, sir?'

'I believe that fear visits many of us in the night; I sometimes wake to the sound of an imaginary barrage. Yet to acknowledge its presence in daylight gives it the victory; an army cannot fight on fear.'

'It is the smell that stays with me from Badajoz. I saw dead men tumbled into a ditch the day after we got into the town, sir, bare feet where the living had stripped their boots. Days after, that sweet smell seemed to linger enough to make a man vomit. I thought I had forgotten it until I saw heaps of the enemy captured by the guerrillas on the way down. The Spanish left them naked with nothing to be dead in.'

'You must attempt, Thomas, not to dwell upon it. There is more to come before we get home, and, besides, once you are there, what will you tell those who wish us to return the same men as we went out?'

When he talked, James was caught by a memory of Camille, the way she smiled and looked past him.

'Perhaps, Captain Raven. We should follow the example of the Major up ahead. He never flags, despite this rain.'

Major Yallop turned when he heard their voices.

'Look out ahead. There seems to be some disturbance.'

They had come into a sodden village. Water poured down a gully in the middle of the path. Despite the storm the doors to the stone houses stood open. Men and women gathered in a crowd round something James could not make out. Many held up knives, sticks and makeshift pikes. A confused sound came off them, half howls, half low groans. A group of women shouted something and then surged forward.

The Major cantered back.

'Best to skirt round the back and leave this business to them.'

'What are they doing?'

'They have a man there. Let us go.'

Before he could turn his horse, James saw Thomas beside him jump down from the mule and run forward.

'Thomas. No.'

Thomas took no notice. James ran after him and tried to pull him away from the crowd, which parted as they ran up.

Out in the street a man lay on a makeshift table with his face pressed to the wood and hands splayed flat beyond. Shackled and broken at the ankles, his feet lay swollen and limp, flecked with blood. At that moment a thickset, powerful man walked to the table. With a single jerk he heaved up the man's midriff and levered up his buttocks with a spade. Another man advanced towards them with a pike. An exultant shout rose from the crowd.

'Stop!' James drew his sword and ran towards the table. Thomas Orde was right behind him.

'Stop in the name of the King. I am a British officer.'

'Es traidor,' a woman shouted from inside the crowd. People surged forward again. Several of the women held babies in their arms.

'Es traidor.' The word came from all sides, flat and simple.

'Stay away. I will kill anyone who comes near.'

The man with the spade looked James in the eye.

'*Es muerto,*' he said and, with a heave, turned the man over and pulled him flat.

Down his front was nothing but a pulpy mass, a hole of blood between his thighs. Next to him James felt Thomas stagger.

Major Yallop walked up, his sword drawn.

'I said come away, James.'

The Major took him by the arm.

'I insist on it. I am still your superior officer. Go now, and we leave.'

James resisted the pressure on his sleeve.

'We cannot walk away. Where is a Spanish officer who can restore order here?'

'Spanish officer! There is no law here but the partisans, you know that yourself. This is not our war.'

Yallop urged James back towards the horses. Some of the men in the crowd followed them. Through the open door to one of the houses James saw a woman. She sat in a corner, her white shift pale against the dirty plaster. A small child clung to her arm, its arms wrapped tight, its bare legs covered in dirt. In the same moment James saw Thomas start towards the entrance.

'No.'

Thomas shouted and ran into the house. As he did so several men came in behind him.

'It is her they will go at now. I know what will happen.'

James ran in too. The room was bare and dark. The woman opened her mouth wide as if to scream, but no sound came out. Her whole body expressed fear and bewilderment. The child felt it; he clung to his mother and screamed. James caught Thomas's arm and felt the rage run through him.

'Do not try to stop me, Captain Raven.'

Thomas tried to free himself from James's grasp and launch himself against the men who stood in silence.

'You do not understand, Captain Raven. I have seen it before.'

'They are her enemies and no friends of ours. Leave them. There is nothing we can do.'

Thomas tried to pull away again. One of the men wrenched the child away from his mother.

'Go, Thomas. I order you to come with me.'

James dragged Thomas after him and waited when they reached the horses for Thomas to mount and start off. Thomas stood immobile by his mule. His rage had subsided and his hands trembled; he could not move or get himself in the saddle. James glanced back to the village, worried that whatever had gone on there might spill out towards them.

'Thomas, get up. We must go.'

Thomas stared at him with a blank look in his eyes, and then swung himself up onto his mule. They set off, with Major Yallop behind them. No one in the crowd moved; their business would wait. James turned his horse the way they had come. They skirted round the back of the village through a quiet meadow with oak trees dotted about it. The air was heavy with silence. Sows nosed through fallen acorns. After a few minutes the storm passed over and great columns of sunshine filtered through the clouds to light up the barren upland ahead. A thousand tiny rainbows stood in the raindrops on the grass. Then, as the light went again, black-birds began to click and fuss in the undergrowth. Behind them, James heard Thomas Orde sob.

~

NATHAN ROTHSCHILD SAT WITH the fat of his back against the hard upright of the family seat at the Great Synagogue in Duke's Place. The beeswax smell that rose up from the mahogany soothed and comforted him. He turned his head over his shoulder and checked the congregation. Men came in hours after the service had begun. That's the way of it now, he thought, we wander in when we choose.

In came Joshua Solomons, whom he had known since his early cotton days in Manchester when he had needed a steady friend in this unknown place. He must remember to greet him on the way out. David Samuel, who shifted and fussed with cushions throughout the service, had already arrived. His two boys walked behind him. He needed a word with Asher Goldsmid over there, and Rav Hirschel, too, Nathan thought, and pressed his hat down tight on his head.

He should love these Shabbos mornings, with the families assembled and the women and girls safe up in the gallery. High windows shut out the world and admitted only a watery spring sky. The clatter of boots and hooves on Duke's Place faded and left the synagogue to float in peace like a ship at sea. The chant was about to begin, solemn and ancient, sung with variations in every synagogue from Frankfurt to Riga or Turin. He felt himself here, in his known world, where the air was benign and suffused with warmth.

Massive stone pillars supported the synagogue's curved roof. Seven great Dutch brass candelabra, branched like trees and weighted with brass spheres, were set above the seats. Three pairs hung above the congregation, with the grandest, triple-tiered and magnificent, over the bima. Their vinegar and bran polish added an astringent note to the beeswax sweetness. Stone, brass and wood; how reassuring in their solidity. To a newcomer—and even after a dozen years in the country, Nathan still thought of himself as a man just disembarked—they should offer a hope of permanence. Yet on days like this Nathan was annoyed by their impenetrable fixity. It served to remind him that his own worth, and his own future, was a matter of paper, built on memory and calculation. One wrong addition, one rash risk, and the whole edifice of his fortune might crash down.

Nathan was impatient, today, with his brothers; Jakob in Paris, first, because he was closest; then Amschel, who sat about in Frankfurt and Berlin. A lack of alacrity and sharpness were their faults. Why not say it: his brothers were lazy, and would be the death of them all if he did not step in. He should not be up to any business on this day of rest; it was forbidden and forsworn. Nathan shrugged; to think about business was not, he liked to think, to do it. What was Amschel up to, for a start, despite their new system of envelopes of different colours to indicate without words when the exchange rate rose or fell—blue for up, red for down? Not much yet, it seemed, though that alone should have allowed him to steal a march on their rivals and buy or sell according to the signs.

All five of them needed to work more closely together now with no father, since last year, to be their lodestar. Calmann shuttled about between Holland and Frankfurt, and Salomon sat square in Amsterdam: those two talked to one another, shared food and prayers. But to him in London who was the centre of all operations (admit it, brothers, I am the general, Nathan thought with a flash of pride, I am the finanzbonaparte of the whole enterprise), to him they were silent for days or weeks on end, at the very moment they stood to make more than ever before. How could he bear it, let alone concentrate on Shabbos?

As if it was not enough to leave him in the dark, his brothers, Jakob especially, accused him of a lack of method, a vagueness in his accounting. What did they know of his labours, and his careful plans to turn the London business to greater good? There was Jakob, that impertinent stripling, who lived in luxury in Paris. He complained of sickness, and in his letters asked, did Nathan not know the fatigue of going from Paris to Boulogne, from Dunkerque to Gravelines, from Amsterdam to Paris again, to take and collect goods from clients? Not to mention the horror of dirty inns? Nathan did not respond. Why should he when his brother was a boy of twenty-one, far too young to tire? Then Jakob wrote to Hannah and directed his ramblings to her, though his English was scarcely intelligible. Jakob had not yet got the measure of his Hannah, had no idea of her steady mind and loyal heart.

Nathan shifted on his buttocks and glanced up at the gallery where his wife sat with her sister Jessie. Hannah's dark brown eyes were cast down under her bonnet; at the sight of them Nathan's face softened. Old Levi Barent Cohen had been a canny Amsterdamer, thirty years in London by the time he died. Levi had married his daughters well, approving their husbands more for their prospects than present fortunes. Mayer Davidson, married to Jessie, was an outspoken man, but surefooted with it. He too had moved to New Court. Nathan saw him come in now, and raised his eyebrows an inch in greeting. Only Judith and Moses Montefiore were absent. Moses was not one of them. He had carried Judith off to worship with the Spanish congregation at Bevis Marks. He looked down on them here, perhaps, though you could not know it from his mild manner.

The thought of Moses sent Nathan back to the business. How much had Rothschilds made in the last year? He alone among the brothers had taken for cashing in London bills of exchange from France and Switzerland of over two million in sterling. As for their dealings in foreign exchange, none of them could say for sure. Much of their money, scattered like the cast of a sower across Europe, was sent out again to fund new purchases of specie and goods or laid out in loans that yielded good commissions and would be repaid with interest. To call in merely the loans they made last year would break several small principalities and might bring more than one larger kingdom to its knees.

It requires a great deal of decision to make a fortune, Nathan thought, and a great deal of caution to keep it. Very well, but the moment for caution has not yet come, whatever Jakob might say. A month ago Russia and Prussia signed a treaty of alliance. That was a start, a hint of what was to come, with Bonaparte on the run. But today, this good March morning, he had heard something better. Prussia had declared war on France. The great surge of war, which had swept Bonaparte to Egypt and Madrid, Piedmont and Moscow, had reached its high water mark and turned. Now, in a maelstrom of retreat, it would suck the French from every corner of Europe back towards Paris. It was no good for Jakob to plead exhaustion: to throw in his hand just when events favoured them. Prussia would look for a loan, the Tsar too, perhaps, and who would provide them?

Familiar chants wrapped themselves round him. The cantor stood at the bima high above the worshippers. Black stripes ran through the white wool of his tallis, and the long fringes brushed across his dark coat. Next to him Dr Joshua van Oven, the surgeon who treated the synagogues' poor, took his turn to recite the blessing that began each portion of the Torah reading.

Ach, well, Nathan grunted, I must be easy with my brothers; it is Shabbos; no time to stand in judgement over other men. Slowly his impatience spread out and dissipated, drained away through the readings and prayers. Lightness filled the gaps his irritation left behind. Prayer made him not so much himself, but a better Shabbos version of himself, equable and kind. He smiled round the synagogue when the service came to an end. It was spring, after all, and the whole family would walk home through the quiet city. Passover would soon be upon them.

AFTER A SLOW JOURNEY through the hills, James Raven and Major Yallop finally fell in with the first outposts of the British army in the villages round the town of Castelo Branco above Badajoz. From there all along the border, in villages and encampments right up the Coa River, and along the Douro, the British army was settled for the winter. As he rode through it, James estimated the area to be fifty miles wide and at least as long; a great swathe of country, dotted with red.

The army was no longer the force that people in England imagined. Though the men marched in formation twice a week to keep discipline alive, they were no longer in ranks, or even companies. Lines and squares did not define the army any more; rather it was made up of clusters of men, ragged groups of a dozen at the most. At night they slept in dirty rooms, in stables, or under carriages and trees. In the day, when the sun was out, they gathered around fires; some cooked, some slept, some picked fleas from the seams of their jackets. Newspapers, two or three weeks old, passed from hand to hand with pleasantry and gossip. Like a great serpent coiled across the land, the army spent the weeks in quiet hibernation and digestion, and made itself ready for a final attack.

Seconded to Headquarters at Freneda, James found a billet some distance from the 9th and it was well into spring before he could set off up the shallow valley in search of his old regiment. A mile or so outside Freneda, on a crisp April morning, he ran into Robert Heaton mounted on his Athena. The pony picked her way with fastidious care through the short grass between rocky outcrops. A brisk wind blew from the east, flattened the grass against the plateau and made Racket shiver. Heaton was dressed in hunting pink.

'Captain Raven. Delighted, and good morning to you. How long have you been back?'

Heaton did not wait for an answer.

'Pity the rest of us, sir, stuck in the country week after week to chew on our pipes and look at the sky. While you diverted yourself in Seville we retreated with nothing but acorns for coffee. I am not a man to fall ill, but many of my company did and I have had the devil of a time to get them up again. It is damned dull now for such as the Major and myself who chafe at inaction. I should have wished to accompany him, but he summoned me from the 44th and then left me to jaunt off to Seville.'

'You have been after a fox, I see?'

Heaton patted Athena's silken neck. He wore new gloves of soft canary-yellow leather, and his boots glowed in the spring sunshine. A large wicker basket was strapped to his pony's rump behind him.

'Had a couple of hunters sent out. I am not fond of any countryside myself, unless it has a racecourse on it. Too green and wet, you understand; but one has to amuse oneself, and there are foxes enough. I am collecting too. Racket has lent a paw.'

Racket put his nose up to his master and his tail began its habitual slow wag. Really, James thought, Heaton's man-about-town way of behaving was intolerable.

'Creatures for David McBride. He is still an enthusiast for the latest advance in science. Since he practised on me it is the least I can do, though I am not sure we should encourage him.'

'Are you going to him now?'

'Come along with me. You look like the ride might do you good. A little down-hearted, if I may say so. I trust nothing untoward happened in Seville?'

'Everything went off exactly as I hoped. A simple negotiation.'

'You found in the famous Señora Florens the patriot everyone expected?'

'She is a firm friend of Great Britain.'

Heaton looked at James from under the brim of his hunting hat. He raised an eyebrow.

'And did she become a firm friend to you also, Captain Raven, and you to her? Word is she was quite a temptress in Lisbon.'

'I am a married man, Captain Heaton. Besides my taste does not run to the Iberian type. If you met my wife you would appreciate my meaning.'

'Ah, that is indeed a pity. I have found Spanish women quite glorious myself, and they do not waste a man's time with tedious preliminaries. If one cannot be in action, why not divert oneself the next best way? I tell you, at Madrid last year, I once had scarcely time to make my intentions known before one of the darlings slipped her hand up my shirt.'

'I was in Seville on duty, Captain Heaton.'

'Very good; so you were.'

That is how humanity carries on, James thought. Who knows what Heaton really thinks or wants; he is mysterious, puts nothing out that a man can pin down. Never speaks of a home, or relatives, and has no attachments here apart from Major Yallop. What does he want from this war? How can one tell; we go on, side by side, grey-faced and alone. In the middle of it all, Thomas Orde, a man born to hardship, breaks down in tears at the thought of a woman violated.

The two men rode in silence up the valley and by mid-morning reached the village where the 9th was billeted. Down the main street a market was in progress and men strolled about. Tubs of salt and tea, barrels of biscuits, sugar and chocolate, stood open on trestle tables. Port, sherry, wine and small beer sat in the shade underneath. Some men and officers wrote promissory notes in return for goods; others paid in cash and got double for their money. At the edge of the village James saw that the men had turned a meadow into a parade ground. A path that wound

up into the hills beyond was widened to make a marching route. Major
Yallop had carried out the General's orders to the letter. James greeted a
man he knew.

'Good morning, Abraham.'

'Mornin', Cap'n Raven, mornin', Cap'n Heaton, sir. You gorn to send us
Thomas back, Cap'n?'

'To be sure I shall send him for a visit. You will be here for a month or
so more, I imagine.'

James warmed to Abraham's slow East Anglian voice. Its familiarity
calmed him.

'Not more'un a month now. That Boney, he be on the run, they say.'

Heaton looked over at Abraham.

'Never underestimate the enemy, that would be my hunch.'

'I ha'n't been in the army for so long to do that, sir.'

Heaton turned back to James and gestured towards the parade ground.

'Ah, there is a beautiful sight. Yallop has everything in perfect order.
Dr McBride lodges in that farmhouse up the hill. Should we make our
way there?'

Halfway up they came across a group of men with their backs to a
stone wall, turned to the south where the sun, even at this early time of
the year, had a touch of warmth in it. From the firesides in the open air,
where the men brewed their tea and cooked up their rations, James heard
laughter and the steady chatter of soldiers who sensed that, whatever the
papers might say, the war in Spain was almost over. One man whittled a
branch; another smoked a pipe. With them was a young soldier, his red
coat patched with squares of blue and brown. Tears streamed down his
face and his breath came in high rasps.

'All all right here, men?' Heaton asked.

The older man took his pipe from his mouth.

'Do not mind Billy, sir. He has been like this since the enemy nearly
got us in an ambush on the way up. We call him Billy Wise these days,
and just sit with him when he cries.'

'Billy Wise?'

'Yes, sir. Not because he is smart, mind you. Cor, no, he don' know
anything, that young bor, his mind's quite gorn; Billy Wise is our name
for a screech owl in Norfolk, an' thas war he sound like now.'

The man put his hand on Billy's knee. James and Heaton watched the
tears fall freely onto the boy's downy upper lip. Every now and then he

drew in his breath and swallowed them, as if he knew they would come round again.

'Nothing to be done, sir. He's a rum un. Says he came face to face with the head of a man at Salamanca and then the other bits of him in pieces all about. Says he sees them when he closes his eyes. Well, sir, you know how it is. He will be better for sure once them tears are out. Then we will turn 'im roun' to face the French again.'

'Odd how things can take a man, sometimes.' Heaton turned to James when they were out of earshot. 'I remember an officer after Badajoz in the hospital up at Elvas. A Hessian. He thought he was blinded. But he could see quite well, and not a scratch on him. Had to be led into dinner and fed by his own servant, though he turned his face to me when I came close to him. Wounded on the inside, you might say.'

James rode on for several minutes.

'Eventually it passes,' he replied and fell silent.

THEY FOUND DAVID MCBRIDE on a chair in a slice of sunshine outside the small stone house that served as his hospital and lodging. He stood up when he saw them, held James's horse while he dismounted and then grasped him by the shoulders.

'James, how good it is to see you. Welcome back.' He turned to Heaton. 'Robert, good morning. You have something for me, I see.'

Heaton took the wicker basket off Athena's rump and smoothed down the damp hide where it had rested.

'Two cubs. Six months old, at a guess. Last of the season I'm sure.'

'Come along in, there is coffee on the stove.'

'No, I thank you. I am going to scout out the Major and take my coffee with him. Come along, Racket. Leave those presents alone.'

Heaton swung himself back onto Athena and rode off down the muddy street at a trot. Racket dashed along by the pony's hooves.

James noticed that David kept his eyes on the wicker basket as they went inside. McBride looked different to him; older and more self-contained, although it was only a few months since they had parted in Madrid. He looked around the small parlour. Papers sat in piles on the floor and spilled from the grate, half-burned. Several phials of brown liquid, stoppered with corks, lay on the desk by a silver inkstand. Books piled up against chair-legs. The room had an air of permanence; David McBride had settled in.

'You keep yourself busy, here, David.'

'I have found that the life suits me. I do my rounds and after that, if there are no new cases that require my attention, I can spend the daylight hours in study. I am surgeon to the 9th, but master of my own thoughts. What greater liberty can a man have?'

He grasped James's arm in excitement.

'I tell you, James, I feel as a man must do who has made a fortune by accident. Most of war, I discover, is waiting, or sitting in quarters as we do now. Since I came out, we have fought one pitched battle, at Salamanca, and laid two sieges, at Badajoz and Burgos. What would I estimate the days of labour to be, if I count the care of the wounded? Three months, perhaps, in all. I tend to the usual camp complaints: abscesses, the itch, and venereal diseases, of course. The army will never be free of those. I have cases of fever and dysentery; but no cholera. With good supply lines to the coast, and cattle brought in from America, the men are fat and well. Then I can continue with my experiments. The work brings me joy. Wrong-headed as it is, I should not complain if the war were to stretch out some while longer.'

James shrugged.

'War is not always as you describe. The retreat to Corunna was a battle every day for those of us in the rear. Then, though this does not concern you as a surgeon, there are two wars in this country, one that we wage against Napoleon, the other that Spaniards fight amongst themselves. That other war has made me long for a decisive action that will get us out of Spain for good.'

As James spoke he could sense David's excitement. It brought Camille back to him, the way a passion grasps the body and pulls it taut. David was not captured by any human feeling, but the effect was the same; to take a man out of himself and into something beyond the envelope of the self, the most powerful feeling that any man can have if he is not a hater. David, James knew, was not a hater; he was a deliberate man transformed by dreams.

David spooned coffee into a tin pot, poured water over it, stirred them together and put the pot onto the fire.

'You know my interest in transfusions. Here I am at liberty to pursue it.'

James found it hard to concentrate his attention on David's words. He saw his friend as if they were separated by a wide empty distance. It frightened him into a reply.

'I should not imagine Mr Heaton thinks much of what you do. He has a tenderness for animals far greater than anything he feels for his own kind.'

'He does not agree with it; but he owes me a debt, and besides, what I have found, James, is that a fox takes perfectly well to the blood of a dog most of the time; or a sheepdog to that of the tiniest lady's pet.'

'A lady's pet?'

'After Salamanca a number roamed about the battlefield; I scooped them up. But Heaton's creatures do not drop dead, whereas a man will die in an instant sometimes, when given another's blood.'

'So you conclude . . . ?'

'That though one dog might be twice the height of another, one pug-nosed, another a hunter, they are connected in some way that we humans are not. We, who look so alike, not one of us twice the size of another or a quarter the heaviness, are divided in ways that make us sometimes fatal to one another.'

'A philosopher or divine—a poet, even—could surely tell you as much.'

'James, I mean to find out why, and to use my discoveries. I should never be able to work unobserved in this way if I were in England, or forced to eke out a living in Edinburgh. The war has set me on my way.'

David grasped his friend's arm.

'Forgive me. I have been too much alone with my own concerns. Tell me more of yourself.'

'More good news came today from the partisans; they are delighted with me at Headquarters.'

'That is a cause for satisfaction, at least.'

'To tell you the truth, David, I find I care little for the approbation of my superiors. I believed I should do, but I take no pleasure in it when it arrives.'

'Something eats at you, James. Do let me listen to you, as a friend.'

It showed still, James thought. He was changed, and not for the better. Before Seville he had been a fine officer and faithful husband; now he could take pride in neither his success nor his probity. The best he could hope for was to go quietly on and hope to regain a kind of balance. His faith in the war was broken, and there was a void in his heart. Already he could sense how dangerous that might be.

David untied the wicker basket and lifted out two fox cubs, one with each hand. The cubs were limp with fear; their legs dangled immobile over David's palms. He held them up to his face and shook them till they mewed.

'Good. They will recover. I shall be back directly; I need to put these outside. I have a kind of stable at the back for my creatures. A few have died, but many are in good health even after two or three transfusions. I mean to release them when we move out.'

While David was outside, James considered whether he should tell him what had happened in Seville. The thought of Harriet stopped him. It was essential that no word reach her; to lose his wife and his standing now would be intolerable. When David spoke about Harriet his face took on a look of concern, as a doctor's does when he knows that a case will afflict a whole family. No, it was better to keep quiet and let the poison drain out in its own time.

'Now, do tell me,' David said when he came back.

'It is just as I said.' James gestured towards the street, where men strolled in the sunshine. 'None of it holds my interest any more. I long to do my duty and return home.'

'There is nothing to be ashamed of in that, James. Is there not something else?'

'No, no. I need to rest, that is all. I am tired, like your men.'

'Rest, then, and come back soon. Now, with your permission I must get on. You have no wish to witness a transfusion?'

'I thank you, but no.'

'Good day, then; good day.'

David leant against the door jamb and watched James ride away. The man seemed diminished, he thought. His muscled body was hollowed out, less leonine and magnificent. They felt uneasy in one another's company; but until James wished to confide in him all he could do was offer him the comfort of an extended hand.

As he rode back to Headquarters James congratulated himself that he had kept his own counsel. Felipe Odonnell had just sent word that Cuesta, a determined and successful guerrilla captain who worked high up in the valley of the Tagus, had come across a detachment of two hundred French soldiers. He had at once got a message to General Hill who was encamped with the cream of the 2nd Division at Placentia nearby and withdrawn to allow the British troops to confront it. This message reassured James that Camille, though she had no use for him, had kept her side of the bargain. He had done all that he was asked to do. Now, like the troops, he had only to wait until General Wellington gave the order to march east.

'HAVE YOU SILENCED THOSE bells for good?' Lord Wellington turned to his staff officers. 'These are worse than at Burgos even. At least there they rang to defy me. Here they are an intolerable irritation, four times an hour. How can I work? Do not answer; I cannot. And do not tell me, Stewart, that I have thirty thousand Spanish troops at my disposal.' Wellington laughed his dry, mocking laugh. 'I have none, or ninety thousand, tell me what you like.'

'My Lord, General Ballesteros's estimate, just arrived, puts the Spanish Army of Castille at fifty thousand.'

'That man always exaggerates his advantages. The fact is his army is in a state of collapse, and no use to me. About as bad as the men here.'

'Your army concluded the retreat with great valour, my Lord,' said General Murray.

'Now you are going to preach to me, Murray, tell me they marched without shoes or rum. I have never seen such want of discipline, or read of anything like it. The officers lost all control of their men; outrages occurred daily. I saw them myself.'

It was Lord Wellington's fault, General Stewart mused, that he bestowed his strictures without thought of their effects. How many worthy officers felt after his latest intemperate circular that they paid the price for the negligence of a few; how many that their daily exertions went unregarded? Admire him as Stewart did, Lord Wellington was a hard man to love.

'Stewart?' Wellington looked at him over the bridge of his nose.

'I would venture to add, my Lord, that you have concluded a successful year with their help.'

Stewart was relieved to see Lord Wellington's scowl fade away. The men in the room stood a little more at ease when they saw the General smile. Staff officers stood round the walls and two or three aides-de-camp made a group by the empty grate. The house was modest, built of local stone and unadorned inside. Lord Wellington slept in the adjoining room on his narrow fold-out bed. From the room where they stood three long windows opened onto a pillared loggia. Between the pillars the offending bell tower of the village church filled half the cloudless sky.

'I thank you, Stewart. True enough, I failed to take Burgos. It was mistaken, perhaps, to leave my best men outside Madrid, and invest a fortress with poor troops.' He tapped a folded newspaper on the table in front of him.

'I do not need the *Morning Chronicle* to tell me that. But Burgos aside, it has indeed been a good twelve months though the newspapers libel me for it and we have had to sit out another winter over the border.'

Several men in the room shifted and stood back; Fitzroy Somerset nodded at his fellow aide-de-camp and leaned towards Lord Wellington. General Murray, who made notes for posterity in his pocketbook at night, sat up straight.

'I have taken by siege Ciudad Rodrigo, Badajoz and Salamanca and our allies have taken other fortresses besides. In the months since January we have sent thousands of prisoners to England; how many, General Stewart?'

'Upwards of twenty thousand, my Lord.'

'Twenty thousand? A very good number, though they take food from the mouths of Englishmen. Besides that, I have cleared the Peninsula of the French south of the River Tagus, and can prepare to push the enemy out of the rest if the government will give me the funds.'

'Do not let us forget the three hundred pieces of cannon we have taken or destroyed, my Lord.' Murray was particular. He wanted to note down the General's response, with a view to seeing it in print one day.

'Yes, point that out to London will you when you next send a memorandum; the saving to the artillery may jolt them into generosity.'

Murray bowed. No matter what his mood, the General was parsimonious with his gratitude. Wellington looked up.

'Another reminder, Murray. Intelligence from the partisans has dropped more supplies into our hands than London had any right to expect. Just add something to that effect.'

Wellington leaned over to Fitzroy.

'I have a mind to go out with the hounds if I can find and intercept them. Let us be brisk; take dictation, Fitzroy.'

'My Lord.'

Fitzroy Somerset sat down at the small writing table. He swept the skirt of his topcoat carefully over the seat as he did so, and pulled up his trousers at the knee. He wore grey twill, as the General did today. Wellington waved a hand to the remaining officers.

'That is enough for this morning.'

Alone with Somerset the General felt his spirits rise. He noted with pleasure that Fitzroy tied his cravat just as he himself did. The boy would make an able general one day. When he went back to Britain he would surround himself with spirited youngsters taut with admiration and the energy of Headquarters. It would dilute the parlour atmosphere.

'Let us get this over as soon as we can, Fitzroy. I see it is a fine day and not to be wasted.'

Fitzroy dipped his pen in the inkwell and held it above the paper.

'I think we shall attack the commissary-in-chief at last, set him on the trail of the money to finish the job. Charles Herries; a man of no family. He has ability they say. Very well, let him show it. Frighten him with costs, and run him down with the sick list and the necessity for specie, especially French. How else shall we buy provisions once we get off this infernal Peninsula and on the road to Paris? Once he has this he will fear for his position and cut along to the City.'

The General laughed his short whooping-cough laugh and Fitzroy grinned. Though it would do him no good to join in, the General was obviously in a good humour now. It was always made better by the thought of another man's discomfort and the profit he would take from it. Fitzroy bowed his golden head and started to write.

Besides the complaints in the London papers that had been delivered today, the General had received in the post a letter from his wife. It lay unopened under the papers Fitzroy wrote on. He had also received, by dispatch, a cipher report from Russia. General Bonaparte had abandoned his army in the snows of Silesia. The Emperor, it was rumoured, had rolled away in his great blue carriage and left his men to die in the ice.

Now, Fitzroy sensed, after three years playing cat and mouse, in which neither the French nor the British had finally got the upper hand, Bonaparte's folly in Russia would secure their victory in the Peninsula. With money and a fresh army, Wellington could prepare his march into France. Marshal Soult might stand in his way with ninety thousand men, ten thousand of the finest French cavalry amongst them, but the French quarrelled about strategy, and the General had his eyes already over the Pyrenees. Somerset stopped his writing and closed his eyes. He allowed himself a picture of organza and pale silk. Tiny slippers and bare, sweet shoulders came into his mind, skin flushed with dancing and desire. Though the General would have the pick of the women in Paris, Fitzroy promised to reward himself with those who remained.

9

London and Spain

SPRING AND SUMMER 1813

In a veil and cloak, a woman in middle age was quite invisible, Kitty found. London was laid out for her, and even the footpads left her alone. One morning in late April she arrived early in the City, left her carriage and coachman to wait by the Mansion House, and walked to the water's edge. Down the narrow cut at Bull Wharf she watched the shallow waves turn over on the shore. An easterly breeze carried the smell of fish and a tang of salt upriver from Billingsgate Market and pushed the water against the stanchions of the wharf. The water's slap and suck mixed with human voices, gulls' cries and the rumble of carts over London Bridge. The river was a brown-blue, laced with grey at its edges. As far as Kitty could see downriver the rust-red sails of London barges and a lattice of masts and spars stood out against the sky.

Beside her two girls, five or six years old, dug through the sand in the shallows and sieved it in the river. They hunt for money, as we all do, thought Kitty, or nails and nuggets of coal, and long for the prize of a brass buckle or half a crown to take home. As she walked back up the narrow path to the street another smell caught her; lemons and onions, just arrived from Spain, and she felt that there was no better place to be than London, by herself.

Later, on Lombard Street, where it joined Cornhill by the Exchange, Kitty's coachman drew up with a jolt.

'I apologise, my Lady,' the coachman called back to her. 'Some fool stepped into the road.'

There was Mr Herries, stock-still halfway off the pavement. Oblivious to carriages in front and the press of walkers behind, he held a sheet of paper out before his eyes.

'Mr Herries, are you in one piece?'

Charles Herries looked dusty and hot, though it was scarcely mid-morning. He appeared speechless and distracted, opened his mouth and closed it again.

'One piece? Yes, I believe so, Lady Wellington.'

'You have been with Mr Rothschild?'

'Ah. Indeed.' Herries hesitated. 'He is a man full of surprises, I find.'

Kitty laughed.

'That is one of the pleasures of his acquaintance.'

Silence fell between them. Herries folded up the paper, put it into his pocket and patted it flat. Kitty bid him good day and drove on. Neither of them wished to share their thoughts with the other.

When Kitty was settled in Mr Rothschild's office, she mentioned her meeting with Herries.

'My carriage almost ran him down. His mind appeared to be quite elsewhere.'

A careful look came over Nathan Rothschild's face.

'We live many lives, do we not, Lady Wellington, and may not wish to show them to all our acquaintance.'

The truth was, Nathan was on edge this morning. From his brother Jakob in Paris came the news that the Emperor Napoleon had joined his armies in the north. It appeared, Jakob wrote, that Bonaparte planned to advance into Saxony and attack the army of the German alliance. It was a setback; Rothschilds, in Paris and in London, had staked a greater sum than Nathan cared to remember on the success not just of the Tsar but also of the German alliance. Over the last year he had made thirty per cent on gold sent to St Petersburg, and he had shipped this year alone bullion and specie worth thirty thousand sterling. He smiled at the thought; what work it was! Just today he had approved the consignment of a boatload of goods to Meyer and Bruxner over there, steady men who would find under the logwood and sugar, the indigo and cochineal, gold coin to the value of five or six thousand pounds, bound for the Russian Mint, to be exchanged for bills on London. Not that the boat would return empty; no, it would pick up tallow and bristles on the way back through the Baltic. There was no need to waste an empty hold or an opportunity. Still, all around Europe so much money was laid out; he had no desire for the Emperor now to compromise his greater plan. He glanced at Lady Wellington. She sat still and waited for him to continue as if she had all the time in the world.

'Few men, I venture to say, wish to acknowledge all their deeds.'

Kitty studied him with a new sharpness in her gaze.

'Do you not agree, Lady Wellington, that we all have, what shall I call it, a capacity for the shadows?'

'I would put it, rather, that goodness does not always serve us well.'

Nathan grunted. The subject already bored him. History, he thought, will always prefer a pat explanation or a pretty story and there is an end to it. I will go my way without it; I like the mess of life. I prefer to run the business with all the figures in my head; there is more satisfaction in letting numbers run free than in a thousand of Calmann's leather account books, initialled and signed. Pin figures down like that and they lose possibility. He ran his hand over his head and shifted in his chair.

'Let us get on. One way or another this war will come to a close, and besides the Continent there are other places to engage us. The Spanish colonies, for instance, Lady Wellington. What do you say to a throw at mining stocks?'

'Is Mr Montefiore interested in those, too?'

Nathan smiled again, a smile that had only an edge of warmth in it.

'These days dear Moses is distracted by philanthropy. I have to drag him onto the 'Change. I need his head; I ask you, Lady Wellington, is it any time for the heart now, when Napoleon himself is out and about again? That is the difficulty with Moses; to keep him at work. That heart of his pulls him out of harness.'

Kitty's heart, she thought, had long ago been given to her children. Ned and her friends took the rest of it. To her mother: duty and affection. To Arthur, now, what remained? The fear she had had of him, the consciousness of her wounded affection, had gone. Her new purpose carried her forwards. Arthur ceased to haunt her.

FREDERICK BENT DOWN AND picked Harriet's stockings and garters from the floor. He slipped the stockings back and forth through his hands, and lingered over the embroidery that ran up their backs. Then he handed them to her and watched while she rolled them up her legs, toes stretched out. He took her garters and tied them with precision above her knees. One by one he held out her other garments; the simple undershift, a soft straight petticoat and her gown. She stood while he pushed thin silk loops round the buttons: eight for each cuff, twenty down her back, and felt, at the end, his lips brush across the nape of her neck.

It was for that touch, gentle and intimate, that Harriet waited between their meetings all through the spring. She felt a delight in her longing and her desire, thought nothing of the risk she ran when she walked out with Frederick alone or rang his bell in Pall Mall in broad daylight. When they walked or lay in bed Frederick told her about new experiments carried out on the Continent that he had read of in German magazines; she replied with news of the Royal Society or details of lectures she had attended. They disputed and laughed; talked over the news and the progress of the war. But Harriet could never draw Frederick out about his family or his plans. As April turned to May his mood soured and, she had to admit it, the joy she took in their meetings began to pall. She took to leaving earlier, or arriving late. Something was wrong, though she did not know if it was in herself or in him, or in the mixture that they had made.

Now, as she drew on her light silk cloak, she was even impatient to be gone.

'Might I ask you, Frederick, is all well with you?'

'It is as well as it can be in this infernal city.'

'But you have found everything in London to suit your ambition. Your business begins to flourish; more and more parishes are turning to gas lighting. It is not just money that you make, but a name for yourself.'

'There you are wrong, Harriet. You must understand. I am a foreigner.'

'A foreigner?'

'Therefore an object of suspicion. But that is simply the excuse; there are men who wish to take the company away from me.'

'Surely you are mistaken, Frederick. Why would they wish to do that when the company grows so fast and you sign new contracts every month?'

'Englishmen will make any excuse to get their hands on something that is profitable; so they declare I am a showman with no knowledge of science. It is even said that a new engineer must be brought in, and you can be sure he will be an Englishman. This talk is a slander, put about to frighten my investors. But I have to lic low.'

Perhaps, Harriet thought, Frederick was more a dreamer than a practical man of science; he poured scorn on fools but craved visions. He longed for the magnificence that the natural scientist sees when he puts his eye to the microscope and a universe blooms before him, but held himself to need no help from others.

Whatever was the case, there was no remedy she could supply. Worse, she knew that her friendship with Frederick did nothing to staunch her feeling of restlessness. Some days she felt trapped as well as restless.

When she left Pall Mall, Harriet took a cab from the carriage stand in St James's Square.

'To Hatton Garden.'

Halfway up the Haymarket, she changed her mind and tapped on the glass.

'Dean Street, driver, if you please.'

Harriet found Mrs Lefevre in her small garden. She sat in her bonnet where the sunlight fell and warmed the old red bricks. Scarlet tulips stood in pots against the wall and pear trees grew inside a box parterre with wallflowers at their feet.

'Harriet, my dear.' Mrs Lefevre put her hand on the bench. 'Sit here.'

Harriet sat down and pulled off her bonnet.

'We will have coffee; but is it wise to risk your skin in this sun?'

'Oh, I hate the feel of my bonnet these days, how it ties me in. I ran about without one as a girl and now I wish to have that liberty again.'

Mrs Lefevre tapped on the glass of the window behind her. The coffee arrived in a golden pot embellished with a portrait of the French King.

'Our late King.' Mrs Lefevre sighed and lifted up her cup. 'The Dauphin, the princes and princesses.' An image of Marie-Antoinette was printed on the cream jug. Harriet began to laugh.

'Is it suitable, Mrs Lefevre, now that they are no longer alive?'

'You forget, my dear. The Princess Marie-Thérèse is with us still.'

'Oh, Mrs Lefevre. I do not wish to touch on that subject; it is all gone, the past. Does it matter if there is never another king of France, or any country? In America they have another government that seems to suit them well enough. Why does everyone think only of restoring what has been lost?'

She felt more angry about the lost king than was warranted by her words. Why could the French not simply accept his death? Like stars, like everything in nature, kings died, and younger, more vigorous monarchs took their places. Napoleon was surely a fair exchange for Louis. Why did Mrs Lefevre cling to her loyalty as if it were life? It was not the case that the King was really a father to his people. A person might choose another king, a more attentive, younger, better king; never another father, or mother.

'Mrs Lefevre, I have come back to ask you about my mother. I find myself returning to thoughts of her. I feel sure there is something you must remember; something you may know that might help me to find her. It is that that I want more than anything else.'

'I have written to you on that subject, Mrs Raven.'

Harriet took the dressmaker's hand and considered it, plump and spotted with age, the wedding ring half buried in flesh. The undersides of her fingers were dry with needle pricks and hard work. Mrs Lefevre had watched her husband marched away by the mob, so Mrs Cobbold had told her, because of his allegiance to the old regime. Mrs Lefevre never saw him again or learned what had become of him. She had not wished to be next, took the boat to London, sewed to survive, and prospered.

Harriet could see all that work in Mrs Lefevre's hands and knew that life had instilled caution in her. Still she persevered with her questions; she did not want sympathy because of her position, because James was abroad and she was alone. No, she asked for it as one woman to another. Her aunt, and now Mrs Lefevre, did not treat with her in that way, but as if she were still a child. They spoke as if time held a secret for all women that she was too young to share.

'I know, and I thank you. But when I came to see you—last year, it must have been and still I know nothing more—you said my mother might wish to remain hidden.'

'I believe I put it another way: undiscovered.'

'Mrs Lefevre, I beg you simply to tell me. Do you believe my mother is alive?'

Mrs Lefevre tapped on the window again. When the maid had cleared the tray, and after another long pause, she shifted in her seat and fixed her eyes not on Harriet but on the narrow gravel walk that led to the end of the garden.

'Diana—your mother—was French.' Mrs Lefevre tipped her chin up with an air of pride and defiance. 'She was brought out, I believe, in the early days of the Revolution; introduced to me as an orphan. Her father had been imprisoned by the King, they said, though I never enquire about such things.'

Harriet started. Frederick had seen something in her, then, when he declared that she had an air that was not quite English. But that was absurd. There was nothing her mother could have passed to her, she remembered nothing given or received.

'She was delicate, and beautiful, Mrs Raven, with your own enthusiasms; the same age as you are now, perhaps. Your father, up for the season, claimed her hand and took her back to Suffolk. Her protectors were delighted that Diana was married and safe.'

'You appear less so, Mrs Lefevre.'

'Indeed not, but your mother was from Paris. She was not bred to the country, especially not to the flat, endless country of your part of the world.'

'She came back to London?'

'Once or twice, and I made her gowns always; but after you were born, they were to measurements. Then I had a letter from Mr Patteson.'

'Mr Patteson?'

'Surely you know him, my dear. He is your father's solicitor.'

Harriet wondered if she had ever heard the name. Nothing came into her head.

'I do not remember, Mrs Lefevre. Perhaps I encountered him, but others took care of my father's affairs. His death was so sudden and such a shock.'

'No matter. There has been an arrangement. Mr Patteson sends a draft each year and a list of requirements.'

'Requirements?' Harriet felt stifled and angry. Mrs Lefevre, and perhaps her aunt, had kept something from her.

'For gowns, shifts, slippers; very simple, but never less than garments for a lady.'

'She is alive. My mother is alive and you did not tell me.'

'I cannot say that Lady Guest is alive, Mrs Raven. I have not seen her for over twenty years.'

Harriet clenched her fists. She stood up and then sat down; the small garden wobbled in front of her eyes.

'She is alive. She is alive, somewhere. Why did you not tell me when I asked? I needed to know!'

Mrs Lefevre looked uncomfortable. She stared along the path. When she spoke her voice was light and considered, the tone she took with émi-grés whose lives she preferred, for the sake of business, to know nothing of Royalists, Republicans, Regicides; those who had fled from that mad-man Robespierre, or, now, the Emperor: they were all here, in London, living out their terrors and feuds. Nothing good would ever come for her if she meddled in it all.

'I told you all that I could.'

'You did not, Mrs Lefevre. You might have spared me such misery.'

Mrs Lefevre's voice hardened now, the voice of a woman for whom silence and survival had long ago come to mean the same thing.

'I had my instructions, and my reputation for discretion to maintain.'

'Your reputation? Did you not think for a moment of my happiness?'

'Your feelings, Mrs Raven, are not my affair.'

Mrs Lefevre drew herself in. Then to her surprise, Harriet leaned towards her.

'No, no; forgive me. The shock has made me think only of myself. I understand; I cannot agree, Mrs Lefevre, but I understand.'

Harriet stood and began to walk up and down the path between the low box borders. The wallflowers that filled the flowerbeds glowed red and golden and orange with her joy. Her mother was alive; all it remained to do was find her. She turned for the last time and came back.

'I do not seek to censure you, Mrs Lefevre. Please tell me, simply, where my mother is.'

'I do not know.'

'You make her clothes.'

'I send them to Mr Patteson's office in the Inner Temple and there is an end to it until the next draft arrives. As I said in my letter, I do believe your father acted for the best, whatever he did.'

'What did he do? Oh, please explain.'

'Mrs Raven, I do not know. Only perhaps that he did not wish you to be like her, or become like her. Perhaps there was some contagion of the blood; some delicacy that might have come down to you.'

'Do you say that my mother was sick?'

Mrs Lefevre pushed her two old hands down on the bench and forced herself slowly to stand. Then she unhooked her stick from the arm of the bench and turned to go into the house.

'Ah, you see how it is. Years at the sewing bench have stiffened me.'

'Do you believe my mother to be in a hospital?'

The old woman looked at Harriet in the same distant way and stopped by the open back door.

'Come inside with me; I can say no more.'

Inside the house, sunlight streamed through the back window and fell down the stairs onto Harriet's shoulders. Mrs Lefevre stopped and steadied herself on the dark curl of the stair rail. She considered Harriet, and noticed the dust on the chenille gown she had made herself. Really Mrs Raven ought to take more care; yet her charm survived her untidiness. In this light she looked so much like Diane, with the lightness and acquired grace of a Parisian.

Mrs Lefevre brushed the dust off Harriet's sleeve.

'Mrs Raven, you are quite at liberty to try Mr Patteson yourself.'

JOHN PATTESON, WHEN HARRIET was shown into his office by his clerk, appeared to be shaken. He stood behind a large oak desk and asked her to sit down.

'Mrs Raven. It is not customary to receive people at this time of day.'

'I cannot wait; I have something of importance to ask you. I think you may know what it is.'

Harriet took off her gloves. Her face was flushed and hot from the walk down to Charing Cross and along the mêlée of the Strand. Dust from dozens of carts and lumbering post-chaises coated the bottom of her gown. Through the windows across the green lawn she saw boats and lighters working upriver against the ebb tide and a brisk west wind. The sun scattered silver lights onto the crumpled surface and the whole silken curve of the Thames, as far as Harriet could see, danced and sparkled through the glass. The busy water drew her eye in; a woman might slip beneath its surface and in a moment disappear, or come up downriver as someone else.

'I have come about my mother. I have been given your name; it appears you have something to do with her.'

'Your mother, madam?'

'Lady Guest. Diana Guest. I believe you deal with my mother's affairs. Is she a Ward in Chancery?'

'I am not empowered to disclose anything material to you, Mrs Raven, but may I say that Lady Guest is not a Ward in Chancery. I administer a trust on her behalf.'

'Why cannot my mother, if she is alive, deal with her own income?'

Mr Patteson looked at her as if he wished to see her out of the door.

'I cannot say; I follow the terms of your father's will.'

Harriet remembered then that she had seen Mr Patteson before. It was the day of her father's funeral. A picture of the church at Bungay came to her, just off the town square with its graveyard on the river side. Mr Patteson was in the church and at Beccles Hall afterwards; a tall man with the alert air of someone at work rather than a guest caught in the drama and sadness. Shock had made her forget, and forget that he had read aloud to her the portion of her father's will that concerned her inheritance, called other members of the family to him, then the servants, and finally left for London. She had not given him another thought and now here he was, determined to thwart her. These older people—no, she must include James, she realised with a shock—swept aside her questions. By what right did they all decide what she could know; and James, her own husband, how could he side with them? She tried again.

'Tell me, Mr Patteson, tell me I beg you, is my mother then alive? Gowns are made for her; a trust administered. She is alive, then. Where is she?'

Mr Patteson stood up and looked down at her.

'I have told you all I am able; your father's will was plain in its wishes, and one of those wishes was that such knowledge should be kept from you, for your own good.'

'I shall ask my Aunt Cobbold, then. Good evening, Mr Patteson.'

Harriet ran down the narrow stairs, past lawyers' offices, two on each landing, marked with gold names on wooden panels, past startled clerks on the ground floor and out by the garden door.

'Harriet, what is the matter?' Mrs Cobbold was shocked by her niece's demeanour when Harriet came into the parlour in Hatton Garden. Harriet did not sit down. She stood by her aunt's chair. The elusive air she usually gave off had gone, replaced by a force that was solid and immovable.

'I have been to see Mr Patteson.'

As soon as Harriet spoke Mrs Cobbold felt an old dread come alive.

'Ah, yes.'

'He refuses to tell me anything. Is my mother living still?'

'Harriet, you must compose yourself. You will do yourself harm if you carry on in this way.'

'I am no longer concerned with any of that, Aunt. I ask you about my mother; please give me an answer.'

'We have attempted to protect you.'

'I do not wish to be protected; I wish to know.'

'Very well. I will tell you what I can.'

Harriet sat down.

'I know so little, my dear. Your mother—your mother lost her reason. William thought it best to send her away.'

'Lost her reason?'

'That is all I know.'

'Very well, so my father sent her away? My father!'

'For your own good, your own good.'

'When? How old was I?'

Mrs Cobbold considered, though she had no need to. She remembered it well, '93, when she lost something so precious that she never spoke of that time again. She thought of the mangled body of her daughter. Samuel never spoke of her afterwards and neither did she; that made it easier, made their loss less a nightmare, more a dream. It was better to forget the child, and in time it happened. Months passed now, years even, without any memory of that day.

'You were two years old, nearly three. It was a difficult time.' Mrs Cobbold looked vague. 'The war had just begun.'

'You never asked where he sent her? How could my father do that?'

'I did not ask, and I do not know. William was always a secretive man, and isolated himself from the world; he liked to do things his own way. We did not always see eye to eye.' Mrs Cobbold sucked in her ample cheeks. 'You must remember that I never approved of his match, and he never approved of mine.' She stretched out her hand to Harriet.

'Believe me, I have told you everything that I know. If Diana is alive, then I know nothing of her whereabouts.'

'You will not tell me.'

'I do not know; believe me I do not know.'

'Mr Patteson will not tell me, Mrs Lefevre does not know. You never sought to find out.'

'Harriet, there are many things I do not speak of. We surely all have sadness to carry through life. I beg you to think of this in that way.'

'I cannot. I cannot forgive what I do not understand. And James; does he know? Oh, Aunt, I am no longer a child. I cannot bear it.'

'You must, my dear, for your own sake.'

Mrs Cobbold looked up with relief at the sound of a clatter of wheels and then the doorbell. A moment later Dorothy Yallop pulled open the parlour door and marched in, her head obscured by a large old-fashioned bonnet. She dropped her bags on the floor and ran over to the sofa.

'A letter, my dears; a letter from the Major sent on from Norwich. Let us open it.'

Mrs Yallop looked around with her wide face full of delight. One by one her features fell as she glanced first at Harriet and then at Mrs Cobbold.

'You have had bad news?'

'Indeed, no. Now do take off your bonnet, Mrs Yallop, and let us hear what the Major has to say. When is his letter dated?' Mrs Cobbold seized this new subject with gratitude.

Dorothy Yallop put her letter down, undid her bonnet and laid it by the door. She sat down, broke the seal on the cover sheet and unwrapped her letter with care.

'From Freneda, on 15th April. Ah, yes, the Major writes on the top, "sent on from Headquarters by Captain Raven." Good, good. Now let us see.' She began to scan down the lines. 'Captain Raven returned from the south. He is well, and impatient to move out and engage the enemy. Ah, here: the Major's men are in good health. Dr McBride gives them oranges which they grumble about.' She waved the paper, brought it to her lips with a smack and shook it out.

'What an old fool I am. Did you ever see the like, and after twenty years with the Major.' She opened her arms wide.

'Oh, but it makes me love this world to see his handwriting, to know he is well and as content as he can be in quarters. Now let us sit down and read it all through. There is a good deal more news.'

Mrs Yallop's delight filled the room. Harriet stood up.

'I must get out of this dirty gown, Aunt. I shall dress for dinner and look forward to a full reading when I come down.' She bent to kiss Mrs Yallop and slipped out. On the way up the stairs she paused. Dorothy's presence soothed her, but there was no denying it; it was not the news of James that commanded her attention. It was that of her mother, her French mother, who must be somewhere still alive. She could not give up the search now; perhaps her mother was close by, in London. As for Frederick, it was for the best, at the moment, that she put him out of her mind.

~

AT THE BEGINNING OF May, a hundred thousand men, with horses, mules, guns, tents, new light camp kettles and carts with cannon balls on beds of hay, began to stir and shift. Like a great animal migration, pulled by a force known in the general memory, the greater part of Lord Wellington's army, ten thousand cavalry, with forty thousand infantry behind them, streamed through the upland passes in the north of the country. Each night the great herd rested; each morning started up and on again.

Major Yallop pulled out his pipe one evening and looked into the constellations flung out across the sky. From horizon to horizon thousands of quiet stars shimmered and winked. The night was moonless and placid. Before he went to sleep, the Major allowed himself the fancy that from up there the red columns of men on the march must make it look as if the earth had opened to show its veins.

The 9th Regiment marched in General Graham's 5th Division. Behind Yallop's men rode the surgeons; behind them the servants and army wives, and Portuguese boys who jogged along on foot. Up in the hills, where the wind was keen and hot and the low trees threw sparse shade to march in, the Major reminded his men to take care against sunburn. Find a moist new leaf, he told them. Lay it across your bottom lip once the sun is up, and smear the top lip with a thumbful of grease from the kettle. Cracked lips burst open in a few days. Apart from the pain, the Major thought, he had his pride. Even with new boots just sent out, his men were a ragged lot, and he did not want them to face the French like a troupe of Gibraltar apes.

Two weeks or so after the 9th set off, General Wellington left his Headquarters at Freneda and put the whole of the right wing of his army, as far down as Placentia, in motion to the east. The village priest, who bowed as the staff left, hurried to his church and sounded the General's departure with a joyous peal of bells. At Salamanca, with the French withdrawn, Wellington joined forces with General Hill. Behind them marched a force of thirty thousand men.

The next morning before they left their lodgings Hill took advantage of the General's good humour to congratulate him on the condition of the army.

'You have amassed a splendid force over the winter, my Lord,' he said with a nod.

'I shall never be stronger than I am now, or more efficient.'

Wellington looked over at Hill. The man was younger than he, but aged already; his chin sagged over his neck. Hill let his hair lie in ragged patches over his scalp, and pulled his trousers up over his stomach.

'I cannot have a better opportunity than trying the fate of a battle. Our intelligence from the guerrillas gives us the advantage of ten thousand men, and I have not known it fail yet.'

'It is odd that you mention the guerrillas, my Lord.' Hill frowned. 'We had an incident a few weeks ago that indicated the contrary, and led me to doubt the probity of Cuesta at least.'

Wellington tapped his gloves against his shins with impatience. Hill could be dull when there was the least call for it.

'We got word from Cuesta that there were a couple of hundred grenadiers up in the hills, foraging no doubt, with an additional brief of ascertaining our strength. I sent five hundred against them, but it appeared that they had been informed of our arrival, and that their numbers equalled our own. A hundred men were killed in the ambush, five good officers among them. I need not tell you, my Lord, that the loss weighs heavily with me. There was no time to make enquiries, but I have lost faith that Cuesta is firmly of our party. Partisans of his sort are fickle, drop in and out as it suits them.'

James, who stood at the back of the crowded room, felt the ground shift under his feet. This was Felipe Odonnell's work; this was Camille. 'Unfortunate, Rowland.' Wellington turned and made his way out into the sunshine. Hill had no discrimination. He cluttered the air with nonsense about a skirmish when one hundred and fifty thousand men prepared to do battle.

In the following days, when he rode behind the General in the middle of the cluster of men who made up his staff, James pursued the idea where Lord Wellington had let it go. Hill had been misled; Cuesta had told him there were two hundred Frenchmen when he must have known five hundred were there. Hill had been lucky; he had sent a generous force, equal to that of the French. Had he only dispatched two hundred they might all have been killed, especially since the French were already deployed. Felipe and Camille had surely worked for the French all along. He was no more than the instrument of her betrayal, one more British soldier to destroy.

But that explanation did not fit. What about the earlier, successful interceptions? The French, Hill had implied, knew that the British were on the way; Cuesta told Hill where he could find the enemy. It was obvious, then; both sides had been duped. Cuesta had told the French that the British had a small force, the British the same, with the calculation that they would be evenly matched. To what purpose but to eliminate troops from both sides; and to what end, now that the forces of France and Britain were on the march? Had it simply pleased Camille to let good men destroy one another, as she had destroyed him?

As the march went on, James let the matter drop. He felt exhausted and confused. Camille had made a mockery of his success. As he rode up through the last hills that ringed the basin of the Zadorra River, where the great French armies had come to a halt on their march north out of Madrid and the south, James longed for the simplicity of a battle, an action in which he might either distinguish himself or be killed.

THE 21ST OF JUNE dawned misty and wet; light rain fell and washed the plain in vapour. The landscape below the General's position on the high ground was indistinct. Stands of wood covered low hills down to the valley bottoms. Thomas Orde, left with James's baggage, knew that dozens of French cannon waited, concealed there behind trees and scrub. Towards the town of Vitoria fields of ripening corn chequered the plain and vineyards rose up the southward slopes. Through the middle of the plain ran the silver ribbon of the Zadorra River.

That was the battlefield. Lord Wellington estimated it as ten miles wide and nearly as broad. It stretched beyond the town of Vitoria to where thousands of camp followers slept amongst all the baggage brought from Madrid. Further still, too far for even a telescope to make out, began the roads to the coast and to France.

Every soldier, that morning, knew it was the day of battle. Thomas Orde was relieved that General Graham, who commanded the 2nd Division and the 9th Regiment, was far away in the hills to the north. He had no fear that he would see any of his friends fall or die. It would be tomorrow before he met any of them and by then everything would be over. Sixty thousand men on each side would march against each other today. This time, Thomas did not volunteer. He had seen enough of war at Badajoz to last a lifetime.

Yet after midday, when the battle, from where he stood, had turned into a running fight up and down the steep hills that led into the city, Thomas could make out nothing much at all. Gunsmoke rose up and covered the hills; it made the mules toss their heads and cough. If the smoke cleared for a moment he saw groups of men load and fire, scurry and charge. In the first hour of the battle he could make out orderly columns of red and blue. Now everything was indistinct and broken up. Beneath his feet the ground laboured and pushed against the boom of the guns, wave after wave, like Atlantic billows. Muskets flashed in the smoke as if a thousand tinders lit up at once.

Snippets of news, shouted from man to man in the rear, told the story of what he could not see.

'General Hill has begun down there on the right. You will see that General Graham attacks on the left while Nosey goes through in the centre here.'

'The attack has been halted to wait for Graham to come down from the hills.'

'The 3rd Division is across the river.'

By the afternoon wounded men began to straggle back. Some cradled shattered wrists or forearms; others limped up without ceremony. Smoke filled the basin; the battle moved across the plain towards France like a great thunderstorm. At a distance of five miles the guns sounded a low continuous roar and the muskets sounded like the tick of crickets on a hot night.

'Lord Wellington is across the river; the enemy is falling back.'

'The Hussars are into the town.'

'Shall we go down, Thomas; take a mule and join the fun. Bill here says word is they have left everything.'

'No, I shall stay here and wait for Captain Raven.'

'It's no time for quiet, Thomas. There is something for all of us down there.'

'I'll not be going.'

THE 9TH ATTACKED THROUGH the mist at midday. In brushed jackets and with shining bayonets the regiment came down a narrow defile through hills that lay between the coast and the plain. They marched four abreast along the road, then straight into a French artillery barrage from the village of Gamarra Mayor. A cannon ball lifted Major Yallop clear of his men, and laid him behind a rock. In the dense smoke and mist he was lost; the regiment swept past him into the French fire, and only later did his men ask where he was.

'My sword arm has gone,' he said to himself when he saw his own body.

He sensed the presence of someone with him, though he could not tell who it was. When he twisted round to have a word with him, the man had gone. Perhaps it was only himself, watching.

I will not be long about it either, the Major thought. He felt it best to die here, on the battlefield, while great things were in the balance. The battle had gone beyond him, passed over and out of sight. Strange that he no longer seemed to mind that it had left him here alone. For some hours he lay quiet. He watched the blood from his empty shoulder pool round the skirt of his jacket. Collected on the ground, its surface was convex, like an upturned dinner plate. The bulge caught the dying sun and the viscous surface glowed.

'If I had my callipers with me I might measure the circumference and so calculate the volume of the whole. That might give me an idea of my blood loss.'

But then his attention wandered to his shattered arm, and singed sleeve.

'Really,' the Major said to himself, 'and I had on my new jacket, brushed clean for this morning.'

He felt no pain yet, just the shock of surprise and a ripple of annoyance especially since he wished to see the outcome of today's action, though he was sure, because the Division had passed by long ago, that the day must be theirs. The shouts and thumps of the battle receded; pain came to take their place, and the Major's mind floated away on it. He felt himself grow weaker and the world about him fade.

But over there was Dorothy. It was quite unremarkable that she was there, without a fuss. If he tried hard enough he would be able to reach her.

'Well,' he said to himself as he went, 'this is it then, Mrs Yallop. The end is nothing to worry about. It is another adventure, after all. Here, take my hand. There is yours, quite warm, as I have held it so many years. Look after yourself, look after yourself, my dear.'

～

MUCH LATER, WHEN THE French armies were in rapid retreat and the British soldiers had already abandoned any thought of pursuit, Robert Heaton walked through the wreckage of Joseph Bonaparte's baggage train. His step was heavy; a message had come from the 9th Regiment that announced its casualties, the Major amongst them. Heaton walked unseeing until he came across the sort of object usually dear to his heart.

'What a beauty of a carriage.' He talked to himself in an effort to lift his mood. 'New by the look of it and perfectly fitted out.'

The carriage gleamed in the near darkness. Two of Heaton's men stood on the curricle-hung seat. Another leaned out over the splashing boards and began to pull off the delicate silver mouldings. A third came over.

'Anything in the trunk there?'

'No, and the sword case is empty too.'

'Look here, now.' Heaton moved forward; but before he could go on, clothes and a mahogany writing case sailed out of the interior, followed by a frightened lapdog with a golden ribbon round its neck. The creature fell at his feet and whimpered. Heaton considered it. A poodle: miniature. That was one dog he disliked; the way its pink hide showed through the white curls, like the hair on an old woman. He made no attempt to pick it up. After a minute the dog scampered off and Heaton watched it run round the piles of loot collected by the soldiers. It barked as it went, and turned this way and that.

You are looking for your mistress, he thought, off you go, and mind you do not end up on the point of a bayonet. Then he felt sadder than ever. The loss of the Major hung about him.

'Soldiers without money become robbers,' he told himself. But the sentiment did nothing to make him feel better.

The carriage door lay open and off its hinges. In the gloom Heaton saw slashes in the crimson damask seat covers. Horsehair poked out, black and tangled. Golden tassels and a heavy fringe, pulled from the window blinds, strewed the polished floor. Heaton leaned in and pulled up a painting that lay face down. He propped it against one of the wheels and stood back.

'And there she is, I shouldn't wonder.'

As he stood there, Heaton saw a party approach; the commander-in-chief, accompanied by three officers. Even Wellington, with such a small suite, seemed insignificant in the scene of devastation. His chestnut horse picked its way with care amongst the debris, as if it were as disgusted as the General by the disorder.

When Wellington drew level with the carriage, he stopped and turned to the pale redheaded officer who rode next to him.

'Colonel Campbell, ask the man's name.'

Heaton stepped forward and saluted.

'Captain Robert Heaton, 44th, my Lord, promoted after Salamanca from a volunteer, and proud to serve you. May I offer you my congratulations?'

'Congratulations? To whom would you offer them, sir? To my army?'

Colonel Campbell looked discomfited.

'I believe Captain Heaton may wish to congratulate you upon your victory, my Lord.'

Wellington looked down at Heaton.

'Very good.'

The commander-in-chief then looked beyond Heaton across the battlefield; past the heaps of clothing and the abandoned carts, to the line of hills that merged into the mountains where Joseph Bonaparte's army had all but disappeared into the blue haze. His face expressed irritation and anger; without saying another word he tapped his horse's flanks, and moved off.

What made him stop, Heaton wondered? Perhaps it was the face of a pretty woman. So that was Lord Wellington, whom he had so long wished to encounter. Now he was indifferent. The day had drained him of admiration; of everything. He was still standing by the maimed carriage when James bumped into him some time later.

'Good evening, Captain Heaton.' James spoke with the same formality he might have used had they run into one another in Pall Mall. He had no wish to talk to anyone now.

At least Heaton seemed subdued, James thought. He himself felt more relief than anything else. He scarcely thought about the battle that was just finished. It seemed unimportant. No battle is ever really won, he thought. Peace is only a surface calm. Perhaps even here another battle would be fought one day. Why not? It was as good a place as any for men to destroy one another.

They moved through a landscape of chaos. On every side lay piles of overturned stores and pillaged trunks. Abandoned mules wandered about. Soldiers, already drunk and with their jackets undone, tossed dresses up and caught them like ghosts on their bayonet points. One wore a pearl necklace, another carried a ceremonial sword. An officer of the Light Brigade sat on the ground, a bottle in one hand and a book in the other. James bent down and glanced across at the spine: Rabelais, in French. He turned over a broken toy cart with his foot. Painted in gay red and yellow, it lay smashed into the ground. A porcelain doll, dressed in the finest muslin stained by the dirt, lay alongside, one leg off. The profligate waste of what had been so carefully packed and collected, the abandonment it meant of homes and happiness, of the innocence of children at play, fitted James's mood. Robert Heaton walked up and stood next to him in silence.

'Did you pick up anything yourself, Captain Heaton?'

Heaton sat down on an emptied trunk. He looked embarrassed.

'I am not here for that sort of trifle.'

'And what is that tucked into your trouser top?'

Heaton looked squeamish, as if James had caught him out in a lapse of taste. With the care of an experienced conjuror he pulled out a cream lace mantilla, diaphanous as a snowflake. Tiny seed pearls hung from every point on the fringe.

'It is not for myself, you understand.' Heaton's face did not move. 'You know the Major was killed in the assault on the bridge up in the north?'

'I am sorry to hear it. The poor man did not suffer?'

James felt nothing beyond a widening of the emptiness in his heart. He brushed a speck of dust from under his eye.

'A cannon ball took his arm off, I am told. He was already dead when they checked on him. You know he had expressed the wish to me many times to go in that manner.'

'Quite so.'

'George told me that Mrs Yallop is quite the lady for a shawl. He always brought her something of the sort back from a campaign. I thought she might find a use for it.'

'She may indeed be partial to a length of fabric; but surely, Captain Heaton, the Major would never have taken such a thing.'

Heaton coughed and looked for a moment as if he might cry. He swallowed and went on.

'You are right, of course; but now that he is not here, I thought to send it to her. I shall do so, on my own behalf.'

Heaton folded the shawl into a soft triangle. The seed pearls trickled into his lap and lay like maggots in an angler's tin.

James and Heaton stared at them. There seemed to be nothing else to say.

After a few minutes James looked up, and his eye caught the portrait Heaton had propped against the carriage wheels. It showed a woman dressed in the Athenian style favoured at the end of the last century. One rope of gold held the folds of her gown under her bosom, another pulled up her hair. Over her shoulder leaned a young girl with a lily in her hand. Something familiar in it made him walk over and pull it onto his knee.

'Pretty, eh?' said Heaton from behind him. 'I knew the artist a little.'

'The painter?'

'Girodet. He painted all of us in Paris; everyone left over when David had finished, that is. This lovely creature has ended up in quite the wrong place.'

James was taken back instantly to Camille's drawing room and the portrait over the fireplace. He saw its golden letters glow through the gloom: Girodet, 1796. Eugene O'Donnell, then, had been in Paris. Camille had never mentioned it.

'You have been in Paris?'

Heaton looked distant, in the way he did when anyone questioned him about the past.

'I was there in '96 and '97. The place seemed full of possibility, then, and I hoped to get on. But there were so many of us, the flotsam of Europe, and then the Irish arrived and rather engrossed the attention of the Directory.'

'The Irish?'

'You are too young to remember, perhaps.'

'Did they support the revolution in France?'

'Only a few of them. There is nothing so provincial as a revolutionary, in my experience. Even the most high-flown of them usually bear some local grudge when you get beneath the words.'

'What did they want, then, the Irishmen?'

'The usual republican things; liberty, equality; as well as freedom from Britain, of course. Many were regicides, wanted the death of all kings. They were poor fighters when it came to the point, wiped out before they got started.'

Heaton looked sad, as if he had missed an opportunity of a good battle in his youth.

'They made up to the Directory, of course, but only to get help against England.'

'Might I ask you another question, Captain Heaton? Did you ever meet a Eugene O'Donnell there?'

'One had to be careful, use another name, and so on. So I may have; then again, it is hard to be sure.'

Had Heaton been a British spy, James wondered.

'They ran around in green, I remember. Every United Irishman wore a green cravat. Very poor taste.'

James saw Eugene O'Donnell again, the green cravat at the very centre of his portrait. So Camille's father had been an enemy to Britain. He had been in Paris in 1796 at the height of the Revolution.

'He is there still, I shouldn't wonder,' Heaton said suddenly.

'Who?'

'Girodet. In Paris. You can look him up. We will not be in this God-forsaken country much longer.'

James smiled at last.

'Spain has been kind to you, Captain Heaton.'

Heaton laid the mantilla carefully aside. James saw that Racket waited, his nose on his master's thigh. Heaton tapped his lap and Racket jumped up. For a long time Heaton sat and looked at the pile of lace beside him.

'Racket and I can never approve of a country where the animal kingdom is held in contempt. Can we, Racket?'

The dog was silent. He sat on Heaton's knees and gazed at James with a look of imperturbable possession in his fathomless brown eyes.

In the afternoon of the next day, when the most urgent cases were dealt with, David McBride walked across the northern edge of the battlefield. He looked for his own wounded at the narrow gate where the 9th Regiment had fought to enter the town of Vitoria. By a turn in the road he came across the bodies of two children, a girl and a boy, one about four, the other no more than two years old. They lay on top of one another, naked limbs twisted as they could never be in life. Beyond one small hand, half buried in the dusty soil, rolled a shattered painted stick, a toy sword perhaps, that performed miracles of imagined glory. Even heaped up, with their rich clothes torn and ragged, the children looked peaceful, and beautiful in the ugliness. How had they got there? Had they run away when the camp followers panicked and ran, separated from their mother? Surely, David thought, they were a brother and a sister, part of a family.

The children, if David did not look too closely, might still be alive. They were indeed yesterday's living, whose presence lay across the battlefield like a cloak of souls. Cavalry officers and infantrymen, muleteers and cooks, brothers, wives and sons lay with them. Every nation in Europe was crammed with their absence; the living would bump up against them for years. After wars the dead talked and talked and the air was full of conversations.

A few hours ago, David thought, those two might have quarrelled over the sword or played at combat by their mother's side. Where was she now? He longed to pull the children up. He might shake them off and breathe the life back into them before night came. He wondered as he looked at them if he would ever have children himself, children like them. A picture of Harriet Raven passed over his mind before he could push it away. Am I a disgrace to my profession, he thought, that I can imagine such a thing by the side of death. Besides this, as a man of science I should not be overcome by their look of innocence; I should know that these bodies are nothing without the electrical charges that give them vitality. Where they lie does not matter; they are gone already.

The notion of the children lying exposed in the dark air unsettled him nonetheless. Perhaps that is why we bury the dead, he thought, and hesitate to burn them. The dead need the safe companionship of the soil; they need quilts of dust and headstones to tell us where to find them. Perhaps he might dig a grave himself, lay the children down side by side, straighten their broken limbs and cover them up. But he had no time or tools, only his scissors, scalpel, needles, bandages and splints. He looked up and down the road in the hope that he might find a spade left by the French artillery who had abandoned their guns the day before. There was nothing except for a heap of ransacked knapsacks. He might find something inside them that the British did not want.

In two of the knapsacks David found French blankets, dark blue and new. The children's bodies were already stiff and cool. Grey settled on their skin and a yellowness had collected under their open eyes. He decided to leave them together and wrapped the woollen cloth as best he could round both of them. Then he pulled out one of his curled needles, threaded it with catgut and sewed the blankets up. His hands shook, he noticed. Why, after so many bodies, did the sight of these two so affect him?

'They are too young to lie out in the open. A terrible thing, too, to find a brother and a sister tumbled over one another. I must at least send a burial party to them, and put up a wooden marker in case their mother should come back. That is as much as I can do.'

As he walked away David began to cry. The tears flowed down his cheeks in the dark.

'FITZROY. PAY ATTENTION. LORD Bathurst had better not get news of victory before this dispatch. Take your pen again.'

He must dampen this mood of elation at Headquarters, Wellington thought the day after the battle. His army wallowed knee-deep in booty. Men wandered the town in the jackets of French officers and Spanish courtiers. The night after the battle, flares lit up the rain-soaked plain where heaps of soldiers, sodden with drink, gambled with rubies and bags of coins. A million sterling had gone into the soldiers' knapsacks; plenty of his own young men had pockets crammed with silver. Not a single senior officer had volunteered to go after the French either overnight or this morning. He knew it: not one of them was worthy of command. He had won the battle, lost five thousand men and allowed Joseph Bonaparte a free passage into France.

'Let us continue.'

Wellington paced the room while Somerset wrote. He spoke just too fast for ease or fine writing.

'We accordingly attacked the enemy yesterday, and I am happy to inform your Lordship that the Allied army under my command gained a complete victory, having driven them from all their positions; having taken from them 151 pieces of cannon, wagons of ammunition, all their baggage, provisions, cattle, treasure etc., and a considerable number of prisoners.'

The room was crowded with men. General Hill, with his lank hair and long face, stood alone by an open window and looked out, his hat tucked under one arm. Several junior officers, who had crowded in to see the commander-in-chief, smiled and glanced at one another, as they heard Wellington speak, as if to indicate that they knew exactly what the progress of yesterday's battle had been. The atmosphere was one of jubilation, suppressed to nonchalance. Though it was early the heat outside had already begun to seep in. Sweat glistened on General Cole's face; every few minutes, he pulled out his handkerchief and wiped it away.

Fitzroy Somerset held his pen with extra care so as to avoid a blot. It was the dream of every aide-de-camp to carry a victory dispatch. Adulation would ride with him if he were chosen. Promotion will come with attendance upon Lord Bathurst, he thought. An honour, even, awaited his arrival at Carlton House or the Pavilion, where the Prince Regent sat with his calves against cushions of plum velvet. Prince George, overcome with gratitude that his throne was safer, would rise and tap him on the shoulder with his ceremonial sword. His title of lord, given him as the younger son of a duke, might be translated into a peerage of his own.

'Fitzroy. Give me your attention. Let us go on.'

Wellington spoke in his light voice without a pause. He would give Hill his due here, why not?

'I am particularly indebted to Lieutenant-General Sir Thomas Graham and Lieutenant-General Rowland Hill for the manner in which they have respectively conducted the service entrusted to them since the commencement of operations.'

Fitzroy Somerset wrote like an automaton. He thought of London in the summer sunshine and his father's house in Piccadilly illuminated for the victory. What title would he take? After all, he was a Plantagenet, descended from Henry II. Broom, he might be Broom; but that had a vulgarity about it. Usk, then, after the family seat? He bent his head over the paper. That had a poor ring to it, like husk, or tusk. No matter, he thought, there will be plenty of time to consider the matter on the journey.

Lord Wellington continued.

'I have frequently been indebted, and have occasion to call the attention of your Lordship to the conduct of the Quartermaster General, Sir George Murray, and am likewise much indebted to Lord Fitzroy Somerset and Lieutenant Colonel Campbell and my personal staff.'

Wellington paused and glanced at Fitzroy who looked up and smiled his sweet, boyish smile. Oh, he had been too indulgent with these young men. They had never known what it was to be alone, or to live with the small inconveniences of life. In India, before the time of his last great victory, he had learned to accept life without a listener, to get on with it by himself. Marriage had made no difference. Kitty's chat and inconsequence drove him further into himself. Fitzroy, though, was confident of his appeal, could look for help. He had always had someone, mother, nurse-maid, tutor, general, to arrange the world prettily for him, and took it as his due. The morning was bad enough without such self-satisfaction.

Who could he send if not an aide-de-camp? A picture came to him of his ride through the devastation yesterday night, and that Captain Heaton, still against the sky. The General disliked volunteers. They were amateurs; charlatans, sometimes; at best men who had no idea of war as a profession. There was no need to do Heaton a favour; still Fitzroy and the others needed a shock, and to send a man like Heaton would certainly deliver it. He gestured to Colonel Campbell.

'Find that Captain Heaton and bring him here. Continue, please, Somerset.'

'I send this dispatch by Captain Heaton of the 44th Regiment, whom I beg leave to recommend to your Lordship's protection. He will have the honour of laying at the feet of His Royal Highness the colours of the 4th Battalion, and Marshal Jourdan's baton of a Marshal of France, taken by the 87th Regiment.'

Fitzroy Somerset felt the blood rise through his cheeks.

'You are in astonishment, Fitzroy? You thought to be the one?'

Fitzroy was about to speak, and then thought better of it. There would come a time when he had the command, and could let the world know his bravery.

'Ah, Fitzroy. By what right do you hope to gallop off?' Wellington looked round at his staff.

'And you too. All of you have purloined something of the enemy's? None of you have self-restraint.' His voice fell to its thinnest and quietest.

'The men they send me are the scum of the earth, and you, who are born to greatness, have shown yourselves to be no better.'

In the silence that followed, Somerset rolled the dispatch papers tight and slotted them into a leather case narrow enough to run down the side of a man's thigh.

'Captain Heaton.'

Robert Heaton walked into the room and up to Lord Wellington. His salute, Fitzroy noticed, was smooth and elegant.

'Captain Heaton, you will take this dispatch to Lord Bathurst and to his Royal Highness.'

'It will be an honour, my Lord.'

Wellington saw that he meant it.

'You are granted leave for as long as you wish to take it.'

Heaton bowed and turned to go.

'Lady Wellington, too. Please acquaint her with the news directly you have been at the Ministry and at Carlton House.'

The General's mood lifted. He had saved himself a letter to Kitty, at least.

10

London and Norwich

SUMMER AND AUTUMN 1813

'My Lord, the dispatch from General Wellington.'

At nine in the morning of the 6th of July, twelve days after the battle, Robert Heaton stood in the summer sunshine in Earl Bathurst's office. He could tell by the earl's air that he already had the news. Somehow, though he had ridden up from Portsmouth and clattered over Westminster Bridge and into Downing Street with only the shortest of stops to change horses, victory had flown ahead of him. No matter, he thought; we will observe the ceremony just the same.

'Captain Heaton, 44th Regiment, at your service, my Lord.' Heaton bowed and handed the dispatch to the Secretary of State.

Lord Bathurst bowed in his turn and took the case. As he opened it he observed the man in front of him. Not young, certainly. Hardly the usual aide-de-camp; but upright, a man who carried himself well. A gentleman. Heaton; he remembered something that attached to the name—good work in Paris, was it?

'Captain Heaton, I thank you. The best news possible. Commend me to the Regent and add my congratulations.'

Earl Bathurst looked out at the houses opposite and frowned. His dealings with the Regent were polite, he trusted, at least on his side; but the Prince always acknowledged his work on behalf of the nation with just a little too much effusion and often accompanied his praise with a pat from his plump hand. On such occasions Bathurst found it hard to leave his own hand outstretched; the Regent's touch was too soft and indecisive.

'Captain Heaton, you may find Carlton House empty. The Regent is customarily at the Pavilion in July.'

Bathurst rang the bell that stood on his desk. When his secretary came in he handed him the dispatch.

'Have this copied and sent to the printers for the *Gazette* immediately. Then bring it back to me.' When the door was closed, Bathurst looked over to Heaton.

'You have time to rest here a little, sir, before you set off. You cannot be there before dark and the Prince seldom conducts official business after dinner. Take some refreshment and give me a first-hand account of the battle. You were present on the field, I presume?'

'Indeed; I will give you as good an account as I am able. One sees little and has to gather the rest, as you know.'

The man has forgotten me, Heaton thought. Memory falters at high altitudes. The idea pleased him; he liked to go through life unobserved. He unhooked his dress sword and sat down in the chair that Bathurst indicated.

'Lord Wellington requested also that I give Lady Wellington the news.'

'Ah, yes. Lady Wellington. You will find her in Hamilton Place. It can be, in a manner of speaking, on your way out of town. Take a fresh horse from the Guards' stable; I shall send them a note to be ready for you.'

Why not, Bathurst thought. Propriety might demand that Heaton go immediately to Brighton. But Lord Wellington was more likely to be of use to him than the Regent; and besides, the news would be in print before the evening was out and it would do him no good at all, as secretary of state, if Lady Wellington learned of her husband's victory from the *Gazette*.

On the way out of the War Office, Heaton gathered up Racket, who waited, nose up, in the entrance hall. The dog had had a torrid journey from Spain, first by sea out of Bilbao, then up full-pelt to London. After the loss of the Major, Heaton wanted to keep Racket with him. So now, in town, Racket travelled squashed into a saddlebag. At Horseguards the two guardsmen who waited with a fresh horse raised an eyebrow at his request, but said nothing. Orders from the War Office were best obeyed even if they concerned a mongrel spaniel and a perfectly good new pair of saddlebags. On the way up the Haymarket Heaton noticed Racket tremble as he poked his head out and turned it from side to side. He feels the absence of Athena, the sensible hound, Heaton thought, and needs time to remember the joys of town. He needed time himself.

As he made his way down Piccadilly, Heaton considered his next visit. Before he left Spain, General Lowry Cole had taken him aside.

'The General scarcely speaks of his wife, Major Heaton, and I happen to know he writes seldom and does not read her letters when they arrive. On occasion he has asked me to look at them and relay any contents that appear to be significant.'

'I am to deliver an account of the victory, merely, General Cole. It is an honour to take the dispatch and will be an honour to hand a copy to Lady Wellington.'

'I merely suggest that if occasion arises you might mention that Lord Wellington has received her letters with pleasure.'

Confusion crossed Cole's face and added to his reticence. 'Something of the sort, at any rate. It is Lady Wellington of whom I am thinking. She is a fine woman.'

In the mews at Hamilton Place Heaton pulled Racket out of the saddle-bag, handed his horse to the stable boy, brushed himself off, walked round to the front and pulled the bell. The butler, with an apron over his old waistcoat and breeches, drew the door back. Heaton took off his hat and tucked it under his free arm.

'Good morning, sir.'

'I have a dispatch from Spain, for Lady Wellington.'

'Lady Wellington is in the drawing room. It is, as you know, too early for visits. But come this way at once, sir.'

Heaton warmed to the informality of the household; it was just the thing for Racket, he thought.

'Could you take my dog when you have shown me in? He is well behaved and will wait in the kitchen.'

The butler grasped Racket in his arms and went ahead up the staircase. By the drawing-room door he hesitated a moment, knocked, and then turned the handle.

'Your Ladyship, a dispatch from Spain.'

At that moment, as Heaton advanced into the room, Racket squirmed out of the butler's arms and launched himself forward.

A captain, with a dog, Kitty thought.

Lady Wellington, on the carpet, with, my goodness, a battalion of boys, Heaton said to himself.

'Racket, come here!'

'A dog, a dog.' Gerald Wellesley ran towards Racket with his arms outstretched. Two other boys followed him.

'He's mine.'

'No, mine.'

Racket wagged his tail and ran between the children. Heaton looked with wonder as his dog licked the toddler's face and then down again at Lady Wellington.

'They understand each other.'

Kitty nodded and Heaton bowed, as if Kitty were not on the carpet but they stood face to face.

'Captain Robert Heaton, your Ladyship, with a dispatch from Spain. I come at Lord Wellington's request.'

Kitty stood up. Her undress gown was rumpled and her hair disordered. It was ten-thirty in the morning and she did not expect a visit. No matter; this Captain Heaton saw her as she was, today.

'I bring the best news, Lady Wellington. Your husband is safe, the army victorious, the French in flight. The road to France is open.'

'I am delighted. Tell me, Captain Heaton, were the casualties heavy?'

A shadow crossed the man's face as he stood before her. He swayed a little and looked round for his dog.

'Many good men died; some thousands on each side, and dozens of officers. I left before the final count was made.'

'Do sit, please, Captain Heaton.'

Heaton handed her the papers he held and sat down. Lady Wellington sat at the other end of the sofa; a small, still woman. Her hair was streaked with grey, though she could not have been much over forty, a little younger than himself. How odd; here he was, with a woman he did not know, in a room full of noise; and over there Racket, who usually shied away from children as much as his master did, lay on the carpet tummy up, with three boys by him.

'Arthur, come and sit with me.' Lady Wellington held out her hand to a tall boy who stood apart from the younger children. He came to the sofa and sat down with reluctance. Lady Wellington smiled at him and then turned back to Heaton.

'My husband's godson, Arthur Freese; one of the family.'

I like the look of that boy, Heaton thought; I like his detachment and watchful air.

'What do you do, Captain Heaton?' The boy wore his curly hair close-cropped in the new fashion. His brown eyes were wary.

'Ah, now that is a good question. I wander about, in a manner of speaking. I went out as a volunteer. I am not a great believer in asking why. But to be present when great things are afoot; that interests me.'

'Did you see great things, sir?'

Heaton paused. Kitty saw the shadow cross his face again.

'Indeed, I did, Arthur; though they are not always what one might think.'

'Did you see Lord Wellington in the field upon Copenhagen?'

'Not in the field. I fought at some distance to the General, but he chanced upon me afterwards. That stallion is a beauty.' He paused. 'Your godfather planned the battle to perfection, Arthur. To be ready; that is also a great thing, I find.'

'Are you brave, sir?'

'Well, that's another difficult question.'

He stood up.

'Lady Wellington, I must go. I have to be down in Brighton as soon as possible. It has been a pleasure to make your acquaintance.'

The eldest of the three young boys ran up to him.

'Sir, if you have to go to Brighton, might you leave us your dog? We do not have one of our own.'

'Ah, I am afraid not; but do come to visit Racket when we return. I live in Arlington Street, just round the corner, and intend to be there, one important visit excepted, for some weeks at least. Racket takes a turn in the Park every morning and insists I accompany him. He is an accomplished beast; can teach you a number of tricks—how to throw a stick, how to drop a titbit into his mouth, that kind of thing.'

He turned to his dog.

'What do you say, Racket? A walk?'

Racket jumped up, wagged his tail, dashed round in a circle and made for the door.

'There, he likes the notion. Always good to ask, I find.'

Heaton bowed to Lady Wellington and nodded at Arthur Freese. 'I shall think about your question, Arthur, consider it with care.'

'You see, sir, I wonder often if I myself would be brave.'

'I quite understand. We all do wonder that at times, I believe.'

Kitty stood up; he noticed her air of amusement and the quiet sense of confidence she carried with her.

'I look forward to our next meeting, Major Heaton.'

Heaton scooped up his dog. He winked at Gerald Wellesley and squeezed Arthur Freese's shoulder. The boy smiled at him with astonishment and joy in his face. Really, Heaton thought, children are quaint animals, in their way; diverting too.

When Captain Heaton left, Kitty sent the children to the schoolroom and went up to dress. The usual chore was more tolerable today, a pleasure, even. She chose a plum-red gown and rubies and while her maid tidied her hair she prepared herself for the ambassadors and the heads of livery companies, the dukes and countesses and well-wishers who would gather in her drawing room as soon as the *Gazette* was printed. She felt light, as she often did these days; not lonely, but alone and alert to the world. Her hair, in the pier-glass, was more streaked with white than a few months ago, but she approved of it.

What had the morning brought? A captain with a dog; a tall, upright dark-haired man, who held himself back. She would enjoy a walk in the Park with him. The victory Captain Heaton announced interested her, of course. She ought to send to Mr Rothschild with the news; but he was sure to have it already. Better to consider, before duty overtook her, the need to write to Harriet to tell her to be ready for a crowd this evening. Better, too, to walk with the children after lunch.

'My Lady.' The butler, dressed in uniform now, was by her side. 'There is a woman downstairs. Not the usual sort of visitor if I may say so. She insists upon seeing you.'

'Did she give you her name?'

'Merely that she came as you had asked when you went to her house some months ago.'

'Show her into the library, and I shall come down.'

In the library stood the madam from King's Place, flustered and defiant. 'Lady Wellington; you said I should find you if something happened.'

'Do sit down. Your name, madam?'

The woman hesitated and then said, 'Mrs Christie, at your service, your Ladyship.'

'Tell me, Mrs Christie, how is Mrs Fitzwilliam?'

'She is dead, madam. I buried her with the last of the money you gave; but there is the child.'

'Yes.'

'Joseph.'

'Where is he now? Do you care for him yourself?'

'I have no wish to.' Mrs Christie stopped again. 'You will understand it is no place for a child.'

Kitty calculated.

'He is eleven months old.'

Mrs Christie shrugged. 'Thereabouts, I should say.'

'Mrs Christie, I gave Mrs Fitzwilliam money as an act of kindness merely. Her child, whatever she may have told you, is none of my responsibility.'

'He is Lord Wellington's son. She told everyone, said to look at his blue eyes and nose. Just like His Lordship, she said.'

'I cannot discuss that matter.'

Kitty reached for her purse. Mrs Christie expected something from her, a reward disguised. She took out several guineas.

'Take this to buy new clothes for him. Though I have no connection with him whatever the case, he deserves my compassion.'

'Very well, my Lady. I knew I could count on you.'

'I bid you good afternoon.' Kitty rang the bell and opened the door for Mrs Christie to leave. When she was alone the horror of death crept over her skin, and Mrs Fitzwilliam's loneliness with it. Mrs Fitzwilliam died with nothing, not even her own name. Kitty saw her as she had been when she came to Harley Street, plump with secret confidence, and then again as she was in King's Place six months ago, hollowed out by poverty and fever, too ill for women to envy or men to desire.

And now, here was Joseph. What shall I do with him, she wondered? Put him in the nursery with the younger ones, or send him to the country to get well? Surely the latter, at least for the moment.

TWO DAYS LATER, ROBERT Heaton rode over Westminster Bridge as night fell. Halfway across he stopped, dismounted, and peered down into the swirling water. A rising tide pushed up against the piers of the bridge. Would the water carry the news of victory up to Windsor, where the old King lived, confined in a small room with his Bible and a cane-bottomed chair? Had the King even been told? Could he comprehend such news, or even care, when his mind struggled with itself?

Heaton frowned and swung himself up into the saddle.

'Come along, Racket. Time to get back.'

From the river, Heaton cut up Whitehall and along the edge of St

James's Park. All the great mansions were illuminated, their windows and doorways ablaze with coloured lamps. With the Regent in Brighton, Carlton House alone was in shade, but wreaths of lights wound round the columns of its great portico, and along the top lamps stood in pyramids. Across the gates the letters G and R shone out. London rejoiced and crowds of people strolled by Norfolk House and Devonshire House to admire the displays.

After the silence of Spanish nights alone in his billet, Heaton was wearied by the noise and delight. He had slept fitfully on the soft horsehair mattresses since his return, and found more comfort wrapped in a quilt on the floor. Now his tired mind wandered through different thoughts and onto Lady Wellington and her collection of children. That odd boy Arthur, who had wanted answers, and wondered about courage, or was it bravery. There was nothing more to that, in the end, than the need to test the core, to make sure that it was true metal. Something like that, at any rate; but no matter. He had never heard a soldier speak of it. Soldiers joked about death, right up to the moment of its approach, when they wept and screamed like other men. Like him, they were silent, or joked again, if it passed them by.

'What shall I tell him then, Racket? That he will know what it is when the time comes?'

Heaton thrust his hand into the pocket of his riding coat as he turned into Arlington Street. His fingers closed round the ball Dr McBridge had extracted after Badojoz. Now, there was his aunt's house, its lantern lit and candles in every window. For a moment Heaton regretted that he could not present her with a title. The Regent had forgotten to honour him as was the custom. He was glad of it. A knighthood just because he had delivered a piece of paper, a flag and a Marshal's baton, laid as close as he could get to the Prince's swollen feet? He preferred himself as he was. Besides, the Regent had been at the card table and the bottle; by the time Heaton was announced the Prince was too befuddled for the task.

'Marvellous, marvellous, my dear man,' the Regent said. He leant over to the equerry who stood by Heaton and whispered, 'Who the devil is he? Could not catch the name.' Heaton bowed again.

'Captain Robert Heaton, your Highness. The 44th Regiment of Foot.'

'Ah, yes.' The Regent peered at him through bloodshot eyes. 'Have I not seen you somewhere before? Newmarket, eh? Cumberland House at the dear Duke's for cards?'

'The former, perhaps.'

'Good, good. Well, I am much obliged.' The Regent turned back to the table. Heaton stood for a moment until the equerry, unable to signal that the ceremony required more, bowed and stepped back. Heaton followed him, and they left the darkened room. With that, his visit to the Pavilion was over.

Heaton reached up and pulled the bell by his aunt's front door. She must have been in the hall as he approached because she opened the door herself and wrapped her arms round him.

'I have kept the illuminations day and night, Robert; and invited all the neighbours to share my joy when I learned that you had brought the dispatch.'

When they went into the drawing room Racket had the run of the house. At first he nosed about with caution, not sure he was home. After an hour the familiar smell of the panelling, the turns of the landings and the ways to outdoors became part of him again. He trotted down the stone stairs to the kitchen, barked for supper and laid himself out to sleep by the range. Heaton found him still there at midnight, stretched out on the flags.

'Well done, Racket old chap. A bed is too soft these days, don't you find? You stay there, then, and I shall see you tomorrow.'

ON A COLD AUTUMN morning, Charles Herries waited at the War Office for Lord Bathurst to arrive. He stared at his accounts and saw his daughter and Lucia. These days women tormented him less. Louisa and Lucia filled his thoughts and spurred him to work. The sooner Lord Wellington got over the Pyrenees and into France the sooner he might—oh, he dared not hope what the end of war might bring. Visions of Paris came to him; the golden stone and a smell of bread, and Lucia, in a small neat apartment in the rue de Grenelles, asleep still, this morning, maybe, her skin dark against the sheets.

Figures remained when his reverie dissolved, etched beneath all his hopes. Six million sterling had gone to the Peninsula in 1810, five million the next year; not all of it for the army or his responsibility, it was true, but much of it through his own office. So it went on, and still he needed more.

Henry Bathurst walked into the office. He looked at Herries with surprise; the man was earlier than was either necessary or decent.

'You are here already, Mr Herries. Good; you will take coffee with me?'

Bathurst rang the bell and settled the wings of his coat tails over the sides of his chair. Everything about him, from his hair, worn short and thinned at the temples, to the Garter star that sat on his breast, was in the best taste. Herries noticed that the earl was trimmed to hunting fitness; his own flesh, in contrast, hung loose over the band of his trousers.

'You passed a fruitful summer, I trust.'

'I have remained as usual in London.'

'Quite right. Time and tide, Mr Herries, one might say.'

Lord Bathurst felt rested. The victory at Vitoria had added a golden glow to his time in the country; from such a triumph the Secretary of State for War cut a slice for himself.

'Now, where are we?'

'Money.'

'Always money.'

'I have shipped out over two million already this year.'

'I am glad to say that the East Indies and India have supplied much of your need.'

'Not enough, my Lord, as you know.'

Why did Lord Bathurst look shocked, Herries wondered. They both knew about his arrangement with the Bank to send out British guineas when foreign shipments could not meet Lord Wellington's demands. Besides, he himself had ordered the Mint to coin half a million in Hanoverian coin for troops in northern Europe. They were both of them way out beyond the letter of the law. He cleared his throat.

'I am aware, my Lord, of the risks we run should victory not attend our—let us call it our circumnavigation of the law. The Prime Minister shares them with us, I believe.'

'I dislike the imputation of something underhand; I do no more than the country demands and yet feel as if I were a common criminal.'

Fawley, who had just arrived, leaned forward with eagerness.

'I hardly think, sir, that one needs to use such language. There is nothing dishonourable, to my mind, in the sensible movement of money. That title, if you must use it, you share with many of the finest men on the 'Change.'

Disdain now crossed Earl Bathurst's face. Charles Herries felt the morning slip away. He needed to rescue it.

'My Lord, the fact is, we and the men in the City turn a blind eye to one another; it suits us all to do so.'

Earl Bathurst sighed, as if he had heard his name coupled with the 'Change quite often enough.

'So, what do you need to discuss, Mr Herries?'

'I have come to doubt the capacity of the government to supply Lord Wellington's needs. I have requested information from the Mint about the coining of louis d'or and Spanish doubloons, but though they are fine craftsmen they cannot make specie out of air. We need help, my Lord.'

Lord Bathurst looked at the commissary-in-chief. Help? The very notion was distasteful. Help implied need and produced control. How could a government that ran the country need help? It might go out and borrow, of course, but that was different, an invitation to the banks and the public to share in the nation's prosperity. Did Herries suggest that the government had run out of resources? That was impossible.

'If the time comes when we need help, as you put it, we will consider where to turn. That is your responsibility, and I leave it to you, sir.'

Herries cleared his throat and then thought better of it. He would not take Lord Bathurst into his confidence until it was necessary, if the man was so determined to let him carry the burden alone.

'Very well.'

'Oh, and Herries, if that time should come, you must understand that any instruction and agreement will be verbally communicated, merely.'

'If we have to procure specie, my Lord, I will need to draw up a contract. Terms must be agreed.'

'Indeed, but such a document will not require the signature of the Secretary of State, merely his acquiescence.'

Herries gathered up his papers, bowed and left the room. Lord Bathurst would be very happy to leave him to hang in the air if such a scheme failed, or victory in the field eluded Lord Wellington. Then, surely, the newspapers would pounce. Where had the money been procured? they would ask; upon whose authority did Lord Liverpool's government flout the law? He would be finished, of course; and what then, with his mother to support?

From the War Office in Spring Gardens he turned into the great sanded square of Horseguards, reluctant to go back to his desk. These days restlessness grabbed him as soon as he was not at work. He moved from club to club or sat at friends' tables over dinner and cards. Often he outstayed his welcome, hot and flushed with wine. He preferred to be out of Cadogan Place as long as possible. Night after night, just before dawn, when the great city began to shift and whisper and the first carriages creaked down the street, he woke to the pounding of his heart. Three or four in the morning, it did not matter, he got up and took his candle to the fire if the embers remained, or fumbled in the dark to get a spark from his tinderbox. In those early hours he clung on to the world with ragged fingertips. Longing for the little household in the rue de Grenelles gripped him. In the half-dark he allowed himself to drift there, talk to Louisa, hold her hand and tell her a story. He believed the truth of his desires in those moments and lay a willing prisoner until the light edged round the shutters and he got up. Once he was at the office, numbers demanded his attention. Thalers, guineas, pistoles and roubles drove him on until evening, when he was alone again and in search of distraction.

EVERY DAY FOR THE last year and a half Dorothy Yallop had walked from her house to the Post Office by the Guildhall in the main square, and every few weeks a letter waited for her. 'Mrs George Yallop, Norwich', the Major wrote in his small neat copperplate on the cover sheet. She read his letters as she walked home, and then again by the fire or in the garden with the tabby cat curled on her knees. 'We are all impatient to be off,' he wrote in the spring. 'The sooner we set out, the sooner I shall be home with you, my dear.' For her sake he pretended not to enjoy the campaign, and often wrote about his idea to go into retirement when it was over.

Dorothy smiled as she read. 'Retire? What would you do, George, tell tales by the fire? Shine your buttons with bran and vinegar? Nonsense, man, I shall accompany you next time. I have had enough of life alone; it has been too long, too long, George.'

Fifteen days after the Battle of Vitoria the *Morning Chronicle* and the *Gazette* printed lists of the dead. George's name had not been there; but the next week, there at the Post Office lay a letter, addressed to her by an unfamiliar hand. She knew immediately, had no need to open it. No pieties, at least, from the Colonel, just the simple truth. 'Major Yallop died from a wound to the shoulder as he led the 9th into battle. A fine soldier and an honourable man, he gave his life to the Regiment, and was buried, as he would have wished, where he fell. Believe me your sincere friend, William Cramer, Colonel, 9th Regiment.'

Now, some weeks later, she went from room to room in the small house. Her duster bunched in her hands.

'What are you doing up there, George?' she asked him. 'In heaven, if we have read it right, there are no battles to fight. Do you hunt down rebel angels and chase them away?'

In front of the fireplace Mrs Yallop thought of her husband as death came to him.

I hope he was happy, she thought, and I hope I was in his mind.

She shook herself. Why should she wish for such a thing? What an old fool; why should it matter that this thought came at her so often, at night, or round corners when she walked into the city centre to find some consolation in the plentiful bounty of the market stalls? The Major was dead. What he thought as he died was unknowable. Why did she talk to him so, she of all people, a soldier's wife, who had prepared herself for this event?

I want that for him, she thought, for him to have been at peace when he died, to have had my love with him.

'That is one thing,' said her other voice, 'but why go on, why talk to him all day?'

'It is because I cannot stop this conversation. I have not the will. While I talk my George is still alive. Or, at the least, he is not gone from me.'

So she let herself talk on.

'No one can overhear me. Our house is empty.'

'Of course it is empty; he is dead. There is no one here.'

'That must be admitted; but, on the other hand, if I speak to him, he replies. And then I see him on the street, rounding the corner of Pottergate or down Elm Hill. When I look again I see men such as he should be, strong men in the prime of life, with bright hair and well-brushed topcoats.'

Some days he mocked her as he lay on the ground.

'Do not imagine, Dorothy,' he said, 'that I am thinking of anything but the progress of the battle.'

Then, at other times, he was tender.

'Dear Mrs Yallop, do not put on the black again. We have always shared a dislike of mourning, have we not? Honour the dead, remember me, if you must; but not with black. Take out the golden shawl, you remember the one, embroidered with roses of many colours. I brought it back to you from India, oh, years ago now. Run and get it from the chest upstairs. Put it on for me so that I can embrace you.'

While Dorothy imagined thus, she and the Major were still together, a married couple. They rubbed along like the others, with jokes and old settled ways. At night she lay against his chest and heard his heart beat, regular and strong.

In the parlour she pushed her duster along the surface of the narrow mantelpiece. The white marble felt cold under her hand, veined with grey. And it is no good, she thought. As much as I long and hope, it is simply to draw out a moment of the old life. I give it to myself because I can no longer bear the new.

'Well, Mrs Yallop, madam,' she told herself, 'you need to look at it squarely, as the Major would do. Tidy your house as much as you wish; imagine him with you if you will. Think of his polished belt and his mellow brown voice. It is not going to pull him back.'

But Mrs Yallop knew that she could not give up the thought. She did not want to be a widow, childless and alone, at the moment of death. One day, but not today, she would release him.

'I want him with me a while longer,' she said to herself, and opened her arms wide to span the width of the fireplace and lean against the mantelshelf.

She felt the Major come back in. Her eyes filled with tears that would not fall.

'Oh, George, allow me my tears, dear man. Though you do not shed them yourself, stand by me and put a hand out.'

Mrs Yallop stood there, with her tousled head on the cold marble. Her tears stayed in her eyes.

'You see, George, I wish to weep, but if I do, what then? There will be an end to it, and I do not wish an end when there is no beginning.'

While she talked on, Dorothy heard a knock at the door. She would not answer it. There was no one she wished to see or talk to. Then came another, sharp and decisive. A knock like the Major's: no nonsense about it. Mrs Yallop walked down the narrow hall.

She opened the door to see a stranger there.

'Mrs Yallop?'

She nodded.

'Dorothy Yallop, sir.'

'Robert Heaton.' He bowed. 'A friend of Major Yallop.'

She started, and put her hand out to the door jamb. The wood was warm with afternoon sun.

'Might I come in a moment?'

He followed her into the narrow hall. Dorothy pulled off her apron and gestured towards the back parlour.

'Do sit down.'

The man sat on the sofa, placed his portmanteau on the carpet and leaned forward towards her.

'You have a fine neat house. The Major appreciated that, I am sure.'

'You know how the Major is; everything in its place. He teases me when I drop things, tries so hard to keep the irritation out of his voice, though I hear it and he knows I do. But then, how I do drop things, and misplace them.'

The man started, looked about as if he missed something, put his hands behind his back, and then leaned forward again.

'Mrs Yallop, George was a man I admired. He died at the Battle of Vitoria; I was not aware that you had not been informed. I am so sorry.'

'I know, of course. It is simply that—well, you know how it is.'

'Indeed so, Mrs Yallop.' He paused and then began again. 'I should like to say that your husband was an example not only to his own men, but to me, who wandered off the street, so to speak, and was honoured to serve with him. We all feel his loss.'

Dorothy said nothing. Silence spread between them; she began to feel a comfort in this man's presence. After a time she raised her head.

'You are also with the 9th?'

'I was for a time; went out there as a volunteer.'

Ah, so that is it, Dorothy thought. The Major disliked the volunteers, complained how they cluttered up the army with servants and baggage. War, he always said, was no business of gentlemen dreamers who had nothing better to do than gawp. But if George had taken to this man he must have been unlike the others. She would venture the question.

'Tell me, Mr Heaton, did Major Yallop die alone? I hate to think so, though it matters little in the end.'

'I was nowhere near the 9th, having transferred to the 44th after Salamanca, so I cannot say. But I feel sure he did not.'

'It would comfort me to know that someone was with him.'

'I am sure that someone was.'

For the first time in weeks, Dorothy felt her heart less squeezed.

'Don't be too kind to me, Mr Heaton. I have been with the army myself. I know death is an unforgiving business; I wish for him to have died easily and with a man by him, but I know it is for myself. That it is so is one of the things that makes me sad.'

She was surprised to hear herself speak such words, and to this stranger; but he looked with steadiness at her. Silence fell again. After a minute, the man opened the bag at his feet, and pulled out a package wrapped in muslin and tied with cotton ribbon.

'George spoke of you often, and with such pride. There was nothing you did not know about a camp kitchen, he used to say. Once he told me that you were quite a seamstress, good with the needle, and with a fine taste in fabric.'

He offered her the parcel.

'I came across this after Vitoria. Please accept it in remembrance of him, though it is booty, and I know the Major never would have approved of my taking it.'

Dorothy took the parcel and unwrapped it with care.

'A shawl. Oh.'

A shock ran through her, as if the Major himself had handed it to her. 'Mr Heaton, you could not have chosen better; I cannot explain why, but I assure you it is so. The Major was a stickler about plunder, it is true, but perhaps he would not mind just this once.' She paused. 'No, I cannot conceal it. George would purse his lips and insist I find its owner, or send it to a Colonel on the other side.'

'You wish me to do the same?'

'No, I want it.' She held the lace in hands that shook. 'I want it in remembrance of him and that place.'

'It is a mantilla, Spanish made.'

'And pearls around the edge.'

Mrs Yallop handed the mantilla to the Captain and walked to the mirror over the fireplace to check her hair. She would do the Major proud, look her best. To her surprise she saw Mr Heaton in the glass come up behind her. He had folded the mantilla into a triangle in the English way and now slipped it round her shoulders. Without a word he turned her round and led her back to the sofa.

The room darkened as they sat there. After a few minutes Mrs Yallop reached out and took Heaton's hand. The tabby cat made his sinuous way round the door and jumped onto Heaton's lap.

'Mrs Yallop, you are not quite alone here, I see.'

'Oh no, Mr Heaton. There is Tabby here, and sometimes another visitor.'

She looked over at Mr Heaton and with her free hand drew the cream lace close round herself. It is the colour of my bridal gown, she thought. Then she began to cry. Great gusts of sobbing passed through her. She tried to push them back, sure that with each sob the Major himself was dragged from inside her, but nothing stopped the tears.

I should have brought Racket, Heaton thought. He is such a help in this sort of situation. He looked round as if Racket might appear, but there was no answering bark, only Mrs Yallop's cries and indrawn breath. Without a thought he put his arms around her, and the two of them stayed there until it was quite dark and quiet. When Dorothy finally sat back Robert Heaton looked into her swollen face and her red eyes and felt at peace.

'Well. There we are.'

His words were just right. Their warmth flowed into Dorothy's heart.

'Mr Heaton, I thank you for your gift, and for your visit. They were just what I needed. I feel sure we shall be friends.'

They both stood up. Heaton took the bag from the floor beside the sofa and made his way in the gloom to the door.

'I feel it too, Mrs Yallop, and that we will meet again before too long.'

Outside on the pavement Heaton took a deep breath of the thin autumn air and buttoned up his coat.

'Well, Racket, old chap,' he said to the empty street, 'I managed it without you. Haven't done that for years.'

IN HYDE PARK, A nursemaid held Gerald by the hand; even at four he often fell headlong in his enthusiasm to catch the others. Now he strained and tugged; the older boys rushed on ahead. At five years old, Charles was sure on his feet and fearless; he followed his older brother out of sight of Kitty and Harriet, only to run back now and again with a fallen leaf or a stone with a pattern he liked. All across the park groups of soldiers in their scarlet jackets stood out against the green. Winter and nightfall nipped at the daylight. A page from *The Times* of 6th November blew about their feet. Across the top of the first column ran the words 'Lord Wellington reaches France'.

Harriet swung her bonnet in one hand, and in the other carried a sheaf of dry horse chestnut leaves. She looked across at Kitty beside her.

'It torments me so, Kitty, that my mother might be alive, somewhere close even, and I cannot do anything to find her.'

'What do you hope for, Harriet?'

'I do not know. Everything I look for disappears. I end up in confusion.'

Kitty paused. She kept one eye on the children as she replied.

'When I feel the same I wonder sometimes if it is simply more fruitful to act, to clear a path through what is before me.' She nodded at the crumpled sheet of newspaper. 'The war may soon be over, now that Bonaparte is pushed back into France from all sides.'

Harriet glanced across at her.

'I have achieved so little in my search for my mother, Kitty. I believe she is alive, but that is all I can say. And then the friendship that I mentioned to you; it, too, seems over the last months to have stopped, or slowed.' She hesitated.

'I believe I sought in Mr Winsor something he could not offer me. It was such an excitement to meet him, to talk of philosophical enquiry with a man who had made it his life's business. But he has changed and so, perhaps, have I.'

'Then there is nothing to regret. Why do you hesitate to bring your friendship to an end?'

Harriet laughed, with Kitty and at herself.

'Because of its pleasures.'

'Then the case is simple, and it is for you to decide when the pleasures no longer outweigh the difficulties.'

Harriet looked over towards the children. Gerald still tugged at the nursemaid's hand.

'Thank you, Kitty.' She raised her voice so that it carried across the gathering darkness. 'Goodbye, children. I must leave you.'

Arthur Freese turned round and ran back to her.

'Mrs Raven, you will come again soon?'

His voice echoed with something that she recognised; her own longing. She put her arm round his shoulders.

'Of course, Arthur. I shall see you next week.'

From the edge of Hyde Park Harriet walked back along Piccadilly and down to Pall Mall. At the door of no. 97 she hesitated for a moment, then knocked.

Frederick opened the door himself. As usual the house was in darkness.

'I did not expect you, Harriet.'

'May I come in?'

Frederick said nothing but turned into the hallway.

'Close it behind you.'

Harriet followed him down the hall and into the library.

'You have not visited me for several weeks and now you arrive without warning.'

'I apologise, Frederick. May I sit down?'

'Do, do. Wherever you like.' Frederick sat on the sofa and looked at her. Harriet chose a small chair, laid her bonnet down and sat. She did not untie her cloak. There was no need to take it off. She would not be long.

The room was cold, and felt empty. She felt round for a pleasantry to help her begin.

'The company expands, so the newspapers report.'

'You have noticed the works in the streets beyond here? In a few weeks all of St Margaret's parish will be lit by gas. But you remember my suspicions?'

Frederick talked on in a voice filled with mockery, as if he knew her intentions.

'A chief engineer has been appointed by the board against my wishes: an Englishman, as I predicted. They will do everything they can to steal my invention. The more so since peace may be on the way.'

'But you too are on the board, are you not?'

'Outnumbered; outvoted. They can see me off if they wish.' He fell silent and did not look at her.

When Frederick and she talked thus, Harriet remembered Mr Herschel's lecture at the Royal Institution. Their friendship, like a dead star, was bleak and cindered. If any light remained, it was light from long ago. Even so, she felt her desire for him gather.

'I need to say that our friendship must come to an end.'

'Your silence has suggested that, Harriet.'

'Can I explain?'

'If you wish to do so.' Frederick shrugged. 'Perhaps it is better not. Why should it matter? I too have more important matters to consider.'

'Frederick, it is not that I do not have affection.' Harriet glanced round the room. 'It is just that I mistook much of it for something else that I wish for.' She noticed him look at her with his familiar sidelong glance, and knew that he wanted her still.

'That was careless of you, Mrs Raven.' He stood up. 'I will show you to the door.'

There was nothing else to say. Tenderness had drained from them. We recoil from one another, Harriet thought; but turn us round and the attraction remains. She glanced back at Frederick from the doorway. He threw up his head as he watched her and stepped back into the shadow. Then she turned and walked up Pall Mall towards the Haymarket, where the city swirled past, and evening excitement filled the air.

For a moment she almost turned back. The shock of what she had done, and the finality of their conversation filled her. She wanted to feel Frederick next to her and she never would again.

At the back of the theatre in Drury Lane Harriet heard the sounds of the theatre musicians as they tuned their instruments before the performance. Snatches of songs came down from the high windows, runs of scales from a flute, a bright trumpet and the cluck of a harpsichord. A singer warmed his voice with popular songs. 'Che farò senza Euridice?' he sang. Harriet stopped to listen. The aria was familiar, sung round the harpsichord for fifty years.

Beside her she noticed a little girl no more than three years old who stood with her back pressed to the theatre wall, a barefoot urchin with a mass of unkempt hair and ragged clothes. She stared at Harriet with curiosity, quite alone and fearless. As the music swelled she began to turn in circles to its time. Love of the music, which moved through her body in the rhythm of life itself, in time with the pulse of the blood, the rise of the tides and the turns of the earth, filled her up. Without a thought for an audience or herself the child danced, and in that moment she was Orpheus, Eurydice, everyone. Harriet watched her and laughed with delight; there was nothing to regret, and everything still to discover.

AMONGST THE INVITATIONS, THE notes asking for money and advertisements for the winter's concert series, a letter arrived at Hamilton Place from Lord Wellington. His thoughts, now he was over the border into France, turned to England, or at least to Arthur Freese:

'The boy has spent too long in the nursery, and in the company of the younger children. It is my wish that arrangements be made for him to enter Eton College at the first opportunity. I myself left the family home at seven and found myself inestimably the better for it. Too many young men are spoiled. For Arthur I intend the best whatever his eventual status in life.'

Kitty rang the bell and asked for Arthur to be brought down from the schoolroom. As he came to greet her Arthur hunched his shoulders and pushed his head forward. He met her eye as if he expected a rebuke. She stepped forward and hugged him. He grinned at her in relief.

'I believed that you might be displeased with me.'

'Arthur, my dear; I have never been displeased with you. Now that you are nearly twelve, we have to talk about your future, that is all.'

'What is my future?'

'I have a letter here from Lord Wellington. He wishes you to be entered into Eton as soon as possible.'

Arthur grasped her hand.

'But I do not wish to go.'

'You have few companions of your own age here, Arthur.'

'Do I require companions, Mama, if I am safe here?' He looked at her with a sudden challenge. 'I have my tutor, and now I am able to talk to Captain Heaton when he visits.'

'Captain Heaton may soon return to the army.'

'Does he come today?'

'He will be here any moment.'

'I still do not wish to go to school.'

Kitty laughed.

'I will consider the matter. Dear Arthur, I will do the best for you that I can. Now be off and finish your history.'

Arthur ran out of the door to Kitty's parlour and left it to swing on its hinges. Everyone senses change in the air, Kitty thought, even the children can feel it.

'Captain Heaton.' The butler bowed through the open door as Heaton arrived. Instead of his scarlet army jacket he wore a chestnut-brown top-coat and white cravat. He carried an ebony cane topped with silver in one hand, a black top hat in the other, and came into the room like a man at ease. Racket ran round Heaton's legs and up to Kitty. His tail flailed with joy.

'Racket is ready, Robert. Shall we collect the children and go?'

Over the last few months Hyde Park had become a space that belonged to them. In the mornings, like today, it was filled with nursemaids who strolled in groups of two or three while children ran about with hoops and sticks. Even so late in the year baby carriages plied the wider paths, handsomely lacquered in grey or yellow, pulled by small ponies.

'Might I ask your opinion, Robert, of the best time to send a child away to school?'

Robert Heaton looked up to where Arthur Freese walked ahead of them, in conversation with a boy about his own age, a neighbour's son he had lately befriended in a tentative way.

'He seems happier, Kitty.'

'He has enjoyed your visits.'

'I have noticed with four-legged creatures, say, that the young amble off when they are ready. A yearling wanders further and further from its mother and one day joins another group. At three or four it recognises her still but rarely returns.'

'That is not much help, Robert.'

'I never went to school myself, you see. I wonder if school merely makes a man an even stranger beast than he is already. Is there really any need?' He hesitated. 'You do not take my frankness ill, I hope?'

'Not at all. I am delighted, the more so since you confirm my own desire. I shall keep him here with me for the moment.'

They walked on. Heaton stirred up frosted leaves with his cane and glanced every now and again at the woman beside him. In months, Kitty thought, the Allies might be in Paris. One way or another there would be peace, and her husband on his way home. Until that day she had her freedom, and Arthur Freese would have his.

'While we talk about boys, I have another on my mind.'

'Another? Really, Kitty, you manufacture boys.'

'You have no children yourself, Robert?'

'None of whom I am aware.' Heaton stopped. 'Travel and boys do not seem to take kindly to one another.'

They reached the end of the path by Kensington Palace. Kitty turned and began to walk back.

'I have a boy in my care, boarded at Merton in Surrey. A kind enough couple who have taken in several children; but he needs a better home.'

'A home? Is he an orphan?'

'An orphan I take an interest in without obligation. He is over a year old now, begins to talk and walk. I should like to find him a place where he might grow up in safety and with affection. He needs love.'

Robert Heaton looked alarmed.

'Love?'

'I mean to say day-to-day affection and care. Love to follow that, perhaps.'

'I see.'

Heaton looked away and into the distance.

'Racket! Racket, come here.'

When Racket bounded up Heaton tapped his cane against his boots. 'Stay here now.'

Kitty looked on. I should like to walk with him through the park for ever. The thought fell into her mind; she had no time to stop it. Robert Heaton had stopped and turned to her.

'I have an idea. But should need to write and enquire.'

'Thank you, Robert.' Kitty stopped and then started again. 'I have a confidence in your opinion.'

'Though I know nothing about boys.'

She laughed.

'On the contrary; I believe you know a great deal about them.'

NATHAN ROTHSCHILD, WHEN HIS carriage arrived in Kensington, still had Charles Herries's note in his pocket. 'Commissary Office, 4th January 1814. I should be most grateful, Mr Rothschild, if you might favour me with a short conversation at my private residence.'

Rothschild had come straight from the Exchange; after the close of business, of course, but with as much speed as he ever got up for any man. Now he and Herries sat face to face in the ground-floor study at Cadogan Place. Herries began as soon as the door was closed behind them.

'Mr Rothschild, now that Lord Wellington is in France and expects an arduous campaign, he demands specie, and it is beyond the capacity of my department to supply it. I have decided to collect foreign coin for his use. The operation must be secret. It is a matter of importance and I need a man to direct it who can guarantee its success.'

Nathan smiled.

'You believe, sir, that I am the man for that task?'

'I am aware that you have extensive operations on the Continent.'

'I am proud to say that Rothschilds has a network of clients and correspondents superior to that of any other merchant banker in the City, or indeed on the other side of the Channel.'

'Exactly.' Herries' anxieties collected in the pause.

'How much do you require?'

'I estimate the sum at six hundred thousand pounds, to be collected in Holland and France and the German principalities and delivered to Bordeaux in two months, and then, if the operation is a success, to continue to supply the army at a rate to be determined by its needs.'

Nathan started. It was a huge sum, far more than even he and his brothers could reasonably expect to gather. Still, a man never got a good piece of business without taking himself at others' estimations. Besides, what other house could even come near his capacities? Barings? Nathan squared his shoulders at the thought. Alexander Baring took no care to make himself agreeable to governments, and was foolish enough to lend money to the government of the United States. Hope & Co., his rivals in Amsterdam? Gone to ground these days, and far too cautious. Risk was his stock in trade and now its moment had come; risk, and information: he had always known they would make his fortune.

'Your department, sir, already employs Mr Reid in such operations.'

'You watch him?'

'I would be foolish not to; as you, sir, appear to have watched me.'

Herries felt uncomfortable. To complicate this negotiation might end in disaster. The fact was he required Nathan in his public as well as his private capacity. He leaned forward.

'We do not think of prosecution, Mr Rothschild. I regard you as the most capable man for the task.'

'Yet we meet in private. Does Lord Bathurst not believe that I am a man to be trusted?'

'Not a bit of it, sir. But this is a delicate matter. Were the newspapers to get wind of the government's need for this sort of money we might see a run on sterling and on government bonds which would be of benefit to none of us.'

'Let us not be polite, Mr Herries. You ask me to take on a very great risk with no indemnity; should I fail, I will be ruined. Both the government and Rothschilds have acted and will act beyond the letter of the law. Besides, I am a Jew.'

'A recent arrival; but the need for care is paramount.'

'Very well, let us agree that I am a foreigner, and discreet. The English, I observe, are proud that their riches bring us here. We make them feel that they are at the centre of the world; yet they do business with us unwillingly.'

'Mr Rothschild, the government believes that there is no family better placed to serve the interests of the country.'

It did not matter in the end; the government, Nathan knew, came to him cap in hand. It could not get money to Wellington without him, and without him Wellington could not advance on Paris. Britain would owe victory in France to the Rothschilds. He would not press the point.

'If I take this challenge, you will forward me the means to pay for the specie?'

'Upon receipt of some surety from you, I will issue government bonds to the face value of the specie that you may deposit and dispense as you see fit when specie is found. I suggest a fee of two per cent as a commission, with the Treasury to pick up the costs.'

Nathan paused to calculate. Twelve thousand pounds sterling for two months' hard work for them all; no, he could do better than that, even if this jewel that now lay close to his hand was just the start.

'The risk is large enough, Mr Herries, to substitute for such costs an extra commission of, let us say, sixpence per ounce.'

'I will consider all such detail, Mr Rothschild, upon your acceptance of the fee.'

'You suggest a written contract?'

'Indeed, sir, though I do not believe it will come to the attention of anyone beyond the Chancellor and the Prime Minister.'

'And Lord Bathurst?'

'Of course. The Secretary for War will, however, not be the signatory. I shall.'

Nathan nodded.

'Very well, sir. I agree. Rothschilds will be as good as my word. You do not flatter me with your trust, since I shall repay it, but I am sensible of it nonetheless.'

'Mr Rothschild, I ask you in the name of business merely. This affair is quite separate, you understand, from our other dealings.'

Nathan laughed. He sounded merry.

'To be sure—a family, and a daughter, are precious.'

'You may have had your own reasons for offering to help me in that matter. The government has of course been aware of your operations in and out of Folkestone for some time. But I do not wish to recall that now.'

Nathan stood up.

'I believe we understand one another, Mr Herries. You will forgive me now if I leave you. I have much to do.'

'Indeed—and I shall look into the matter of the commission, Mr Rothschild.'

Nathan Rothschild took Charles Herries's hand and shook it in a formal way. He would get his commission. There was no doubt of it. He nodded at Herries.

'I shall let myself out; no need to stand on the ceremony, as you English say.'

LESS THAN A WEEK later, Charles Herries sat with Mr Rothschild and Earl Bathurst in the War Office in Spring Gardens. Bathurst took one side of the table, Herries and Nathan the other. Bathurst picked up the top sheet of the pile of papers that lay between them.

'The government of Lord Liverpool, all of us here, will overlook the means by which you transact your business, Mr Rothschild. I shall assume you are a man who wishes to see tyranny overthrown, understands that the restoration of Europe's monarchies is good for business as well as the people. We know that you are a man who wishes to uphold . . .' he paused, 'English liberties.'

Nathan sat impassive.

'You have prospered, Mr Rothschild, and we applaud your industry. Mr Herries has determined that you alone, amongst all the bankers now operating in the City, are in a position to work to supply the government needs.'

'I am confident of Rothschilds' abilities, my Lord, and anxious to serve the country.'

'You are familiar with Hellevoetsluis, I believe; you work out of that port a good deal.'

'There is enough deep water there, my Lord, for a ship of the line to enter with ease. I have agreed with Mr Herries that my consignments will travel at my risk, but in a British naval vessel. My own transports are quite unprotected and not robust enough for the Bay of Biscay.'

'Very well. We need not linger upon the detail. Mr Herries here has it all written in the contract.'

Lord Bathurst inclined his head and pushed away the papers in front of him. The business appeared to have been concluded; his part at least was finished. Good manners merely demanded a few pleasantries.

'You live where, exactly, Mr Rothschild?'

'I am planted at the Exchange on Tuesdays and Fridays. For the rest you may find me in my offices at New Court. I live above them.'

Bathurst looked vague.

'Oh yes, indeed, I am sure you are well set up and snug there.'

Nathan started. His English may have been imperfect, but he could hear the music of a word even if its meaning passed him by. Lord Bathurst, who had once owned Apsley House, would never have described that honey-coloured residence as snug. Apsley House on Piccadilly, 149 Piccadilly if he had it right (and he did, since he never forgot a number): the last house before the park, the best of its kind, with its gatehouse and forecourt and garden behind. The Secretary for War had sold it to Richard Wellesley a few years back. A retrenchment, perhaps, but Bathurst still owned much of Gloucestershire; villages, acres, wooded valleys.

Nathan had estimated the man's worth; calculated it as a good deal less than his own, but, he had to admit, a handsome sum. And then there was the title and all that meant to the English. He, Nathan, had no need of a title, as if he had to lean up against something to stand tall. But here in England it made a man bigger than he was. Therefore, he concluded, such an earl as Bathurst did not esteem the modest or the convenient; and snug, in English, meant small, and tight: heimlich, indeed. Nathan had all the time in this world for heimlich, for geliebte Hannah and the children shouting above his head, Moses ruining the peace with his trumpet across the court, and Meyer Davidson too; but what Lord Bathurst really meant was that it was best for all of them that Rothschilds should live out of sight and out of the way.

Lord Bathurst's dark blue eyes rested on Nathan; they expressed open and transparent courtesy. Nathan looked back into them. A fortune, he thought with his sudden decision, was not enough. No longer would he mix about coins in his pocket when hopeful composers came to visit him, and say, 'This is my music.' No, he would have musicians compose him songs and sonatas to sleep through. An artist would draw him up a symbol for the firm that befitted the family name, with a sign for all the brothers. Rothschilds would be known through every principality and in every great house not just in Britain, but in all of Europe.

Nathan smiled at Lord Bathurst.

'Ah, I am snug indeed, as you so say. This London is a place of wonder.'

When the war is over and the price is a good one, he said to himself, I shall buy a house on Piccadilly right up close to the corner of Hyde Park and to no. 149, some grand mansion with steps and columns and a marble hall to shrink the visitors. Hannah and my girls will have footmen and parlourmaids, carriages and jewels. Artists will paint them in shining oils and enclose them in gilded frames. I shall have a country house; near enough to London to receive guests, splendid and grand. I will live my holy days dull, surrounded by acres of grass, with chestnuts up the drive and sheep to graze as I pass by. I will be honoured by princes, and they will remember with envy that I am far richer than they could hope to be.

'My Lord,' he said and held out his hand.

'Doesn't bow, that man, does he?' Bathurst remarked to Herries when Nathan had taken up his hat and left.

PART THREE

11

London and Suffolk

So it happens, the restoration of our beloved monarchy, and I, Goya, painter to the court for twenty-six years—as loyal a subject as any office-holder, you can say—am here to see it. A few months ago the British hopped over the border after the French. Lord Wellington led his armies like the piper, over the Pyrenees and out of Spain. He left the carcass of my country, picked white for peace. Paris surrendered, and by April Napoleon was emperor no more, plonked on the island of Elba like a child in a playpen. And here, after six years of war, Spain has bowed to the Bourbons. The idiot Fernando is back in charge!

Our Fernando scuttled into the empty space Lord Wellington left, was back in Madrid by May to throw orders about: repeal the Constitution; annul all its laws; dissolve the Cortes and give the fat priests their Inquisition back. It has all been done, with subservience and speed, just as I, Goya, do my bit for the illustrious monarch with my oils and brush. Two commissions to paint his portrait before the spring was out. Instructions from the city of Santander where undesirable ideas swim into the port on every tide: the councilmen want an allegory with their portrait. They demand a crown and sceptre, a marble figure of Spain to look over Fernando and a lion to chew on the broken chains of servitude. Nothing equestrian to annoy me, and I would not honour the King with the loyalty of a dog. Yes, I said, I'll sign right away. And I rushed it out in fifteen days. Eight thousand *reals* for me; and, for them, no stinting on the rascally look of the dear restored monarch.

Madrid might seem peaceful now that Fernando is back. Its citizens pretend to rejoice and so do I. But under the palace runs a river of blood, thick and scarlet beneath the mellow stone. Sooner or later it will come to the surface. All over Spain the souls of the dead will rise up. The monster of war will stride over the land, a pitiless colossus who devours all humanity. And I, Goya? I am past seventy, deaf and have money to make.

∾

ALL THROUGH THE WINTER and into the spring Harriet lived in Hatton Garden, gathered into herself. Day by day Frederick receded and London became again the busy grey city she remembered from her arrival two years ago. One December evening, when she walked down Whitehall from Charing Cross, she saw the lamplighters turn on the jets and light up the new gaslights. She watched each glass globe turn green, then a dense white and finally lucid enough to see the gas jet as it burned upright and unwavering within. By the end of the year all St Margaret's parish was lit by gas. Thieving, the *Morning Chronicle* reported, had all but disappeared from the streets of Westminster, and pickpockets moved to other parts of town. The editor recommended that other parishes adopt the new lighting as soon as possible to rid London altogether of the scourge of crime.

When Harriet read the newspaper or saw the new gaslights, Frederick came back to her; the way he attended when his interest was caught or the feel of his skin against hers. In the New Year she read under the heading 'National Light and Heat Company News' that Mr Winsor had been given a pension and appointed to the board, a new chief engineer appointed and the company renamed the Gas Light and Coke Company. Everything Frederick predicted had happened. Harriet wondered if they used his genius and discarded it because he was a foreigner, as he thought; or if he was a dreamer who lost interest once his idea demanded the tedious attention of business. It did not matter to her now, though the memory remained of his oddity and beauty.

WHEN LORD WELLINGTON CROSSED the Pyrenees Mrs Cobbold insisted that they follow his progress on a map, and mark the army's route towards Paris with glass-headed pins. On the last day of March, when Paris surrendered to Marshal Blücher, the newspapers reported that Lord Wellington marched towards Toulouse. Mrs Cobbold moved her pins, one for each division of Wellington's army, right up to the cluster of blue-topped pins in Toulouse that represented the exhausted army of General Soult. The April day that Wellington entered the city he heard that Napoleon had abdicated. When this news reached London, Mrs Cobbold took the blue pins out of the board and placed them round the periphery of France.

'That is to represent the French troops, Harriet; for surely they will creep away now that the Emperor has saved his own skin. The 9th will soon be home. I expect you will wish to return to Suffolk to wait for him there.'

'No, Aunt; since we cannot tell when he will arrive, I intend to stay here in London. I have no idea if James wishes to stay in the army. He may be put on half-pay or sent immediately abroad.'

When Harriet spoke of James, the shadow of Frederick fell over her. She had to digest that secret and make it a part of her; she would never speak about it again, even to Kitty. Yet she was sure that her voice had a new note in it, a disharmony that was the residue of her passion. Mrs Cobbold, who had known her longer than anyone else now alive, must hear it, and wonder. But she never asked Harriet what had happened to her friend; instead she spoke of James's homecoming and her hopes for the future.

At the beginning of May, after peace was declared, James wrote from Toulouse. 'My dear Harriet. You will have read of the Peace of Paris. I have learned this morning that the 9th is to be sent home and disbanded, the officers to go on half-pay. The regiment will embark at Bordeaux and I shall send Thomas Orde home with it. I myself have business in Paris, but intend to come to London as soon as it is concluded. I remain your loving husband, etc.'

When Harriet read James's note she could find in it no trace of the ardour and affection that had filled his early letters. She waited with defiance for him to knock on the door in Hatton Garden. Until he came she would continue to visit Kitty and stroll with her in the Park, to walk home by herself in her old silk cloak and without a bonnet, and all the time to watch out, in case she saw her mother in the street. Despite Mr Patteson's refusal, Mrs Lefevre's ignorance and her aunt's apparent indifference, she still believed that one day she would find her. Was it not possible, indeed, that her mother looked for her, might seek her out in Hatton Garden or had already gone to Beccles Hall only to find it shut up? For her mother might know nothing of James, or of Sir William Guest's death and Harriet's marriage; and if Mrs Cobbold had had any letter from her in the last twenty years then she had chosen to reveal nothing to Harriet and surely would not do so now.

THE 9TH FOOT BUMPED up to Suffolk in carts, discharged to early summer heat and shortage. Lacy drifts of cow parsley covered the verges and sparrows gathered in the hawthorn. By the Butter Cross in the square at Bungay, Thomas Orde turned to his friend and shook his hand.

'You now gorn home, Abraham?'

'I am that, and what to say to my ol' mother?'

'At least that you are home and all paid up. How much do you have, then, at the end of it all? How much to show for them years with Nosey?'

'Twenty pound to the good I reckon.' Abraham smiled and pulled a golden cross and chain out of his pocket. 'Twenty pound 'n' all that I got from the baggage at Vitoria. Must be worth a bit, melted down. Keep me gorn for a year, maybe.'

Abraham picked up his knapsack and slung it round his shoulders. He wore his scarlet jacket still, torn at the cuffs and with most of its buttons gone. Dozens of the men were home already, dropped off in villages along the road from Lowestoft. When the cart had come into Bungay children ran alongside it in excitement and people came to their front doors to watch. One by one the men jumped down by their cottages; when the cart reached the main square only a few were left. From the new mill by the river, a clatter and hum rose up into the silence. It was a month since they had marched down to Bordeaux to sail up the French coast and across the Channel for Great Yarmouth.

'Be off with you then, 'Ham. Strange, though, to be home. Does not feel like home to me, though I know every door and every window here.'

'We will get used to it soon enough, Thomas. Well, I must be off. There's young Samuel there ready to go with me.'

'Your brother.'

'Little devil; just the same.'

A boy pulled at Thomas's sleeve. Nelson; taller and thinner, silent with excitement or apprehension.

'Father, it is you?'

'Nelson. Dearest boy.'

Thomas swung Nelson into his arms and hugged him to his chest. Nelson shrank away, uncertain and frightened.

'Mother said to wait and bring you home.'

Thomas put the boy back onto the ground and took his hand.

'Come on then; home. Like the wind.'

They ran hand in hand out of the square and down the hill, then turned into the lane that led to the cottage. By the door there was Mary. She watched them approach, quite still, with the evening sun behind her.

'Mary. Mary, here I am.'

Thomas hung back at his own door, unable to approach. He might look the same, though brown as mahogany from the long march up France in the heat of early summer; but inside he was different, a stranger. Did Mary feel as awkward and odd as he? She was his wife; he ought to kiss her.

'Come inside, Thomas. I will put the water on to heat for a wash, and while you wait there is bread and cheese, new made. Come in, come in. You are home at last.'

All the windows and doors of the cottage stood open on their hinges and hooks. Thomas walked across the front room where his loom still stood by the window and into the kitchen. He peered up the cupboard staircase, and then out into the garden where the bright flowers of climbing roses stood from their green leaves. Down the path beyond the washhouse, the cowshed door was open. Orange marigolds flowered against the cracked plaster. Behind him Mary had set the table with brown Lowestoft plates and bread and cheese under a muslin cloth to keep the flies off. He turned and curled his arms around her and then stood back.

'Come and eat.'

'You got the letter I sent from France last month; knew I was on the way?'

'Yes, Thomas, I got that letter. You are tired no doubt from the journey.'

'I am not tired, Mary. I feel the need to get started right away. What work do you have on? What orders are in?'

Thomas felt, in his own house, too big for the tidy space that Mary and Nelson had lived in together, without him, for the last two years. Nelson looked at him with apprehension, his only son, so dear to him. Yet he could think of nothing to say to him, no comfort to offer either of them, no way to make this day like every other day.

A wasp settled on a raspberry in a small blue bowl. Its curled body pulsed with anger. Thomas waved it away.

'I should like to wash, Mary, before anything else. Warm water: that is the greatest treat a soldier can have.'

'Have you been a soldier, Father?'

'Servant, soldier: both, Nelson; though I am glad to have served Captain Raven and no one else.'

'Has Captain Raven come home too?'

'I left him on the road to Paris; he sent me on ahead, wanted to spend a few days alone, he said, and then find his wife in London. So we are scattered. Besides I have to start work.'

Mary Orde went outside to the wash-house and brought back a large bowl of hot water from the copper. She set the bowl on the kitchen step and Thomas unbuttoned his grimy shirt; a simple action, something he had done a thousand times before. When he pulled off his britches he felt awkward again, conscious of his nakedness and Mary's eyes upon him. He knelt by the bowl, threw water over his bowed neck and back, scrubbed, rinsed and took the stiff square of cotton Mary held for him.

'Word among the men was that work is scarce and prices high.'

'Everything has changed, Thomas. There is no work for the weavers any more. The mill has taken it. Men work there, the old weavers, and women for lower wages. Children tie up the broken warp, run up and down under the looms in the noise and dust.' She handed Thomas a clean shirt and trousers. 'I kept your loom going as long as I could. But you see it idle now.'

'No machine can do the work I used to do. It is too fine, and requires more skill than any machine can have.'

'They say the worsted is of just the same quality, and anyone can work in the mill; you or me as well. The learning is only a few weeks.'

Thomas looked round the kitchen. After all the time away, every object—the tin cups and pine table—and the view from the window down the garden that had once been so familiar and so comforting—everything around him stood out in high relief. The furniture was paltry and ugly, the cottage not much better than some of his billets in France. Once the guineas in his pocket were gone, he and Mary would be penniless; was that all his reward for the hardship of war? To go out because prices were high and work scarce and to come back and find the work gone and prices higher? The peace had brought prosperity, but for Mr Watney, not for such as he. Most of all, everything that was once so dear repelled him; the most ordinary things and the most lovely were cut off from him; or he was denied them.

He sat down at the table and cut a thick slice of bread from the loaf. Mary poured small beer into two tin cups. When she put the jug down she stretched out a hand to his. Her pale hair was tied up with a simple ribbon; several strands had escaped and hung over her shoulders. Even Mary looks unfamiliar, Thomas, thought; unfamiliar and far away. I feel nothing for her, when I had expected everything, like a story book when the heroes return. I might as well be in France again; I had come to feel more myself with the 9th than here in my own cottage. He withdrew his hand, put it down on his lap and ate the bread and cheese with the other that was beyond Mary's reach.

'I must go out, Mary.'

'It is not much of a homecoming, Thomas. I hoped for more.'

'And I, Mary.'

The light faded as Thomas walked back towards the town. Away to his left the bulk of the new mill stood above the river, and drew him towards it. The windows stood open; as he approached he heard the hiss and clatter of the steam engines and power looms inside. A fine cloud of dust coated the grass underneath the windows and the water of the river eddied slick and grey with oil and scraps of fibre. Thomas sat on the bank and watched a family of moor-hens make their way through the sludge, their dark feathers laced with grey.

A bell sounded, sudden and insistent in the still summer evening. The doors and gates of the mill opened and the mill-hands came out. Thomas knew so many of them. They nodded to him as they passed. 'Evening, Thomas. You back, then?' 'Thomas, what you doin' here, then?' One man stopped. His neighbour Sam Bobbitt, tall and fair-haired with a lopsided smile and freckles over his nose and forearms.

'Thomas, here you are, then. Will you work here?'

'We are weavers, Sam, not Mr Watney's slaves.'

Sam looked down at his dusty boots.

'Oh, it is not so bad. My Dora and Charlie work here, too. Together we make up my old earnings. The wages come reg'lar, too; cash every Saturday.'

'And you did it without a murmur, gave up your freedom just like that?'

'Thomas, you have been away with Nosey, sent money home, maybe. What choice did I have when the piecework dried up, what with bread double the price and four children to feed?'

'Prices will come down now we have peace.'

Sam shrugged.

'There is no other work in town.'

'Never. Never, Sam.'

On the way home, Thomas walked into the market square. Bungay appeared deserted, but here and there oil lamps glimmered and he saw that men loitered in groups, heads together. There was a tension in the town. The murmuring voices had an angry edge, not the old slow Suffolk drawl that he had left behind.

When he got back the cottage was in darkness. Mary was already in bed. Thomas pulled his clothes off in the kitchen and made his way up, familiar with the turn of the stairs and the metal latches on the doors. He tiptoed through the first room where Nelson slept and into the bedroom that led off it. Mary did not move when he slid under the coverlet. How often he had thought of her like this in Spain and France, curled up in her pale solidity. He ought to take her in his arms. He turned towards her in the darkness and his face brushed against her hair. He lay rigid. Instead of joy, anger rose in him. Everything was wrong: Bungay, the lifeless loom downstairs, Mary most of all. He could not kiss her or pull her to him.

'Thomas.' He could see nothing in the darkness, not even his own hand. 'Thomas, what is it?'

'You have changed.'

He began to shout, then stopped himself. Nelson was asleep through the thin slatted door.

'It is all different.'

'No, Thomas, it is just the same. I am just the same; perhaps I appear older. The war takes its toll.'

'There is no work; the mill has made the men mere goods; it is not any different from the army, where men are given over for territory.'

He wanted to tell Mary something, but he was repelled by her paleness and softness.

'I must sleep.'

'It will get better once you are used to it.'

Thomas said nothing. Not a single person here could understand what he had seen; not a single person had so much as asked, and had they done so how would he have replied? He had no words for it.

And then this town; he had hoped at least that Bungay would take him back and that with peace his life might be resumed and his pride with it. Nothing here was the same, just as surely as nothing inside him was the same. The two no longer fitted.

To Mary, he was unable even to say goodnight. They turned away with their backs to one another. For a second Thomas felt her spine touch his own and they were joined bone to bone; then there was space and silence between them. In the room next door Nelson wept. It was the first time he had slept alone for years. I do not want you here, Father, he whispered to the closed bedroom door. Go away again, Father, back to that war; go away for ever.

IN LONDON, A COUPLE of weeks after the 9th arrived back in Britain, David McBride noticed James McGrigor in the hallway of the new headquarters of the Royal College of Surgeons. The Inspector General called him over.

'Dr McBride! Glad to see you.'

McGrigor turned to the two men who stood with him.

'This young man—surgeon to the 9th and a very good one—has been busy out in Spain. Believes transfusion has something to do with the humours; do you not, Dr McBride, eh?' McGrigor's eyes twinkled.

'I have simply noticed—Oh, let us drop the matter for the moment.' David bowed to the two doctors with McGrigor. 'I intend, sirs, to present a paper on my findings and hope it will convince you of the importance of my work.'

McGrigor nodded.

'Good. Good. I hoped to goad you into something of the sort. You will set up in London, no doubt?'

'I am at present with my father in Bushey.'

'Ah yes, the asylum. Do remember me to him; we have not met but I have sent him men from time to time; officers for the most part returned from war, with families unable to understand their conditions.'

David bowed.

'Indeed, sir. War can break any man. Or peace, for that matter. You will excuse me; I have a call to make.'

IT WAS EASY TO find Robert Heaton's house in Arlington Street.

'That's the one; Mr Heaton, of course.' An old man, immaculate in a black coat and top hat, pointed David across the street. 'You are a friend?'

'His doctor.'

'Robert? A doctor? The man is strong as an ox. Nothing wrong with him, is there?'

'Not as far as I know. I treated him for a wound in the Peninsula and am come to see how he is.'

'The Peninsula, yes. We had all hoped for an account of his adventures; but he has not said a word about the war since he came home, though he has a captain's jacket on his back. He is a charming man, but in and out, you might say. We have all grown quite used to his voyages; as for his latest goings-on: well, you will see. I bid you good day, Doctor.'

David pulled the bell of Heaton's house. A uniformed footman opened the door and took him up to the first floor. A toddler sat in the middle of the room, on a very fine carpet. The boy was getting on for two years old. A tottering pile of wooden bricks rose in front of him.

'Oh.' David stared at the boy. Everything he had imagined about Robert Heaton dissolved. For a moment he thought he must have mistaken the house.

'Dr McBride; delighted. Here I am.' Robert Heaton turned around from a writing desk at the far end of the room.

'Mr Heaton, I do apologise again. I had no notion you were a married man; in fact I remember . . .' David's voice tailed off. Surely he had asked Mr Heaton before he administered the transfusion, or at least when he found that he would live, if he wished to write to his family? He shook himself.

'It would give me great pleasure to meet your wife, and your son here.'

Heaton laughed and came to shake David's hand.

'Wife? Good Lord, Dr McBride, you have got ahead of yourself. I have no wife; and see, Racket likes the idea no better than I do.' Heaton knelt down by the tower on the carpet. Racket advanced from under the writing desk and sat down, paws out, at a distance from the boy.

'How does the tower progress, Jo?'

The boy held out a wooden brick. His pale face was solemn; ringlets stood out from it in all directions.

'Thank you.' Heaton took the brick, added it with care to the trembling stack and stood up.

'How is that?'

Jo kept his eyes on Heaton. When he was sure that he had his attention he swept a hand through the tower of bricks and pushed himself to his feet.

'Again!'

'Very well.' Heaton piled up two or three bricks, then handed one to Jo.

'This is Jo. Racket is jealous, as you can see.'

''Acket. 'Acket.' The boy dropped his bricks and put his arms tight round the dog's neck. Racket's eyes implored Heaton to stop it. David waited for Heaton to rescue his dog, but Heaton watched the boy with a rapt smile.

'Jo seems pretty well acquainted with Racket.'

'Of course he is. We have seen a bit of this dear—' Heaton stopped. 'We have visited this child, in Merton where he has been lodged.'

'Is he yours, Robert?'

'No; I have merely watched over him a little.'

'And now he has come to live with you here?'

'No, indeed. I am to take him tomorrow to a new lodging; one that will prove a safe haven for him.'

'Forgive me, Robert. I came to enquire about your health and perhaps to ask your advice as a man who knows London. I had no idea about this odd mission.'

'I undertake it for a friend.' Heaton paused. 'Though I have to say, this creature is quite an amusement now he begins to talk; which accounts for Racket's jealousy.'

The two men sat down on a cream brocade sofa; David taut and dark, bent forward with eagerness; Heaton thicker-set, soft and relaxed, languorous against a cushion.

'You look very well, if I may say so, Robert.'

'Never better.'

'You have felt no ill effects of the transfusion, nothing remarkable; no eruptions on the skin or faintness with exertion?'

'Good Lord, no. I never thought of it again after Badajoz. I am quite all right. It must count as a great success, Dr McBride, though I am not quite willing to give you the credit of my life. Do you think to continue here in London or go on with those experiments?'

'Transfusion is still a risky business; one failure and I would be ruined.'

'So you think to continue in the army?'

'I have left my post.'

'Tired of war?'

'It has served its purpose. And you, Mr Heaton?'

'It was most interesting; but for the present I am out to grass like my dear pony Athena up at Newmarket. She had seen enough, perhaps.'

Heaton looked vague.

'Odd though, the way the present closes over the past with a death. Like the ocean over a sinking ship: one suck and it goes to the bottom, nothing to be seen. Life continues, and yet . . .' Again Heaton seemed to have left the room for a moment before he recollected himself. 'Do you not find the same sort of effect?'

'For myself there is nothing I wish to forget. But I sympathise with your idea: we must look to the future. My idea is to set up in practice here in London. What do you think? You know the world of fashion. Dr McGrigor urges upon me the example of Ranby, who came from the army to become Surgeon General to the King.'

'My dear Dr McBride, you do need to consider.' Heaton was all attention again. 'The King is beyond hope. No man would wish to be his doctor. As for the Regent; I cannot think he would be anything other than a disappointment as a patient.'

He stood up. 'Well, I shall have to give the matter some thought. Let me see you out, for today. Jo and I have a post-chaise to catch later on; you will forgive me.'

DOROTHY YALLOP LEFT CAPTAIN Heaton's letter open on a table in the parlour. At first she read it several times a day; even now she touched the paper as she went past, to pin it down.

'I shall take the Thursday coach from Charing Cross, stop a night at Newmarket, and be with you the day after.'

'What do you think, George?' she had asked the Major when the first letter came.

'Do what you like, Mrs Yallop; you will know what best to do.'

'I shall teach him to dance—teach him myself. You counsel against it? No, no, remember how nimble I am even if I am scatty.'

At the beginning she thought, It is not because of the child. She had never been a woman to cluck and crow at children in their mothers' arms. No, it was because of Captain Heaton. There was no fuss to him. Although she had been so sad, he did not ask why. That was the first thing; but more than that, the Major had liked him even though he was a volunteer. If she took the child she might say to George, you made a good choice; you discovered an honourable man.

Captain Heaton had sent a letter. He wrote to enquire about her and mentioned a boy; the son of an officer and his wife, both dead, boarded and supported by a friend. He had undertaken to find the boy a better home. Did she know anyone who might take in a child of a year and a half? It need not be a permanent thing, but would be better so; a sense of home, a mother, even—Joseph Fitzwilliam (Heaton mentioned his name) had need of those things above all else.

Out of gratitude to Mr Heaton, Mrs Yallop looked about. She asked one or two of the officers' wives and enquired amongst her acquaintances in Norwich whether there was a respectable family who would take in a child. But after a few weeks she gave up the search. She knew it was not in earnest. From that moment on, a vision of Joseph Fitzwilliam settled in the house in Pottergate. It was not, Dorothy told herself, that she decided absolutely to have him, but that his presence took hold of her and the empty house. Besides, the Major gave the idea his blessing.

So Joseph arrived, bit by bit. A nursery was painted and stocked ready on the first floor behind Mrs Yallop's own bedroom. The quilt of Sir John Moore, completed with Anne Cobbold last year, now covered a new bed, made low enough for a toddler to scramble onto. Several sets of clothes, sewn by herself after consultation with her neighbour who was mother to a large family, lay folded in the chest of drawers. A rocking horse stood in the back parlour and a hundred lead soldiers, painted in the colours of the British, Spanish and Russian armies, lay limb over limb in a wicker basket by the fire. In the kitchen a new set of cutlery lay alongside Dorothy's knives and forks: a silver spoon with a fat handle and, instead of a sharp-pronged fork, a pusher like a tiny broom without bristles, so Joseph could learn to eat by himself.

And now, here he would be; dark, fair, short, plump, agitated by the journey or excited by Mr Heaton's house and stable at Newmarket: she did not know. He would be Joseph and she, at least for the moment, some sort of mother.

'Well, George, you liked an adventure and me to share it, so here we are.'

And then, there they were, Captain Heaton, off the coach, and Joseph. Dorothy, in the front parlour, with the door open, heard them outside.

'Now, Jo, I shall lift you up and you can pull the bell. Ready?'

''Eady.'

'One, two three—up. Now, pull!'

The bell clanged down the hallway. Dorothy waited for a minute and then opened the door herself.

'Mrs Yallop; good day; here we are.'

Heaton still held Jo at shoulder height. The boy looked at Dorothy then turned and buried his face against Heaton's travelling coat. His ringlets brushed against Dorothy's face. Joy filled one half of her heart, apprehension the other. She turned to her maid.

'Mr Heaton and I will take tea in the back parlour, with hot milk for Joseph too.'

In the parlour Heaton pulled a bag of wooden blocks from his travelling case and handed it to Jo.

'Show Mrs Yallop how to build a tower.'

The child knelt down and began with solemnity. Every now and again he turned and checked that Heaton was still there. Heaton drank coffee and gazed at Jo, for all the world, Dorothy thought, as if he were his father.

'I have a letter here for you, Mrs Yallop, that will explain Jo's situation.'

Dorothy took the letter Heaton drew from his pocket. The cover was sealed with wax stamped with two letters that curled together: K and W.

'My friend Captain Hon. Rbt Heaton, 44th, has recommended you as a suitable person to take care of Joseph Fitzwilliam, who was born this September two years ago. His mother was already ill and subsequently died. For his upkeep I shall send you quarterly by post a banker's draft for the sum of ten guineas, which I trust you will find sufficient. If it is not then I beg you to send me your accounts, made up; and I will review the arrangement. Joseph is in my care; but if after an interval you find that his company is agreeable then you may wish to adopt him as your own. I have great faith in Capt. Heaton's judgement and am therefore delighted that you have agreed to take the child and certain that you will provide a good home for him. Kitty, Lady Wellington, Hamilton Place, Piccadilly, London. 1st July 1814.'

'Lady Wellington! Agreed to take the child! Captain Heaton, I am aghast. It seems that you had me in mind all along.'

To Dorothy's surprise Heaton looked solemn.

'Indeed; but for the best of reasons. I know your heart, Mrs Yallop, and then, forgive me, your situation. Besides, I have grown fond of Jo, and shall like to visit from time to time. That is, if you and he will have me, eh Jo?'

Jo ran to Heaton and climbed onto his knees with a practised air.

'Well, I must leave; I intend to take the coach back and you know it waits no more than a couple of hours.'

Dorothy watched Captain Heaton take Jo in his arms, stand up with him and kiss him. Then, as the boy began to cry, he handed him to Dorothy.

'Goodbye, Jo. Racket and I will be up before too long.'

Silence fell on the house in Pottergate. Dorothy picked Jo up and put her arms round him. She felt conscious of herself in her own home, as if Jo observed her. Minutes passed. Jo stopped crying and struggled down to the floor.

''Acket. 'Acket.'

'Who is Racket, Jo?'

The child looked at her. Despair, and then tears filled his large blue eyes.

''Acket.'

Dorothy glanced at Tabby, who sat alert on the sofa.

'Now sit here, Jo.'

Dorothy Yallop sat Jo on the chair, and picked up the cat. His legs hung stiff over her outstretched hand, but he did not protest.

'This is Tabby. Do you like cats?' She put Tabby on Jo's lap and after a while Tabby sat on his haunches, his tail curled round his forelegs, and began to knead with his paws. Jo laughed and put his arms round the cat. Tabby's tail twitched once or twice and then he subsided and closed his eyes. Dorothy saw Jo's eyes close too. In a minute he was asleep, slumped askew on the armchair with Tabby on top of him. For a few moments Dorothy watched him. Then she lifted Tabby off and gathered Jo into her arms.

~

WHEN THE 9TH REGIMENT left Toulouse for Bordeaux and embarkation to Portsmouth, James took a coach to Paris. In the small towns Bourbon lilies, white against a blue ground, fluttered on flags from the fronts of the town halls; but the countryside was sullen and undefeated. Whatever the people of France wanted, and James could not guess the mood of the country from the guarded small talk at inns and on the coach, it was not occupation by the British or Germans. Paris, with a king in the Tuileries again, was full of returned exiles who wanted to be the first in line for government offices. French officers who had declared for Louis XVIII walked the streets in groups in new coats of Bourbon blue. Austrian and German soldiers, who occupied the capital, walked by them and sometimes bowed. A fine dust of civility settled on the stone buildings of the grand arrondissements, underneath, the inhabitants of Paris squabbled and seethed. Some welcomed the monarchy back, and the loans that backed it; some fretted for the days of the Directory, or the Emperor. Others kept quiet and skimmed along with the uneasy peace.

Girodet, when James enquired, was easy to find. He had worked through all the years of the Republic and the Empire; a steady diet of generals and officials in uniform or in family groups. A painter of republicans and Napoleonists might sensibly go out of town until he judged how he might fare under Louis XVIII, and his house appeared deserted when James found it. He rang the bell and waited. After a few minutes a window opened above him.

'Yes.'

'I am looking for Monsieur Girodet.'

'What do you want with him?'

'I have come to enquire about a portrait he painted many years ago. It is of particular importance to me.'

'I have never painted a British officer, or any of your countrymen.'

'An Irishman; Eugene O'Donnell.'

The casement was shut and bolted. James waited. In a few minutes the front door opened.

'I am Girodet. Come in.'

Girodet was a small man of perhaps fifty with dark curling hair that stood back from his forehead. He wore a voluminous white shirt of fine cotton with a layered wide collar that showed his naked chest. Or perhaps, James thought, he was still in some sort of nightshirt and had been disturbed in his sleep.

The stone house was gloomy and quiet. In the bare studio on the first floor, Girodet peered at James for a minute and then offered him a wooden stool.

'Eugene O'Donnell, eh? A relative of yours, Monsieur?'

'Yes, yes; it is a family matter.'

Girodet glanced at him. His eyes, under the overhang of heavy brows, were wary.

'Ah well; it is a long time ago. Of course they all left, the Irish; some in '97, if I have the right year; others in a hurry in '98. Look here.'

A great stack of unframed canvases stood at the far end of the room, faces to the wall. Girodet began to pull them towards him. After peering down over four or five canvases he hauled one up and turned it round. It showed a small man, white-haired and frail, with the same green cravat that James remembered on Eugene O'Donnell, and bright blue eyes that stared at the viewer with defiance.

'Wolfe Tone. The man was a great talker. Even though I paint at night and he should have been asleep he never stopped. He disliked silence, perhaps; a difficult subject, but a man of great charm. You knew him?'

'Indeed not. Though I know that he will not return for his picture.'

'Who do you take me for, young man? I am aware he died a republican death.'

Girodet paused. 'O'Donnell paid for his portrait; a model client; but he never came back for it either.'

'Why not?'

'I thought you knew the family. He went with Tone.'

It was just as Robert Heaton had hinted. O'Donnell was a United Irishman, a sworn enemy of the British.

'And after the failure of the rebellion in Ireland, he went back to Seville.'

Girodet interrupted with impatience. 'Went back? Of course not. He was killed. General Stewart was it not who commanded your army then? A better fate than Tone's, I have heard. If nothing else it is easier to die by an enemy bullet than by one's own hand do you not think, as a soldier, monsieur . . . ?'

'Captain Raven; James Raven.' James was determined not to let the painter divert him. 'Yet I have seen your painting of Monsieur O'Donnell, sir. It hangs in Seville.'

'Of course. Madame his daughter came for it some years ago. She reveres her father, as you will know.' Girodet now glanced at James with mistrust. 'I perhaps speak out of turn. You do not work for the British government?'

'I assure you, sir, that it is for myself that I enquire. I knew Camille; worked with her to rid her country of the French.'

'By the look of your jacket you are a British officer.'

'And Señora Florens worked on behalf of the British government.'

Girodet laughed. A look of scorn crossed his face.

'You are mistaken. Camille Florens had little time for us French, it is true; but she hated the British. Why should she have any love for the country against which her father fought? Eugene O'Donnell gave his life for Ireland. You think his daughter is any different? No, sir, she too is a patriot and republican. All she desires is a Spain that is independent and free of all kings. That is why I was so happy to see her take the work away. She wrote also that with the peace she would return for Tone himself.' Girodet picked up the picture again and turned its face to the wall, as if to tell James that he had said enough. 'I could do with the fee.'

Everything was clear. Camille had tricked him: that much he knew, but now he understood why. Revenge: that was what she had wanted. Revenge against the nation she held responsible for her father's death; a desire that other men should die as he had done. And then to continue Eugene O'Donnell's mission; to bring the republic to Spain. For himself it did not matter if she succeeded. She had duped him, and turned his heart into an instrument of betrayal. Dozens of soldiers, English and French, had died because of that weakness. Yet he had lost the will to chastise himself. The world was indifferent, and so was he.

James thanked Girodet, saw himself out, and headed back towards his hotel. Was he indifferent now to his wife? Yes, also to Harriet. Nothing attached to that name, no memory of her body or sound of her voice, no feeling of happiness or safety. He could face her with equanimity because there was nothing there, or nothing of any significance. To London, then, and the days that stretched out ahead.

~

'HARRIET, HARRIET! HE IS here; come down.' Mrs Cobbold ushered James into the house. In the wide hall she turned towards him.

'Now let me look at you.' James was haggard, she thought; older, too, though that was to be expected. 'We have a house stocked with provisions; you can take your ease here and eat the best of everything. Oh, how delightful to have you home and not a scratch on you that I can see.'

Harriet, at the turn of the stairs, saw her aunt and her husband together, one so small and solid, the other tall and fair. She stopped and looked at James. Everything about him, from the slope of his shoulders to the straight-backed way he stood, with only his head inclined towards her aunt, was familiar; but she felt no desire to quicken her pace, to run and throw herself into his arms. No, she hung back, motionless for a minute on the half-landing. Then she came down, step by step.

'Welcome home, James.'

James let go of Mrs Cobbold's hand. When Harriet was close to him he bent down and kissed her first on one cheek and then on the other.

Mrs Cobbold ushered them towards the parlour.

'Oh, it will take a while to get used to one another again, to be sure; but in you go and sit down. I must arrange for your portmanteau to be brought in and unpacked, James. I will order coffee for you.'

With that Mrs Cobbold shut the door. Harriet and James stood side by side in the bright room. Silence ran round the walls.

'"To Calais, and to England then."' Harriet touched James's sleeve. He smiled a formal smile.

'You are still at that game, Harry?'

'It amuses me.'

'Yes.' James looked distant and sad.

What I have done is my secret, Harriet said to herself. James must never know it. The knowledge would be a humiliation to him, a blow to the pride he had a right to. It was her duty to spare him that, and to live with her secret, surely? It was the uncomfortable price she had to pay. In time she would forget Frederick. Then she might love James again, or at least live in affection with him.

'You have been away a long time, James. My aunt is wise to counsel that it may take us weeks to remember how we used to be.'

I can never open my heart to her, James thought. She cannot know that it is not the passing of time that separates us, or even the war. It is what I have done and have become. But she is my wife still; I will be as far as I can, an honourable man.

That night, James lay on the new fine sheets Mrs Cobbold insisted should make up the bed and watched Harriet as he used to do before he left for Spain. Harriet unpinned her hair in silence and shook it out. Her body was folded into itself; she hurried through her undressing, turned away from him. When she came to bed she slid under the coverlet and lay still. James sensed the heat of her body. Although he felt nothing, it drew him to her.

'Come here, Harriet. Let me kiss you.'

She turned towards him; enough that he could put his arms around her and turn her to face him.

'Why will you not kiss me?'

'I cannot; not yet. Dear James; do not think it is because of your absence. It is something quite different.'

James put his mouth to hers. His tongue, when he pushed it out, met the barrier of her teeth; there was no answering softness, no moment of closeness and unity. Harriet did not yield. She lay rigid. When she opened her eyes and looked at him he felt a gulf between them, as if they stood either side of a wide avenue with no way across. Then as her glance dropped away, nothing.

'Why are you so cold to me, Harriet?'

He knew the answer. Harriet could sense in him the lack of conviction, that it was his body alone that wanted and desired her. His heart was void. Why should that not be so? Harriet was his wife, whatever had happened in Spain. She would do her duty; not today, perhaps, but soon enough. He did not deserve her disdain or the way she flinched when he touched her. He had transgressed no more—a good deal less, indeed—than most officers and men. Every officer's wife knew that her husband would take his satisfaction where he could find it. Think of the Duke of Wellington; a married man who made no secret of his conquests in town after town, who flaunted them in front of his aides-de-camp. Those young men, Fitzroy and the others, admired the Beau for his lovers; would have taken nothing less, some of them, in their commander, and sought to show that they, likewise, could catch a woman. His heart had been involved, it was true. Worst of all, he was compromised and betrayed. Harriet need never know; he could hide it for ever. But that she should spurn him in this way was unjust. He had a right to her and intended soon to use it.

'Very well. Let us agree to behave towards one another with the dignity that every man and wife should observe.'

'Yes, James, we must. We can have a hope, then.'

But I have no hope, Harriet said to herself; not for this. She felt with certainty that she would not love James again as she once had, and for a moment despair gripped her. She pulled up her knees inside her night-gown and wrapped her arms round them. But then it came back, the jet of anticipation, the certainty that something would happen and everything around her change.

'Now, it is a very good morning, Lady Wellington. In former times my father, on such a morning, walked out always in the sunshine of Frankfurt. And do you do the same, Lady Wellington?'

'I have taken a house at Weymouth for the summer. The children have gone down; I remain because I have word that the Duke of Wellington will sail from Calais today or tomorrow.'

Nathan had already had word from Jakob of the Duke's departure from Paris, and of his appointment as ambassador to the court of Louis XVIII.

'And so you wish to tidy your accounts?' Nathan gestured to a notebook that he had propped up on a pile of ledgers that stood on his desk amongst a mass of scribbled sheets of paper.

'I should like to know my balances, and profits, and to hear what you advise now that peace has come. The Russian bonds that I bought over two years ago have risen as you forecast. Should we sell?'

'Ah, it depends on what you plan.'

Nathan Rothschild was less inclined to plan than to seize the opportunity. Take this very year of 1814; not yet finished, he acknowledged, and not altogether a surprise; but unexpected in its success, even for him. The very day after he had agreed with Mr Herries to furnish Lord Wellington with specie, he had dispatched Mayer Davidson to Amsterdam to begin the work. Of course the word soon got out that Rothschilds was buying all the coin to be had in Hamburg, in every corner of France and the Spanish Netherlands; all over northern Europe, Nathan remembered with a flash of pride. That had raised the price a little, no doubt, but they had no time to quibble. What a triumph it had been, though he had had to send letters to them every day and work himself, God (and Hannah) forgive him, on Shabbos. Money went with the letters; bonds to the value of fifty thousand pounds from Mr Herries, placed in a new account, and his own money too, plenty of it, for how else were they to pay for the specie but with his own drafts? There was the risk and there the joy; never had he planned and executed anything like it, to make all the figures in his head cohere and leave him with the profit he desired. Mayer and Jakob had hired coaches and suffered poor inns; they had written notes to all the partners they had, every broker in out-of-the-way corners where specie might be found. Yes, they had worked hard, but he had been there at the centre, still the great General, the Commander-in-Chief.

And so quick; he had astonished even himself. In less than two months they had got the specie to Hellevoetsluis, and sailed it into Bordeaux, four hundred thousand pounds of it. Not the six hundred that Mr Herries demanded, but they went on, until quite suddenly (and too soon for business) Paris surrendered. Off went Bonaparte to Elba and back came King Louis. Which all left him, and Rothschilds, with more specie on their hands than they could dispose of at a good price.

What to do now he had asked himself in May, when peace seemed about to spread across the Continent. Sell his specie? No, he would rather take a risk, bet that Napoleon plotted to escape and try again.

If the Emperor made it back to France, how many would rise? Nathan's mind turned back to numbers. Of course this idea of Napoleon's ambition suited him. All that cash that he had on his hands would be needed the moment the alarm was raised. But even allowing for his own desire, his bet was a reasonable one. This was Napoleon after all, a man who commanded the devotions of millions. He would hang on to his specie, wager that it would hold its value or be called for by Mr Herries. Furthermore, he was in no hurry to buy French bonds as others did.

Did Lady Wellington, he wondered, share his view that the Emperor was too close to shore?

'Nathan, I cannot look too far into the future. I should like to know what my worth is now.'

'I see you are in no mood to indulge me, Lady Wellington, and that is quite right. This morning I made a total as you asked and reckon that your bonds and the shares you have bought would be worth some ten thousand pounds if sold.'

Nathan gave Kitty a mischievous nod.

'And the money you laid out on the National Light and Heat Company has added as much as fifty per cent since the lights went on in Westminster. Allow me to congratulate you; I did not believe that young man had it in him.'

'Herr Winsor, as no doubt Mr Montefiore has told you, is no longer actively in charge. My investment, however, was never in jeopardy and I had faith in his notion.'

'Ah yes, to pipe gas underground; too slow for me, as I said; but I am delighted for you, and for Moses also. Meanwhile, Lady Wellington, what do you plan to do with your account?'

'It is in safe hands, Nathan, and I wish for no more than to leave it with you and let it work.'

Nathan closed the notebook in front of him. Kitty saw, as he did so, that it was blank. Had Nathan any idea of what he had bought and sold on her behalf? It was hard to tell; but her own estimation was not far off what Nathan had come up with. Perhaps that trick with the notebook was to tease her or to invite a challenge. No matter.

'I may not see you for a few months, Nathan. I have much to do in that time.'

'I wish you well, Lady Wellington, and look forward to the resumption of our adventure, perhaps when Bonaparte tires of life at the seaside.' He stood up and gave Kitty his hand.

'It is all my pleasure, Lady Wellington. Or, as I must now say, your Grace.'

ROBERT HEATON, WHEN HE walked between Arlington Street and Hamilton Place later that day, did not encounter a single person. Through the open windows of a house in Clarges Street he saw two paper-men at work on a new scheme of decoration. Further on a house was obscured with a wooden scaffold; the smell of oil paint drifted down from the upper floors. Mayfair was gone out of town for the summer.

At Hamilton Place, Racket bounded up the stairs and stationed himself on the sofa in Kitty's dressing room on the second floor. Kitty and Heaton sat either side of him.

Kitty noticed that Robert Heaton carried an air of formality with him this morning, as if there were another person in the room.

'Lady Wellington, I congratulate you on the Duke's arrival at Dover. You expect him any moment, I am sure.'

'I am not here to sit and wait. I am glad you made this visit. Do tell me your news, Robert. One novelty I see; a new summer coat.'

'Ah, yes; indeed. Delivered yesterday.'

'I am glad you wore it today.'

Heaton threw his head back and ran his hand down Racket's back. He saw how upright Kitty sat, and how still. He reached over Racket, picked up her hand and kissed it. His lips passed over Kitty's cameo ring; it was rough where the stone was carved into ridges, cool on the gold mount.

'Thank you, Kitty.'

They sat together in silence for a minute, as the air gathered around them. In such a situation, Heaton had always felt, it was time to leave, to pack away the past and the present; to throw into a portmanteau only the future, fasten the leather straps and set off. It was not as if England held him. He got up and went to the window. The dusty street was deserted. Well then, he might go; stroll down to Piccadilly and hail a hackney carriage. Or, he could stay, for a bit; London had not treated him so badly these last few months. There was always Italy, now the Austrians were back; but that adventure could wait. He walked back to the sofa, sat down and then after another minute said, 'Now, a letter. From Dorothy Yallop, about Jo.'

Kitty unfolded the letter with gravity, as if it were more than a crumpled sheet of writing, and read it through.

'Dear Captain Heaton, I write as you requested, to tell you of Jo's progress. He is a dear boy, though frightened for the first weeks at everything. He is very fond of my cat, and the wooden bricks you brought with him. He eats as well as possible, and plenty of garden stuff. Please do assure Lady Wellington that the funds will be more than sufficient. I thank you for the child; he has pitched camp in my heart, so to speak, and takes my mind from loss. I remain yours, Dorothy Yallop.'

Kitty folded up the letter. Heaton was surprised to see tears in her eyes.

'That is very good news.'

'It makes you sad?'

'No, happy; very happy. I think, Robert, we can leave Jo to Mrs Yallop. I shall not disturb him again. He need never know more about his mother than that she died in London if Mrs Yallop believes that to be the best in the end.'

Heaton put the letter back in his pocket and nodded.

'I shall nonetheless keep this in case Jo wishes to read it when he is older. A little history never did anyone any harm; I have suffered from a lack of it myself.'

'For that reason also you took the wooden bricks down with him.'

'Indeed so, Kitty. I wished him to have something from me. It was either them or Racket.'

'You joke about Racket.'

Heaton caught Kitty's eye.

'My sentiments for Racket are far too tender to part with him. But I am sure you know that, Kitty.'

Racket lifted his head to their laughter and stood up on the sofa. His tail began to wag. A footman came in.

'The Duke of Wellington is in the hall, my Lady.'

'We will say goodbye, Kitty.' Heaton stood up. 'Ah, I forgot.'

He felt about in his pocket and drew out a musket ball, polished to a dull brightness.

'It went into my shoulder at Badajoz, and was given to me as a souvenir. I had an idea Arthur Freese might like to keep it for me.'

'I will ask him. Good day, Robert.'

She turned to the footman. 'Please show Captain Heaton out and the Duke of Wellington into the library. I shall be down directly.'

The Duke of Wellington, when he heard a tread on the stairs, came to the door of the library behind the drawing room on the first floor. Who was that dandy in a new frock-coat on the way down? He looked the man over; there was something familiar about him, and his mongrel of a dog, too.

'Captain Heaton, 44th, at your service, your Grace. Welcome home.'

Heaton bowed; though his bow was not, Arthur noticed, much more than a dip of the head.

'Good day, Captain.'

Wellington turned back into the library and shut the door. He stood by the empty fireplace for a minute, then went out of the room. Kitty was on the stairs a few steps above him. A long look passed between them, back and forth. It was the look of their whole life together. It gathered all their estrangement, Arthur's time in India and return, the five years they had just spent apart, all the women he supposed her to be in ignorance of, and the way in which, now, civility took the place of affection.

In Arthur's eyes, when the look had passed, Kitty saw shock and withdrawal, and something else that perhaps only she had ever caught: fear; Arthur's fear of age, of confinement and loneliness. For a second, compassion filled her.

'Ah, Kitty.'

Wellington considered his wife. She was old, of course; greyer than ever. Neat, too, he acknowledged, and more alert than he remembered. A curtsey or a kiss for him? No, her glance promised nothing, contained no prospect of comfort or pleasure. Revulsion and disdain returned to him as if he had never been away. But there was something else: that caller. Was it possible that she had received such a man? A captain: well turned out, too, a man who knew how to dress? And on the very morning she expected him; perhaps even because she expected him?

'Good morning, Arthur. Welcome back to London.'

Kitty, Arthur saw, would not mention her visitor. Very well; they could agree on that.

'So, Hamilton Place; it suits you, I trust?'

'It is convenient for the Park.'

'Good.'

Silence fell for a moment.

'It will be a sadness to you that you will not have Ned.'

'Indeed, I have longed for his safety.'

Kitty put out her hand to an armchair. Ned Pakenham had accepted command of the British forces in North America, and must soon sail for Canada.

'I must hope that without French support peace will be concluded there as well.'

Wellington shrugged. It had been high time that Ned left his side. He glanced round the room. It was cluttered and untidy. A pile of school-books lay on a table by the door. In front of the fireplace stood a dappled grey rocking horse, with reins, stirrups and a hair tail that reached to the ground. Worst of all, the piano lid stood open, so that the keys gathered dust and heat. A violin lay across the top of the piano. Did no one in the house care to have things put away?

'The boys?'

'They have been down at Weymouth this past month.'

'Without any instruments to practise upon?'

'May they not have a month to run about without a care?'

'I never had such a time in childhood; idleness can do a child no good. Is Arthur Freese gone with them?'

Another look, which acknowledged this time Arthur Freese's place in their life and Amelia Freese as well, rehung by Kitty in Arthur's new study.

'Yes, he most of all had need of sea air.'

'Why did you not go also?'

'I have had business in London.'

Again, the captain. Wellington was shocked, before incredulity wiped the idea away. It was impossible that Kitty could carry on an intrigue. No: it was impossible that any man would wish to carry on an intrigue with her. Besides she was his wife, and what man would have the effron-tery to compromise him now?

'You must get the boys up; I shall not be able to stay very long. I am here to carry out my public duties, as you know; but am wanted in Paris by the autumn.'

Times had changed since the beginning of the wars with France and since he had been in the Peninsula. Enthusiasm for reform, religion, the

influence of meddling women; who knew what it was, but these days no
man could appear in public dead drunk as Pitt had used to do or dangle
courtesans on his arm like the wretched Fox. The Regent was held in
contempt. Even Lord Byron, so idolised a few years ago, had run into the
headwinds of scandal. Wilberforce and his friends had softened the
country, sobered it up, that was it. Being good was quite the fashion.
Dull, respectable and on their knees; that was how England liked its
politicians now. I may do what I please in private, Wellington thought,
but I must ring myself with a wall of propriety so high no one can see in.

'I shall not trouble you, Kitty, with any attention. I presume that that
is what you too prefer?'

He did not wait for Kitty's answer, but went on, 'I shall stay here.
Decorum demands it; besides I have some thought, as I have written to
you, of a political career now that war is over. I shall require a wife and
family; absurdly, the Regent, and the country, demand it.'

'I will have your things taken to your bedroom.'

'Good. Well, Kitty, I shall take my leave of you for now. I will be back
for dinner, with company.'

'You will send me word how many?'

'Indeed, and I expect that you will dress as the occasion requires. I
want no histrionics, no effusions on your part. I hope we understand one
another?'

Kitty nodded, though the Duke could not tell by her gesture if she
agreed with him or merely understood his demand. As ever, she was
closed. Wellington picked up his things and went down the stairs two by
two. By the front door he dropped his cape onto a chair, buttoned up his
jacket, pulled a cane from the stand and, with the same brisk movement,
walked through the open door.

'You require your horse or carriage, your Grace?' The butler held the
door open and bowed.

'Can you not see? I shall walk by myself.'

DAVID ACKNOWLEDGED TO HIMSELF that even after several weeks in
London he had made no progress towards the establishment of a practice. The time was right. Hundreds of officers had arrived home. Many
had wounds that lingered; balls that had lodged in ribs or wandered still
round their bodies; amputations that needed attention. Others, perhaps
most, looked for another sort of care; the company of men who had

served with them, the opportunity to talk in the clipped shorthand of soldiers who had seen too much. A surgeon in David's position would gather clients with ease, especially if he set up in Lincoln's Inn, St James's or one of the squares north of Oxford Street. He had the money, too. Arrears of his salary, settled in the last weeks of the war, would pay for the lease on a couple of rooms and advertisements in *The Times* and the *Chronicle*. Robert Heaton had offered his recommendation and he had called on Captain Townley, who winked and said he required a discreet doctor from time to time.

But still he did nothing, and did not know why. Perhaps he ought to omit all reference to the blood in his advertisement? The question held him up. If he did so would his interest in transfusion be lost in ordinary work? Would a bolder man be the first to announce a successful transfusion of human blood? One by one the reasons for hesitation advanced and the ambition he had discovered in Spain burned less bright. Discouraged, he began to spend more time helping in the asylum at Bushey. In the company of his father's certainty he felt again his old lack of distinctness.

One morning after his rounds, David found a note from James Raven amongst the letters collected from the Post Office. James expressed a wish to see him. He was still in London, had been there since his arrival from Paris. Could David come to Hatton Garden and spend a few days with him? In a bound David's enthusiasm returned. He took leave of his father and set off the next day.

Through the window of the coach on the Great North Road, David saw discharged soldiers from time to time, alone or in small groups by the roadside. One or two were accompanied by women. They sat with bundles at their feet, some on the verges by crossroads, others by coaching inns. What did they wait for, David wondered? For peace to sweep them up and set them on their feet? For the times of plenty to bring them work?

From Charing Cross where the coach set him down, David walked back to Hatton Garden. He wore a wide-brimmed straw hat and a simple brown linen topcoat. After years of discomfort and making-do, he strode fast, his head held high and hair about his shoulders, with the air of an alpine traveller or an artist in search of a subject. To his surprise he noticed as he walked that even in the press of London he attracted the gaze of passers-by. Once or twice someone turned to look again at him as they walked past, as if he were a person with a secret or of special beauty.

David shrugged off this attention; his coat must be of an unusual cut or his hair worn in an odd way. He looked about with unfeigned interest. Here, too, he saw old soldiers everywhere. Their rust-red jackets coloured the streets, patched and repatched, bleached by Spanish sun. Some begged for money; others stood and watched as carts and coaches, gigs and hackney carriages rolled past. In their presence London brooded, baked by summer sun and coated in dust.

'David. How good it is to see you.' James, to David's eye, looked haggard. His fine cotton shirt hung loose on his frame; he seemed hurried and restless.

'Come in, come in.'

They went into the parlour. Mrs Cobbold jumped up and introduced herself. 'Ah, Dr McBride, we have heard so much about you, and have been so grateful for your letters from the Peninsula. Harriet will be delighted you have come.'

Where was Harriet? In that instant David knew why he had answered James's letter without delay. For two years he had gone about Spain with Harriet in his mind; not at its centre always, and in the midst of the hardest work or in his experiments it had faded; but there somewhere nonetheless. He had come to keep his friend company; but he had also come to test his new sense of purpose against the picture of Harriet.

James began to talk at speed on the subjects of the day: the continued high price of grain; the news of unrest amongst the weavers in Suffolk; the difficulties of returned soldiers. He himself had thought of making an application to the Duke of Wellington for a place on his staff in Paris; but after a few days in that city had realised it did not suit him. Then he broke off.

'My dear David; I have not asked how you are, and how your father goes on?'

Before David had time to speak James rushed on. 'You will stay for a few days? I should welcome your presence.'

'I shall be glad to.'

'Good. You must tell us how your work progresses and what plans you have. Now I must dress for dinner. Find Harriet, too. Do make yourself at home.'

Mrs Cobbold stood up.

'Dr McBride. I have put you on the second floor. My housekeeper will show you up and my maid attend.'

'Ah, no need, Mrs Cobbold. I thank you, but I have no need for a maid. For years I have shifted for myself, and cannot now shake off the habit. I shall wash and be down directly.'

When Harriet came into the room David was dressed and stood alone at the window. He looked at her, he was sure, with equanimity. Was she beautiful or not? Her shoulders, held well back, and her long neck; they were good, undoubtedly. The cut of her dark blue gown—was it the low curve behind that drew his attention to her naked back? Did the success of any dress lie with the dressmaker or the form of the wearer? All he could think was that Harriet had a dressmaker who was an artist, who had created a gown that lay against her slender form in such a way as to promise fullness and warmth.

She looked older, he noticed, no longer a girl. When she smiled at him the two crevasses either side of her mouth deepened. Something had changed in her. Of course, David thought, the war has stamped its passage on all of us. It is not merely time that leaves its mark, but the extremity that war brings to every life; for her the waiting and the silence; for him the excitement and the regret that followed on each death he might have prevented.

Yet when Harriet darted towards him with her old quickness he remembered the girl she had been. Surely, he thought, it was stillness and self-possession that were held to be irresistible; why then did he find the same in Harriet's hurry?

'Dr McBride. David. How glad we are that you have come. We do hope that you will stay on for a while.'

Harriet welcomed David like an old friend; his letters had made him seem so, and his service with James. I am quite poised, she said to herself. They stood by the window and looked out at the pools of light in the dark street. Harriet's restlessness, her habitual sense of hurry, fell away from her. It was a comfort to stand like that, with no thought of before or afterwards. How odd it is, she mused, that we seem to understand one another without the need to say a word. It must be a way David has, from his profession, of certainty. A doctor learns to offer a sense of safety and hope whatever he might privately think.

They began to talk about David's experiments, though later Harriet could not really remember the detail of their conversation. Ease was what she thought about afterwards, when she lay by James's side, restless again, and wide awake; their ease and the ordinariness of their talk.

'HOW GOOD TO SEE you dressed,' Mrs Cobbold said when she came back into the parlour. 'It is quite like old times. Harriet and I, these last years, have so seldom changed at all, the whole day.'

'We have scarcely ever had a guest, Aunt, except for Dorothy, and we never did dress when she stayed.'

Mrs Cobbold busied herself with dinner; it was delightful to have young men in her house. These two could not take the place of her own boys, whose letters she awaited with a secret fervour and for whose return she prayed each Sunday with a passion that belied her sanguine chatter about their success. But there was no doubt that men changed the atmosphere of a house; brought the outside in, slammed doors and filled rooms. James had been listless since his return. He wanted a friend such as this young doctor, who had a sense of purpose about him, and anything that roused James would surely help Harriet too. She rang the bell for the maid with decision.

'Sit here, James, at the head of the table, and carve the meat when it arrives. You take the other end, Dr McBride. Harriet and I will sit between you and make the foursome.'

Mrs Cobbold had opted for a fashionably late dinner, to please the young people. She herself preferred to eat early, at the time of the last century, but it seemed that those days were gone for ever. Still, she had insisted on a proper table, though it was August and many people gave up all formality at the end of the season. In her childhood, they ate fish brought up the river, meat from the estate and vegetables from the kitchen garden. Here she had to make do with Billingsgate and Smithfield, but the beef, she was sure, would be excellent nonetheless. She looked forward to the dessert that would follow the meat: a fool made this morning and laid on ice.

As he cut the tender roast into thin slices and spooned the rendered stock over it, James felt more content than he had done at any time since his arrival from Paris. The smell of red wine, beef stock and rosemary rose into the room from the platter of meat. There was David, whose presence took the edge off his sense of emptiness, and here on his right Mrs Cobbold with her sense that there was always something to be done. Then, to his left was Harriet, and he could look at her as she lifted her glass, with admiration and equilibrium. It had been a good idea to invite David up; they might talk.

'YOU WILL ALL COME to the Grand Jubilee tomorrow?'

It was after the beef. Mrs Cobbold had loosed the sash under her bosom. Her mood was ample; she wished the world, and especially these young people, well. 'Yes, I was sure of it. I have bought tickets for the enclosure by Buckingham House. It is from there that the balloon will ascend. The papers have been full of nothing else. A hundred years of the House of Hanover, that is one great thing to celebrate. But the advent of peace; that is surely more. It is fortuitous that the two come together.'

David looked mischievous.

'As a Scot, Mrs Cobbold, I may perhaps be allowed to toast the memory of our legitimate kings.'

'Come, come, Dr McBride, with the Stuarts we should surely have had the horror of revolution like the French; no colonies, no trade, nothing.'

Harriet leaned across the table.

'Of course we will come, Aunt. James proposes to go early to the Park; there is to be a naval battle on the Serpentine, stalls for everything, then a castle that will transform itself into something I have forgotten, but it is written in the newspaper.'

'Well, I shall wait for you all by Buckingham House. My old person will not bear the crush of the Park. Now, shall we have the fool?'

AT SIX THE NEXT evening, the Duke and Duchess of Wellington stood just outside the ropes of the enclosure by Buckingham House. The Duke was dressed in a dark blue coat, his usual grey trousers and black boots. Since the Jubilee celebrated the peace he had put on a top hat; it threw his aquiline nose into prominence. He heard but did not acknowledge the whisper of approbation in the crowd behind him. The Prime Minister, Lord Liverpool, an insignificant figure in black, accompanied the Duke, while government ministers stood to one side. A gilt chair, brought out of Buckingham House, stood empty. The Regent was late. Further off, the Duke's staff officers bunched together. Fitzroy Somerset looked without interest at the firing of the balloon. He would rather be at Almack's or at the opera; but he put on a face that contrived to be both amused and serious, as the occasion demanded.

Slowly, just after the hour, the balloon ascended. Mr Sadler, in the car, waved his hat once he had risen above the crowd. He prayed for enough wind to get at least beyond the confines of the Park, and hoped to sail south of the river to land with decorum in a market garden.

The flags of the allies fluttered round the car; Russia, Austria, Prussia, Great Britain, and the arms of enough German princes to complete the circle. It was unfortunate, Mr Sadler thought as he placed his hat at his feet to avoid any mishap with the guy ropes, that his passenger, Mrs Johnstone, had had to be left on the ground. He could not guarantee a safe passage over the trees with so little wind. The actress, prettily dressed in red and white, held a dove in her hand, for peace and charity. She looked annoyed and discomfited; what was she to do now that the balloon had abandoned her?

The Duke of Wellington gazed at Mrs Johnstone; she was the only thing of interest in the whole scene. It was a mercy that she had not floated off; if she had gone in the balloon all his attention would have flown with her. He glanced across at Lord Liverpool.

'An indifferent performance, with a device of insignificant size. Why was the car not large enough for two?'

Lord Liverpool opened out his palms, as if to suggest that since his government was not responsible for Mr Sadler's incompetence, he should say nothing. The Duke bowed at the crowd and then to the Prime Minister.

'I shall take my leave of you. The duchess may wish to accompany me.'

Kitty turned to her husband.

'I thank you, Arthur, but I shall stay a little longer. I am to meet friends, and a tent has been prepared for me near the bridge in Green Park. I have a particular interest in the pagoda, prepared by Mr Winsor, which is to be lit with the new light as it gets dark.'

'You are acquainted with this Mr Winsor?'

'Indeed, I have an interest in the new light also.'

Wellington glanced at his wife. As so often now, she surprised him. He nodded at Mrs Johnstone in a way that made clear his admiration, and walked away, Fitzroy Somerset by his side. The Duke had declined any other escort. His modesty delighted those who called his name and pressed forward to touch him. Wellington kept his silence as he walked to his carriage; inside he pushed down the window, leaned out and lifted his hat twice. Then, at his signal, Fitzroy called to the coachman to drive off and pulled up the blinds.

By eight in the evening the Jubilee had taken on the feel of a great festival. All round Hyde Park the booths with food and drink were empty and the great crowds milled about in search of diversion. Thousands of servants released for the evening, shopkeepers and traders finished with their day's work, clerks and printers, women of fashion, beggars and old soldiers walked about in groups, all mingled together in one crowd that ebbed and flowed along the wide walks and round the Serpentine.

Though it was high summer by the calendar of the season, the light in the sky told another story. Autumn was just over the horizon; August was a month of elegy for a summer already past, for endless days, and nights so short that the light lingered in the sky to meet the dawn. Very well then, Kitty decided as she sat under the linen awning prepared for her to see the lighting of the pagoda, she would celebrate what was to come, the future.

The pagoda rose into the sky in four tiers, tipped up at each corner. Now, as darkness fell, men climbed aloft to light the hundreds of wicks inside the globes that ran in lines round the edges of each storey. A sigh ran through the watching crowd as the whole pagoda glowed under the new gaslight. Faces in the crowd, and the red coats of soldiers returned from Spain, were illuminated in their turn. The pagoda was so bright it made its own reflection in the water below that trembled in the breeze.

'There.' Kitty turned to James who sat next to her. 'Splendid, do you not agree, Captain Raven? While you have been away a whole new world of illumination has been created here in London. I am confident it will soon be found in every capital on the Continent and in America, too, once peace is declared there.'

Before James could reply he saw that Kitty's attention had turned to a man who now stood before them, and bowed.

'Mr Winsor. My congratulations. A triumph.'

'Your Grace, I hope that the pagoda fulfils the expectations raised of it in the press.'

'Indeed, it is a great advertisement for the new light, and for the company.'

Frederick bowed again. Harriet shifted in her chair and held herself tight. Here was Frederick in his midnight-blue suit. In the light of the gas lamps his body seemed insubstantial, but his face was lit up; the fine straight nose and the white streak of hair.

He turned then, looked at Harriet, and held her gaze. She took a deep breath. Frederick's beauty struck her not as something remote, but as if for the first time. She could feel herself drawn towards him, and saw that he knew and felt it, too. Harriet determined to wait for the moment to pass. But Frederick came right up to her and held out a hand so that she had no choice but to take it. He brought her hand to his lips and as he did so moved his gaze languidly over her to James at her side. Phosphorus, she thought in distraction, as Frederick's lips touched her skin and the old desire rippled through her. More than ever that is his element. He is Lucifer, the bringer of light.

Frederick looked at her again, over the top of his hand, with veiled eyes. Beside her she sensed James sit up, replete with new knowledge.

'Mrs Raven; a pleasure. It is some time since we met.'

'Indeed, Mr Winsor. Might I introduce you to my husband, Captain Raven, and Dr McBride, who served with him in Spain?'

James nodded. He sat up in his chair and buttoned up his coat right to the top. That man toyed with his wife. He treated Harriet as if he owned her, or had once. James had caught his look, a glance that went under Harriet's clothes, took them off right in front of everyone here. How dare he? Who was he, this upstart Mr Winsor? He and Harriet knew one another, that was quite clear. More than that, James had felt Harriet respond. The way she raised her chin, tipped her head back: he knew it. He had loved it, that wanton look on her face, as if she disappeared into her own body. He had believed it was for him alone.

James gripped the sides of his chair. Another second and he would strike the man. He forced himself to sit quite rigid though his mind jumped about. That was it: Harriet dissembled, though she had always seemed so rigorous in her honesty. His own wife deceived him.

'Gentlemen, good evening to you. The pyrotechnics are about to begin, and require my attention.'

Frederick bowed to James and David with a little too much deference, and then turned back to Kitty. 'Your Grace, goodnight.'

'Goodnight, Mr Winsor; I wish you the best in your new endeavours.'

'Next month I leave for Paris, to introduce the French to the rewards of progress.'

Frederick held Harriet's gaze again for a moment. Then he raised his hand to her and began to walk towards the pagoda. As she looked he seemed to dissolve into its brightness and disappear.

As the fireworks hurtled upwards, James's thoughts gathered pace. That look, the way Mr Winsor toyed with him, as if he had won a hand at cards, thrown them on the table and walked away with no need to collect his winnings, could only mean one thing. Harriet had been his mistress. No, worse; they had been lovers. That explained everything, not just his anger now. That was why Harriet was so cold to him, and why there was a gulf between them. It was not what he had done in Spain. That was to be expected. It was what Harriet had done, her betrayal of her marriage vow. For a moment James thought he might challenge Mr Winsor to a duel. But such theatrics were futile. He would say nothing. He would maintain the dignity of silence until the time came to speak.

THAT NIGHT, WHEN THEY had said goodnight to Mrs Cobbold and waved David up the stairs to the second floor, Harriet and James sat on in silence in the parlour. Harriet watched the flames in the grate sink lower and collapse into the glow of embers and ash. Then she forced herself to begin.

'You know, do you not, James?'

'What do you suppose that I know?'

'You will not help me?'

James looked away from his wife, stiff and implacable.

'Harriet, you do not talk sense.'

'About Mr Winsor. You know that I have already made his acquaintance.'

James said nothing.

'James, do not make me spell it out.'

'You should spell it out, though I have no need that you do so. I do not wish to hear anything more. It is enough that you have betrayed me. To force me to greater knowledge, to ask for my forgiveness even: no, you ask too much of me.'

'I have much to chastise myself for, James, and do not expect your immediate forgiveness; but he talked of things that I loved, and I looked upon it all in the light of an adventure.'

'An adventure, to betray me?'

Harriet looked over at James and longed to lie in his arms as she used to do, to break down the wall between them. Surely it was possible now that she had admitted what had happened? Not all at once, perhaps, but little by little, if he would yield to allow it.

'Can you understand what I attempt to say? Now that I have told you, that is to say now that you know, I feel that there may be hope for us. Oh, dearest James, you must know yourself the longing that grows in one when alone. I do not ask what might have happened in Spain. I seek only your understanding.'

James felt the anger rise in him and the old sense of displacement, as if he stood outside himself.

'Do you suggest that I entered into a similar commonplace liaison?'

'I do not know, James, and do not seek to know. I ask you only to enter into my feeling, and to treat me with generosity. I suggested only that if you had had a similar longing in Spain I am quite sure I would not hold you to account.'

'Quite without justification you insinuate that I have compromised you. How dare you, Harriet, when we have stood only a few hours ago with your lover?'

'No, no; please do not misunderstand me.'

'I have done nothing. Nothing at all. Do you hear me?' James drew himself up to his full height and stood over her.

'No, Harriet. There is nothing that I need to regret and nothing to confess if that is what you urge upon me. It is you who must demand forgiveness and I give it, if I can.'

'I do, James.'

James stood up, took a lamp from the mantelpiece and walked to the door.

'I do not wish to talk any more upon this subject. Besides, I have decided now that we should leave London.'

'And go to Suffolk?'

'There is no reason for me to stay here now, and every reason for us both to leave. I cannot feel that the influence of the metropolis upon you has been a good one. The friends you have made, who promised much, have evidently condoned your behaviour. Nothing is therefore to be expected of them.'

'If you believe we will be happier in Suffolk, that we might start again there, then I understand. But what will you do?'

'I have been in correspondence with the North Suffolk militia. They have asked me to act as Colonel. It has been represented to me that the times are insurrectionary and demand a man of experience. There may no longer be a threat from Napoleon, but discontent has spread all over the country. I had not until this evening given the matter much thought, but now I am inclined to accept. I shall leave within the week. You may follow me when you wish; but I expect you in Bungay by the end of the month.'

'And David? He has only just arrived.'

'I shall invite him to extend his visit with us to Suffolk. You may choose to travel with him if he agrees.'

James still looked down at her.

'There is just one thing more. I do not wish to know why you did it. The man himself is beneath my notice. You will remain silent upon the subject from tonight: with me, and with everyone.'

'James, how can you ask such a thing of me? I rebel against it.'

'I ask it as your husband; you will observe it as my wife.'

There seemed, for the moment, nothing more to say. James left the room without Harriet. He climbed the stairs with new energy; he felt purified and exonerated. It was a matter of indifference, in the end, whether he drew a promise from Harriet or not. It mattered only that she behave to the world as a wife was duty bound to behave. That, for the moment, was what remained to them.

12

Suffolk and London

One night, soon after David arrived in Suffolk, he was woken by a repeated knock on his bedroom door.

'Doctor McBride! Please!'

David jumped out of bed and glanced at his pocket watch in the bright moonlight under the window. It was two in the morning, the time when the body was most defenceless and death crept up. He threw on his trousers, a shirt, a dressing gown over the top, and his shoes, then opened the door. One of the kitchenmaids stood outside, a candle in her hand.

'Sir. It is a child; she is with Lizzie downstairs in the kitchen, sick. Come down I beg you. We fear for her.'

By the range in the kitchen a woman sat with a girl of perhaps two years old in her arms. The child was limp, her eyes rolled back and her mouth open. She breathed with difficulty, and with each breath the room filled with the sound of a wave as it runs up a gravelled beach and withdraws; a rasp and then a slow rattle. The kitchenmaid and the child's mother looked at David. No one spoke; the sound transfixed them. They knew its message, and lived it breath by breath.

David knelt down by the chair and lowered his voice.

'Lizzie, she has the croup.'

Lizzie nodded. Everyone feared the croup. There was nothing to be done for it; the body fought itself in those gasps for air. Some children lived, some died in the space of a few hours.

'I will use a remedy that I learned of in Madrid. I shall need your help.'

'Yes.'

'Speak to her softly, so she can hear your voice.'

Lizzie was beside herself; she looked at David with bewilderment.

'Try to calm yourself. It will not help your child. What is her name?'

'Ruth.'

'That is a fine name; she is old enough to know it. Whisper to her and make her as tranquil as possible.'

David turned to the maid who had woken him. He spoke as if he had all the time in the world.

'And your name?'

'Sarah.'

'Sarah. Good. Is there any cornmeal?'

'No, sir.'

'Oatmeal?'

'Yes, yes.'

'We must use that and hope it will do as well. Bring me a muslin cloth and a towel. Then get a bottle of red wine and mix it with water on the stove. When it steams add the oatmeal as if you are to make porridge. Make it thick enough to stay together in a mass.'

'Yes, I understand.'

Sarah brought the muslin and the towel. When the mixture was hot David spooned it onto the cloth and tied up the corners. Then he laid Ruth down on the kitchen table, opened her shift and placed the hot poultice on top of the towel on her bare chest.

'Now, Ruth, stay as still as you can. Just stay calm and breathe.'

David drew up a chair to the child as he had so often to wounded men in the Peninsula and untied the corners of the muslin. Fumes of the red wine, heated by the hot porridge, came off the poultice, heady and thick. At first Ruth turned her head away, but David spoke to her softly.

'Breathe in, Ruth. It will do you good.'

The child sensed his sincerity; her pond-green eyes held onto him as she gasped for air. After a few minutes the rasping came just on the intake of breath, and little by little fell away. In an hour Ruth was asleep; hot and flushed but at peace. Lizzie looked up, bowed with exhaustion.

'What did you do, doctor?'

'The wine has relaxed Ruth's throat. The swelling troubles her less and her breathing is eased.' He smiled. 'It is true she will feel the effects of the wine when she wakes, but it will do her no harm. The crisis is over. Bring her to see me tomorrow.'

AFTER RUTH, OTHER PATIENTS began to arrive at the house and by the beginning of winter David had established a practice without, as he said to himself, any effort on his part. Well-to-do farmers and men of property began to consult and pay him. He took rooms in the centre of town and told himself it was temporary, and for want of anything better to do. Yet he acknowledged to himself, when he rode out round the flooded water meadows in the river valley, that although the work interested him and sometimes brought him joy, he stayed in Suffolk to be close to Harriet.

David sensed that, in the evenings, when he sat with James and Harriet at dinner, and afterwards by the fire, they were grateful for his presence. It bridged some silence between them. The stories that he brought back, though they were of failure and sorrow more often than success, lifted the atmosphere.

James listened to David's talk and sometimes spoke. But in the daytime his feeling of weariness and loss persisted. He sat for hours in an armchair and stared out at the leafless trees, a book on his knees. Sometimes Harriet sat with him, but often he wished to be alone. Once, when David drew up another chair and sat alongside him, he roused himself and began to speak.

'David, you are a doctor. What would you have me do? My house, my garden: I feel nothing for them. Plaster and grass.'

David got up and walked over to James's chair. Sympathy and impatience filled him. Why, when the world beyond his windows had such need of him, did James sit on, hour after hour?

'Believe me, James, I feel for your situation though I do not know its cause; but do you not wish to find your place in whatever peace brings?'

'I care little for what is out there.'

'What is in here, then.' David forgot his habitual caution. 'Your wife, James, and a family to come. Many of us long for that.'

James sat up with decision. He threw his arms up and over the back of his chair and stared at David as if he had waited for this moment. His blue eyes sparkled like a cold sea.

'Ah, Harriet.'

'Harriet?'

'I have observed you in her company.'

David said nothing.

'I see that you admire her.'

James's voice took on a sardonic edge that David had not heard before.

'Do not trouble yourself about it, David, or compromise yourself with a false reply. I see how it is and why you are here. Harriet is my wife. You cannot have her; but it is all a matter of indifference to me.'

He smiled and looked past David into the park as if something had caught his interest.

AFTER THAT DAVID SPENT most of his time in his lodgings. He promised himself that he would soon move back to London and set himself up there as he had planned. But the only change he made was to go to dinner less often at Beccles Hall, and to take care, when he did so, never to be alone with Harriet. Once or twice James got up and left them. He taunts me, David told himself, before another idea came to him. No, it is worse; he trusts me never to reveal my admiration and wishes me to know it.

Harriet had come to rely on David's presence at dinner and now she missed the respite that the evenings brought. Most days she was restless again. Her father's quizzical presence still filled the Hall, yet her search for her mother drained away. Though she wanted to ask James about her father's will, his melancholy forbade it. At night James demanded that she be his wife; in the day he expected, but did not request, her company. He gave no indication that he resented her conduct or thought about the last two years.

Sometimes they spoke about the house, the militia or their servants. Words without conversation, Harriet thought with sadness. One morning in March she could bear it no more.

'James, we seem no longer to talk with ease. Is there anything you wish to say to me?'

To her surprise James leaned over and took her hand.

'I have no need to discuss your conduct.'

He seemed to want to say something else, but stopped.

'There is another matter?'

James dropped her hand.

'No.'

'Then I wish to speak on my own behalf: about my mother. I have spoken to Mrs Cobbold.'

'Your father would not have wanted you to do so.'

'Also to Mr Patteson. I know she is alive.'

James hesitated. He ought to take this opportunity to speak. If he told Harriet everything now, balanced her need to know about her mother with his own wish to have done with his past, might they not forgive one another? Surely they could. James saw a future in that moment. It was a future chastened but alive with possibility. What did the world's opinion matter weighed against that? All he had to do was begin.

In that instant the tall figure of Frederick Winsor walked into James's mind. That man! How insouciant he had been; bowed at him with a smile and all the while held his knowledge of Harriet behind his back. Why had Harriet given herself to him; how had he possessed her? No. He deceived himself. Why should he crawl along the ground like a guilty man? Harriet had played with her marriage vows, toyed with two men as if they were playthings.

James forgot all about Lady Guest. Disdain, no longer subdued by his frail imaginings of happiness, marched back in.

'You flout your father's desires, and betray me also. Is that the consequence of my absence?'

'It has nothing to do with it. The two matters are not connected.'

'I believe they are; no matter. I honour your father's wishes; it is best that you do the same.'

'I cannot; my father sent my mother away, that much I have discovered. James, I need to find her.'

Again James seemed to hesitate. Harriet clenched her fists, the thumbs tight under her fingers. She forced herself to wait. James stood up; he observed her as he walked to the window, his shoulders back, and stood there, stretched to his full height. Regret washed through her; James was her husband still.

James turned round.

'No. Your father acted for your own good. It is my duty to exercise the authority he passed to me, and that is what I have done. That chapter is closed. There is nothing more to be said.'

James turned back. Harriet started up; she refused James's statement. She did not wish it to seep into her. Already she hesitated; but she had done enough, at least for today. It was better now to leave.

Out in the corridor she met David, who carried a newspaper in his hand.

'James is inside.'

'You will join us?'

'I thank you; not now.'

Harriet made for the laboratory, where the bottles and jars stood familiar on their shelves. She walked along, as she used to do, and touched them one after another. In the stove, coals waited on a lattice of sticks. With the fire lit she might stay and read for a bit.

IN THE DRAWING ROOM David walked over to the window and put his arm on James's back. When James turned round David was surprised to see not the dead eyes that had greeted him for months now, but an expression of infinite sadness.

'Is there something wrong? Is there something I might do?'

James looked down at him.

'No indeed.' His voice took on an edge of mockery. 'Everything is just as it should be.'

'Then I will not press you. I have some news at least, in the *Chronicle*. The French telegraph reports that Bonaparte has left Elba, landed in France and declared his intention to march on Paris. He is already at Grenoble. Every regiment he encounters goes over to him, and not a shot fired.'

James took the newspaper and shook it out in front of him. He did not read anything in it, or turn the page over.

'And James, there is trouble here too. I ran into Thomas Orde on my way here; he has called a meeting at Watney's mill.'

'To what purpose?'

'He is to speak to the men put out of work by the new looms. The mood is ugly. Machines have been smashed in other towns. Everything has been made worse by talk of these new parish workhouses where whole families will be forced if they need relief.'

'There are no such plans here. I should know it if there were.'

'A rumour is enough. I have come to know these men a little. They will endure great hardship, but confine them, separate them from their wives and children as the new workhouses will do, and they will rebel.'

James tapped the paper.

'Thomas Orde was changed by Spain. He seeks to right what went wrong there.'

'I do not believe so, James. It is not the returned soldiers merely who agitate. Mr Orde has lost his self-respect along with his employment; he wants it back.'

There was a knock at the door, and a maid came in.

'Mr Watney is in the hall, Captain, and asks to see you.'

'Very well.'

James stood up and turned to David.

'Thomas is a fool. Nothing will bring those old ways back. You will excuse me; I must go.'

Mr Watney waited for James with impatience.

'Captain Raven, I am here to appeal to you as head of the militia; to ask you to act. No one is safe with these agitators in town. My mill is threatened, and the mill-hands too.'

James sighed. Insubordination and disorder were everywhere.

'I will do what I can. I can promise no more than a few men.'

When Mr Watney left, James went up to his bedroom and put his uniform on. He sent a servant to call out the nearest of the volunteer militiamen. From a cupboard in the gunroom he took a rifle, his powder box and pouch, and left the house.

IN HIS COTTAGE DOWN the lane, Thomas Orde prepared to leave. As if there was no bustle around her, Mary sat at the kitchen table, a long white pinafore over her grey serge gown. She pulled the blowsy outer leaves off a winter cabbage taken from the vegetable patch. Slugs had eaten them to a purple filigree. Three bloaters with glazed eyes lay on an iron tray. Mary pressed salt on their scales.

'So much better than a kipper.'

She looked over at her husband, who stood in his stockings on the flags.

'Shall you come with me, Mary?'

'I have much to do here.' She smiled. 'Food, for when you return. Besides, I do not think it wise.'

'You do not agree with my work?'

'Work, you may call it, Thomas, and I am sensible of your good heart. But you have had no work all winter. We have scarcely seen you.'

'You have been shut up in the mill.'

'Without me there what would we eat?'

Thomas took a step towards her.

'Mary, I have no wish to fall further into a dispute. You know that. Yet I must stop these looms. Do come to the meeting.'

'I shall stay with Nelson.'

After an hour or two Mary went out of the cottage. Shouts drifted along the river. Nelson tugged at her hand.

'Is that father? I can hear his voice.'

'Perhaps it is.'

'Can we go to him, mother?'

'Yes, indeed, Nelson. Run and find your jacket. We must urge him to come away.'

JAMES WAITED IN THE town square for the militiamen to arrive. They came in ones and twos, their uniforms neatly pressed in parade ground order. Although he had ordered one or two sessions of shooting practice over the winter, James commanded men who had joined the militia more for pleasure of brass buttons and evenings in the hotel than from any belief that they would ever be called on to defend their town. A couple of them, local farmers, were good shots when a partridge flew up; but many had scarcely kept their guns oiled since the end of the war.

When he had twenty men, James ordered them to march down and halt in the shallow rise above the river. The crowd by the mill was much bigger than James expected. The gates stood open; the men massed by the doors. Most carried weapons: axes, stakes and spades. At the sight of the militiamen, a great shout went up. In their midst James saw Thomas Orde. Though he could not hear what Thomas said among the noise, he saw him gesture towards the doors of the mill.

'Form up. Load your weapons.'

The militiamen bent over and began to load their muskets. James looked at them with impatience. Property was threatened and he had only amateurs. They looked confused.

The noise from the crowd grew louder. Several dozen men ran up the slope towards the militia, turned and from their position just above the wall of the mill hurled stones through its first-floor windows. In the confusion James noticed Mary Orde and Nelson, who stood off to the side in a crowd of townspeople. As he glanced he saw Harriet arrive, and then David. He shouted over to them.

'David. Please ask the people to move away. They are in danger. This is a riot, can they not see?'

Smoke began to rise from in front of the mill. Harriet turned to Mary Orde.

'I came because of the shouts, Mary. Can you see Thomas there?'

'I can see him! I can see him!'

Nelson tugged at Harriet's cloak and pointed. Thomas's fair head came and went in the crowd. It was impossible to know if he urged the men on or tried to calm them down; by now the crowd had its own life.

They will force the doors of the mill, James thought. Once inside they will destroy the looms and smash the steam engines. He had to prevent them. He turned to the militia.

'I must disperse the crowd. I will order you to fire in the air above their heads. Do you understand?'

The men nodded.

'Raise arms!'

One by one the men lifted the muskets to their shoulders.

'Fire!'

At that moment Nelson saw his father. He dropped Mary's hand and began to run down the slope.

'Father!'

'Nelson, come back!'

Harriet heard the snap of musket fire as the shot flew over the men's heads. A cloud of smoke rose into the air above the militia and blocked out the silver trunks of the birch trees on the other side of the river. Underneath the smoke Harriet saw puffs of dust rise off the side of the mill as a couple of bullets, badly directed, hit the stonework. Men ran in every direction away from the bullets, some round the back of the mill and some towards the bridge over the river. Others tried again to break down the door of the building and reach the safety of the inside.

At that very moment Harriet saw Nelson stop short in his run, and fall headlong to the ground. From below, Thomas glanced up, saw his son drop, and began to run up the slope towards him. He and Mary reached Nelson at the same time.

Nelson lay where he had fallen. At the sight of his parents he lifted one arm into the air and let it fall. Thomas put his hand on his son's chest.

'Nelson, Nelson: speak.'

Nelson looked at his father without recognition. Fear ran through Thomas; a fear worse than any he remembered. They would lose him, their only child, on whom all Mary's hopes rested, and the only joy they had known together since his return. With a lurch of his stomach he acknowledged that he had brought all this about.

I have killed my own son, he thought, as surely as if I held the musket myself.

Mary knelt down and held Nelson's hand.

'Find Dr McBride, Thomas. Please run and find him.'

Thomas glanced again at his son. Nelson's foot lay at an absurd angle, twisted and limp. It dangled off his leg, and through the stocking Thomas saw a bulge where the broken bone pushed through the surface of the flesh.

Thomas ran further up the hill from the river; in a minute he saw Dr McBride come down towards him. He must have heard the shots and then the screams of the men; but Nelson had not screamed, had not made a sound. Perhaps someone else had fetched the doctor. Thomas's thoughts flew about, disjointed and nonsensical.

'Doctor, please come. It is Nelson, my son. He is shot.'

'Take me to him.'

In an instant David felt as if he were back in the Peninsula at the moment the first wounded were brought in. The anxiety that had filled him drained away.

'We must get him inside. I need to find the ball if it is still in his body and then set the leg.'

Thomas Orde looked as if he might lose consciousness. David turned to see Thomas's friend Abraham Greene run up.

'Can you find me a cart, Abraham; bring it up? I need a man to lift the boy.'

'I can do it myself, Doctor.'

'Very well; take care. Come down with him as soon as you can.'

David bent down to Nelson.

'Nelson; I am Dr McBride. I intend to set your leg so that you can walk again. You will be quite well. Do you understand me?'

The boy looked at him with blank eyes. David turned to Mary.

'Mary, please tell him again. I must go now.'

By the mill gates a carriage drew up. Mr Watney jumped out, a whip in his hand. David walked up to him.

'Mr Watney, I require a room inside. A child is injured and I must operate.'

'Open up my mill?'

'Now.'

'To let in this rabble? I will not. They will destroy my looms.'

David heard himself speak as if his own voice was far away.

'You will. I have a life to save.'

'Do not shout; I am not compelled to listen to you.'

'Open the doors or I shall order the men to knock them in.'

Mr Watney turned to his manager. He clenched the whip handle.

'Do as he asks. Unlock your office.'

Next to him, David sensed that Thomas and Mary had arrived with Abraham, who now carried Nelson in his arms. Blood soaked Nelson's stocking; it dripped down over his shoe and onto the flagstones by the mill door. Behind Nelson, David saw Harriet. James and the militia had left; the men dispersed. In a few minutes they would be alone.

He gestured to Abraham.

'Come in, come in. Lay him down and then find a length of cloth. Cut one off a bolt and put it down here on the table. I shall need some strips of linen, or something that may serve to bind his leg and wounds also.'

In the manager's office, David laid out his instruments on the manager's sloped desktop with the methodical care that came to him without a thought. When he looked round he saw that Harriet had come into the room.

'I am almost ready, Harriet. If I ask you, can you hand the instruments to me as I need them?'

'Are they in the order you will require?'

'Yes, I will hold my hand out. Take the used instrument with one hand and with the other hand me the next in line. Then wipe off the used instrument and put it back in its place. I may call for it again, by name.'

'I understand.'

Abraham returned with a manager's linen coat and a length of worsted in his arms. He folded the worsted, laid it on the table and then lifted Nelson onto it. Then he pulled open the desk drawer, found a pair of scissors and cut the skirt of the coat into long strips.

Mary Orde, who had pulled a chair up to the table, spoke up.

'I shall hold his hand, Dr McBride, and wish that he may get comfort from the sight of me.'

No sound came into the mill from outside. Beyond the open door the rows of great machines stood silent. The light drained from the windows as David worked; the gloom added to the tension. When David made the first incision, and found the path of the ball through the artery, Nelson fainted away. Mary gasped and looked across at the doctor.

'It happens often that the patient faints; he will come round later, and it is perhaps better so, to have no memory of the pain.'

David spoke with the assurance he knew he must give to everyone in the room. The knowledge that Nelson might die quite suddenly and not from the effects of the wound must be carried by him alone. When he had sewn up the two small incisions where he had extracted the ball, he straightened up and looked around the room.

'Now I must set his broken leg.'

David reached over and picked up the two thick wooden rulers that leaned up against the manager's desk. All he could do was to align the smashed bones, bind Nelson's leg so that it stayed rigid, and give the boy hope, when he came round, that he would walk again. It was as well that the boy could not feel what he did. David felt for the bones; the breaks above the ankle were clean.

'Good. Hand me the strips of linen, Abraham, one by one.'

It was quite dark now. Harriet found and lit the oil lamp. She held it while David worked. At the moment the golden light fell on his face, Nelson stirred. Mary squeezed his hand; he opened his eyes and looked at his mother. Silence hung over the scene like a kind of warmth until David broke it.

'That is the best I can do.'

He looked down at the boy.

'You need to rest now, Nelson. Your parents will take you home.'

He gathered up his instruments, turned to Thomas and handed him a small phial of liquid.

'I shall visit you in the morning. I advise a few drops of laudanum for the pain. It may bring violent dreams with it. Calm him as best you can, and watch to make sure he has no fever. I feel sure that he will make a full recovery with rest and time. Good evening to you. The cart and horse are still outside. Carry him gently.'

When everyone had left, David walked back up the hill to his rooms in the centre of the town. As he turned the lock in the heavy old door, weariness crawled over him. War had come to Suffolk. One group of men imposed their will upon another by force. War never finishes, he thought in distraction, and never will. It simply moves about the world like the ocean current that touches now one country, now another. Why? Because in the same way that a rash upon the skin is merely a symptom of a fever that rages in the body underneath, war is only the visible shape of all the forces that nature has planted in us. To declare peace; to think it is ever possible? All that is folly.

UPSTAIRS IN THE COTTAGE Nelson breathed through his dreams. Flames crackled in front of his eyes.

But my eyes are closed, he thought. The fire is my dream.

No matter what he said, the fire burned on. It devoured fields and exploded houses—pouf, they went, each one in a shower of sparks; and all the time he could see himself here in the cottage, asleep on his bed. The fire came up behind him. He could feel its heat. It coloured the brass balls on the bedstead a dangerous red. It roared like the lion in his story book and soon it would rush into the room. Terror came to Nelson then, a red dream-terror that dipped and spun and never stopped. Time after time he woke up and then sank back into sleep.

In the room next door Thomas lay awake; he could hear Nelson shift and moan. Once or twice he got up, felt his way through the open door and laid a hand on his son's cheek in the darkness.

'Are you awright, son? It's a dream just as Dr McBride said. I am here. Try to sleep. The dream is the laudanum; it stops the pain.'

Nelson was almost eight; he could understand. The boy gripped his father's hand.

'I will stay with you until you sleep again.'

But Nelson was asleep already, gone out as if he had received a blow. What were his dreams? Thomas wondered when he was back in bed. Were they of the shooting and the pain, or perhaps something happy, with sunlight, or a jaunt to the sea? Whatever they were, he had brought them on Nelson. Fear slid through again.

As he lay there Thomas sensed Mary turn to face him in the darkness and for the first time since he was home he was grateful that she was beside him. She had been quite calm all through the operation. Not once, then or afterwards, as she wiped Nelson's face and body with a cloth dipped in warmed water, and spooned a few drops of laudanum down his throat, had she reprimanded Thomas or made any reference to the riot, or the events of the last weeks. How generous she is, Thomas thought. Tenderness passed through him like a wave that left him stranded.

'Try to sleep a little, Thomas.'

'Mary, you know I cannot. I feel myself responsible for his life. He is all we have.'

'We have one another, Thomas.'

Mary came towards him and her hair fell round his hands as they lay against her soft face. The feeling of relief that Thomas had had since the operation suddenly gave way in him, as if a wall collapsed. Pictures of

Badajoz passed before his eyes one after another until he saw as clearly as if he were there again the curls of soft black hair in his hands, heard the sob of the girl and his own scream of hatred and joy.

Mary's hair still covered his hands. He tried to swallow and could not. Something pushed up the other way. Then he began to cry. His tears were for everything that had happened; for Mary and himself, for the destruction and scramble of their life since his return, for Nelson, for the shame of the last hours.

'Mary?' His voice trembled.

'Thomas.'

'Mary, I have remembered something; something I did in Spain. I must tell you about it.'

As he spoke he kissed her. The touch and softness of her lips disarmed him, overcame him; she yielded to him and allowed him back. In that simple gesture and the way she put her arm over him and joined herself to him with it, he felt and absorbed her forgiveness, and his body shook with gratitude.

'You need not tell me now, Thomas.'

'It was something of which I am ashamed. I had forgotten it until this moment.'

'I can wait until another day, when Nelson is well.'

Then she kissed him in return and they lay together with their limbs entwined. Thomas ran a hand up Mary's back and felt the solidity of her body, its warmth and safety. Everything, he knew, would follow from this. Perhaps he would never tell her all that he had done. Perhaps she knew already, or had guessed nearly enough why he had held himself aloof. What had happened had changed him, he knew. He could not tell now if they could make something new from the disaster of today and his past; but hope had come back to him, reticent and fragile, like a light across the marshes.

BY THE EVENING THE town was quiet; shock had overcome it. With the rioters dispersed the militia went home too; respectable men disturbed by the fears they had found in their own hearts. In the half-empty square, a few people nodded to Harriet as she passed through, but no one approached her.

At the Hall Harriet noticed an unfamiliar carriage by the portico. James was in the drawing room, pale and still. Two men stood with him.

One was Mr Watney; the other she did not know. James listened to Mr Watney speak.

'I find it intolerable, Captain Raven, that you arrested none of the rioters.'

'Mr Watney, your property is saved. That is enough. I decline to arrest men on suspicion; it was impossible to distinguish one from another and I cannot arrest a whole mob. Besides I have not the powers.'

'But I am a magistrate, sir. I have those powers and would have wished to use them.'

James glanced at his other visitor and nodded at Harriet. Despite his pallor a firmness had returned to his voice and he was more animated than he had been for months.

'Harriet, this is William Paston, Colonel of the 44th. It seems that the Allies will declare Bonaparte an outlaw. We will be at war again in a very few days. Colonel Paston has been called to make up the deficiencies in the 44th, the 9th being stood down and dispersed. He leaves for Harwich tonight. My orders are to accompany him.'

'Tonight?'

William Paston hitched up the travelling cloak that lay over his arm.

'I am sorry to bear such news, Mrs Raven. It is important that I mobilise the reserves of the 44th as quickly as I can, and I have asked your husband to assist me. Might I wait in the library while your husband packs his necessary items? His trunk can follow later.'

'Of course, Colonel.'

Harriet rang the bell and the two visitors left the room together.

After a pause James came close to Harriet. He pushed her disordered hair back over her shoulders.

'Harriet, I have considered everything in the hours since Nelson's shooting. I am very tired; tired of everything. When I get back I will explain it all to you. There is not time now; I want merely to say that nothing that has happened is important. I forgive you everything and I wish that you may be able also to forgive me.'

'Forgive you?'

'Yes.'

'Please tell me now.'

'Harriet, I cannot; but let me say I have behaved no better than you. That will do until I come back, and maybe no more need be said. This way we may at least part as friends.'

Harriet felt exhausted. Were they friends? She let the question go; the day had been too long already. James took her hands.

'There is another thing also, but it too can wait. You will help me pack, select a few shirts and ferret out my best trousers? I wish to face Bonaparte looking my best, at least.'

An hour later he was gone.

As soon as David was sure that Nelson's wound was healed and his broken bones had begun to knit together, he gave up his rooms in Bungay and moved to London. To remain in Suffolk was impossible; he must take himself in hand and establish the practice in London that he had always planned.

In Leicester Square he found a neat set of rooms and took them for a year. He called on Captain Townley at the Albany and Robert Heaton in Arlington Street. In a very few weeks Townley's friends began to consult him. He prescribed them mercury tablets and weeks at home on a simple diet for venereal diseases. Robert Heaton passed him on to the bachelors and widows of Arlington Street. Gout, stiffness in the joints and dropsy plagued them. For the dropsy David could offer little but his visits; for the rest he dispensed the willow bark he had used in the Peninsula, with excellent results. To his surprise daughters and nieces of his elderly clients also began to insist on his services, especially, he noticed, when nothing more ailed them than too little to do. 'You must come, Doctor,' they would say, 'I am a victim of headaches', or 'Doctor, my son is behind-hand with his walking. Will you examine him?' Though he charged them high fees to discourage such wasted visits, it made no difference. The mothers of Mayfair found him delightful.

Robert Heaton shrugged when David told him.

'So you are to become a society doctor. Here is a tip. Stay clear of the grandest houses; Cumberland House, Northumberland House, that sort of place. Not worth your trouble. One incurable condition there could destroy you.'

'It is not what I had expected.'

'Nothing is, it seems. To take myself as an example: here I am bedded down in London as if it were my home. And what keeps me here? A woman.' He looked alarmed. 'A friendship, rather.'

'A tender friendship?'

'Can you credit it, I believe you are right.' Heaton laughed and David heard pure gaiety in his voice.

WHEN JAMES LEFT, HARRIET, too, felt that there was nothing in Suffolk to keep her. After three weeks she shut up Beccles Hall and made for Hatton Garden. Mrs Cobbold welcomed her with a kiss on both cheeks.

'How good it is that you have come; and see who is here also.'

There was a clatter along the hall and a sturdy little boy ran into the parlour and came to a halt in front of Harriet. He carried a trowel in his hand, covered with soil. Dorothy Yallop came in a second later, red with effort and her gown hitched up at the waist.

'My goodness how you gallop, Jo. Your poor mama is quite out of breath.' She put her hands on her hips and panted with loud exaggeration.

'I won, I won.' Jo jumped up and down, then ran and hid his face between her legs.

'So you did, Jo, so you did.'

She turned the boy round.

'This is Mrs Raven. Go and greet her.'

'Mrs 'Aven.'

Dorothy smiled.

'No, try again. You are able to say it: Mrs Raven.'

'Mrs Raven.' Jo pronounced her name with solemnity. Mrs Yallop ruffled his tight brown curls and kissed him.

'Well said, Jo. What a fine talker you are. Run along to the kitchen now. There is bread and honey laid out. Take your trowel and leave it on the kitchen step.'

Dorothy watched Jo out of the door, loosened her gown so that the skirt fell back to the floor and turned to Harriet. Life sparkled out of her. The hem of her gown was covered in dust.

'That's my Jo, as pleased as I am to see you.'

'Dorothy, he is charming. Mrs Cobbold tells me he is yours.'

'Not mine, no. I should not put it that way; just that he lives with me, and you see how it is.'

'I do indeed.'

'And this afternoon we go to Piccadilly to pay a visit to Captain Heaton.'

Mrs Yallop chuckled.

'Look at my dusty skirts. I shall change and then you will tell me all your news. We will follow the Duke every day with our map, as before. He has left Vienna for Brussels already, and we mark his progress on the board. Jo is quite the master of the little flags, knows the colours of all the armies, too.'

Later, when they sat round the parlour table where the great map of France and the Low Countries was laid out, Jo jumped up and down with excitement. But he moved the pins with care. Now that the Duke of Wellington had so many allies, they had pasted tiny flags onto the pinheads: scarlet for the Duke of Wellington and the rump of the British army, orange for the troops of the Netherlands. The Prussians had yellow flags, the Austrians and Russians grey and light blue. Around Paris Jo planted a forest of dark blue.

Day after day they waited for Napoleon to move. Harriet could only say to herself that James was somewhere near Brussels. He did not write and she made no attempt to write to him; everyone knew the battle would come soon, but no one knew when. Life settled into the routines of the year before, as if the peace had been just an interval that was always bound to end.

After a few weeks David began to call at Hatton Garden in the afternoons, an old friend with whom Harriet could pass the time. Each day, when it was fine, they took a different walk: down the gentle incline to the river, up to the fields around Islington, or through Lincoln's Inn among the lawyers in their wigs and gowns.

One afternoon they paced round the square base of the Monument and looked up to see its crown of copper flames flare into the sky. The door to the staircase stood open. Harriet turned to David.

'Shall we climb up?'

'It is three hundred steps, at least.'

'Three hundred! Nothing! I am sure I can do it without a stop.'

'Show me. I shall follow hard on your heels and get past you if I can.'

Harriet picked up her skirts and ran in, with David behind her. They laughed at their success when they reached the open top without a pause and pointed out the buildings spread out below them. To the west rose the great dome of St Paul's and away to the south the thicket of masts on the river.

Harriet slipped her hand round David's arm as he leaned against the rail.

'There, look, down there, is Hatton Garden.'

'We cannot see it, Harriet, it is surely obscured by the Bank.'

'Smithfield, then, and the Great North Road that runs away from it.'
David put his free hand over hers.

'Just for today, I shall see what you see. Tomorrow I shall tell you that
you talk nonsense.'

'When do I ever talk nonsense, David?'

'All the time; but not today. Today you talk plain good sense.'

It was a sign of friendship, Harriet thought, to curl her arm through
David's as they turned out of Hatton Garden; and to talk to him about
her father, and her mother. A sign of friendship, too, to enter into David's
plans for his practice and listen to stories of his visits as she had in Suffolk. But then she had known him, surely, for many years: one need not
count them. By the time May turned to June and the days stretched out,
Harriet became impatient if David arrived late. Without a thought she
devised longer walks to suit the length of the evenings. Night might find
them still out, but were there not constellations to find and fix in the sky?

On 12 June Napoleon left Paris. After three days, when the news
reached London, Jo moved almost every blue flag north to the Belgian
border. On 22 June, after breakfast, when news of the victory at Waterloo
went from house to house, Dorothy Yallop sat Jo on her knee.

'Let us pull out all those flags, Jo. The Duke has the victory; but sixty
thousand men, they say, are killed and wounded.'

They sat at the table while Jo took out the pins, and put them in their
box so that they lay one on top of another, blue and red, grey, orange and
yellow flags all mixed together.

For Harriet it ended when Mrs Cobbold's maid found her in the garden a few days later. It was a beautiful day, summer blue, with climbing
roses out.

'Colonel Paston is in the parlour, Mrs Raven. He asks to see you.'

There was no need to go in, to walk up the path, wash her face in the
kitchen, take off her apron and extend her hand to the Colonel. She knew
already that James was dead.

JAMES RAVEN WAS BURIED on the battlefield of Waterloo near the
walled farm of La Haye Sainte. Colonel Paston explained to her that he
was killed when the 44th Regiment charged into oncoming French
infantry in the middle of the day. General Picton had died at the head of

the charge and Captain Raven had followed right behind him, he had been fearless, and brave. The Colonel added nothing to that, but Harriet knew in her heart that if James had not exactly wished to die at that instant, he had nonetheless thrown himself at death, met it head on and felt no regret.

When Colonel Paston left, Harriet sat in the parlour alone, until she felt another presence in the room. She looked up to see Dorothy Yallop by her, solid and safe.

'Oh, Dorothy.'

'Would you like me to sit with you?'

'Yes.'

Dorothy put her arms round Harriet, and Harriet laid her head on Dorothy's chest.

'Please do not leave me.'

'No, my dear, you shall not be alone. I shall stay with you as long as you want me.'

It was Jo, a few days later, who demanded that Harriet look up and come back to herself. When he saw her cry first his own blue eyes filled with tears.

'No, Jo, do not cry.' Harriet hugged him. Jo pulled her sleeve.

'Outside, Aunt Harriet, come outside to my house.'

Harriet followed Jo into the garden, where, the evening before, he had collected a dozen snails, dropped them into a wooden box and shut them up for the night. Mrs Yallop, who wished Jo to understand that no creature should be confined without food, had taken the lid off when Jo was in bed.

'See, my house.'

The box was empty. Jo sat down on the garden path and turned the box over. He looked up at Harriet and his upper lip trembled.

'Gone.'

Harriet laughed and knelt down beside him.

'Do not cry, Jo. We will collect some more tonight and give them some food. Is that a good idea?'

'I want the old ones.'

'They have escaped. But we can ask the gardener which leaves snails like.'

Jo considered the idea and then jumped up.

'I will find him.'

The next day, at breakfast, Mrs Yallop handed Harriet a note with her coffee.

'I see Dr McBride will call this afternoon.'

'Dorothy, I have not asked him to call.'

'But I think we would welcome a visit from him; it is a week now, and you have not gone out. Dr McBride has written several times and offered yesterday to accompany you on visits should you wish to make them, or on a stroll through town.'

'I ought not to need him.'

'What do you suggest, Harriet? There is no ought about it. Dr McBride is concerned about you. It is impolite not to receive him.'

She turned away and offered Jo a slice of toast spread thick with butter.

'Besides, my dear, you may find he is the best cure of all.'

So, dressed in a gown dyed black for mourning, Harriet walked out with David again. One afternoon she told him about Frederick.

'You noticed, perhaps, at the Jubilee? It was after that I tried to explain to James what had happened. He never forgave me; but at the end, before he left, he said he wished to tell me something also. Then there was no time. I blame myself much for what happened and am tormented by it.'

David took her hand.

'One thing Captain Heaton said: matters take turns we do not expect. We must all live with them.' He stopped. 'I, for instance, find myself in an unforeseen situation.'

'What is that?'

'No matter. I mean to say that you will never know what James wished to tell you in return. Might it not be best to leave it thus, in the knowledge that you parted friends?'

'Yes, it is all that I can do.'

Another day, they sat in the Park side by side. Harriet had thrown off her bonnet. She shook out her hair, lay back on the grass and looked up into the sky. The Park was full; crowds came everyday in the hope of catching sight of the Duke of Wellington, though he never appeared and they had to make do with his staff officers who strolled in groups and bowed to right and left.

Summer seeped through Harriet's skin. She had come from a visit to Kitty and the children.

'You have no idea how Gerald has grown; and then Arthur Freese, he will soon be a young man.'

David lay by Harriet's side and watched the clouds fly backwards over their heads.

'How can I have an idea? I have never yet met them.'

Harriet turned towards him and propped herself up on an elbow.

'Perhaps that idea, to give up what I cannot know and remember the best of what has passed, holds good for my mother, too.'

'Your mother?'

'You know she left when I was young. I have longed so much to find her, and tried so hard. My father sent her away; I hated him for it. Now I wonder. He did what he could, and that was all. Perhaps it is time to let her go and to look forward without her.'

'Do you wish for that now?'

'I am not sure; it is merely that the feeling of restlessness I have had for so long has faded.'

David sat up and looked down at Harriet. How could he say that at that moment he longed to kiss her, to hold her, to have her for himself?

She sat up too, and took his hand.

'When we go back to Suffolk, we will find my father's instructions; James's too, if he left them. I think we should wait until that day comes.'

'When we go back?'

Harriet did not seem to hear him.

'I think to keep the Hall, and the laboratory, but there are enough bits and pieces to furnish a house and we may like to pick them out before we close it for the winter.'

'Before we close it?'

Then Harriet turned to him.

'Yes.' She kissed him with decision. David felt her lips, and her mouth open to his. He had to speak.

'Harriet.'

'Yes.'

'Are you? Will you?'

Harriet laughed her robust laugh.

'David, yes, and yes, I will. Next year. Until then we can remain thus.' Harriet laughed and threw herself down on the grass.

'It is all quite simple in the end. You see, it seems not as if we are to be married in the future, but as if we have been married many months already.'

David pushed himself onto his side and looked at her. He picked up her hand and kissed the fingers one by one.

'You know that I have loved you for a long time?'

His voice trembled. Harriet laughed again and then fell silent. She brushed her fingertips across his lips and over his eyelids, came towards him and kissed him. She threw her head back and David felt her yield.

A FEW WEEKS LATER, down in Suffolk to shut up the house, Harriet sat at the desk in James's study and pulled open the drawers one by one. The papers were piled up without order, bills, account books, his commission papers from years ago, even a copy of a novel in French: *Corinne*, by Madame de Staël. It did not take long, however, to find what she looked for. In the second drawer, on the top was a letter still in its cover sheet, with James's note written along the top, 'Mr Patteson. Replied. 16 Dec.'

Harriet unfolded the cover and flattened out the letter inside.

'Inner Temple, 13th Dec., 1814. Dear Captain Raven. It is with regret that I write with the enclosed letter from Dr Thoday at the Hitchen Asylum, which carries the news that Lady Guest died there last week. I leave you to pass this sad notice to your wife and her aunt, and send my own condolences to them and to you.'

A blow struck Harriet, of horror, then disbelief. She did not stop to think, or read on, but opened the drawer again and pulled out a smaller letter. It was dated a week earlier and addressed to Mr Patteson. As she began to read, the knowledge forced itself on her. Her mother was dead, and had been for many months. 'Dear Sir, I write to inform you with sorrow that Lady Guest died here last night, a victim of the fever that has spread through these parts and claimed several of my patients. Her end came so quickly that there was no time to inform you, and she scarcely had time to suffer unduly. She will be buried in the churchyard here, a wild spot that she loved to sit in. I trust you will inform her relatives and look forward to receiving your instructions as to her effects. I remain yours, Edmund Thoday.'

The letter shook in Harriet's hand. Her mother a patient in an asylum. Buried in a churchyard. A wild spirit. She picked up John Patteson's letter again. There was little more. He would write to Mrs Lefevre, settle all the accounts, arrange to have Lady Guest's effects distributed amongst the poor of Hitchin.

Harriet dropped the letter and stood up, went to the window with the thought that she might see David in the garden, came back to the desk and sat down. In a single moment she had found her mother and lost her. She felt a shock, then a sadness, but the anger she expected did not come. James had begun to tell her, perhaps. But that did not matter; for now that part of her life, and her life with James, was over. Only to her mother did she wish she could speak.

'I shall visit you when the time is right, Mother. I will keep you in my mind and sit with you when I can. Perhaps you will know that I have come. That is all I can say for now, except that I am to be married again, and hope to have children.'

Harriet stood up. David was somewhere in the house and she wanted to go to him. They would make the journey to Hitchin together. She need no longer go alone or feel that what she sought was always just around a corner. David would be with her. She folded up the letters, laid them in the drawer and pushed it shut.

TWO MONTHS AFTER THE news of Waterloo reached London, Nathan Rothschild rose as the sun came up, threw on his silk dressing gown, sat down in his study and took stock of the last three years. What can I say more, he thought, than that they have been good; happy, interesting and profitable. Many believe that I have made a fortune on the 'Change from victory at Waterloo: some tale of couriers, boats waiting, pigeons, and my arrival at Lord Liverpool's house with the news. The first to know! Perhaps so, how can I tell? Rothschilds has made little from the end of the war. I am left holding specie still; I believed the Corsican would have a longer run. But let the story stand: why not? A myth is as good as a profit, I find. Sometimes better, if it enhances a man's reputation.

Apart from that miscalculation it had been a good war, concluded Nathan as he stirred several spoons of sugar into a thick cup of coffee. He wished his father might see him now in the moment of his glory. Nathan remembered Mayer Amschel with tenderness and impatience. Perhaps he had a point when he criticised his accounting, but had it mattered? Not a jot; Mayer could have no more complaints. And today he had no complaints of himself. The world was on the turn, and for the better.

When all was said and done, he liked London. It had given him his Hannah and round them they had grown not only their little family but the bigger one; Mayer Davidson and Jessie, Moses and Judith and all the children to come. London glowed like a new city, glazed with victory, the envy of the world.

Meanwhile those restored princes, and archdukes and kings, what did they do but turn to Britain and hint that a throne was one thing, a solvent ally another? Might his Majesty's government now lend them enough to refloat? Who better placed than he and Mr Herries to organise such loans? No one, not now. So the great work was begun, bigger than anything he had so far attempted and with the promise of proportionate reward for the whole family.

Ah, the family. Across the way, the door of no. 4 swung open; the genial figure of his brother-in-law emerged. A black top hat added to his height and his chest strained the buttons on his topcoat. Nathan knocked on the window.

'Moses!'

Moses Montefiore waved a hand. Nathan pushed up the window and leaned out. His dressing gown flapped in the summer breeze.

'Moses; a cup of coffee before you march off so busy.'

'Business, Nathan?'

'Just this once, on a day of work, let it be for the pleasure of your company.'

Moses turned and went in at the open door of no. 2. Nathan had something up his sleeve, perhaps; he had never known him to sit about in the morning. Still, it did not matter. Nathan and coffee, with a slice of sweet cake in the saucer, made a good start to the day.

WHEN MOSES LEFT, NATHAN found a stray sheet of paper and wrote a note to Charles Herries.

'New Court, 15th August 1815. Mr Herries. The loans we have discussed to the Allied powers advance as we have agreed and at a commission of two per cent as before. I shall wait on Mr Vansittart at the Treasury in the morning, and understand that you go to Paris yourself soon to further the same matter.

'To speak further, and for the last time, of Paris, your acquaintance there has been quite safe. They ask that you go to them upon your arrival and offer you a room in the rue de Grenelles whenever you wish it. I wish you the pleasure of their company and remain, your friend, Nathan Rothschild.'

~

THE NEXT DAY AT five in the afternoon Wellington waited for Kitty in Hamilton Place. They had fixed upon five to meet and Kitty was late. When she arrived he noticed with annoyance that she wore a gown he had not seen before.

'You wear the latest fashion, Kitty.'

'It was time for something new.'

'It would look better if you dyed your hair also.'

'No, Arthur, I shall not do that. I shall keep my hair as it is.'

'I wish you to cover the grey. It shames me.'

'Ah, but I do not wish it.'

'You must.'

'No, Arthur. There you are mistaken. No power can force me to it. I have decided to live in my own way.'

Wellington struggled to keep his voice from rising as it did so often when he spoke to his subordinates. He disliked his wife's contained self-possession, her tidy outline. He felt regret rise in him and pushed it away; he would never indulge in such a soft sentiment. No, one acknowledged an error and lived around it.

'You are obliged to live as I desire.'

'Not any more.'

'Are you in rebellion against me? You are my wife.'

'Indeed, and shall remain so. It is merely that I intend also to live as I want, and that is with grey hair, if it is grey hair that is the bone of contention between us.'

Wellington noticed the challenge. He would pass it by.

'How will you live? How? You cannot contravene my wishes.'

'While you have been away, Arthur, I put the time to good use.'

'I see no benefit from it. None at all.'

'I invested my pin money, and such surplus as remained from the quarterly housekeeping that you allowed me.'

Wellington thought of the millions that the army had walked on in France.

'What possible gain could you make from such paltry sums?'

'I have taken it to the City; it has been invested there by a capable banker, some in consols, some in foreign currencies, some in stocks. Then

I have made other investments of my own in businesses that seemed to me to look to the future. My investments have grown to a useful sum.'

'How much?'

'Arthur, I do not intend to tell you; but enough for me to live the life I wish.'

Arthur was silent. How could Kitty, who never bothered with money, and had been accustomed to annoy him about the smallest expenditure, have become interested in figures, and mastered such language?

'If you really have made such sums as you suggest, it is your duty, and my request, that you hand them over to me. A married woman, as you know, cannot hold money on her own account.'

'I think it would be unwise of you, Arthur, to persist with that request.'

'Do you threaten me?'

'No. I have no need to. The fact is, I have had dealings with a friend of yours.'

The Duke looked at Kitty with incredulity. His anger rose.

'A friend? What friend?'

'Mrs Fitzwilliam.'

'I know of no Mrs Fitzwilliam.'

'Arthur, I believe you do.'

After a minute Arthur spoke again.

'I am not aware that there is any particular objection to the way an army commander spends his leisure time. Besides, you know I care nothing for public opinion about private matters. Mrs Fitzwilliam is a fool if she tries to blackmail me.'

'Mrs Fitzwilliam is dead.'

Arthur remained impassive. Kitty could not see any change in his expression.

'And therefore?'

'It is not about her, but about him.'

'Captain Fitzwilliam? He is beneath my notice. He offered me his wife in exchange for a promotion to headquarters. She came to me anyway. Does he now intend to challenge me to a duel, or something else equally absurd?'

'Captain Fitzwilliam is dead also. I mean the child.'

'The child?'

'I do not know, Arthur, if he is your son. How could I, or any man? He lives quietly in the country with a woman who takes good care of him. However, I let it be known that I pay for his upkeep. For though the world cares nothing for that boy, and quickly forgets a lovely woman who falls from grace, a man's honour would shrink, would it not, from the disclosure that his bastard son was supported by his wife?'

Another silence. Wellington knew that she was right; the same newspapers that praised him now would be quick to find fault as soon as he signalled an intention to enter government. Worse than that, there would be those, gentlemen all, who would suggest that a man who could not take care of those he was responsible for had no business in Parliament.

'What is it you want, Kitty?'

'My life.'

It seemed to Kitty at that moment a great thing, but as soon as she said it she realised that life alone was not enough; she wanted Arthur to acknowledge that she was free to do with it as she pleased.

'No, I wish for more: my life, but also my money and a private separation with terms agreed, drawn up and signed by both of us.'

'If you intend to ruin me I shall give you nothing.'

'Indeed; that is to be anticipated. Then let us come to an agreement. In return for what I ask I will offer you my services as a wife on the occasions your duties of state require it, and, more important, my silence. You may do as you please without any fear of me. I believe we will be able to live in harmony. To a casual visitor the surface of our lives will seem as smooth as an egg.'

'You appear to have thought about this a good deal.'

'Another blessing of war; it gives women a useful quantity of time without domestic life, time to consider the future.'

She has outmanoeuvred me, Arthur thought, backed me into a corner when I did not even know that an engagement was in prospect. He was speechless and disbelieving. He had underestimated her.

There was a soft knock on the door.

'Yes.'

The butler came in.

'Captain Heaton is below, my lady.'

'Show him into the library. Please tell him that I have finished my business and will be down very shortly.'

Kitty turned to her husband.

'You will consider my offer, I am sure. Now I shall leave you. Good day, Arthur.'

Then she was gone. Arthur heard the door to the library open, a man's firm greeting, a bark, and Kitty's reply. After an interval, the front door opened and closed. They have gone together, the Duke thought, they have left my house side by side, with that wretched dog.

He did not mind that Kitty no longer cared for him; that might have come as a relief from the burden that he had carried with him for so long. What enraged him was to lose; or, more precisely, that his own wife should get the better of him in this calculated fashion. Kitty! How was it possible! Then, this matter of the captain. Had she planned it? Or was it luck, the sort of luck that a commander finds when he does not know the lie of the land but nonetheless finds himself on a bluff that overlooks enemy forces. Then he remembered: Captain Heaton. The Honourable Robert Heaton, indeed. He himself had picked him out, sent him with the Vitoria dispatch and delivered him into his wife's hands.

He threw his head back and laughed out loud his mocking laugh. Volunteers; they always caused trouble in the end.

The Duke of Wellington sat on in the empty room. Why, he wondered, did I command the army, surrounded by fools; why watch the life drain from those I loved, live in comfortless lodgings and risk my life for twenty years in the service of the King? For one reason only. Nothing for myself; but to keep England as it has always been and as I wish it to be. And there is an end to it.

What now? The Duke looked up and saw Arthur Freese's violin on top of the piano. The bow, he noticed with irritation, lay across the music stand that stood nearby.

'Still tightened, by the look of it.'

He lifted the violin, tucked it under his chin, balanced the bow in his right hand and began to play.

'Out of tune; what do those boys get up to?'

At once, as if he had never stopped playing, he steadied the bow and began to tune the violin. He sounded the A string, then the strings in pairs, tightened some and loosened others, until, when he drew the bow across them, he was satisfied.

He played a tune that came to him without a thought; one of Ferguson's Irish melodies. He heard and felt it as clearly as if his father was in the room with him, or as if they were together in the house in Merrion Street thirty years ago and it was the easiest thing to play as he had then, without a care, and in love with the music.

In Hamilton Place Mr Sant, a clerk in the Treasury Office, paused in his walk, and rested his cane on the ground. He lifted his head to hear the music's lilt and follow the practised movement of the phrases. The violinist was a master who made his instrument a part of himself. His playing was unhurried and precise; now decisive, now languorous, now splendid with lament.

Mr Sant felt tears start in his eyes. The simple melody filled him with all the longing and all the pity in the world. He crossed the road and craned his neck to look into the open window. The sash was up and a muslin curtain blew in the evening breeze. A man stood alone, upright and with shoulders back. He held the fiddle under his chin tipped up a little, and gazed away from it as if he looked at something in the room.

Mr Sant started.

'Well I never,' he said out loud, 'the Duke of Wellington himself. Now there's an odd thing, to be sure.' He tapped his cane on the ground, walked on, and in a moment turned the corner out of sight.

Dramatis Personae

denotes historical figure

HARRIET RAVEN, née Guest, b. 1792.

JAMES RAVEN, Captain, 9th Regiment of Foot, the East Norfolk Regiment, b. 1788, her husband.

MAJOR GEORGE YALLOP, Major, 9th Foot, b. 1764.

DOROTHY YALLOP, b. 1765, his wife.

THOMAS ORDE, servant to Captain Raven, b. 1787.

MARY ORDE, his wife, b. 1787.

NELSON ORDE, their son, b. 1807.

DAVID McBRIDE, surgeon of the 9th Foot, b. 1788, Bushey, Herts; educated Edinburgh University.

*ARTHUR WELLESLEY, LORD WELLINGTON, b. Dublin, 1769, 3rd son of Garret Wesley, 2nd Earl of Mornington, Professor of Music, Trinity College, Dublin. Spent early life at Dangan Castle, County Meath. Educated at local school in Trim, County Meath, and Eton College. Joined army aged 17; proposed to Kitty Pakenham, 1793, and was rejected. Went out to India, made fortune and reputation at the Battle of Assaye, knighted, returned 1805. Proposed to Kitty and was accepted. Married April 1806. April 1807 became Chief Secretary to the Lord Lieutenant in Dublin; lived Phoenix Park. Commander-in-Chief of the British army in the Peninsula April 1809, and successively Viscount, Earl and Duke of Wellington. Returned to England briefly after the abdication of Napoleon, summer 1814, then proceeded to the Congress of Vienna and, after Napoleon's escape from Elba in January 1815, to Waterloo. Returned to England summer 1815. Entered the government 1818, and bought Apsley House, Hyde Park, from his brother Richard. Prime Minister 1828. Supported Catholic Emancipation, 1829; opposed Parliamentary reform; resigned 1830.

*KITTY, LADY WELLINGTON, b. 1772. Born Catherine Pakenham, at Pakenham Hall, Co. Westmeath, Ireland, daughter of 2nd Baron Longford. Married Sir Arthur Wellesley, Dublin 1806. Lived briefly in Dublin, then moved to London, first to no. 11 Harley Street then to 4 Hamilton Place, Piccadilly.

*HON. ARTHUR WELLESLEY, b. 1807.

*HON. CHARLES WELLESLEY, b. 1808.

*ARTHUR FREESE, b. India, 1802, son of Wellington's mistress, Mrs Freese. Adopted by the Wellesleys, 1807.

*GERALD VALERIAN WELLESLEY, b. 1809, son of Arthur's brother Henry. Adopted, 1809.

*EDWARD PAKENHAM, GENERAL, b. 1778, Kitty's brother and Arthur's brother-in-law, known as Ned. Killed at New Orleans, in command of the British army, Jan. 1815.

ELIZA FITZWILLIAM, a woman about town.

HON. ROBERT HEATON, b. 1771, Florence, Italy, a gentleman volunteer, or amateur. Racket, his dog.

ANNE COBBOLD, née GUEST, b. 1758, Harriet's aunt.

*FREDERICK WINSOR. Born Friedrich Albrecht Winzer, Brunswick, Germany. Lived Berlin, Paris, before arriving in London c.1803. Founder of the National Light and Heat Company, subsequently the Gas Light and Coke Company. Conceived and executed the idea of a central gas plant and a distribution system via underground pipes. Granted charter 1812. Removed from day-to-day running of the company winter 1813/14. Left London for Paris, Jan. 1815.

The Gas Light and Coke Company expanded rapidly to become the biggest supplier of coal gas—or town gas as it was popularly called—in the country. It was nationalised with the rest of the gas industry in 1948, and became part of the Gas Board.

*NATHAN MAYER ROTHSCHILD, b. Frankfurt, 1777, in the kingdom of Hesse, 3rd son of Mayer Amschel Rothschild, 1743–1812. Settled in Manchester 1799, and London 1806. Lived at 2 New Court, Bishopsgate, from 1810. Spoke a heavily accented English all his life. Cotton trader and then banker, who, with his four brothers, Jakob, Calmann, Amschel and Salomon, provided the specie to pay for the running of Wellington's army 1814–15, and then organised a series of huge loans to Allied powers. Refused a knighthood, 1815. In 1816 bought country house at Stamford Hill in Middlesex; 1826 moved to 107 Piccadilly; 1835 bought Gunnersbury Park, Ealing, former home of Princess Amelia, daughter of King George II.

*HANNAH ROTHSCHILD, née BARENT COHEN, b. 1783, his wife.

*JOHN CHARLES HERRIES, b. London, 1778, Treasury official, commissary-in-chief to the British army. Studied banking on the Continent; lived 21 Cadogan Place, Kensington.

*WILLIAM HERSCHEL, b. Friedrich Wilhelm Herschel, Hanhover, 1738, astronomer who in 1781 discovered a new planet in the solar system. Named by him the Georgium Sidus after the reigning monarch, it is now called Uranus.

*HON. CHARLES STEWART, b. 1778, Dublin, half-brother to Earl of Castlereagh. As Lieutenant-Colonel of 5th Royal Irish Dragoons fought and routed disorganised Irish rebels at the Battle of New Ross, 1798. General; Adjutant-General in the Peninsula from 1809.

*LORD FITZROY SOMERSET, FIELD MARSHAL, b. 1788, aide-de-camp and then military secretary to the Duke of Wellington. Created 1st Baron Raglan; became infamous for his part in the Charge of the Light Brigade in the Crimean War, 1854–5.

*DR JAMES MCGRIGOR, b. 1771, Surgeon General to Lord Wellington's army in the Peninsula.

*COLONEL GEORGE MURRAY, b. 1772. Quartermaster General.

*ROBERT HUGH KENNEDY, b. 1772, General; commissary general in the Peninsula, 1810–14.

*SIR THOMAS PICTON, b. 1758, General. Wounded in the escalade at Badajoz. Killed at Waterloo.

*ROWLAND HILL, b. 1772, General, second-in-command in the Peninsula.

CAMILLE FLORENS, b. 1780, a hostess in Seville, daughter of Eugene O'Donnell, Irishman, b. 1750, Kildare, Ireland.

*FRANCISCO JOSÉ de GOYA Y LUCIENTES, b. 1746, Spanish painter. Painted Duke of Wellington in Madrid, summer 1812. Infra-red photographs of this painting, now in Apsley House, London, reveal two earlier figures underneath the portrait of Wellington, thought to be Joseph Bonaparte and Manuel de Godoy, Prime Minister of Spain until 1808. Goya's portraits of the Spanish royal family and Godoy are now in the Museo del Prado, Madrid. While working in Madrid he also produced his series of etchings of the war, *Los Desastres*, 1812–15.

*HENRY, 3rd EARL BATHURST, b. 1762, from June 1812 Secretary of State for War and the Colonies in Lord Liverpool's government.

*SIR MOSES MONTEFIORE, b. 1784, stockbroker and philanthropist. Married Judith Barent Cohen, June 1812. Lived no. 4 New Court, London. Captain, 3rd Surrey Local Militia 1810–14. Founded Imperial Continental Gas Association and Alliance Life Assurance Company. Retired from active business 1824 to devote himself to good works.

Acknowledgements

I owe a debt to Gill Coleridge and Jenny Uglow that is greater than I can say. Gill first encouraged me to write fiction, or, rather, drew out an idea I had kept in the shadows for too long, and has been with me through every chapter and draft not just as my agent but as a friend on whom I have relied constantly for advice and support in the last three turbulent years. Jenny Uglow has been my editor for twenty years now, through the tenures of successive fine publishers at Chatto & Windus: Carmen Callil, who first bought my work; Jonathan Burnham; Alison Samuel, whose literary judgement and surprising knowledge of military arcana hugely improved this book; and Clara Farmer, who has steered it to its publication with skill and grace. To all of them, my thanks, and thanks also to Dan Franklin who has been there all along. To Jenny, my love and admiration, and heartfelt thanks for countless suggestions, improvements, readings of the manuscript and moments of encouragement. My thanks also to Cara Jones at Rogers, Coleridge and White for her patient fielding of calls and emails, and at Chatto to Parisa Ebrahimi, Jenny Overton, Fiona Murphy, and Sandra Oakins for the map, and, over the years, to Roger Bratchell, Rosemary Davidson, Rachel Cugnoni and Richard Cable. In New York I would like to thank Melanie Jackson, and Frances Coady and the staff at Picador.

Many friends read the manuscript, talked things over with me and helped me with love and support while I was writing. Since so many of them are also professionals, as well as professors, in fields about which I know little, my thanks not only for their friendship but also their expertise to Hugh Macdonald, Simon Schaffer, Ruth Erlich, Elden Croy, Cherry

Potter, Jo Budd, Lisa Jardine, Peter Mandler, Jamie McKendrick, Xon de Ros, Martin Murphy, Valeria Frighi, Davide Lombardo, Deborah Colvin, Hal Cook, Charlotte Brewer, Peter Bowman, Aldo and Gabriella Zaccagna, Grayson and Flo Perry, Romilly and Charles Saumarez Smith, Lucy Heller and Rachel Watson. An especially kind group of friends read, corrected and made invaluable suggestions about the typescript. David Crane, Honor Clerk, Elizabeth Green, Min Stacpoole and Anthony Pakenham (who between them have read all the books fit to print and many not), Simon Schama, Claire L'Enfant, Sam Brearly, Juliet Gardiner and Philippa Perry; you have made this a better book and given me confidence to persevere. To Philippa, you have done good with love, wisdom, Jane Austen and coffee. To Simon, my thanks for Hebrew and your baggy monster of a heart. To John Brewer my love over many years, and to Grace and Lori, my gratitude for your love, laughter and just being yourselves in Italian and English, every day.

For expert advice I would also like to thank first and foremost Ian Fletcher of Ian Fletcher Battlefield Tours, who unfailingly and generously offered me his knowledge of all matters Wellingtonian and Napoleonic, and saved me from more than one military howler. Michael Crumplin advised me on medical matters in the Peninsula, Melanie Aspey showed me thrilling material about Nathan Rothschild in the Rothschild Archive, and Christopher Gray took me to Trim and told me about Dangan Castle. Thanks also to Aron Rodrigue and Herbert Kaplan; the staff of the Royal Norfolk Regimental Museum at the Britannia Barracks in Norwich, the Royal Mail Archive, the Museum Judengasse in Frankfurt, the London Library and the British Library. Finally I would like to thank Julie Cummins, Mary Heffernan and David Levins at Farmleigh, Dublin, where I spent summer 2009 as OPW Writer in Residence, and where the first part of this book was substantially rewritten.

I consulted many books in the course of writing mine, but the following were of particular help to me: Humphry Davy, *Elements of Chemical Philosophy,* 1812; Niall Ferguson, *The World's Banker: The History of the House of Rothschild* (Weidenfeld, 1998); Ian Fletcher, *In Hell Before Daylight* (Tunbridge Wells, 1984); Christopher Hibbert, *Wellington: A Personal History* (HarperCollins, 1997); Boyd Hilton, *A Mad, Bad and Dangerous People? England 1783–1846* (Oxford, 2006); Richard Holmes, *The Age of Wonder* (HarperCollins, 2008); Robert Hughes, *Goya* (Vintage, 2004); Anthony Brett James, *Life in Wellington's Army* (Allen & Unwin, 1972);

Herbert H. Kaplan, *Nathan Mayer Rothschild and the Creation of a Dynasty* (Stanford, 2006); Elizabeth Longford, *Wellington* (Abacus, 1992); Eliza Pakenham, *Soldier Sailor: An Intimate Portrait of an Irish Family* (Weidenfeld, 2007); E. G. Stewart, *Town Gas: Its Manufacture and Distribution* (HMSO, 1958); Wellington's dispatches, Lady Holland's *Journals* and William Napier's *History of the War in the Peninsula* (all in various editions).

About the Author

STELLA TILLYARD was born in Britain and educated at Oxford University, where she studied English Literature. Her Ph.D. on twentieth-century art criticism, completed in 1985, was published as *The Impact of Modernism* in 1987. In 1981, she became a Knox Fellow at Harvard and subsequently taught English literature and art history there and at UCLA. She moved to Florence, Italy, in 1993. *Aristocrats*, her biography of four eighteenth-century sisters, was published in 1994, won the History Today Award, the Fawcett Prize and the Meilleur Livre Étranger, and it was made into a BBC/WGBH Masterpiece Theatre series in 2000. Her subsequent books include *Citizen Lord*, the life of Lord Edward Fitzgerald (1998, shortlisted for the Whitbread Prize) and *A Royal Affair*, about George III and his siblings (2006). In 2005, she became visiting scholar at the Centre for Editing Lives and Letters at Queen Mary, University of London, where she taught the history and practice of biography. She has written for many newspapers and magazines and has sat on several prize juries, most recently the 2010 BBC Johnson Prize for Nonfiction. Tillyard lives in London and Florence and has two children, aged fifteen and twenty-three. *Tides of War* is her first novel.